Hope is the *Sunday Times* bestselling author of
al Miner's Daughter. She was born and raised in
Durham and worked as a nurse for many years,
fore giving up her career to raise her family.

Also by Maggie Hope:

A Mother's Courage

Maggie Hope

EBURY
PRESS

3 5 7 9 10 8 6 4 2

Ebury Press, an imprint of Ebury Publishing
20 Vauxhall Bridge Road,
London SW1V 2SA

 Penguin
Random House
UK

Ebury Press is part of the Penguin Random House group of companies
whose addresses can be found at global.penguinrandomhouse.com

First published in 1997 as *Blow the Wind Southerly* by Inner Circle Books
This edition published in 2018 by Ebury Press

www.penguin.co.uk

A CIP catalogue record for this book is available from the British Library

ISBN 9780091957407

Typeset in India by Integra Software Services Pvt. Ltd, Pondicherry

Printed and bound in Great Britain by Clays Ltd, St Ives PLC

Penguin Random House is committed to a sustainable future for our
business, our readers and our planet. This book is made from Forest
Stewardship Council® certified paper

Chapter One

'Please, missus, can you not spare a bite for me little sister?'

Eleanor heard the plea as she came through the baize door into the kitchen with the orders for cook from Grandmother Wales. Grandmother was not feeling well and had decided to rest in bed until the dinner hour at three.

'You will be so good as to give cook the menus for the day,' she had said to the fifteen-year-old Eleanor, more of a command than a request, thought Eleanor rebelliously; after all, she wasn't a servant.

'Yes, Grandmother,' she replied meekly enough, though she was wishing she was back at the Wesleyan School for Young Ladies in Houghton le Spring. But she was too old for school, her mother had said; it was time she learned about household duties, how to look after a husband and a family, and about managing servants. How else was she to find a gentleman willing to marry her? For Eleanor was a little too plump and plain with her straight black hair, which, though thick and glossy, had to be tied up in rags every night to produce the ringlets that girls her age wore. A line of anxiety would appear between Mama's brows whenever she looked at her daughter, her ninth child, and the one it was going to be most difficult to get settled in life.

I don't want to be married, Eleanor told herself as she closed the door from the hall behind her and walked into the kitchen, lifting her crinoline skirts slightly so as to negotiate the narrow path between the dresser and the large scrubbed table that stood in the middle of the room. What she wanted to do was go on with her studies and one day get the chance to go to university and become a doctor – an ambition she had learned to keep to herself, for if she mentioned it to anyone at all they thought she was very droll and couldn't possibly mean it. Young ladies definitely did not go to university to study anything; their poor minds were not up to it, her father had said when she first broached the subject.

Eleanor sighed and looked towards the back door where Mrs Green, the cook, was standing, holding the knob of the door in one hand ready to close it.

'Go away, Mary Buckle,' the cook was saying. 'You know I can't give you any food, I could lose my position here if I did. You should be ashamed, begging at the door like this, can't you get any work like respectable folk?'

'Mary Buckle!' Eleanor cried and moved to the door. She knew Mary Buckle – hadn't they been in the same Sunday School class years ago when they were both small? That had been when Eleanor had stayed the whole summer here in Hetton-le-Hole with her grandparents.

Mrs Green halted in the act of closing the door and stood back. 'It's Mrs Wales's orders, miss,' she said, 'no handouts at the door.'

'Mary,' Eleanor said again, ignoring Mrs Green for the moment. She stared at the other girl, who was about five feet tall, very thin, and the cotton dress she was wearing, despite the cold north-easter that was blowing up the yard, barely reached her calves. The shawl that she had over her shoulders was also wrapped round the tiny girl she carried on her hips, a sickly-looking child of about two years old. But it was Mary's face that shocked Eleanor for although they were the same age, Mary's could have been that of a woman in her thirties.

'Mary, you remember me, don't you?' Eleanor said at last, trying to wipe the shock from her face. 'I met you at

Sunday School years ago, when I was here for the summer, can you remember?'

'Aye, I can. I remember you all right, miss,' answered Mary. The child in her arms squirmed and sniffled and she hitched her higher on to her hip. 'Be still, Prue, will you?' she admonished sharply before turning back to Eleanor. 'She's hungry, like, we both are. We've had nowt to eat since yesterday. There is a supper at chapel the night, miss, but it's a long time till seven o'clock, like.'

'Oh!' Eleanor stood back from the door, distressed. 'Come in, do, sit by the fire and warm up, you must be frozen. I'll get you something to eat.'

Mary stepped forward immediately, walked past the scandalised cook and sat down in that lady's chair by the range, with its blazing fire, piled high with best household coal in order to heat the oven for the evening meal. There was a smell of new bread baking in the oven; cook must have the bread rolls for dinner in there now.

'Miss—' Mrs Green began but Eleanor interrupted.

'I'm sure there's bread left from yesterday's baking, isn't there, Mrs Green? And is there any cheese in the pantry? And two of your excellent jam tarts, I'm sure the baby would like one of those.'

Mrs Green didn't move. 'There are only enough tarts for the mistress's tea,' she said, her whole being exuding disapproval that Eleanor refused to acknowledge.

'Well then, a fairy cake, I know there are some fairy cakes, Mrs Green.'

Reluctantly, the cook moved to the pantry and came out a moment later with two pieces of bread and cheese and two dainty fairy cakes on a single plate.

Prue sat up straight on her sister's lap and stared at the food, her eyes gleaming. A tiny drop of slaver appeared at the corner of her mouth and ran down her chin and she raised a tiny hand, rubbing it away impatiently. She did not reach for the food when Eleanor first proffered the plate, however; first she looked up at her sister, her eyes large with hope.

'Go on, Prue,' Mary said gently. 'It's all right to eat.'

She herself waited until Prue had picked up bread in one hand and a piece of cheese in the other before taking a piece of bread herself. She ate carefully, a small bite at a time, concentrating wholly on the food. But the child tore the bread with her hands and stuffed it into her mouth, chewing quickly and barely swallowing one piece before taking another.

'Careful now, Prue,' Mary said warningly. 'You'll choke.' The child slowed for a moment but soon forgot and resumed ramming the food into her mouth.

Eleanor watched, dismayed, while Mrs Green stalked off into the pantry and could be heard banging pans about. Prue coughed and put a hand to her chest, obviously finding the food too dry but determined to eat it anyway. Eleanor found two cups in the dresser, filled them with milk from the jug on the table and offered them silently.

'I'm grateful to you, I am, God bless you, Eleanor Saint,' Mary said quietly and sipped daintily from her cup. Prue regarded the milk suspiciously and looked at her sister again, seeing she was drinking the milk but unsure whether to follow her example.

'It's all right, Prue, it's milk, it's good for you,' Mary reassured her.

'Do you mean to say she hasn't seen milk before?' asked Eleanor, shocked.

'Not since Da was killed in the pit.'

'Oh dear, I'm so sorry.'

The words hung in the silence, inadequate, banal. Eleanor tried again. 'I mean, I know how awful it is, my father died too. Last year.'

'More?'

Their attention was taken by Prue's request; she had climbed down from her sister's knee and was holding the plate out to Eleanor. The plate was empty so she must have eaten Mary's cake as well as her own. She still hadn't touched her milk; the cup was perched on the steel fender before the grate. Eleanor looked down into the intent brown eyes, almost too large for the pinched little face, and nodded, unable to speak for the emotion welling up in her. Emotion that was a mixture of the old, aching sadness over the death of her own father and pity for these two, so much worse off than she was herself. For her own father, though he had begun work as a miner, had been a colliery agent when he died. The family circumstances were now straitened but they were certainly not so badly off as Mary seemed to be.

'No, Prue, don't ask for more,' said Mary. 'You've had enough.'

'I didn't,' the child asserted, shaking her head.

'I've told you,' said her sister firmly. 'We'll go home now.'

'I didn't,' insisted Prue. 'I hungry.'

'Perhaps just another piece of bread?' suggested Eleanor and behind her, from the pantry, she heard Mrs Green snort and mutter something about most folks having to work for a living.

'No, thank you,' said Mary and rose to her feet, catching hold of Prue's hand. She stood before Eleanor, her head held high despite her rags and the fact that Prue was dragging at her hand and whimpering.

'Thank you,' she said simply. 'I won't forget your kindness to us.'

'Would you like some to take home? I could easily put some in a basket for you,' said Eleanor.

Mary hesitated before answering. 'Mam wouldn't like it,' she said at last. 'We're not supposed to ask for anything, but Prue was so hungry and I thought—'

She broke off as Prue suddenly stopped struggling and turned a nasty shade of green.

'I feel bad,' she whimpered.

'Don't you be sick in here,' cried Mary and rushed her off to the drain in the back yard where Prue promptly relieved her stomach of its contents. 'Never mind, pet,' Mary whispered to her. 'You'll feel better now. Mind, you shouldn't have eaten both the cakes, it was over much on an empty stomach.'

'I could have told you that would happen, miss,' commented Mrs Green, folding her arms across the white expanse of her apron and nodding sagely. 'Cakes is too rich for them by half. Such as them's not used to cakes.'

'Seems to me they're not used to eating anything, let alone cakes,' Eleanor was stung into replying. She would have said more but from inside the kitchen a bell began to ring insistently. She looked up at the row of bells and saw it was the one from Mrs Wales's bedroom. 'It's Mrs Wales,' she said when Mrs Green didn't move.

'I cannot be leaving the kitchen when I've bread in the oven and strangers in the yard,' said the cook. 'And Jane's gone for the messages and Phoebe's busy in the drawing room. Mebbe you can answer it, miss?'

Eleanor seethed. She almost retorted that she wasn't a servant, that it wasn't her place to answer the summons of the bell. She glared at the cook but Mrs Green stared implacably back and in the end it was the fifteen-year-old Eleanor who dropped her eyes and turned towards the door that led into the downstairs hall. Passing the window, she noticed that Mary and Prue were going out of the gate, Prue straddled on her sister's hip and her head lying on Mary's shoulder.

'I'll find out where they live and go to see them,' she said aloud as she went upstairs to her grandmother. Standing before the bedroom door, she smoothed down her dress and patted her ringlets in place before going in. Grandmother could be quite cutting if she thought her granddaughter looked at all untidy.

'Where have you been, Eleanor?' Grandmother's voice was petulant. 'And where are the maids? One would think the house deserted, it makes one wonder why we keep such lazy good-for-nothings. What they need is a firm hand; if only I felt better and was able to oversee them properly things would be different, you'd see.'

'I'm sorry, Grandmother, I was in the kitchen giving cook your orders.' Even as she said it, Eleanor remembered she had done no such thing. Oh well, she would do it as soon as she could. 'Jane has gone on an errand for cook and Phoebe is still cleaning the drawing room. Can I get you anything, Grandmother?'

'I have a headache,' said Margaret Wales fretfully. 'I need more lavender water to soothe it, it's the only thing that helps. Why was I not informed that Jane was going out? She could have bought some at the apothecary's. Here am I, mistress of the house, and no one tells me anything. How am I to run it properly?'

'I can go, Grandmother, it's not far, it won't take long.'

'I don't know.' Margaret bit her lip doubtfully as she regarded Eleanor. 'It's not proper for young ladies to be out on the streets on their own.'

'I'll only be ten minutes, Grandmother.'

Margaret nodded, wincing as she did so. 'Oh, my poor head. I suffer so from these dizzy spells. Go, then, but don't dawdle and don't speak to anyone. Remember you are a young lady now and should behave as such.'

Eleanor sped down the stairs and gave the belated orders to Mrs Green. Tying on her bonnet before the looking glass in the hall, she grimaced at her reflection. The plain brown bonnet with its demure brim and matching ribbons did nothing for her, except perhaps to hide the fact that her heavy hair was already beginning to drop out of its ringlets. Still, at least her cloak hid her plump arms and neck, she thought, grinning as she turned away. She was so looking forward to getting out of the house, even if just for half an hour; the air inside was so stale for, after October, Grandmother insisted on all the windows being kept closed.

The street outside was muddy and there was no footpath so she was glad she had remembered to strap on her pattens.

At least they raised her skirts above the mud and she was still young enough to enjoy the satisfying squelching sound they made as she walked along to the corner and turned into Front Street for Mr Herrington's apothecary shop.

She bought two ounces of lavender water from Mr Herrington's apprentice, a young boy who blushed and stammered and fumbled with the wrapping paper as he made a parcel of the tiny bottle. Eleanor stood demurely waiting, holding her lips together primly so as not to burst out laughing as she pretended not to notice how inept he was.

'Good morning, Miss Saint – it is Miss Saint, is it not?'

Eleanor looked up as she heard the minister's voice. She knew him well, for Mr Nelson served her home chapel besides this one in Hetton. 'Good morning, Mr Nelson,' she answered. 'How are you today?'

'Very well, thank you, Miss Saint. You are staying with your grandmother and uncle, I take it? How is Mrs Wales?'

Fractious and ill-tempered, Eleanor thought, but otherwise in fairly good health. Aloud she said, 'Tolerably well, thank you, Mr Nelson, apart from a headache. I must go now, she's waiting for this lavender water.'

'Of course, Miss Saint,' said the minister, nodding his head so that his grey-speckled beard went up and down against his white collar. 'I may expect to see you in chapel on Sunday, then?'

'Yes, of course, Mr Nelson,' Eleanor replied and escaped into the street. The winter sun was glinting on the coloured bottles through the small panes of the apothecary's window and she looked up at them, pleased with the jewel-like colours. Reluctantly, she walked slowly along the street, almost deserted at this hour, as the whistle from Lyon Pit had just blown its message over the pit rows that fore shift was loosing, and the men and boys were coming home. The womenfolk would all be busy preparing a meal for them, thought Eleanor, or setting the back shift off for their ten hours in the pit. Dreamily, she imagined them in the tiny cottages in the rows, happy families even if they were poor. Though the mines were doing well and the pitmen were all in work and earning good money, according to her Uncle John.

Eleanor was almost to the end of the village and regretfully she turned the corner to the lane that led to the Lyon viewer's house out of the village, away from the dirt of the pit yard and colliery rows. As she passed the end cottage she noticed the door was open and she couldn't resist peeping inside, for she had remembered that this was the Buckles' cottage. A flagstone was in place before the open doorway and a rag mat lay on top to keep the worst of the mud at bay. Eleanor paused, staring into the room, which had a brick fireplace with a smoking fire and a ladder up to a hole in the rafters, presumably leading to a bedroom. The only other furniture in the room was a bed in the corner, covered by a patchwork quilt. The floor was made of bricks laid end to end and there was another rag mat before the fire.

Fascinated, Eleanor forgot herself and leaned in past the door frame to get a better look. The bricks had been scrubbed only that morning, she could tell, for they were still damp and there was a distinctive smell of lye soap. The walls were lime-washed, as indeed she had known they would be, for Uncle John had issued an order that all the cottages had to be as a guard against the cholera. He even supplied the powdered lime, as it could be bought cheaply from a shed in the colliery yard.

'Who's there? Is that you, Mary?'

Eleanor jumped back as the quilt on the bed moved and the thin figure of a woman appeared, sitting up against the black-painted bars of the bedhead.

The woman peered at the door. 'Mary? Did you find any mushrooms? By, I could really fancy a few done on the griddle with a bit of bread. Have you got the bairn with you?'

Eleanor stepped forward into the room. 'I'm sorry, Mrs Buckle, it's not Mary, it's me. I was just passing and I—'

'Come closer, will you? I can't see a thing in this half-light, that window gets covered in mud every time a cart passes however often Mary washes it. I'm sorry, I can't tell who it is from your voice, like.'

'Eleanor Saint, Mrs Buckle, I used to go to Sunday School with Mary. I'm here visiting my uncle at the viewer's house.'

'Betty Wales's lass are you? I remember Betty Wales when her da was nobbut a pitman. He did well for himself, he did.' Mrs Buckle had slid down the bed and her voice was becoming weaker and more threadlike. The brief interest she had shown in Eleanor was fading and she said fretfully, 'Our Mary should have been back afore now. I wonder where she's got to? I'm fair clammed for a cup of tea.'

'Well, shall I put the kettle on for you? I can make you some tea,' offered Eleanor. Mrs Buckle roused herself to give a short laugh.

'Aye, I'm sure, lass, an' if you can find a few tea leaves in the caddy you can do it.'

Eleanor looked about her for the tea caddy. There was a wooden shelf over the fireplace and a battered wooden box standing on it but when she looked inside it was quite empty. She felt a fool.

'Oh, you mean you have no tea,' she said, a little lamely.

Mrs Buckle was lying back, her eyes closed and her face as white as the bleached flour sack that acted as a pillow slip but she managed to smile faintly and nod her head. Eleanor was at a loss; she could go back to the village and buy a twist of tea – Grandmother had an account with Mrs Lambton's grocery shop just as she had with the apothecary and Mr Sweeney the book seller. She hesitated, knowing she was already late in getting back with the lavender water. But surely it was her Christian duty to do something to help Mrs Buckle? Her dilemma was ended as Mary came in the door, holding little Prue's hand. She had a cloth bag slung around her neck bulging with what Eleanor took to be mushrooms and in her other hand she carried a pail of water. Prue was hanging back and whimpering softly to herself but the sisters both came to a halt as they saw Eleanor, standing awkwardly by the bed.

'Miss Saint!' exclaimed Mary, the first to find her voice. 'What are you doing here?' She placed the pail of water by the hearth and the cloth bag on the table. Prue clambered on to the bed beside her mother and turned hopeful eyes on Eleanor.

'Cake?' she asked.

'No, no I haven't—' Eleanor began but Mrs Buckle interrupted.

'Prue, don't ask for nowt, I've told you before,' she said sharply.

'I have nothing,' Eleanor finished, 'or I'd gladly give it to you.' She turned to Mary, who was regarding her steadily even while she was ladling water from the pail into the iron kettle and settling it on the smoking fire. 'I ... I've been on an errand for Grandmother, your door was open as I was going past, so I ...'

'You came in, miss. Well, that's all right, our door is always open like most of the folks' around here, but for the gaffer's, like.'

Eleanor blushed, remembering the reception Mary and Prue had received earlier at the back door of the Lyon viewer's house before she had intervened. But she held her head high. 'I thought to help your mother,' she said simply.

Mary sighed. 'Aye, I'm sorry, miss. But I have a lot to do. Ben, that's my brother, he'll be coming in off the fore shift and you can see how Mam's held, her sight's going now and her head's bad all the time. Laudanum helps, but we can't buy much. The doctor says something's growing in her head as shouldn't.'

'Oh, how aw—' Eleanor gave a horrified glance to the woman in bed, who seemed to have dropped into a doze, forgetting her fancy for mushrooms. Looking down at the parcel in her hand, she had an idea and held it out to Mary.

'Grandmother swears by this for her headaches. I'm sure she won't mind if I give it to Mrs Buckle when she is so ill.'

Mary looked doubtfully at the parcel. 'What is it, miss?'

'Just lavender water. It may help. You should dampen a cloth with it and smooth it on to your mother's temples. Look, I'll show you.' Eleanor opened the tiny parcel and looked around for a cloth. Seeing none, she took out her own dainty handkerchief, wet it with lavender water and, going over to the bed, gently wiped the invalid's head. Mrs Buckle sighed gratefully and opened her eyes for a moment. Eleanor was shocked to see how cloudy they were, how sightless they looked. The smell of lavender hung in the air, overlaying that of lye soap and damp.

'I'll leave it here, Mary,' said Eleanor and placed the bottle on the table. 'I have to go now, Grandmother will be waiting.'

'Thank you, miss,' Mary said simply as she went with her to the door. A small boy was just entering. Ben, Eleanor supposed, for he was dressed in old clothes stiff with coal dust and on his head he had a leather helmet with a holder for a candle. Though there was little to be seen of his skin through the layers of dirt, his eyelids were drooping wearily and his shoulders bowed like those of an old man.

'This is Miss Saint, Ben,' said Mary and the boy nodded and walked past them to the chair by the fire and slumped down on it.

'It's a long shift for him, he's only eight, Miss,' Mary apologised for him. 'He's a trapper boy, like, down the Lyon.'

Eleanor nodded; of course, she had seen many young pit lads, she saw them every day. It was a hard life for a boy but trapper boys were necessary in a mine; Uncle John had explained to her they were needed to keep a flow of good air in the tunnels of the mine. She said goodbye to Mary and sped back to the apothecary's shop in Front Street.

*

'What have you been doing, Eleanor? You've been gone almost two hours!'

'I'm sorry, Grandmother.' Eleanor stood before her grandmother in the dining room. Uncle John was already sitting at table and Jane was serving him beef soup from a large tureen.

He looked at Eleanor's face, pink with rushing back up the lane on her clumsy pattens, and smiled. 'There's no harm done, Mother,' he said. I'm sure Eleanor has enjoyed her morning out in the fresh air instead of being confined to the house all day. Perhaps she met a friend, someone her own age to talk to.'

'You haven't been mixing with the people from the colliery rows, have you, Eleanor?' Mrs Wales asked sharply. 'Did you meet someone and talk?'

Eleanor studied the red roses in the carpet before answering. If she said she had been talking to a friend from Sunday School it might do but Grandmother might ask who it was and then there would be trouble – she would probably be confined to the house for the rest of her stay. Her mind flew back over her outing and she remembered the minister.

'I met Mr Nelson. He inquired after you, Grandmother. I thought I would offer to help at the chapel supper tonight, if you will allow it.'

'There, you see, Mother. A perfectly innocent outing. Now do come to the table, Eleanor, the soup's getting cold and I'm ready to say grace.'

Uncle John drove her to the Wesleyan chapel that evening, on his way to a meeting of his fellow colliery managers. The night had turned cold and frosty and Eleanor was glad of her warm cloak and the rug to put over her knees. As they came to a halt before the chapel, she saw there was quite a queue of people waiting and the stewards were ushering them forward into the schoolroom.

'I'll come back for you, my meeting won't take more than an hour,' said Uncle John as he handed her down on to the flags at the entrance and walked with her to the door. Eleanor was very conscious that all heads were turned towards them as they went past the queue. Why didn't the stewards let them in faster? she thought. It was so cold outside, the mud in the lane was already icing over, and some of the children had bare feet.

Inside, the schoolroom trestle tables were set out with barely space for two people to pass between them. The benches around them were filling up rapidly and Eleanor had to gather her skirts around her to make her way down to the serving table by the platform.

Mr Nelson stood by the table with Mr Briggs, a portly man with side whiskers and thatch of grey hair. Eleanor knew him slightly, for he was a lay preacher and she had heard him preach in the chapel at home. Beside him stood a young boy, half a head shorter than she was herself, fresh-faced and earnest-looking

The smell coming from the cauldron of broth that stood in the middle of the table made Eleanor feel slightly queasy: boiled turnips and cabbage mingling with the greasy ham bones.

'Oh, Miss Saint,' said Mrs Nelson, who was standing behind the table, enveloped in a large apron and with a ladle in her hand. 'Have you come to help? God bless you, my dear. We are few in number tonight, the weather being so bad. Some ladies don't like to venture out in the dark winter nights. And there is quite a crowd to serve, is there not? You know Mrs Herrington, do you?'

The apothecary's wife paused in her task of cutting thick slices of bread and piling them on plates and smiled at Eleanor. 'Perhaps you will serve the tea?' she said.

'Of course,' said Eleanor. She took off her cloak and hung it on one of the hooks to the side of the stage. Putting on the apron she had brought with her, she took her place behind the copper tea urn.

The schoolroom was full by this time and the stewards were ushering the last of the queue into the chapel itself, where extra tables had been erected. At last, everyone was inside and the doors closed. The buzz of conversation died down and all eyes looked to the platform as Mr Nelson climbed up, followed by the young boy.

'Good evening, friends,' said the minister. 'Some of you will know Master Francis Tait, grandson of Mr Briggs. I am happy to announce that he has decided to give his heart to the Lord and become a lay preacher. I am sure you will join with me in wishing him every success. Now, Francis will offer thanks for God's goodness in providing this food for our use.'

Eleanor stole a quick glance at the boy on the platform before bending her head for the prayer and was surprised to find him regarding her with steady brown eyes. Their gazes locked for a brief second before he turned calmly away and began to speak.

Chapter Two

'I believe we have a thief in the house, John,' said Grandmother Wales.

Eleanor stopped eating her breakfast of bacon and eggs and placed her knife and fork carefully side by side on the plate. Cautiously, she looked up at her grandmother to find that lady not looking at Uncle John, but staring icily at herself. Blushing furiously, she raised her napkin to her face.

'Surely not, Mother,' Uncle John said, sounding very surprised. 'The maids have been with us for years and they have always been honest before, haven't they?'

'I'm not talking about Phoebe or Jane,' said Mrs Wales, still keeping gimlet eyes on Eleanor. 'Nor Mrs Green.'

'Who then?'

Instead of answering her son's question, Mrs Wales spoke to Eleanor. 'Have you something to tell us, Eleanor?' Pointedly, she picked up two accounts that had been delivered with the morning post. Miserably, Eleanor saw the headings: one was from Mr Herrington, the apothecary, and one from the village grocer.

'Eleanor? What is this all about?' asked Uncle John. Eleanor was dumb, though her mind was racing furiously.

'Someone has been acquiring goods at the village shops and putting them on my account,' said Mrs Wales. And I'm sorry to say, it must have been Eleanor as it is she who has undertaken the marketing this last month.'

'Eleanor? Come now, you can tell us if it's not true, perhaps the tradesmen have made a mistake.' Uncle John wiped his moustache with his napkin and waited for Eleanor to speak. He ignored his mother's loud snort.

'I ... I can't say that, Uncle John,' Eleanor said at last. 'I'm sorry, I just didn't think—'

'You didn't think you would be found out?' Grandmother said, her voice heavy with sarcasm. 'You think I am so bad a housekeeper that I don't check the accounts? You are a thief, girl, you will burn in hell! Though God knows what you wanted with a pound of candles and a stone of flour. Not to mention a bottle of laudanum from Mr Herrington.'

'I'm not a thief! I will pay you out of my allowance, it's due any day now. I needed the goods for a friend, someone who is ill. Doesn't the Bible tell us to feed the hungry and help those who are ill?'

'How dare you speak to me like that! Preaching to your own grandmother about the Book! Go to your room, girl, you can stay there until I can arrange for you to go back to your mother. Perhaps she will have more success than I in controlling you.' Mrs Wales was trembling with rage, she clutched her napkin so tightly in her hand that her knuckles gleamed white in contrast to the alarming flush that enveloped her face and neck.

'Mother, Mother, calm yourself, you'll be ill,' Uncle John said urgently. 'You know the doctor said you must stay quiet with no excitement.' He looked across at his niece. 'Eleanor, do as she says now, go to your room. I will speak to you this evening, when everyone has calmed down. Go now.'

'I'm not a thief,' said Eleanor stubbornly.

Mrs Wales started up from her chair, raising her hand as though to strike her. 'No, and you're not too old for a beating, my girl! By, if I was but a few years younger I'd—' Her face had turned an unhealthy shade of red and her usually carefully cultivated speech had slipped, her vowels broadening

17

as her voice rose. Eleanor remembered that Grandmother's father had been a hewer down the pit.

'Mother, sit down.' Uncle John kept his voice calm and deliberately low as he moved to his mother's side and put his arm around her and forced her back into her seat. 'Eleanor, go now, I say.'

Eleanor stood for a second, her face flaming, her mouth open to protest, before turning on her heel and racing out of the room and up the stairs. She banged the door of her room shut behind her and flung herself on to her bed. Rage flooded through her, a rage every bit as high as her grandmother's and all the more so because she knew herself in the wrong. But what was she supposed to do? She had no money of her own and since her mother had gone to live with her older brother Tom and his wife Charlotte, earlier in the year, her allowance had been cut drastically; it barely covered her dressmaker's bills, small though they were.

She thought about Grandmother's threat to send her back to her mother – surely she would not do so. In Charlotte's house she would be worse off than she was here in Hetton-le-Hole. She would be expected to act as unpaid nursemaid to her spoilt little niece and nephew, Alice and Albert, and she couldn't bear the thought.

'Please, God,' she prayed aloud, 'don't let Uncle John send me away. I won't put another thing on Grandmother's accounts, really I won't.' She paused for a moment and shook her heavy hair back from her forehead, the better to be able to think. What would happen to the Buckles if she couldn't help them any more? Ben was growing older but it was still a long time before he would be earning a man's wage and the few shillings he got as a trapper boy were not enough to keep the family. And Mary, now, she could work, it was true, but what about young Prue and her mother if Mary wasn't there to see to them? Truly, it was a great problem, one she couldn't answer.

Rising from the bed she went to the window and looked out on the green paddock that lay at the back of the house with trees and bushes at the side planted by Grandfather Wales to screen the ugly pithead and slagheap and, most especially, any view of the colliery rows.

If only she had been born a boy, she thought miserably. Then she could have gone to Durham University and become a doctor – oh, how she had wanted to do that. She had thought that Uncle John would understand, he was so different to how her father had been – until the day she mentioned it to him and he had smiled gently at her and told her it was impossible. He had explained to her that men liked 'good' girls rather than clever ones and she had had to clench her hands until the nails bit into her palms to stop herself from screaming at him. Here they were into the second half of the nineteenth century and women in England were as much slaves as those poor black folk in America.

'Flaming hell!' she said loudly and then looked apprehensively at the door. Had someone heard her? And if they had, what would happen then? She'd likely be turned out of the door without a penny, why she might have to earn a living on the coal screens at the pit head. She had seen girls there, as black as the stones they were picking out of the coal; in fact, it had been from them she had heard the swear words. The upstairs hall was silent, however; no one had heard her. 'Flaming hell!' she said again, quieter this time. The words expressed how she felt so perfectly and she didn't care how wicked they were. Shaking her hair back from her face yet again, for it had already fallen out of its restraining ribbons, Eleanor glared out of the window for a moment before going back to her bed and flinging herself down on it again. She was still there when Uncle John knocked at the door at four o'clock.

'May I come in, Eleanor?'

'Just a minute, Uncle John.'

Eleanor jumped to her feet and smoothed down her dress, which was all wrinkled and creased from the hours she had spent on the bed. Her stomach rumbled; there was a delicious smell of food coming from the hall and not only had she left half her breakfast but she had had no dinner sent up to her at three o'clock. Grandmother's orders, no doubt.

'I'm ready now, Uncle John.'

Her uncle came in, closing the door quietly behind him, and came to stand in front of her. For a moment they looked at each other silently. He was a mild-mannered man, tall and earnest-looking. She thought he looked more like a college professor than a mine manager though she knew he ran the pit efficiently.

'Well, Eleanor.' It wasn't really a question, nor even a greeting, just a statement. 'Your grandmother has retired to her room, she is upset and feeling ill.'

'I'm sorry for that, Uncle John,' she answered. 'I will pay for the things I bought, just as soon as I get my allowance from Mother. I always intended to. The things were for poor Mrs Buckle, she's dying, Uncle John, and I couldn't let her die in the dark for want of a candle, could I? And they were hungry, so I thought flour for bread—'

'Sit down, Eleanor.' Uncle John waited until his niece sank into one of the two small armchairs by the window and then he took the other. 'Eleanor,' he said quietly, reasonably. 'We cannot look after all the destitute in the village, not you nor I. We simply cannot.' It was typical of him that he did not ask who Mrs Buckle was; he knew everyone in the village, even though there were hundreds of men working in the mines and living with their families in the colliery rows. 'I have given the boy employment, he is a trapper boy in the pit, isn't he? And though we are short enough of cottages for our workers, I allowed them to stay in their home after Mr Buckle was killed. I think I have done my duty. I must remind you, I am but the viewer here not the owner. I am like the servant in the parable of the talents who received five talents from the master. I have to manage the affairs of the mine wisely and make a profit for the mine owner.'

20

Eleanor raised hot eyes to him. 'But Mrs Buckle is so ill, Uncle John. I want to help, I went to Sunday School with Mary, it's our duty to help those less fortunate than ourselves. And I have been reading about Florence Nightingale in the *Ladies' Home Journal*. I can do what she does, after all, she is a lady and—'

'I know well who Florence Nightingale is,' said Uncle John. 'A lady of independent means, I understand. You cannot compare yourself with her, Eleanor, you are still a child.'

'I am not a child, Uncle John. I am almost sixteen. Why, when Grandmother was my age she had been earning her own living for almost ten years!'

Uncle John coughed dryly. 'Hush, Eleanor, do you want to upset her further? You know she does not like to be reminded of it.'

Eleanor subsided; she was indeed well aware that Grandmother Wales was very sensitive of the fact that she had never been to school but as a child had worked alongside her brothers on the coal screens, for her family was large. She had learned her reading and writing in the schoolroom at the Wesleyan chapel on Sunday mornings.

'Be a good girl, pet.' Uncle John changed his tone to one of persuasion. 'I would be sorry to see you sent back to your mother, you're a ray of sunshine in this dreary old house, you are. Now my mother has retired, I'll send you up a bite of supper so you don't lie awake with night starvation and tomorrow evening you can come with me to the missionary meeting.'

'Thank you, Uncle John.'

Eleanor's tone was meek, in contrast to her earlier rebellion, for she could tell Uncle John considered the episode finished. Any thoughts of following in the footsteps of Florence Nightingale were to be consigned to the midden, along with her earlier hopes of becoming a doctor. She stared for a moment at the door, which he had closed behind him, and then returned to the window, staring out into the black night that was lit only by a red glow to one side, behind the trees, where the colliery continued its ceaseless working. Though she was frustrated in everything she wanted to do, she told herself, she would do something, oh, she would, she would make her mark in the world and show them all. She would find some way, yes indeed.

Francis Tait was at the missionary meeting. Eleanor saw him as she came through the door to the schoolroom along with Uncle John, and she felt his eyes upon her, calm and steady and velvety brown. When she returned his gaze, he inclined his head gravely in the manner of a man twice his age, yet it did not make her laugh as it might have done in any other young boy.

'I see young Master Tait is here,' said Uncle John, looking down at her. His sharp eyes had missed nothing of the silent exchange of greetings between his niece and the boy preacher. 'He is apprenticed to learn business and commerce at Newcastle upon Tyne, perhaps he has a holiday.'

There was no time to say more as the meeting was called to order and Mr Nelson rose to introduce the guest speaker. There was a general rustle of anticipation, for it was Mr Mee, a visitor from the Australasian mission field, a man who had worked among the heathen of the savage islands they had heard such tales of – unspeakable tales of pagan rites, the wicked butchering of babies and more, the sin that the people of Hetton hardly dared breathe to each other. Eleanor watched and listened, enthralled, her mind taken completely off her own mundane trials and troubles as Mr Mee described fierce warriors, naked as the day they were born but for a few feathers in their hair, and armed with tall spears, warriors who would kill and eat you as soon as look at you.

Eleanor felt someone's eyes upon her and glanced along the row, catching Francis Tait watching her. She lifted her chin and gazed at him loftily, and he blushed, quickly turning his attention on the speaker. Eleanor smiled to herself, feeling strangely pleased even though he was just a boy, years younger than herself. She was glad she had bothered to put on her new straw bonnet with its fringe of lace that hid her unruly hair.

The next minute she had forgotten all about Francis Tait and everyone else around her as she listened enthralled to Mr Mee describing how the natives had no real doctors, only heathen witch doctors and when they fell ill of even such mild illnesses as the common cold they often died because the witch doctors used the most horrific remedies, which seldom worked.

For half an hour Eleanor gazed at Mr Mee, but she wasn't seeing the missionary, she was seeing herself going among sick natives like an angel of mercy, like Florence Nightingale, dispensing medicine and wise advice and saving them from the wicked witch doctors, and they would all adore her and call her the Lady from Heaven. Oh yes, she could be a medical missionary, or at least a nursing missionary, and the heathen hordes would all be converted to Christianity and become civilised human beings.

'Eleanor, wake up, child.'

Uncle John was taking hold of her arm and the people were getting to their feet. For a moment she was disorientated, her mind still in distant lands, and she didn't know why they were standing.

'The grace of our Lord, Jesus Christ, the love of God—'

Oh, yes, of course, the meeting had ended, as always with the saying of the Grace. The members were moving about and beginning to chat among themselves and suddenly Francis Tait was standing before her.

'Good evening, Miss Saint,' he said. 'Good evening, Mr Wales.'

'Hello, Francis,' said Uncle John. 'You will excuse me, won't you, I wish to have a word with Mr Mee.'

Francis and Eleanor were left looking at each other. He has grown, she thought abstractedly, realising his eyes were on a level with her own now.

'Did you enjoy the talk, Miss Saint?' he asked politely.

'Oh yes, indeed, Mr Tait,' she answered, full of enthusiasm.

Francis smiled at her animation, encouraged. 'I intend to enter the Wesleyan Missionary College in London as soon as I am seventeen. I am greatly drawn to the work.' He would have sounded impossibly pompous except that his voice broke during the last statement and became almost a squeak.

Eleanor, however, hardly noticed it. The animation was fading from her face and she turned abruptly from him. 'I must find Uncle John, it is time I was going home,' she muttered and pushed through the crowd away from him, leaving him staring after her looking suddenly young and dismayed. Why did his voice let him down at the important times?

It's not fair, Eleanor was saying to herself as she waited for Uncle John to stop speaking to Mr Mee, her eyes fixed on the scrubbed boards of the floor. He was a boy; he could go away to college and become a missionary, he would have all the adventures, he could do anything. What could she do? Nothing, that was what, nothing at all, except be a good little wife to someone and stay at home and never make a name for herself, never have any fun. That was if anyone would have her and, according to Grandmother Wales, even that was doubtful. She would never be able to follow her dreams, never, she might just as well settle herself to it.

'Come along, Eleanor, it is time we were going.'

'Yes, Uncle John.'

She followed her uncle out of the hall, not even looking to see if Francis Tait saw her going. What did she care if he did or not; waves of envy were sweeping over her and in that moment she hated him.

Chapter Three

Eleanor stood by Mary and her young brother and sister as the minister recited the burial service and the plain deal box, which was all the Poor Law Guardians allowed, was lowered into the grave. It was the corner of the churchyard where all those who were buried on the Parish were laid to rest and it was behind the church, out of sight of the imposing tomb-stones of the more affluent dead.

Prue was whimpering, for the corner was dark and damp, and what could be seen of her feet between the patches of mud was blue with cold. Automatically, Mary bent down and swung the child up in her arms and rested her weight on one hip. Mary's face was set and white but she did not weep and neither did nine-year-old Ben; he simply stood there and watched as his mother's body was laid to rest.

The service was over and the small gathering of neighbours began to move away, most of them glancing curiously at Eleanor, the viewer's niece, in her plain black dress and poke bonnet. But the day was cold and they didn't linger. After all, there would be no funeral tea to send off poor Mrs Buckle, no, and no doubt it would be the workhouse for the little lass too, for the family had no kin left to help them. Young Ben might manage to get a family to give him house room, as he was used to the pit now and in a year or two would be earning good money as a putter or even a hewer of coal. Housewives with more girls in the house than boys looked appraisingly at Ben and both Eleanor and Mary knew exactly what they were thinking.

'Come, Mary, we should go now,' Eleanor said when everyone had left and the minister had given them his condolences and gone back to his manse. 'At least Uncle John has agreed to let you keep the house for now and there's coal in the coal shed, Prue can get warm.'

'Aye, Mary,' said Ben. 'Let's away, I have to go down with the night-shift men the night.'

At first Eleanor thought Mary hadn't heard, she was standing so still, simply looking at the grave. Then, holding Prue with one hand, Mary delved inside her apron and pulled out a bedraggled bunch of snowdrops and laid them at the head. Shaking her head, she turned away, her mood completely changed.

'Now then,' she said. 'We'd best get back out of this wind or we'll all be taking our beds.' She started to stride towards the gate and then stopped and looked at Eleanor. 'Do you need me up at the house today, Miss Eleanor? I can leave Prue on her own now, she knows not to do anything daft, she'll be all right at home in the warm.

'No, no, of course not Mary,' answered Eleanor. 'Tomorrow will be soon enough I'm sure.' Though she would have to explain to Grandmother that she had given Mary the rest of the day off, thought Eleanor ruefully as she turned away and started to walk home on her own. She had been going to accompany the family back to their cottage but some instinct told her now that they wanted to be by themselves to mourn in their own way. At least there was bread in the house, she knew that, for Ben had been paid his fortnightly wage yesterday, along with the rest of the men.

Mary walked back to their tiny cottage in the row with Ben and Prue, her thoughts bitter. Poor Mam, these last years had stretched out for her, filled with such pain that her daughter had longed for her to go. Yet when the end did come it had filled Mary with a wild anger and sorrow. Why had it had to happen? Was it not enough that Da had been taken in the pit? What did God have against them? Why was He punishing them? God didn't care, she decided. He probably didn't even know the Buckles existed. If He was there, that is. Maybe He was just an invention to keep the poor folk down, folk like them.

There was Eleanor Saint an' all. Thought she was a proper Lady Bountiful, dishing out lavender water to Mam as though that would cure what was eating away her head, bringing them flour and dripping and beef tea when Mam couldn't eat bread — all she had wanted was strawberries, she'd murmured about them all the time, remembering when she and Da was young and Da had taken her into Durham and bought her them in the market. Eleanor could have got her strawberries, of course she could. Eleanor had plenty money even if that old witch Margaret Wales plagued her all the time. But when Mary had asked her, she had tut-tutted and said strawberries were too expensive and unnecessary.

No, thought Mary as she opened the door of the cottage and stepped in, keeping her eyes averted from the empty bed in the corner, Eleanor knew nowt really, she didn't. She was just playing at being a Saint by nature as well as name.

'Howay then,' Mary said sharply to Ben. 'Get your pit clothes on, we can't afford for you to miss the cage going down the day.'

Mary knew she was being unfair, both to Eleanor and Ben, but she couldn't seem to help it. She was full of rage against God and the world.

Ben's face was white and drawn, his eyes full. Listlessly he changed and picked up the battered bait tin containing his jam sandwiches and slipped the water bottle into the pocket of his coat.

'I'm off then,' he said and went out of the door, joining the stream of night-shift men making for the pit head.

*

It had taken Uncle John to persuade Grandmother that Mary was suitable to be her maid, mused Eleanor as she walked home.

'What does the chit want with a maid?' Grandmother had asked. 'It's a waste of money, that's what it is, and mark my words, she'll be putting on airs next, think she's as good as the gentry.'

Which was a bit much coming from Grandmother, who put on airs all the time and was always disciplining Eleanor for mingling with the pit folk.

'Miss Barnes has a personal maid,' Uncle John remarked slyly and that silenced Grandmother. For Miss Barnes was the daughter of the agent, the man who oversaw all the mine managers such as Uncle John, and Grandmother tried to follow the agent's wife in all things.

'She'll have to help in the kitchen as well then,' Grandmother had said and so it had been agreed. Mary had come to the viewer's house to work and was allowed to sleep out to enable her to see to her family, although it turned out that in practice she was more of a kitchen maid than a personal one.

As Eleanor took her cloak and bonnet off in the hall of the viewer's house, all her sad thoughts disappeared. There, propped up on the hall table, was a letter. A letter from London – oh, it had to be a letter from Florence Nightingale, surely it would tell her what to do, how to break out of her narrow, boring little life. Snatching it up, she carried it upstairs to her bedroom and closed the door so she could read it in privacy. Her heart beat fast as she stood with her back to the door and opened the letter, noting the address: the Institute for Sick Gentlemen. Seeing the notice in *The Times* that Florence Nightingale had been appointed superintendent of the Institute had been the spur that had prompted Eleanor to write to her. Oh, she was ready to run away to London tomorrow to join Miss Nightingale; she was willing to scrub floors, clean out bedpans even, anything, if only she could train as a nurse, a proper nurse.

Miss Nightingale did not want her. That was the gist of the letter. Set out in forthright terms, it told her she was not educated enough, she was not old enough, even that she was not quite of the class from which Miss Nightingale intended to draw her nurses. And it advised her that even if she had been she would need written permission from her guardian.

'Miss Nightingale suggests that if you really feel you have a vocation then you will find a niche in your own community.'

The ending was polite but curt and it wasn't even signed by Florence Nightingale but some secretary whose name Eleanor couldn't decipher.

Crushing the letter into a ball, Eleanor threw it under the bed and herself on top where she beat at the pillow with her fists, anger surging through her. So she wasn't good enough to train as a nurse, that was the nub of it. Well, she'd show them, oh yes she would, she'd show them all, Miss Florence Nightingale, Grandmother, Uncle John, everybody. She would train herself, work among the pit folk, help Dr Andrews, send away for books out of her allowance. Turning over on to her back, Eleanor set to work making plans. Florence Nightingale had started on her own, hadn't she? Well, of course, she had gone to Germany to undertake some training, but what could the Germans teach Eleanor that she couldn't teach herself?

Francis was in his lodging house in Newcastle packing his bag, which stood open on his bed. At last he was beginning to realise his ambition, at last he was giving up the world of commerce and dedicating his life to the service of God. He paused for a moment, a spare pair of stockings in his hand, and gazed out of the window of the lodging house on the quay, over the river to Gateshead, though he wasn't seeing the Tyne or the coal staithes dropping their coal into the keel boats. No, he was seeing the Thames at Richmond and the Wesleyan College where he was soon to begin his training. A river as different from the Tyne as ... as heaven was from earth, he thought.

He fingered the soft brown down on his chin pensively; would it ever grow into the full beard so many of his fellow preachers sported? Turning to the small looking glass hanging on the back of the door, Francis gazed into it anxiously, not seeing the high forehead and symmetrical features gazing back at him but only that, in spite of the beard, the youthful roundness of his cheeks was still obvious to anyone. No wonder Miss Saint thought of him as still a boy, he thought ruefully. But that wouldn't last, oh no – when he came back from London he would be a man of the world, ready to set out on the great adventure of converting the heathen and he would marry her and take her with him. For a man needed a wife, especially a missionary man, he needed a woman's aid. Unaccountably, Francis blushed, feeling strangely excited. What was he thinking about, today of all days? His mind ought to be on God, he should be giving thanks to his Maker for this chance to serve Him. God would always come first with him, he told himself, and it would be only fair to make that plain to Eleanor before they married.

Folding his long legs, he sank to his knees, clasped his hands together and resolutely concentrated on prayer. It would be years before he was in a position to marry Eleanor and until then he must keep his thoughts clean and pure. It never occurred to him that Eleanor might not wish to wait all those years for him or even marry him at all.

Rising to his feet, Francis finished packing his clothes and placed his Bible on the top where it would be easy to get at. He smiled and ran his fingers over it, enjoying the sensuous feel of the calfskin-bound volume, the distinctive scent of new leather. It had been a gift from the chapel at Hetton-le-Hole when he gave his farewell sermon there only last week and it replaced the battered old copy he had had as a Sunday

School prize years ago. The leather felt so rich— Abruptly he snapped the bag shut and turned to put on his coat and hat. Perhaps he liked rich things too much?

As he picked up the bag and ran down the stairs and out into the icy air of the quayside, the slightly guilty feeling was swamped in the gladness that flooded through him. The great adventure was about to start. Well, at least the training for it was. He turned into Castle Chare, which climbed steeply up from the quayside and on to the railway station.

Chapter Four

Eleanor glared at her reflection in the looking glass as Mary struggled to mould her heavy hair into the loops and twirls demanded of the fashion of the new decade. 'Oh, leave it, Mary, you're never going to get it just so, it's too heavy. I can't be bothered with it, just pin it up under my cap. Mother and Fanny will be here any minute and if I'm not downstairs to greet them that will be something else for Grandmother and Mother to complain about.'

'But—' Mary began and Eleanor glanced impatiently at her reflection, her attention arrested for a moment by the contrast between Mary's blonde, biddable waves and ringlets topped by a plain starched cap, and her own unruly locks.

'Oh, go on, Mary, I know you have work to do in the kitchen, go and get on with it,' said Eleanor, slightly snappish. She rose to her feet and moved away from the dressing table, smoothing down her pale blue taffeta gown as she did so. Lord, she looked sallow in blue, she thought; the dress was more suitable for Mary's colouring than her own. But it was Grandmother's idea of what a young girl should wear, gleaned from the pages of the *Ladies' Home Journal*, which Grandmother had delivered every month. In vain had Eleanor protested that she preferred plain, dark colours or maybe a dark green for evening wear.

'I'm almost twenty-four, Grandmother,' she had pointed out. 'Not a young girl any more.'

'No, and you're fast becoming a bitter old spinster!'

'I don't wish to be married,' Eleanor had said patiently, as she had said every time Grandmother had invited a young man to dinner or Mother had written inviting her home to meet a promising man. No doubt that was the reason Mother and Fanny were coming for the weekend; Grandmother probably had a man coming to dinner and they were invited too to make it look like a dinner party.

Grumpily, Eleanor pulled on her white lace evening gloves, snagging the lace on the rough skin of her fingers. Rough skin caused by the carbolic acid she had bought for Mrs Simpson, a miner's wife with twelve children and no strength to keep them clean and healthy even though the neighbours did what they could to help. Eleanor had seen the angry red bug bites on the new baby and rolled up her own sleeves and demonstrated to the oldest Simpson child how to make a 1-in-20 solution of the acid and scrub the walls where the bed bugs lurked.

Thinking of it, Eleanor smiled grimly. It was just as well Grandmother didn't know about that, she thought. There was enough trouble as it was; Eleanor's 'meddling' with the miners' families, as Grandmother called her work, was a constant complaint.

'It's hard enough trying to find a man willing to marry you when you won't even try to improve your appearance,' Grandmother lamented often enough and Uncle John would frown at his mother if he was present. 'But what man wants a wife who risks disease and the Lord knows what else going among the riff-raff? I tell you, Eleanor, it's not womanly!' When in fact it was very womanly, and just what the Bible exhorted one to do, thought Eleanor rebelliously, but it was no good saying that to Grandmother Wales.

Sighing, Eleanor opened her bedroom door. She could hear the murmur of voices and clatter of dishes as Mary and Prue worked in the kitchen, for Prue was thirteen now and was often brought in to help Mary when the Waleses entertained. That meant there was another guest apart from family and Eleanor's spirits sank as she started down the stairs. It was so humiliating when she was paraded in front of a possible suitor like this; it made her feel like one of the horses the gypsies ran up and down the green during the horse fair.

It was not as though she hadn't something better to do – there was the chapel tea and bazaar to organise for Saturday and everyone else made such a muddle of these things. It was in aid of Overseas Missions, and it was very important that it did well. For wasn't it specifically to help send Francis Tait, who had finished his training at the Wesley College at Richmond Hill and was coming to preside at the tea on Saturday, to the Australian mission field? The familiar pang of envy went through her at the thought, but she was used to the idea that she couldn't go herself. Oh, why had God made her female?

Eleanor was frowning blackly as she flung open the door of the parlour, which Grandmother called the drawing room, and strode in, only to come to a sudden halt when she realised there was someone there. A tall, broad figure, dressed totally in black except for a snowy-white clerical collar, rose to his feet and stepped forward.

'Oh! I'm sorry, I didn't realise—' said Eleanor.

'Miss Saint.'

The strange minister's voice was a firm, assured deep baritone and Eleanor gazed up at him as he came within the circle of the lamplight. And even though she had just been thinking of him it took her a moment to recognise Francis Tait.

'Oh, I'm sorry,' she repeated. 'It's Mr Tait, isn't it? I'm afraid I didn't recognise you, it's so long since I saw you.'

Fleetingly, the image ran through her mind of the time when he spoke to her in chapel, trying to be oh so grown up, and his voice had wobbled and broken. Well, he was certainly grown up now, she decided, as he took her hand in his and held it for a moment longer than necessary. She looked up into his face, half obscured by the bushy beard that seemed to be almost part of the uniform for Methodist preachers, a beard that was a rich, deep brown, though not so rich and deep as the colour of his eyes.

'I'm so sorry you have been left on your own, Mr Tait. If Mary had told me I would have come down sooner.' Where was Uncle John? Surely he would not have left a minister of the church sitting on his own?

'No, no, I have been perfectly all right,' said Francis. 'It's my fault, my train got in a little early but I have only just arrived, I assure you. Mr Wales was here but he was called away, something to do with the mine, I believe.'

Eleanor was suddenly conscious of her pale blue dress and badly dressed hair; she must really look a sight. 'Do sit down,' she mumbled and took a seat on the opposite side of a table covered with an ornate, fringed cover, which managed to hide most of her dress. Not that it mattered, of course it didn't – why should it matter what any man thought of her appearance?

'I hear from your uncle that you take a keen interest in the mining folk and their welfare,' said Francis. 'Besides your work for the chapel, I've heard you are also an indefatigable fund-raiser for the missions.'

Eleanor looked down at her lace-covered hands, twisting them in her lap. So even Uncle John had been coerced into helping to find her a husband, she thought.

'Your reputation is to your credit, Miss Saint,' said Francis, rather pompously, she thought.

'Not at all,' she murmured. Heavens, if this was the extent of his conversation it was becoming very boring. She looked up in relief at the sound of the front-door bell. 'Oh, that will be Mother.'

Sure enough, a moment or two later Mary opened the parlour door and Mrs Saint swept into the room, her youngest daughter Fanny following in her wake. She bent her head in acknowledgement to Francis. 'Now then, Minister, how are you?' she said, hardly waiting for his murmured reply before crossing to Eleanor and pecking her on the cheek. 'You look healthy enough, Eleanor,' she said, as her daughters greeted each other.

'Yes, of course, Mother,' said Eleanor, surprised. 'You know I enjoy good health.'

'But not good enough to visit your mother too often. It is quite three months since you came to see us.'

'I have been busy, Mother,' said Eleanor. 'There has been much sickness in the village and I—'

'Oh yes, of course. The pitmen and their black-faced brats have to come before your own mother and sisters.' Mrs Saint's voice was hard and bitter. Fanny, who had hardly spoken a word as yet and not moved from her mother's side, looked quickly at Francis, her brown eyes, so like Eleanor's with their dark lashes and straight brows, embarrassed.

'Mother, perhaps we should sit down?' she said and in an attempt to change the subject added, 'How is Grandmother Wales, Eleanor?'

Her mother flicked her hand at Fanny as though she were a bothersome fly and Eleanor noticed, not for the first time, how like she was to Grandmother Wales.

'Don't interrupt me when I'm talking to your sister, Fanny,' Mrs Saint said peremptorily.

'I don't wish to contradict you, Mrs Saint, but it's my opinion that Eleanor does excellent work among the poor. And after all, Jesus said that anyone who did anything for little children did it also for Him.'

Eleanor shot Francis a grateful glance. The evening had got off to a bad start – what was her mother thinking of, ranting on like that before a guest, a minister at that? And surely it hadn't been so long since she had visited her? Well, thank goodness her mother seemed to have recollected herself and was sitting down, thus allowing everyone else to do so.

Uncle John came into the room. He shook Francis's hand, apologising that he hadn't been there to greet him when he arrived. 'The pit, you know, so many problems,' he said before greeting his sister and niece. 'Shall we go in?' he asked, preliminaries over. 'I took Mother straight into the dining room, Elizabeth,' he added to his sister. 'I'm afraid you'll see a big difference in her since you saw her last, she's becoming unsteady on her legs.'

The company trailed through the small hall to the dining room, John with his sister on his arm and Francis bringing up the rear behind Eleanor and Fanny. Eleanor gazed at her grandmother, already seated at the table; indeed she was frail; why had she not noticed just how frail? The old woman was shrinking in on herself somehow.

There was nothing frail about her temper. 'How good of you to come to see me, Elizabeth,' she said to her daughter, her voice heavy with sarcasm. Fanny caught Eleanor's eye and smiled faintly, for Mrs Wales sounded so much like their mother, even down to the same complaint. But Uncle John, ever the diplomat, quickly steered the conversation into more pleasant channels, questioning Francis about his proposed missionary appointment far away in the Australasian field, involving the women in the conversation.

Eleanor, seated next to Francis, was very conscious that he was there; occasionally the serge of his black coat brushed against the bare skin of her arm as he reached for his glass of raspberry cordial or leaned sideways a little for Mary to serve the roast beef and Yorkshire pudding. The sensation could have been pleasant but Eleanor was also conscious of the unbecoming blue dress and the fact that her hair had escaped its pins and was dangling down on her shoulders. Yet what did that matter? she asked herself; it was not her purpose to net him for a husband, was it?

The beef was succulent and rare and the pudding light and airy; Francis ate heartily as did the rest of the company with the exception of Eleanor. She normally had a good appetite but this evening it had unaccountably deserted her and she was absentmindedly pushing the food around her plate.

'What on earth's the matter with you, child? Eat your dinner, everyone's waiting for you.'

Her grandmother's voice made Eleanor start and she hastily cut a piece of beef, put it in her mouth and swallowed it, choking a little so that Francis became concerned and offered her a glass of cordial. Lordy, what a fool she was, and all because Francis Tait was asked to dinner and why shouldn't he be? He was off to far-away places to work among the heathens soon.

It was at that moment the idea was born: why shouldn't she get Francis to marry her, then she would go with him on his adventures? She would be away from the restrictions imposed on her by English convention and surely among the natives she would find sufficient scope for developing her medical and nursing skills? Eleanor turned a brilliant smile on Francis and began to eat her meal with a new appetite.

'I believe I am quite hungry suddenly,' she said.

Francis was encouraged, to say the least. He put up a quick hand to brush back the lock of hair that persisted in waving across his forehead and smiled quickly back at her. Sitting up straighter, he resumed his conversation with Uncle John but his mind was on the girl at his side.

Oh yes, he had been right. God was drawing him to Eleanor; it was meant to be. She was just exactly the helpmeet he needed in his new life; he had known it all along. A good girl, a life-long Methodist as he was himself, and strong and healthy too, which was important in the mission field. The superintendent would approve his choice, he was sure of it. He cast a swift glance at her as she laid her knife and fork side by side on her plate and sat back in her chair, touching her lips with her napkin.

A fine-looking girl, he thought happily. Such lustrous brown hair, such a white skin touched so delicately with rose. And her air of vitality—

'When exactly do you expect to go, Mr Tait?'

Mrs Wales's question broke into his musing and he looked up, a little embarrassed that he had let his thoughts wander off the conversation. Eleanor's mother and grandmother exchanged knowing glances.

'Oh, I haven't an exact date yet, Mrs Wales,' he said. 'All will be arranged shortly.'

He was expected to take a wife, he had been told that plainly.

'Have you a lady in mind?' the superintendent had asked and Francis had replied that he had, even though his courtship was all in his mind so far. But now it would begin in earnest. As the meal came to an end and the company looked to him to give thanks, he rose to his feet and bent his head.

'Thank You, Father, for the food You have given us in Your bountiful mercy this evening. And we thank You for Your eternal goodness to us, Your servants, and especially for the gift of Your Son, Jesus Christ, our Lord.'

The company adjourned to the parlour, only now Francis held Eleanor's arm with a touch so light she could easily move away if she disliked it. Eleanor, however, did not. Francis looked down at her, noticing the blue gown for the first time and hoping she was not fond of pale taffetas; the proper dress of a minister's wife was black serge with perhaps a small touch of white at the neck. What was it John Wesley had said on the subject? Something about a woman needing no other adornment than the goodness of her soul shining in her eyes. A tactful word to Eleanor on the subject perhaps? Well, all in good time. Oh yes, he thought, the courting would start now. A pleasurable feeling of anticipation ran through him.

'Mr Tait, miss,' said Prue.

It was the following morning and Eleanor was just finishing breakfast. She was on her own in the dining room, for Uncle John had long since left to present his report to the mining agent and Grandmother Wales always breakfasted in bed nowadays.

Eleanor put down her cup and rose to her feet. 'Thank you, Prue. Will you ask him to wait in the parlour? I'm coming directly.'

Prue went out without a word or a curtsey and Eleanor pulled a wry face. She was trying to teach the girl so she would get a good job in another household as Grandmother had made it plain there was no room for her in the viewer's house. But it was uphill work, for Prue was too independent a spirit to make a good servant.

Glancing at her reflection in the ornate looking glass that hung over the fireplace, Eleanor tucked her hair more securely under the plain white cap she had faithfully copied from one worn by Florence Nightingale in a picture taken on her return from the Crimea. In it she was wearing a plain black dress with narrower skirts than was the fashion, as a crinoline hampered her movements when she was working among the sick. And today Eleanor was visiting Mrs Brown, a woman who was lying-in after the birth of her thirteenth child, and both mother and baby were sickly. Well then, she thought, Francis might not be struck by her beauty but he would see what a capable woman she was and how eminently suitable as a missionary's wife.

Francis had had time to be settled in the parlour, she judged, and with a last glance in the looking glass, she went out and through the small hall to the parlour. This was a very important meeting and casting her eyes upwards as she laid her hand on the door knob Eleanor sent up a quick prayer: 'Please, God, let me do everything right, let Francis think I am the wife for him.' Excitement lent a sparkle to her eyes as she went in and Francis responded to it immediately, going forward and taking her hand confidently.

'How well you look this morning, Miss Saint,' he said. 'I hope you don't mind me calling so early?'

'Not at all, Mr Tait, I am very pleased to see you,' said Eleanor, smiling up into his eyes in a way that would have made Grandmother Wales snort in displeasure and order her to her room. And the attraction Francis had always felt for her grew into a powerful force.

At Eleanor's invitation, he accompanied her on her mission, walking with her and carrying her basket as she went to see Mrs Brown. Together they went through the pit rows, greeting the miners' wives who came to their doors, curious at the sight of the young minister walking with the viewer's niece. They were used to seeing Eleanor; she was in amongst them every day and not always as welcome as she thought she was by the miners, for they were suspicious of her as one of 'them'.

The wives were not always welcoming to her either, or her habit of coming and overturning customs that had served them for generations. There was her passion for fresh air, for example, when the cottage windows had been kept shut at all times to keep out the stink of the coke ovens and the middens. Why, she had even persuaded the colliery joiner to mend windows that had been nailed shut for years. The viewer had soon stopped that after a deputation of wives had gone to the colliery office to put their case.

The minister, though, was welcome. It was true he was a Wesleyan and many of the pit folk were Primitive Methodists, but it could not be denied that in the hard times the Wesleyans put on a good soup kitchen and the chapel suppers were not to be missed. So the women nodded and murmured a greeting to Francis and Eleanor as they walked through the muddy streets and the children clung to their mothers' skirts and stared.

The Browns were a Wesleyan family and Jeremiah Brown, who had been sitting at the kitchen table about to start a meal of bread and a couple of boiled eggs, rose to his feet as Francis and Eleanor knocked at the open door and went in. He was black from the pit, except for where rivulets of sweat had run down his face, making channels through the coal dust. As he rose, coal dust jumped from his clothes, shimmering in the sunlight coming through the small window.

'Minister!' he cried. "By, we never expected to see you. I thought you would have been on your way to convert the heathens by now.' A thought struck him and he faltered. 'Are you collecting for the missions? Eeh, I don't know, it's not paynight till next Friday, but mebbe I can spare a copper.' Turning to the fireplace, he started to reach up to the high mantelpiece but Francis stopped him.

'Oh no, Mr Brown, indeed, I know you will have already given what you can spare. No, Miss Saint was coming to see your wife and baby and I decided to come with her, I hope you don't mind. I am at leisure until I go away and it's a good opportunity to meet and thank the people who have supported me.'

You will forgive me, Lord, Francis prayed silently, fleetingly. I would have visited all the members before I left, of course I would, it is not really a lie.

The miner turned back to the table, not bothering to hide his relief. Two little boys, dressed only in the flannel shirts they had worn for bed, came to his elbow.

'Da, Da, can I have the top off the egg?' they clamoured, staring fixedly at the boiled eggs on his plate.

'The wife's in the room,' said their father, as he topped the eggs and gave a piece each to the boys, along with a piece of bread and dripping. 'She's not so good today.'

'I'll go straight in,' said Eleanor briskly. 'Perhaps you will wait for me here, Mr Tait?' Taking an apron out of the basket, which Francis had placed on the table, she went into the sitting room and closed the door behind her. After all, Mrs Brown was in bed in the sitting room and it wouldn't do for Francis to see her, him being a single man.

Mrs Brown was pale and wan and lines of exhaustion on her face made her look nearer fifty than the thirty she actually was. When she spoke her voice drifted weakly on her shallow breath.

'Good of you to come, Miss Saint.'

'Are you feeling worse, Mrs Brown? Did you take the beef tea I left with you yesterday? You'll never get your strength back unless you eat properly, you know.' Eleanor was put out, quite irrationally she knew, but when she helped anyone she liked to see a result almost immediately. Mrs Brown nodded her head, not wasting any energy on talking. She watched as Eleanor went to the drawer standing on two chairs by the bed and looked down at the baby. The same drawer had been used as a crib for all thirteen of the Browns' babies in their turn.

The baby was asleep, a tiny drop of milk at the corner of his mouth. He was small, probably no more than five or six pounds in weight, Eleanor surmised, but he was a good colour.

'I'll bathe him,' said Eleanor and Mrs Brown looked alarmed. Finding a little strength, she lifted her head from the pillow.

'No, no, my neighbour has done it all, washed him and seen to me an' all. Don't wake him, he's just got to sleep.'

'Oh, very well.' Eleanor stepped towards the bed, leaving the baby reluctantly. She strongly suspected the baby had been wrapped in strips of rag 'to keep his limbs nice and straight', as she had heard so many old wives say, in spite of her explaining they were better left to nature. But there was a great deal of rickets in the village and every mother was worried about bow legs or knock knees. Swaddling was their remedy for it and it was no good arguing with the mother now; Mrs Brown wasn't up to it.

'You look tired,' she said instead.

'I was up with the two littlest ones, both of them are teething, that's all,' said Mrs Brown. 'I'm all right now Jeremiah's in, I'll be able to get some sleep. Like I said, my neighbour's been in and done for me.'

Eleanor realised she was being told to go away and for a moment she was hurt; hadn't she done all she could for the family when they couldn't afford a doctor at the birth and the old woman who usually 'did' for Mrs Brown was in bed with an ague?

'I'll leave you to sleep while you can then,' was all she said and she stripped off her pinafore and rolled it up ready to put into her basket.

Mrs Brown put out a hand and touched her lightly on the sleeve of her black dress. 'I am grateful for what you've done, Miss Saint,' she said softly, her eyes already closing. Mollified a little, Eleanor went out of the room.

As she and Francis walked back to the viewer's house, she was noticeably quiet, the sparkle in her eyes dimmed. They had called in on Mrs Simpson but that lady was busy washing clothes in the back yard. It seemed no one wanted Eleanor's services this day and she had been so anxious to show Francis how good she was with the poor and sick.

'It must be good to find your ministrations are no longer needed,' said Francis as they left the colliery rows and turned into the lane.

'Well, I—' Eleanor began and stopped, not knowing how to carry on.

'I mean, you must have been so very successful in what you did for them before that they needed little help today,' he went on and smiled down at her. 'And isn't it a blessing? It means you and I can spend the afternoon together. I have some papers on Fiji I would like to show you, even some illustrations. Would you like that? With your grandmother's permission, of course. I could bring them over after lunch if I may.'

Eleanor's heart lifted as she acquiesced eagerly. There now, she thought, she had made an impression on him, her plan was working and he was interested in her even though she was such a plain-looking girl. At last things were beginning to happen in her life.

It was only a week later when Francis proposed to her as they were walking on the edge of the woods one Saturday afternoon. The brilliant colours of the changing leaves shone in the late autumn sunshine and the grime of the pit village seemed a world away. Eleanor's hand was laid lightly on Francis's arm and he was gravely silent so that she stole a glance at him, wondering what he was thinking.

'The trees are so beautiful, aren't they?' she said at last, more to break the silence than anything else.

Francis helped her over a stile before turning her to face him.

'Will you marry me, Eleanor?' he said and Eleanor beamed all over her face.

'Oh yes, Francis, I will,' she replied and waited for him to kiss her but Francis merely took her hand and replaced it on his arm.

'You have made me so happy, my dear,' he said. As they walked on she could feel the slight tremble in the arm under her fingers and his face was slightly flushed; whether with success or agitation she couldn't say. Strangely, neither of them noticed that no word of love or even affection had passed between them.

Chapter Five

Eleanor stood beside Francis on the deck of the *Liberator*, watching the small group of black-clad people from the Missionary Society, their white handkerchiefs fluttering in the wind that was sweeping up the channel, dashing the waves against the quay and rocking the ship even as it weighed anchor and began to move away. Eleanor shivered, as much from the excitement of finally getting under way as from the icy December wind.

The missionary party stood close together, quietly watching England slip away. The wives – all young women and all wrapped up in voluminous dark skirts and cloaks – stood closer to their husbands as the reality of the sailing sank in. The men smiled and nodded to each other, masking the fact that they were as uncertain as the women now that the time had come.

Eleanor looked further along the deck to where Mary and Prue were standing, just the two of them, Mary with an arm around her young sister. She made an involuntary movement towards the girls and would have liked to have gone over to join them for this last glimpse of home but a glance at Francis stayed her. He was watching her, a slight frown appearing between his eyes as she stepped forward, and she stood still.

Francis hadn't wanted her to bring Mary and Prue. But what was she to do? Grandmother Wales had made it plain that when Eleanor went she had no use for Mary, let alone Prue.

'Flibberty-gibbet, that girl Prue is, any road, mark my words,' Grandmother had declared. 'I won't have her in the house, making eyes at the menfolk, it's not decent.'

In vain, Eleanor had protested that Prue was only thirteen and she didn't realise the effect her bright curls and impish smiles had on the opposite sex; she was only a child.

'Thirteen she may be, but she has the ways of a woman and a scarlet woman she'll become, I'm sure. But she'll not shame my house, she won't get the chance.'

Eleanor watched Prue now, the only one of them all who didn't seem saddened by leaving England. In fact, she didn't look at all sad. Prue was looking at the group of sailors working on deck as the sails unfurled and the ship gathered speed in the freshening wind. And more than one of the men spared time to glance down at the two sisters and especially at Prue who was smiling broadly now.

The little by-play had not escaped the notice of the group of missionaries and their wives and disapproving looks were cast at the girls.

'Go below at once, Mary, you too, Prue,' said Francis harshly and Eleanor bit her lip. He was right, of course; it was a mistake to offend their companions right at the beginning of the journey, and heaven knew, the voyage would be long enough. Although she had paid for the girls' steerage tickets herself out of the small legacy left by her father and which she had come into on her marriage, she was painfully aware that the money rightly belonged to Francis now and he had been against the idea.

'Steerage passengers should not be on deck,' said Miss Tookey, the schoolteacher of the group. She sniffed and stared down her thin nose at Eleanor while the Reverend White and his dumpy little wife nodded in agreement.

'Perhaps we should all go below,' said Reverend Gibson diplomatically. 'The wind is blowing cold and we all need to conserve our health for the great task ahead.'

'Prue is only a child, she meant nothing by smiling at the sailors,' said Eleanor defensively as she and Francis entered the tiny cabin allocated to them and closed the door behind them. Of necessity she spoke in an undertone, for only a very thin board separated them from their neighbours on either side.

Francis sighed as he removed his long woollen scarf and, for want of anywhere else to put it, laid it on the upper bunk bed.

'I can't help but think it was a mistake to bring Mary Buckle and most especially Prue. However, it's too late now, we must make the best of it.'

Eleanor took no notice. She had meant to bring Mary and she had got her way; women got precious little of their own way in this year of our Lord eighteen sixty. She wasn't going to let the opinions of the other missionaries spoil this great adventure for her, no, not even Francis. She set about unpacking their belongings and laying them in the chest that was bolted to the wall by the beds.

'Shouldn't Mary be doing that, as she's here?'

'There's hardly room for her when we are both present,' Eleanor pointed out.

'Well, while we're here, perhaps we should give thanks to God that we have been granted the privilege of serving Him in the mission field,' said Francis and sank to his knees by the beds and folded his hands in the attitude of prayer. He looked up at her expectantly and she was struck again by how incredibly fine his eyes were, how clear-cut his chin. He had looked at her just like this as they stood by the communion rail in the chapel at Houghton le Spring on the day of their wedding. Putting down the bundle of neck cloths she had unpacked, Eleanor knelt beside him.

'Dearest Father,' he began and Eleanor's thoughts slipped away without her even realising, back to her wedding day, or rather, her wedding night. What a fool she had been, what an ignorant, foolish girl for all her twenty-six years.

She had thought she knew it all, having worked in among the mining folk for so long, observing how husbands and wives were together, seeing men practically naked but for the half-trousers they wore in the pit as they bathed in tin baths before their kitchen fires. She had even seen a baby born, helped at the birth; she thought she knew everything all right.

Eleanor opened her eyes briefly and peeped up at Francis. His forehead was smooth, his face untroubled as he communed with his God, so different from that night. She rested her chin on her hands and slipped away again, something she did more and more when Francis was praying though she was well aware he would be horrified if he knew.

'Are you sure, Eleanor?' Fanny had asked the week before the wedding. Fanny was staying with her sister to help her prepare and she was going to be Eleanor's bridesmaid.

'What do you mean?' Eleanor had replied impatiently. 'Am I sure about getting married, do you mean, or sure about going with Francis to minister to the heathen?' She smiled at her younger sister. Fanny was such a timid little thing, Eleanor couldn't imagine her ever having such an adventure.

'No. Are you sure you are in love with Mr Tait?'

'In love? Of course I am,' said Eleanor. 'Why shouldn't I be?'

'I don't know. It's just ... I think you have to be very much in love with a man to live with him on such ... such intimate terms.' Fanny had stopped abruptly, blushing.

'Oh that, I'm not at all worried about that,' Eleanor had said, thinking of Francis and how he hadn't even kissed her on the lips as yet. She wouldn't mind at all if he did that when they were married. After all, it would be his right, wouldn't it? And he was such a good-looking man, and his breath didn't smell at all and his teeth were white and even.

Eleanor smiled wryly as she knelt by Francis and remembered. What an ignorant fool she had been – if only she had thought the whole thing through. She had known how babies came out, she could have worked out how they got there in the first place. And it was all so ... so embarrassing, such an invasion of her secret places; it wasn't her fault she had felt so outraged when they had got into bed on their wedding night and Francis had turned to her and fumbled with the buttons on her nightie. He had begun to breathe heavily and impatiently pulled up the gown. When she realised what he was going to do, she could hardly believe it, and pressed her legs together, protesting in as loud a whisper as she dared without waking his uncle, who was in the next room. But Francis was deaf to her entreaties; his face was red and like that of a stranger as he pushed his long fingers between her legs and then invaded her body.

Afterwards, when she had jumped out of bed and pulled a wrap haphazardly round her and fled the room, she had sat on the stairs and cried. For how could such an indecent practice be right? How could a man of God, a man who was so respectable, so upright during the day, behave like that during the night? Maybe if she were to tell someone she would be able to get an annulment – but who could she tell?

'Eleanor?' The door of the bedroom opened and Francis came out dressed only in his nightshirt. He reached out a hand to her and she shrank back against the banister. 'Eleanor, I'm sorry if I hurt you, really I am, but you can't sit out here all night, you'll catch a chill. Come inside, I won't hurt you again.'

Eleanor looked doubtfully at him; he seemed so normal, not at all the excited red-faced man who had attacked her in bed.

'Come now, Eleanor, you don't want any of the family to find us out here in our nightclothes, do you?'

Slowly, she got to her feet. The thought of his uncle coming out of his room and finding them there was a powerful incentive to return to the bedroom. Silently he held open the door and she walked past him, careful not to touch him, and sat down in the chair by the window.

'You will be warmer in bed,' said Francis.

'I'm all right here, thank you.

'In bed, Eleanor,' repeated Francis. 'You will remember your vows taken before God only this morning?'

She did indeed. Reluctantly she got into bed, lying as far away from her husband as the width of the bed permitted. But Francis moved towards her and, propping himself up on his elbow, he leaned over her. The flickering light of the bedside candle revealed little of his expression as he gazed down at her solemnly

'It is natural, Eleanor, and necessary for the procreation of children. If I hurt you it is because I am as lacking in experience as you. But we will learn, Eleanor, my dear, we will learn.'

Eleanor realised he had fooled her, that he had every intention of repeating his actions.

'In the name of our Lord, Jesus Christ, amen,' said Francis, but Eleanor was still lost in her thoughts. 'Eleanor, if you wish to continue praying—'

'Amen,' said Eleanor hastily. 'I'm sorry, Francis, I was adding a small prayer for myself, that I would be worthy of this great task.'

'I'm sorry, Lord,' she said as Francis went off to seek his friends for a turn round the deck, some fresh air before sleep. She considered calling for Mary to finish the unpacking and help her prepare for bed in the tiny box of a cabin but changed her mind and did it herself. She had lied to Francis but the fact was that she would much rather pray on her own, offer up her own thoughts; she wasn't used yet to having her husband praying for her.

It was a little strange climbing into the narrow bunk and lying there, staring up at the bed above. She would not be sharing a bed with Francis for weeks, not until they reached Sydney, so at least that particular problem could be shelved for a while. Her thoughts wandered back; thank goodness she had time to think at last, everything had been such a rush in the weeks between her marriage and the time they set out for the south and the ship to Australia.

It was Mary who had reassured her, Mary, who was unmarried herself. But Mary was so worldly wise, in some ways so much more mature than herself. 'Men always act like that, it's natural,' Mary had said and Eleanor forbore to ask how she knew. So there had been no question of an annulment then.

Turning over on to her side, Eleanor blew out the candle and endeavoured to sleep. It could be a difficult day tomorrow with the other missionaries' wives seeming so disapproving of her and especially of Mary and Prue. Thank goodness they wouldn't all be stationed in the same place once they got to Fiji. Or at least she hoped they would not.

When Francis came back Eleanor was already asleep. He lit the tiny lamp that was secured to the wall of the cabin with a bracket and gazed down at her. She was an enigma to him, he admitted to himself; she seemed so transparent sometimes, so full of vitality and enthusiasm for the 'Great Adventure' as she called it. Then she would say something that indicated that she did not think of it as giving her life in God's service, but just that, a great adventure.

He thought of a remark she had made only that morning as they rose to their feet after morning prayers, a remark that even made him wonder if she had been completely with him as he prayed for the Lord's guidance.

'I hope to be able to practise my nursing among the natives,' she had said in almost a continuation of her amens. 'Don't you think, Francis, it will be almost as good an opportunity for me as Miss Nightingale had in the Crimea?'

'We will be there primarily to convert them to Christianity,' he had said heavily and even to his own ears he sounded pompous. 'You must not forget that, Eleanor.'

'What? Oh no, of course not,' she had answered quickly.

Eleanor stirred in her sleep and flung back the bedcovers. Francis drew back, putting himself between her and the light so that it did not disturb her more. Slowly he began to undress, folding his clothes neatly on the chair by the bunks and putting his shoes underneath. Wearing only his long shirt, he began to climb up to the top bunk before remembering the lamp.

Before he blew it out he took a last look at his wife. Although the covers were thrown back her shoulders and arms were covered to the wrists by her voluminous nightgown, but the top button was unfastened and gaping a little, showing the rounded curve of her neck. Perhaps she would catch a chill.

Francis knelt by the bed and carefully, so as not to wake her, he put his hands on the tiny buttons, only instead of closing them he found himself undoing more. She was his wife, he told himself, what evil was there in him seeing her breast? Eleanor was always so careful not to let him see her naked body; their lovemaking was done under the bedclothes, all touching and feeling and no seeing. Francis felt himself getting heated, he should not – oh, but how could he stop? The Lord gave a man these urges, did He not?

The buttons loosed, he turned back the collar of her nightgown and looked for the first time on her full breast and the dark circle around her nipple. Forgetting altogether his intention not to wake her, he slid his hand over the breast and ran his thumb around the nipple, feeling it magically spring up and harden under his touch, feeling his own response surge through his veins.

'Francis? Francis, what are you doing?' Eleanor moved suddenly, clutching at the neck of her gown, squirming against the wooden partition wall, unable to move far because of the narrowness of the bunk.

'It's all right, my love,' Francis said thickly, nuzzling her bare breast with his lips, reaching down to pull up her gown. The bedcovers were already falling to the floor.

'No!' cried Eleanor, and then remembered where they were and lowered her voice to a frantic whisper. 'No, we can't, please, Francis, the bed isn't large enough for us both. And the Gibsons will hear us, think of it, Francis, please!' But Francis was past the stage where he might have been able to stop voluntarily; he was groaning with pleasure as he proved that, in an emergency, the bunk would hold two.

'At least put out the lamp,' cried Eleanor despairingly, but her cause was lost, Francis had already accomplished his end. And strangely, Eleanor found herself disappointed when he finished and collapsed on top of her.

Chapter Six

Both Eleanor and Francis barely left their cabin in the next few days as the *Liberator* sailed through squalls of rain and bounced up and down on waves that seemed to Eleanor to be mountainous. She lay on her bunk, filled with nausea as the world revolved around her, unable to rise without being violently sick. Her nightgown and bedclothes were stained and sweaty and the tiny cabin stank as she struggled to stifle her groans, wishing she could only die.

She should not have felt so ashamed that Francis should see her like this, for his condition was as bad if not worse than her own; yet she did, pathetically trying to hide the state she was in whenever he staggered down from the top bunk to retch into the chamber pot in the corner.

Mrs Gibson looked in, offering to help, but Eleanor waved her away, wanting only Mary. But it seemed that Mary was in an even worse condition than herself or Francis and quite unable to leave her own cot in steerage. A steward came every night and morning and left two bowls of salty, greasy soup accompanied by small hard loaves of dark bread, the smell making Eleanor's stomach heave yet again. One day Prue came, her blue eyes twinkling merrily and her curls bouncing as she skipped about, making Eleanor's head ache even more than it had. But at least she brought a dish of cool water and bathed Eleanor's face, ignoring Francis as he lay on the top bunk. Prue helped her change into a clean gown, brought the brush from Eleanor's bag and dragged it through her tangled hair.

'Jack says not to worry, everyone gets seasick in the Bay of Biscay,' Prue said. She smiled kindly at Eleanor. 'Jack says—'

'Jack? Who do you mean, Prudence?' Francis poked his head over the edge of the top bunk. He must be feeling better, Eleanor thought, to be taking an interest in what Prue was saying.

'Why, Jack Allan, the steward,' said Prue, looking up at him, all dimples and fun-filled eyes, in the way she always looked at men. She just didn't seem able to help it, thought Eleanor, despairing.

'You must not associate with the seamen, Prudence!' said Francis. He meant his voice to be stern but somehow it came out all weak and wobbly. He lay back on his pillow, exhausted.

'You have to speak to them sometimes, sir,' said Prue. 'It's not polite not to.'

Eleanor listened but she hadn't the energy to intervene and in any case she felt so ill, what did it matter? What did anything matter?

The next morning the ship sailed out of the Bay of Biscay and into calmer waters as it began the long descent along the coast of Africa to Capetown. And suddenly Eleanor couldn't stand the stifling atmosphere of the cabin for another minute. She splashed water on her face and neck and dressed in a clean gown. Realising she was ravenous, she broke off a chunk of bread from the night before's loaf and chewed it, washing it down with stale water. Francis was still sleeping so she slipped out quietly and made her way on deck.

It was barely six o'clock and there was no one to be seen apart from the helmsman and a solitary sailor high up in the rigging. Walking to the rail, she looked out on a sea turned from foaming grey to gentle blue. The ship swayed only softly and the air was fresh and invigorating. Oh, it was grand not to feel ill any more; happiness surged through her and she lifted her face to the sky in a prayer of thankfulness that the bad time was over.

She was standing there when she became aware that there was someone else beside the helmsman at the wheel; she heard his deep voice say something and then a girl's giggle.

'Oh, come on, now, no one's about, you can let me have a go,' said Prue. 'Look, you can stand behind me so and just put your hands over mine if you're feared I can't do it right.'

Eleanor gasped. What was Prue up to now? If Francis found out she was being so familiar with the crew there would be trouble and if the other missionaries found out, why, goodness knows what would happen. Thank goodness it was so early in the morning; the rest of the passengers were still in bed or at their morning prayers. She started towards the small flight of steps that led up to the wheel house but her heart sank as she felt a hand on her shoulder.

'Leave this to me, Eleanor,' said Francis. Of course it was Francis, she thought dismally, now he would go on about how he had not wanted the two girls to come in the first place and he had been right, hadn't he?

Eleanor stayed at the bottom of the steps as Francis strode up them and into the wheel house. The seaman and Prue looked down at her, the dimpling smiles gone from Prue's face at the sound of Francis's voice and the seaman scowling behind her. Too close behind her, thought Eleanor, Francis would go mad and not surprisingly. The seaman's arms were around Prue's body, and his hands clasped over hers on the wheel.

'Come away from there, Prudence Buckle,' said Francis, his voice stern and tightly controlled. 'Go below to your sister and stay until I tell you otherwise.'

'Hey, what right have you to order the lass about, she wasn't doing any harm, I was just learning her how to …' the seaman started to argue. He did not move away from the girl and Eleanor could see that Francis was becoming even more incensed.

'Prudence, go below,' he said harshly and the girl looked at Eleanor, who had moved nearer.

'I wasn't doing nothing,' she said sullenly. But nevertheless she moved away from the wheel and out of the seaman's embrace.

'I bet you fancy the lass yourself,' said the seaman and Francis went purple.

'How dare you!' he spluttered. 'I shall speak to Captain Molar about this, you insolent brute! Why the child is barely fourteen and she is in my care!' He turned back to Prue and his voice rose to a shout. 'Go below, I say! And don't come back if you know what's good for you.'

Prue burst into tears and fled, whereupon the seaman growled and stepped forward, leaving the wheel to take care of itself, his hands bunched into fists. He was about to attack Francis and, to Eleanor's amazement, Francis took up a fighting stance, looking as though he could handle himself, Eleanor saw as she gazed wide-eyed at the pair. Fortunately, Captain Molar chose that moment to appear, no doubt roused by the commotion.

Captain Molar was a hard man, typical of his breed, and the argument came to an abrupt end. 'Take the wheel, Simms!' he roared. 'What are you about, man, are you drunk? I'll have the skin off your back! And you, sir –' he turned to Francis – 'I'll thank you to retire, sir, I'll have no passengers up here.'

'I was protecting a young girl of our party, Captain,' said Francis stiffly.

'Were you, then,' Captain Molar said. 'If you mean that saucy chit who hangs around my men all day, I wish you luck.'

'She is only fourteen, Captain.'

'Aye? And already far along her chosen path, I'd say,' commented Captain Molar. 'Well, keep the chit down below, that's my advice to you, Minister. I'll not have her causing trouble among the men, do you understand me? Else she'll be put ashore at Capetown.'

Eleanor gasped. She had opened her mouth to argue with the captain when she caught her husband's eye and subsided. Francis took her arm and as they were descending the steps to the deck they could hear Captain Molar bellowing down the speaking tube.

'Bo'sun! Look alive there, I want you up here now and Simms's relief with you. You can take Simms below till I have time to deal with him. The charge is fighting with a passenger.' Francis half-turned towards him and Captain Molar fixed a steely eye on him. 'You have something else to say, Minister?'

'No.' Flushing slightly, Francis walked Eleanor rapidly away to the opposite end of the deck where a few of the missionaries and their wives were beginning to congregate for morning service, some of them by now casting curious glances at the quarter deck. The sun shone warmly down on the company, lighting winter-white faces and glittering on the sea.

'You see?' Francis whispered through clenched teeth. 'That girl almost had me brawling on deck!'

There was no time for Eleanor to reply, for the service was already beginning. They sang a hymn of thanks to the accompaniment of a travelling harmonium and, in spite of Prue, Eleanor's spirits lifted. Now she felt better she would watch Prue, give her things to do so that the girl wouldn't have time to flirt with the crew. Not that she was really flirting, she was still a child, but with men on their own away from their wives, well, a child's friendliness was easily misunderstood.

The Reverend Johnson's view of Prue was not so tolerant. Mr Johnson was a small, slight man with a luxuriant dark beard threaded with grey and his beard was the only luxuriant bit about him. Privately, Eleanor thought he grew it as a statement of his masculinity, his figure being smaller than most women's. Mr Johnson and his wife were in their forties. Childless, they had been in the mission field for fifteen years already and were returning from home leave. Unfortunately, his years of service made him the senior missionary and he took his position very seriously indeed.

Some days later, as the *Liberator* sailed south into the Tropics, Mr Johnson drew Francis aside after morning prayers.

'A word with you, Mr Tait, if I may,' he said, his tone rather peremptory, Eleanor thought.

'Of course, Mr Johnson,' said Francis and the two men drew away, leaving Eleanor with Mrs Alice Johnson, a rather plump lady who would have made two of her husband.

'I'm pleased to have this opportunity to have a talk with you, just the two of us,' said Mrs Johnson. 'We'll take a stroll round the deck, shall we?'

'Well—' said Eleanor, thinking of Prue and wondering where she was, for neither she nor Mary had been present at morning prayers. 'I was going down to see Mary Buckle and Prue,' she went on but Mrs Johnson took her arm and led her to a secluded part of the deck.

'It was about Mary Buckle I wanted to talk to you,' she said.

'Mary?' Eleanor was surprised; her worries had been all about Prue.

Alice Johnson turned to face her. 'Did you know the boatswain and she were becoming, well, to put it mildly a little too friendly? It's a mistake, my dear, to allow servants to have followers and especially on board ship. Take my word for it, dear, I am more experienced in these things and I should put a stop to it. No good can come of it, Joseph Rae is a sailor, an ungodly man and even if he weren't—'

'Yes, thank you, Mrs Johnson, I can deal with it myself, if what you say is true,' Eleanor said.

'Oh, it is, my dear, it is. And that sister of hers is quite brazen, ogling the men with her blue eyes, she's immodest, Mrs

Tait, really. I know you are young and possibly you were worried about going into a heathen country without a female servant but I was against it from the start. There are always plenty of servants to be found among the natives. If I were you, I'd send the both of them packing as soon as we reach Capetown.' Mrs Johnson paused as she caught Eleanor's eye and realised that her audience was far from sympathetic.

'Thank you, Mrs Johnson, I'll deal with it,' Eleanor said again. She turned on her heel and went immediately in search of the Buckles.

'Hoity toity!' said Mrs Johnson but her disapproval was carried away on the breeze and in any case, Eleanor was already on her way below.

Mary and Prue were sitting on the bench that ran along the side of the ship and was all the furniture provided for the steerage passengers. The atmosphere was thick and stale, redolent of bodily odours and something else, something Eleanor couldn't place and didn't want to.

Mary was brushing Prue's curls vigorously and Prue was squealing loudly at every tangle caught in the bristles of the battered old wooden brush. Looking at her now, seeming such a baby with tears in her eyes, Eleanor could not believe she was grown up enough to know what effect her friendliness had on the seamen. In any case, she hadn't had the chance to be friendly these last few days with Eleanor keeping her busy all day from morning prayers until she sent her to bed in the evening. People just had suspicious minds, she thought. But Mary and the boatswain, that was different.

'Good morning, Mary, Prue,' said Eleanor. 'Prue, will you go up to our cabin and sort out the dirty linen? I thought we might wash today, it's such good weather.'

Prue pulled herself away from Mary and the hairbrush, dashing the back of a grubby hand across her eyes before casting a resentful glance at Eleanor. 'Aye, miss,' she said sullenly and flounced out.

'You weren't at prayers this morning, Mary,' said Eleanor.

'I was tired, we both were,' said Mary. 'The air down here is foul an' all, it's worse than being in the coke ovens back home in Hetton. I don't know why Prue and me can't come up on deck more. The others do.'

There were three families of emigrants sharing steerage accommodation with the Buckles, young Methodist families with small children, bound for Sydney, and it was true they were allowed up on deck when it wasn't inconvenient for the crew. Of course, it was a part of the deck separated from the rest but it was in the open air.

'I'm doing my best for you, Mary,' said Eleanor heavily. 'It's the seamen, that's the trouble. Mr Johnson thinks young girls are a temptation to them and Captain Molar doesn't like it either. And now Mrs Johnson says you are too friendly with the boatswain. You're not, are you, Mary?'

'No, I'm not,' Mary answered. 'People like the Johnsons think pitfolk have no right to live, never mind owt else. I can't pass the time of day with a man before they're saying bad things about me.'

Eleanor bit her lip. 'Mary, the Johnsons haven't even met any pitfolk, of course they don't think like that. It's just because you're young girls, that's all. And sailors have a bad name, I suppose. Come on, now, we'll do our washing on the deck, it's all right if you're with me. And the fresh air will do you both good.'

Up on deck the girls set to work with lye soap and sea-water on the flannel petticoats that had been shed as they sailed into the warmth of the Tropics, and drawers and shifts odorous from the days of seasickness. Grudgingly the captain had detailed Jack Allan, the steward, to haul up canvas buckets filled with seawater and they set to work with a will.

It was when they strung a line along the deck to hang the washing on that trouble appeared in the outraged person of Mrs Johnson at the head of a band of missionaries' wives.

'Mrs Tait! How could you!'

At the scandalised tone Eleanor looked up from where she was soaping a grimy line on the inside of one of Francis's neck cloths. Sighing, she laid down the article and dried her hands on her apron. 'What is it now, Mrs Johnson?'

'Hanging up your personal washing for all the men to gape at! No wonder they fall into temptation. Mrs Tait, take that line down at once!'

Eleanor looked at the washing and then around at the deck. Not a seaman in sight that she could see, not at this end of the deck; they were hidden from the main part by the bulkhead. 'There are no seamen here, Mrs Johnson,' she said evenly.

'What's that, then? Or should I say, who is that?' Mrs Johnson nodded her head in the direction of the rigging and there, right at the top, looking like a peg doll from that distance, was a man and he was indeed looking down at them curiously.

'Mrs Johnson—' Eleanor began, but when she was interrupted by Francis, who strode up to her with a face like thunder.

'Eleanor, take down that line and go below, I wish to speak to you,' he said.

'But—'

'Now, Eleanor. And bring those two with you.'

The worst part about it was the way the missionary women stood back in a line and watched Mary and Eleanor collect their dripping washing and pile it into the canvas bucket. They carried it along the deck and down to the cabin, Prue trailing behind. And then just as they were about to disappear from the deck, the seaman in the rigging shouted.

'Now then, Prue, me darlin', keep your chin up and don't let the holy joes get you down!'

'Mr Rae!' yelled Captain Molar from the wheel deck to the boatswain. 'Bring that man to me at once! I'll teach him a lesson he won't forget in a hurry!'

Prue, her eyes sparkling with fun and her cheeks flushed by the sun and the fresh air, was still grinning as they entered the tiny cabin, dripping water from the clothes all over the floor. Francis glared at her as he closed the door behind him and turned on them furiously.

'Did a seaman bring rum down to the steerage last night and were you both drinking it with him? Now, tell me the truth, for I won't have you lying.'

'No, no, I didn't,' cried Prue, shaking her head vigorously at the same time as Mary looked stonily at him and admitted it.

'It was a bit of fun, that's all,' she said. 'I haven't signed the pledge even if you have.'

'You have the gall to stand there and say you were drinking strong liquor and worse, with a seaman and in the place where you sleep?'

'Aye, we did. Well, it's good for you when you're at sea, all the seamen say it is.'

Eleanor shuddered as she looked at the girls; she was quite bereft of words. They were in for it now.

Chapter Seven

Francis stood at the rail of the main deck of the ship as the *Liberator* edged its way into dock at Capetown, the first landfall since leaving England. For the moment he was on his own; Eleanor and the Buckle girls were still below, preparing for the trip ashore. He sighed as he thought about the Buckles, bitterly regretting agreeing to Eleanor bringing them with her.

He stared out over the bay at Table Mountain with its 'tablecloth' of low cloud and the castle, its flagpole flying the Union Jack. Eleanor should have been up here with him; they should have been enjoying the magnificent sight together and instead she was below, no doubt chattering with Mary Buckle. Oh yes, Mary Buckle had been a mistake; he should have put his foot down from the start. Eleanor was too close to the girl; she treated her, if not exactly as a friend, not as a servant either. It just wasn't right.

At least there had been no more trouble with the crew. Francis shuddered as he remembered that morning when Mr Johnson had brought to his attention the gossip about Mary and Prue and the seamen.

'The emigrants in steerage are decent family folk, Mr Tait,' Johnson had said. 'It's not right that they should have to witness licentiousness and drinking, not right at all. It is a great pity you agreed to the Buckles coming on the journey. It's my advice to you to send them back on the first available ship from Capetown.'

But even if Eleanor agreed to it, where was the money to come from for the girls' fares? Even with them travelling in steerage it had taken a lot of money to bring them in the first place – no, they couldn't go back. Of course, he was master in his own family and if he should insist then Eleanor would have to let them go. If they had the money. As things were, the Buckles would have to go on with the rest of the missionary party but thank goodness the Johnsons were getting off at Capetown.

'Francis?'

He had been so lost in his own thoughts that he jumped when Eleanor's voice sounded close to his ear. The passengers were all coming on deck, he saw, ready to go ashore, dressed in lightweight summer suits and dresses as they had been advised by the Missionary Society, though the colours were dark grey and black as befitted Methodists.

'Francis?' Eleanor said again. 'Mary and Prue are going ashore too, I told them that would be all right. They want to go on their own, just to have a look around. After all, they may not get another chance to see Capetown.'

If Francis had a few misgivings about allowing the girls to stroll about a strange town on their own, he soon overcame them. He would be with Eleanor and only last evening Mr Gibson had suggested they make up a party with him and his wife. Eleanor was looking at him in her direct way, waiting for his answer. Well, he would forget the Buckles today, let them do what they would.

Excited anticipation rose in him as he took his wife's arm and led her towards the gangplank, a feeling that was shared by the rest of the party, an eagerness to leave the confinement of the ship. They took a carriage up Adderley Street, Mrs Gibson and Eleanor chatting together happily. Thank the Lord for the Gibsons, the only ones who hadn't turned a little cold towards the Taits on account of the goings-on of the Buckles.

Francis kept glancing at Eleanor as she sat there, looking all around her at the sights, her face alive with interest as she exclaimed at the mountain and the coachman told the tale of Mynheer van Hunk and his fight with the devil and how he was spirited away to Hades.

'Superstitious nonsense,' murmured Mr Gibson and Francis nodded his head gravely. But the talk of legends and ghosts had led naturally to a discussion of the famous Flying Dutchman and how he was condemned to try to round the coast for ever because he had cursed the Almighty. 'God is not mocked,' said the older minister.

They saw the castle and heard the noon gun boom out over the town and Eleanor was enthusiastic about everything. If only he could get her away from the Buckles, what a perfect minister's wife she would be, mused Francis.

It was when they returned to the ship, tired but happy, full of the sights and sounds of Capetown and Francis was paying off the driver, that they saw a strange man, dressed outlandishly in checked trousers and pale-grey frock coat and sporting a large-brimmed hat on his head, approach the ship and bound up the gangplank at a rate of knots that showed his unlimited energy. The missionaries and their wives in their sober dark clothes stopped talking and all four followed his progress with varying expressions of surprise.

'He must have the wrong ship,' said Francis at last.

'Extraordinary,' murmured Mr Gibson, though they had seen and even spoken to a bewildering diversity of human beings during their day in the town.

Eleanor made the first move. 'Well, if he has boarded the wrong ship he'd best be getting off pretty quickly, it's almost time for sailing. Come along, we must board ourselves if we don't want to be left behind.'

There was no sign of the stranger on deck and Eleanor wasted no time in looking around for him; she was anxious to discover whether Mary and Prue had returned safely. She excused herself to the Gibsons and hurried below but there was no sign of the Buckles either in their quarters in the steerage or anywhere else she could think of. She hurried back to the cabin she shared with Francis and found him sitting at the tiny table writing up his impressions of Capetown while they were fresh in his memory. He regarded Eleanor gravely as she told him the girls were missing.

'But what can I do about it?' he asked and calmly went back to his writing.

'But, Francis, supposing they miss the boat? What will they do, two girls on their own in a strange city?'

'If they miss the boat it will be their own fault,' he said, privately thinking that it might be a good thing if they did; it would certainly solve a lot of problems.

'Francis! That is just not Christian!' cried Eleanor and ran from the cabin and up on to the deck where Captain Molar and his men were beginning to prepare for sailing. She approached him and began talking all in a rush but he waved her aside impatiently.

'Get off my deck if you please, ma'am,' he said, brushing past her and almost knocking her off her feet.

Eleanor recovered herself and tried again. 'We can't go yet,' she cried. 'My maids are not aboard yet, we can't leave them here.'

'Time and tide wait for no man, no, nor maid either,' snapped the captain, 'now I've told you, ma'am, get out of my way or I will have you removed.' His tone altered to a bellow as he shouted to a seaman on the quay. 'Get ready to cast off!'

Eleanor despaired. She ran to the rail and peered down at the shore in the gathering gloom – was that them coming? A group of people were hurrying along, waving urgently at the *Liberator*.

'Wait!' she cried but the captain ignored her. Seamen were already moving towards the gangway, ready to draw it on board. Frantically, she ran to them, pointing out the two girls, for now it could be seen who they were.

If a seaman had not noticed that one of the men with Mary and Prue was the steward Jack Allan, they would have been left behind, but the sailors hesitated for the minute it took the group to reach the ship.

'Oh, thank you, God, thank you,' Eleanor breathed as they hurried up the gangplank and gained the safety of the deck.

'Put that man in irons!' roared the captain, the moment the gangplank was secured. 'I'll deal with him tomorrow.' And Prue's face crumpled as she began to wail.

'It wasn't his fault!' she cried. 'It was me that got lost, he was looking for me.'

The captain merely roared, 'Take that squalling brat below or God help me, I'll have her in irons too!' and turned back to the business of getting the ship under way.

Eleanor watched as Mary dragged a sobbing Prue away, thankful that the two girls were aboard at least. She would have to punish them, or at least give them a good talking to, she determined.

'Well, Eleanor!'

At the sound of Francis's voice, Eleanor turned to confront the row of missionaries and their wives, all on deck to watch the departure from Capetown and all of them staring at her unsmiling. Her heart sank.

'I think I'll go below, Francis,' she said. 'I feel a headache coming on.'

Chapter Eight

It was not until next morning when the passengers assembled for breakfast that they saw again the man who had come aboard the evening before. They were now twelve hours out of Capetown on the last leg of their journey to Sydney and though it was only seven o'clock the sun was hot in the sky and the Englishmen and their wives looked hot and uncomfortable in their sombre clothing.

'Captain West,' the newcomer introduced himself to the Taits. 'Morgan West, at your service, ma'am, sir.' He looked cool and elegant in his white calico suit and thin-leathered boots; he was broad-shouldered and lean-hipped with eyes startlingly blue in his tanned face and straight dark brows contrasting with his sun-bleached hair.

All this Eleanor noticed in the few seconds it took Francis to say who they were and as Captain West took her hand in a cool, firm grasp. She looked up into those surprising eyes and stood quite still until Francis cupped her elbow and moved her forward towards the table where the Gibsons were already sitting. As she sat down she saw that Captain West was greeting Miss Tookey, the schoolteacher, and that lady was curtseying awkwardly, the tip of her long nose glowing pink.

'American,' murmured Mrs Gibson in her ear. 'I wonder how he gained passage on this ship.'

America, of course, thought Eleanor, that's where his strange drawl comes from, his free yet courteous manners.

She glanced at Francis and saw he was wearing a slight frown as he gazed at the man.

'What is it, Francis?' she asked.

'I don't know, just there's something about Captain West,' he replied. 'I'm sure I've heard his name mentioned somewhere.' But Captain Molar had entered the room and was taking his place at the head of the company. There were fresh exotic fruits on the table and the water supply had been replenished at Capetown so it was no longer stale on the tongue. After a short grace, the company became more interested in breakfast than in Captain West.

There were mangoes and bananas, and oranges that tasted nothing at all like the oranges that Francis or Eleanor had been used to receiving in the toes of their Christmas stockings, so fresh and full of juice they were. And limes of course; they had all been instructed to eat limes as a guard against the dreaded scurvy.

Later the upper-deck passengers were joined by the ones in steerage, the emigrant families and the Buckles. The two girls took up their position to the side of Eleanor and Francis, though slightly behind, both looking pale and subdued after the censure they had received the evening before from Francis and the downright bawling out from Captain Molar.

Prayers were about to start when Morgan West approached the group and casually joined them, nodding a greeting to the steerage passengers. Seeing the position of the Buckles, part of the circle yet not quite in it, he took Mary's arm and led her and her sister forward.

'Come now, ladies, I'm sure these good folk will make more room for you,' he said and the congregation had perforce to do so. Francis felt put out; it was as though he and his fellow missionaries had been taught a lesson in manners but he managed to smile politely at the man.

'Of course,' he said. 'All are equal in the sight of God.' And the way that he said it implied that it was not necessarily so in the eyes of Englishmen, not even English clerics.

Francis opened his eyes once between the prayer that the ship might avoid all perils on its voyage to the Antipodes, and the prayer that the company would be blessed by the Lord and carry out His will as good and faithful servants in their mission to convert the heathen, and his gaze fell upon Prue. Her hands were clasped in front of her as piously as her sister Mary's but she was smiling her dimpling, red-lipped smile and her small face was turned bewitchingly to one side.

She was gazing at Captain West, using all her wiles on him. If Mr Gibson wasn't at that moment beseeching the Lord for guidance in all they did this day he would— Morgan West caught his eye and grinned, nodding at Prue as though sharing a joke, and Francis hastily closed his eyes and concentrated on the words uttered by Mr Gibson. He had allowed the minx to distract him, he thought savagely. Dear God, the wickedness of women! For Prudence Buckle was a woman in spite of her years and well on the way to being a harlot, he was sure of that. And yet again he bitterly regretted allowing Eleanor to bring the Buckles.

Mary herself was beginning to wish the same thing as Francis. Oh, how excited she had been at the prospect of leaving the coal-ridden county of Durham and travelling to the opposite side of the world, what a life she could carve out for herself in a new country, a country where a person could climb out of her class and make something of herself without the need to be a servant to anyone. Not that Eleanor had been mean to her or her family – quite the opposite really; she had helped them when they were in desperate need and Mary was grateful to her, she really was. But still, there was no getting away from the fact that Eleanor was the mistress and she was the skivvy. Though how could she have brought up Prue without Eleanor's help? At least she wasn't like her grandmother, the viewer's mother. Mrs Wales's father had worked at the coalface himself, Mary had heard it muttered many a time in the village when the old lady acted as though she were the lady of the manor.

Who does she think she is? Mary would think when Mrs Wales complained about her work, or made nasty remarks about Prue, not even bothering to lower her voice. She was glad to get away from Mrs Wales and everyone else, even Ben. For Ben was courting and he wanted the cottage to bring his wife to when they were married and there would be no room for Prue and Mary.

Prue didn't mean anything when she flirted with the seamen, it was just that she was developing as a woman and enjoyed testing out her new powers. She would be all right without the restrictions imposed on her by the missionaries and their wives. Well, when they got where they were going they would perhaps be able to branch out on their own; everyone said Australia was less class-ridden than England and why couldn't they find their fortunes there? Or at least a rich man apiece. And in the meantime it was so deadly boring on the ship with prayers twice a day and the top-deck passengers looking down on them all the time even if they just passed the time of day with a seaman. Poor chaps, they went months without seeing a woman, why shouldn't they have a bit of fun now?

Mary chuckled to herself. By, they'd had a good time in Capetown yesterday, that was one thing about seamen, they were generous with their pay if they liked a girl and there was no doubt that Joe Rae liked her.

Mary's thoughts shifted to the man who had come aboard at Capetown, the American; now there was a man to dream about with his bonny eyes and bright hair and his air of assurance, his way of looking at a girl and somehow showing he was interested, wicked-like, as though he knew what she was thinking. And his clothes, so outlandish and yet so good and well-cut, he must be worth a bob or two, that fella.

'He's a bit of all right, isn't he, Mary?'

Prue, sitting beside her on the bench they shared in the cramped steerage part of the ship, broke into her thoughts.

'Who?' asked Mary though she knew very well who it was.

'That Captain West, o' course, who do you think? Morgan West.' Prue rolled the name round on her tongue, savouring it. She looked dreamily at her sister, a very adult look in her eyes.

'Prue!' snapped Mary and Prue giggled mischievously, suddenly a little girl again.

'I never meant nowt,' she said, 'I was only funning. Anyway, you know I like Jack.' She sighed, remembering that Jack Allan was in trouble over being late back to the ship last night. 'Do you think Captain Molar will let him out today? It wasn't his fault we were late.'

'No, it wasn't, it was yours, you young minx,' said Mary. 'If you hadn't dawdled about the shops trying to get him to buy you something we would have been back in plenty of time.'

Prue pouted. 'It's so boring on the ship and Mr Tait thinks me and you don't have the right to any fun, him and those others. Jack reckons those holy joes are right hypocrites and he's right an' all.'

'They did let us come, though, didn't they? You have to give them that. Why, man, Prue, what sort of a life is it we would have at home? Marrying some pitman would be the best we could do and likely end up like Mam, widowed and with a houseful of bairns. Australia or even this Fiji they are talking of going to, well, they're bound to be better than that, aren't they?'

Prue sighed and flounced across to the ladderway that led up to the deck. 'Well, I don't know, I tell you, I'm sick of this damn ship.'

'You'd better not let anybody hear you swearing like that,' warned Mary. 'Come away from there, any road.'

'I won't, I want some fresh air, I have a bloody right—' began an unrepentant Prue but her petulant tone altered immediately when the boatswain, Joe Rae, appeared.

'Eeh, lass, you'd best not let them holy joes hear you swear, they'd have you walking the plank, they would,' he commented cheerfully as he clambered down the steps and brushed past Prue. He walked over to Mary, picked her up bodily from the bench and kissed her soundly, one arm holding her tightly to him as the other plunged down her neckline, putting a fearsome strain on the buttons.

'Joe! Behave yourself this minute,' Mary said, struggling out of his arms. Look now –' as the top two buttons popped off and skittered across the floor – 'I'll have to sew them on now, you great lump.'

'Aye, but it was worth it, wasn't it?'

'No, it wasn't. Any road, who said you could take liberties with me like that? Get away from me, go on, you're coarse, that's what you are, I'll not have it.' Mary's irritation was turning to fury as she went down on her hands and knees and scrabbled about looking for the buttons.

The boatswain frowned. 'What's that you say? After all I spent on you yesterday, you and that little whore of a sister of yours?'

'You never did, you bloody liar,' Prue cried, 'you never spent a penny on me. I was with me own man, for what would I go with an old man like you? And besides, I'm not a whore.'

'Are you not?' Joe laughed harshly. 'I'm beginning to think the pair of you are fresh out of the gutter. And it's because of you that poor old Jack Allan is where he is.'

Mary got to her feet, her eyes flashing and her face pink with anger. 'Get out of here, Joe Rae, or I'll scream the place down. Don't you come near me nor my sister again, do you hear me?'

Joe stared at her for a moment, then lifted a hand and placed it squarely on her chest where the material of her dress gaped open. Grinding his hand against the soft flesh, he pushed her violently against Prue so that the two girls went sprawling, Mary banging her head against the iron support of the bench. Without another word the boatswain strode past them and on up the ladder to the deck.

Mary was dazed, her head swimming, and she put up a hand to her temple and felt the stickiness of blood. Shaking, she managed to sit up and look about for her sister. Prue was sobbing quietly, her face pale but, as far as Mary could see, she wasn't hurt.

'Come on, pet, you're all right,' said Mary. 'We'd better make ourselves presentable before we go up to see if Mrs Tait wants us to do anything.'

Snuffling, Prue got to her feet and brushed down her dress with her hands and Mary dabbed at her temple with a cloth dipped in a cup of water from the bucket provided for drinking. She peered at the cut in the mirror that one of the emigrants had tied to an upright. It wasn't so bad.

'It doesn't look bad, does it?' she asked Prue and the younger girl shook her head. 'I'll tell them I fell, do you hear me, Prue? There'd only be trouble if we said Joe was in here.'

'Aye.'

Prue had stopped crying at least, Mary thought as she looked out her sewing box and replaced the buttons on her dress. She winced when her hand caught her breast as she fastened them again. Joe had bruised it, the rotten sod. Well, there was one thing for sure, she didn't want any more to do with the likes of him.

That American, Captain West, now he was different, a gentleman. He'd been ever so nice to her even though he knew she was just a maid and she'd heard Australians were like that an' all. Maybe Australia was the place for her and Prue. What would it be like married to a man like Morgan West? The very thought made her feel warm all over. Suddenly the prospect of the voyage from Capetown to Sydney no longer seemed boring.

Chapter Nine

18th March, 1861. A red letter day, thought Eleanor. Australia, at last. She was elated as she descended the gangplank with Francis by her side and Mary and Prue behind her. She wanted to shout it aloud, dance a jig on the quay, do something to mark the day.

'Aren't you excited?' she asked Francis, who was walking sedately by her side, and he smiled wryly.

'There's a fair way to go yet,' he replied. 'This isn't Fiji.' But Eleanor could see a little extra colour in his cheeks not put there by the sun and his eyes shone.

There was a noisy, bustling crowd on the quay as porters touted for custom and hackney carriages, which had been standing in line waiting patiently for customers to disembark, filled up and threaded their way through the crowds. And above the din a brass band was playing.

Eleanor paused and looked back at the ship for a moment but Francis was eager to get on and he rushed forward to hail a cab.

'Come along, Eleanor, we don't want to keep the others waiting,' he said, holding open a cab door as he turned to see what was holding her up. Sighing heavily, he saw she was with Mary, an arm around the girl as though she was comforting her, and Mary was holding her face with one hand, evidently distraught.

'Eleanor!' he cried sharply. Exasperated, he let go of the cab door and strode over to them. 'Come along, we haven't time for silly regrets now. Anyway, where is that girl Prue?'

'She's gone, that's where she is, she's run away,' sobbed Mary. 'The minute her feet touched dry land she was away and how will I find her in this place? Look, she pushed this letter into my hand and she went!'

Mary had a grubby piece of paper clutched in her hand and she held it out to Francis, who took hold of it rather gingerly and with some difficulty read the unformed handwriting. Well, there was little doubt, Prue Buckle had run away and what's more she had run off with a seaman.

Dont worry about me, Ill be all right. Jack luvs me an he ses hell look after me an buy me a new dress a cotton one that's not too hot an some shus an all an I can throw these ugly old boots away. Luv Prue.

'Oh, Mary, I'm sorry,' Eleanor said helplessly. She turned to Francis, her brown eyes beseeching. 'Can't we go in search of her? She can't have got far.'

But Francis shook his head. 'Certainly not. I'm not running around a strange city after a chit of a girl who doesn't want to be found. We haven't the time, Eleanor. Who is this Jack, anyway? Is he that steward she was always getting into trouble? If he's jumped ship the captain won't have him back.'

'Francis!'

He paused at the reproach in his wife's voice. 'Now, Eleanor, we have to go, there's the reception at Wesley Hall and the others have already gone, we'll be late as it is.'

Eleanor stood her ground. 'She is fourteen years old, Francis. It is our Christian duty.'

Francis reddened, though whether it was with shame, annoyance or frustration she didn't know. He stared at her for a moment, his lips compressed, then across at Mary, who was controlling her tears by this time and looking at him hopefully.

'Dratted girl!' he exploded; it was the nearest he ever got to an expletive.

'Just a child,' murmured Eleanor, pressing her point.

'Oh, very well, we'll take a cab and look around the streets before we go to the hall. But I must say we stand very little chance of finding her if she doesn't want to be found, especially if she's with this seaman.' He snorted as he handed the women up into the cab. 'She's no child, either. Prudence Buckle was born with a woman's wiles.'

Mary opened her mouth to protest but a warning glance from Eleanor stopped her. Instead she confined herself to gazing about her from the open-topped cab, oblivious to the heat that poured down on the road and the dust that was raised by the horse cab, and the smell of hot, sweaty humanity and hot, sweaty horseflesh.

By the end of the morning even Mary had to admit defeat. They had searched the area around Circular Quay and the rocky ridge nearby, which the cab driver helpfully told them was known as the Rocks, up and down streets of private dwellings and around bonded warehouses. But of Prue and her seaman there was no sign.

'It's too late now to go to Wesley Hall,' said Francis. 'We might as well find our lodging.'

Not a very good beginning to their new life, mused Eleanor as she unpacked their overnight things in the pleasant bedroom of a house in a newly-built terrace overlooking an unlikely village green. She had sent Mary to her own room at the back of the house, for she looked exhausted and ready to drop. Francis had removed his coat and was washing his face and hands in the china basin on the washstand. He reached for the towel on the side rail and patted himself dry before turning to her.

'I know, I shouldn't have brought them,' Eleanor said quickly, defensively.

'Yes.'

She watched him change into a clean shirt. 'Is that all you're going to say?'

'What else is there? Come now, Eleanor, it's almost three, we must go down to dinner. The others will be wondering where we are.'

He's glad Prue's gone, she thought. He wanted to dismiss her and Mary besides as soon as we arrived, didn't he say so? Well, I'm keeping Mary with me, I am.

She followed him down to the dining room, her chin set in determination. Only a few days and the *John Wesley,* the missionary ship bound for the Fiji islands, would sail with them aboard, Mary included though she might be reluctant to leave Prue behind in Sydney. After dinner, when Francis was safely occupied with his fellow missionaries, she would slip away and persuade Mary that it was the right thing to do and that if Prue had eloped with Jack Allan, she would not want her sister trailing after her.

Mary was not in the lodging house, however; she did not appear for dinner and when Eleanor went to her room in search of her she found the tiny room that had been allocated to the sisters was stifling hot and airless, the curtains had not even been drawn and there was no sign of the maid or her bag. At least Francis would be pleased, thought Eleanor bitterly as she made her way to their own room and flung herself on the bed. She felt hot and horrible, the greasy mutton she had consumed at dinner was repeating on her and her mouth tasted like a colliery tip. She sat up and poured herself a glass of water from the jug on the dressing table but it was warm and brackish and increased her queasiness.

Ingrates, that's what they were, the Buckles, they never thanked her for anything. Oh, but she would miss Mary – here she was going to a strange land and there was only Francis. Bile rose in her throat and she swallowed it determinedly and after a few minutes she felt better. Conscience pricked her; of course Mary would be worried about Prue, she had most likely gone in search of her. She would come back. Closing her eyes, Eleanor fell into a light doze.

*

Mary was running through the streets of Sydney, not knowing where she was, only that she had to find Prue. She was clutching the shabby black bag that held her few possessions in one hand and as she ran round a corner the bag swung out at an angle and caught against a post, wrenching her shoulder and almost bringing her down, but she ran on. Her breath came in panting gasps; sweat streamed down her face and neck, trickling down between her breasts. People in the street turned to watch the crazy girl who was running in the heat of the afternoon.

'Prue! Prue!' she cried once when she saw the figure of a young girl walking on the arm of a sailor, a girl with fair hair and a blue dress and just that way Prue had of looking sideways at a boy and laughing with him, but when she caught up with the couple and stretched out a hand to them, it wasn't Prue, nothing like her. How had she thought it was?

"Ere, what's up wi' you?' the man growled. Mary muttered an apology and fell back. He shrugged and whispered something to his companion and she was laughing as they walked on.

Mary sank down on a low wall outside an inn and put her bag on the ground by her feet. She was panting for breath and a red mist was swirling in front of her eyes. After a while the stitch in her side eased and her heartbeat slowed. She found a handkerchief in her pocket, wiped her face and neck and pushed her hair away from her forehead.

Looking up at the inn sign, she saw it was called The Jolly Sailor and, remembering Prue was with a seaman, a wild hope filled her. It was likely Jack was in just such a place as this, near the docks, and he would make straight for where he could get good ale on a hot day like this, wouldn't he?

Forgetting her bag, she went in, following the sound of raucous singing into a smoke-filled bar stinking of male body sweat and stale beer. She had to stand for a moment or two to let her eyes get accustomed to the darkness and then she peered round the room but, as far as she could see, the only woman there was behind the bar. Still, maybe Jack was further in. She started forward to get a proper look in the alcoves but suddenly her arm was seized by a brawny hand, which swung her round to face the man it belonged to.

'Oh no you don't, my lass, there's no women allowed in this bar, men only this is and you can go and ply your trade somewhere else!'

Mary gasped. 'What? What do you mean? I—'

'Aw, don't tell me you don't know what I'm talking about, I know your sort.' Without more ado he propelled her out into the bright sunshine to the accompaniment of jeers and obscene calls from his drunken patrons. None too gently he pushed her away from the inn into the dust of the street and she would have fallen but for the man she cannoned into.

'Mary? It's Mary Buckle, isn't it? Are you all right?'

Mary was almost sobbing with humiliation and anger as she looked up into the handsome face of Morgan West. 'Oh, Captain West!' She struggled to compose herself, pushing her hair back from her forehead and searching for her handkerchief to dab her face. Oh, she must look a proper sight, she must indeed.

'Did that man hurt you? I'll have a word with him, how dare he treat a lady so?'

Even in her distress, Mary was proud that he had called her a lady.

As Morgan West started for the door of the inn, she called after him. 'Please don't! Really, he didn't hurt me at all, look, I'm all right, I shouldn't have gone in there but I'm looking for Prue, you know, my sister Prue? You haven't seen her, have you? She's ran away, I'm desperate to find her, anything could happen to her, anything at all.'

'Come now, don't upset yourself, we'll find her.' He came back to her and took her arm. 'Look, we'll hail a cab and go somewhere quiet and cool where we can talk about it.'

Even as he spoke he was looking about the street and miraculously there was a cab with soft seats and a top to shade them, open-fronted so that when the driver clucked to his horse and they began to move, a small breeze played on Mary's over-heated body.

Now then, what were you doing in The Jolly Sailor? You didn't think Prue would be in there, did you?'

Mary had to admit that Prue hadn't just run off in a fit of pique or that they'd had a row or anything like that but had run off with a seaman. Jack Allan, in fact, the steward from the *Liberator.*

'And she's only fourteen, she's never been on her own without me before, never.' Mary took out her by now grubby handkerchief again and wiped her eyes.

Morgan put a comforting arm around her shoulders. 'Don't worry so much, Mary, I'm sure Prue's all right. She may be only fourteen but as I remember she's quite grown up. In any case I noticed Jack Allan is besotted with her, he won't hurt her. Do you know, in my part of the world, girls sometimes marry as young as twelve or thirteen.'

'But if I could only see her, make sure she isn't in trouble, oh, where is she, Captain West?' Mary was conscious of his arm around her suddenly; she could feel the heat from his body through the thin clothing between them. She looked up into his face, her blue eyes damp and beseeching, and his own darkened, became intent. He bent his head towards her.

'You're a damn fine-looking woman, Mary,' he drawled softly. 'Let me comfort you.'

The cab had slowed to a stop on a headland high over the bay and a sea breeze freshened their hot flesh as he gently touched her lips with his. In front of them, the cab driver sat stoically, his back to his passengers.

Chapter Ten

The trouble with Captain Morgan West, thought Eleanor as she watched him pause on his morning walk round the deck of the *John Wesley* and raise his hat to one of the ladies, was that he was too charming, too courteous, too … too … oh, altogether too much. He was extravagant in his dress, his hats were too big and flourishing, his smile too wide and what's more he had all the ladies on the ship, even Mrs Calvert and Mrs Gibson, twittering and simpering when he bent in greeting to them and lifted one of those hats with such an air of assurance and something else, something almost indefinable, exciting. No, not exciting, wicked.

Oh, yes, look at Mrs Calvert now, such a dumpy little woman with a double chin and no waist yet, as Captain West spoke to her, Eleanor was close enough to see how her face softened and tilted to one side when he bent over her.

'Good morning, Mrs Calvert,' he said and that lady blushed and fluttered her fan as though she saw some hidden meaning in the greeting. Eleanor turned away feeling sickened. She would go back to the cabin; she certainly wasn't going to show herself for a neddy in front of the other passengers by being charmed by him. Thank goodness they were almost there; another day and the ship would berth at Lakeba.

'Eleanor? Where are you going?'

Drat, it was Francis. His meeting with the rest of the missionaries must be ended; now she wouldn't be able to escape before Captain West got to her.

'I thought I would just go below ...' she began but already Captain West was standing beside her, lifting his hat and looking down at her with those intense blue eyes under their startlingly black brows.

'Mrs Tait, how are you this beautiful morning? And Mr Tait, of course?'

'We are both well, praise be to God,' said Francis stiffly. Was that amusement lurking in Captain West's eyes? wondered Eleanor. What on earth did he find so amusing about Francis? She glanced at her husband and was surprised to see him staring unsmiling at the American.

'Is something wrong, Francis?' she asked when Morgan West had gone on his leisurely progress round the deck.

'That man is not all he seems,' answered Francis. 'We have been discussing him just now. Do you know, we suspect him of blackbirding? Why on earth the captain agreed to give him passage I don't know.'

'Blackbirding?'

'Bringing in natives from some of the other islands to put to work on the plantations. They are virtually slaves and what's more, no regard at all is paid to their moral or spiritual welfare.'

'Really?'

'Really. Well, at least he is not getting off the boat at Lakeba, he is going on to Viti Levu. It's this trouble over slavery in the American South, they think the cotton trade will be affected and scoundrels like Morgan West are finding new places to grow cotton. At least, that is what I have heard.'

If Eleanor wondered where he had heard anything about anyone in these last few weeks while they had been at sea, she said nothing. No doubt Francis had his sources. Suddenly she felt quite queasy and a little dizzy and longed for a short rest on her bed.

'I think I will go below, Francis,' she said. 'I have a slight headache.'

'Will you be all right? I can come with you.' But his gaze was wandering to the group of his friends that was gathered in a corner of the deck engaged in a discussion. In any case, she wanted to be on her own. Shaking her head, she went to their cabin.

This was the third time she had felt like this in the mornings, she mused as she opened the door. Perhaps she was sickening for something. Mary was in the cabin, singing softly to herself and packing their clothes ready to disembark at Lakeba.

'Can't you leave that now?' Eleanor said grumpily. She felt decidedly out of sorts and the other girl's glowing health and shining blonde curls did nothing to help. And anyway, Mary had no right to look so happy either; did she not care at all that her young sister had run off when they were in Sydney?

'You look very pleased with yourself considering what happened to your sister,' she said, sitting down heavily on the bottom bunk and knocking the back of her head against the top one in the process.

Mary's smile faded. 'I don't know that anything has happened to Prue,' she said, biting her lip. 'Jack Allan thinks a lot about her, he wouldn't have left his ship if he didn't. He'll look after her. And any road, Morgan says that lots of girls marry when they are fourteen and even younger where he comes from. Aye, I bet Prue's wed by now, she'll be all right.'

Eleanor had her eyes closed and was rubbing the bump on her head, only half-listening to Mary. But suddenly she realised what the other girl had said and she jumped to her feet, forgetting the pain.

'What? What did you say?'

'I said Prue's likely wed—'

'No, not that, you said Morgan, you're calling that – that American by his Christian name, are you? You forward besom, you! By, I'm beginning to think Francis and Mr

Johnson were right about you, you and your sister are both alike, so you are.' Eleanor's voice rose shrewishly; she could feel the rage rising in her yet felt helpless to control it. Her hands clenched by her sides.

'He calls me Mary, why can't I call him Morgan?'

'What do you mean, he calls you Mary? Of course he would call you Mary, you're a servant, that's why he calls you by your first name, you know very well why. But him, he might be an American, but he's a gentleman—'

Eleanor paused momentarily as she remembered what Francis had said about him that morning. But still, he was a gentleman born, surely?

'He told me to call him Morgan.'

Mary's flat statement made Eleanor's rage rise even more. 'He told you? Do you mean to say you've been meeting the man? Flirting with him, I dare say, rolling your eyes at him like a common—'

'He likes me!'

Mary was shouting now, standing there before her and shouting at her, oh, why on earth hadn't she listened to Francis, why had she brought these two miner's brats? He'd been right, they'd been nothing but trouble.

'I forbid you to talk to this man.'

'What for? Because you like him yourself? I tell you what, *Mrs Eleanor Tait,* I'm sick to death of you telling me what I can do. You think because you helped me out when Mam was so bad, you think you own me, aye, an' Prue an' all. Why do you think she ran off then? It was because of you, if it hadn't been for you she'd still be here with me, but you couldn't let her have a beau like normal, could you? Oh no, you think lasses like us has no right to our own lads. Well, I'm telling you, I like Morgan and he treats me proper like I'm a lady.'

'Mary! After all I've done for you!'

'Well, it suited you, didn't it? There you were playing at being Florence Nightingale and everyone in the colliery rows laughing at you. Miss Know-It-All, that's what they called you behind your back because you know nowt, that's what. But it's different here, this isn't England, I'm as good as you here, I'm telling you. And if I want to go with Morgan West, I will, and I won't ask you if I can or not. I only hope he asks me, I'll go like a shot. Any road, you're only jealous, you fancy him yourself '

Eleanor was staring at her in stupefaction; all these years she'd known the Buckles and she'd never guessed what they'd been thinking.

'Mary! I'm a married woman, don't say such wicked things!'

'No, but you can say what you like to me, can't you? Fancy saying I don't care about my own sister!' Mary's voice began to wobble and her face crumpled as she rushed from the cabin, leaving Eleanor speechless.

She lay down on the bunk and put her hand over her eyes. It was true; what she had said was unforgivable, of course Mary cared about Prue. She had got into such a rage though, even before Mary had opened her mouth. What had made her so angry? She was shaking still and a pulse was pounding in her temple as she fumbled for the bottle of lavender water that was on the packing case by the bed. She would just put a little on her forehead; perhaps it would help. And when she felt better she would go and apologise to Mary.

'Eleanor? Are you all right? I thought I heard shouting in here, did something happen?'

She opened her eyes wearily. Oh dear Lord, she had used too much lavender water; the smell of it was overpowering, making her feel sick. Francis was bending over the bunk, his brow puckered in concern.

'I'm not well,' she said faintly, scrabbled for the chamber pot and vomited copiously.

'Shall I get Mary?' he asked anxiously, backing to the door hastily.

'No!' she cried, lying back and wiping her face with her handkerchief.

'But—'

Eleanor struggled to a sitting position and after a moment her head ceased its swimming. She began to feel better and it was then that it came to her almost as a revelation.

'No, Francis, I'm all right now, it's over. Most women feel like this when they start a baby.'

Slowly the ship edged its way into the bay at Lakeba and tied up at the recently constructed jetty. All around the vessel, natives paddled canoes, looking to be in imminent danger of being run down. Francis and Eleanor stood close together on the deck, staring at the dense tropical vegetation that ran down right on to the beach, coconut palms and tall ferns and grasses. Right in what looked to be the centre of the island rose a mountain – a volcano was it? – covered in dense vegetation, lush and green.

The noise was tremendous, men and women shouting and holding up things they wanted to sell, dogs on the beach barking hysterically and running into the waves and out again, birds shrieking and crying and rising in great clouds from the trees before settling back again. The only animals ignoring the coming of the ship were the pigs, grunting and rooting about in the sand and mud.

The ship slowly nosed its way alongside the jetty and at last they had arrived. There were last-minute goodbyes, for the rest of the party was going on to other stations and the *John Wesley* was staying only long enough to drop supplies for the mission house, and the Taits and their baggage, as the ship had to leave before the tide ebbed. Francis and Eleanor watched from the shore as it drew away again almost immediately. Glancing at Francis's set smile as he waved, Eleanor guessed he was feeling almost as forlorn as she was herself. Tucking her hand under his arm in a gesture she hoped was comforting, she lifted her chin and turned towards the line of natives waiting in the hot sun to greet them with a black-coated minister at their head.

Neither of them noticed the look of despair on Mary's face as she trailed after them. She had been so sure that Morgan would take her with him to the island of Viti Levu or at least say that he would send for her when he had concluded whatever mysterious business he had on Bau. Last night, as she lay in his arms in a secluded corner of the ship, well away from the prying eyes of the missionary party, she had waited for him to say he would send for her at least, even if he couldn't take her with him immediately.

He had not. Instead he had said he was sure they would meet again soon. 'It's a small world, Fiji,' he had said softly as he kissed her goodbye. 'I'm sure to be visiting Lakeba one day soon. Be a good girl while I'm gone.'

She was struck dumb at first; she thought she hadn't heard aright. And by the time she had gathered her thoughts to protest he had disappeared, to his cabin no doubt. She had lain awake for most of the night after that, sobbing quietly to herself, and now her head throbbed unmercifully.

'Mary! Do come along,' Francis said sharply, pausing at the end of the jetty and looking back. Mary's heart burned with resentment though she quickened her step and followed him ashore. Her shoulder began to ache from carrying her own bag in the sticky heat and she changed it to the other hand. Of course the Taits had a native porter to carry their luggage. Mary looked at him now: a Tongan, that's what he must be; he was different from the black men in the canoes, not so wild-haired and he was even wearing a shirt and a sort of wrap-around skirt over his loincloth.

Mary sighed as she saw there was a reception party on the beach waiting for them. All she wanted to do was get inside out of the hot sun and wallow in her misery. If only she had had Prue with her, she thought, feeling sure she should have stayed in Sydney to look for her young sister. Guilt rose in her; by, Mam would have been past herself if she knew that Prue was left to God and Providence in a strange city on the other side of the world from Hetton-le-Hole. Mary had felt bad enough leaving Ben though he was a man now and earning a hewer's wage at the pit. But Prue—

Her thoughts were interrupted by the realisation that everyone had stopped talking and was moving off, the minister who had led the greeting and prayers of thanksgiving leading the way. Miserably she followed, halting once to look back at the ship that was bearing Morgan away from her. It was because of him that she had left Sydney, she admitted to herself. He would come back, she told herself, she knew he would, hadn't he said so?

A bare brown arm reached down by Mary's side and took a firm grip on her bag, making her jump in alarm. 'I carry,' said the owner of the arm, his voice deep and guttural. Petrified, Mary released the bag, staring at the fierce-looking man, who was wearing nothing but a piece of cloth round his middle. And what was that stuck in his waist band, a club? If this place was so civilised, why did they need to carry weapons? She looked at Eleanor and Francis; at least she wasn't on her own amongst these heathens, thank God for that. But to her horror, Francis was telling Eleanor he was just going off with his predecessor to view the church.

'I'll be back in plenty of time for supper, dear,' he was saying. 'It will give you a chance to get settled in.' Mary moved closer to Eleanor, telling herself not to be a fool, these native servants were Tongans and Tongans were Christians, weren't they?

'Oh, God preserve us all,' she prayed under her breath, fighting to keep down her sudden panic. No matter how fierce they looked, Christians weren't going to turn on them and kill them, of course they weren't, not these ones at any rate.

They were striding away along the well-trodden paths in the sandy soil and before long they reached the house, a long, low, wooden building with a plaited palm roof and small fenced garden in front. It was part of a compound with half a dozen similar buildings and one slightly taller, which she surmised must be the chapel because Francis and his friend were just disappearing into it. Well, she was here now, she told herself as she looked at the house. The Tongans carrying the luggage had disappeared round the side; she only hoped they hadn't taken off into the hills with the luggage.

She must make the best of it, she told herself. Maybe Morgan had been telling the truth and would come back for her, he might, he might. And maybe there would be a letter from Prue the next time the boat came in. Mary smiled grimly. 'When the boat comes in,' she murmured; the phrase reminded her of home.

'Did you say something, Mary?' asked Eleanor, who had gone out of her way to be nice to Mary since the row of the previous day. They had entered what looked to be the main living room of the bungalow and, without waiting for a reply, Eleanor went on, 'It's quite nice, isn't it?' Eagerly she inspected the furniture, a mixture of old wooden pieces that must have been brought in over time, since the mission was established thirty years before, and bamboo tables and chairs made locally. There were homely touches, cotton cushions and curtains that must have been made by previous female occupants.

And they had moved on from here, Mary thought, so this wasn't a life sentence; it just felt like one.

Chapter Eleven

At least she was beginning to tell the difference between the native Fijians and the Tongans, thought Eleanor. The alarm she had felt every time she had come across a black man, naked but for a loin cloth made from bark or sometimes a piece of cloth and tied round the middle, had begun to quieten. She sat down heavily on a bamboo chair on the verandah, one hand across her swelling stomach and the other waving a fan slowly before her face.

A rivulet of sweat trickled down between her breasts under the voluminous coverall she wore over her dress to hide her pregnancy and another ran down her back. Lordy, she could do with a drink, even a drink of that sickly pineapple juice that seemed to be the main beverage of the island. She looked out over the compound, hoping to see Mary or at least Matthew, the Tongan houseman, both of whom had disappeared soon after breakfast, leaving her alone in the house. She debated whether it was worth her heaving her bulk to her feet and going out to the kitchen or whether it was just too much effort even for a drink of water. Lovely cold water.

Closing her eyes, Eleanor thought of the water that was piped to the viewer's house in Hetton, pumped up from the pit it was, cold as melted snow and sparkling clear, tasting faintly of minerals, iron and coal. She put her tongue between her lips, remembering the taste of it. Sighing, she opened her eyes and gazed out over the compound again.

Mary was coming out of the store, a basket over her arm. From the chapel in the centre came the sound of singing; Francis must have almost finished his prayer meeting. Knots of islanders strolled about or stood in groups, the Tongans separate. The locals didn't like the Tongans and Eleanor remembered Francis saying that the Fijians considered them arrogant interlopers who looked down on the native Fijians, quite mistakenly from the Fijians' point of view, for they were convinced that their islands were the centre of the world. Not even when they were shown maps and globes by the first missionaries to reach Lakeba, William Cross and David Cargill, had they believed any different.

Eleanor shuddered as her attention was diverted by a fat black rat. It emerged from under the verandah and made its leisurely way across to the lush undergrowth just a few yards away. Instinctively, she gathered her skirts around her shins in spite of the sticky heat. There was probably yet another nest down there; she would have to get Matthew to clear it out.

'Rat no hurt you,' Matthew would say, shrugging his shoulders in amazement at the strange fancies of the minister's woman. He would get rid of it in the end, but not before Eleanor had persuaded Francis to order him to.

'Rats are vermin,' she had insisted the last time this had happened. 'Florence Nightingale says they carry dirt and disease.'

'Oh, Florence Nightingale,' Francis had said, humouring her. 'What has Florence Nightingale to do with life in Fiji? All right, I'll tell Matthew to clear them out, I don't want you upset, especially not now.' Which was as near a reference to her pregnancy as he ever got.

Oh, what had happened to her dreams of looking after the natives, nursing them when they were sick, teaching them hygiene? Her work was going to be as important as that of Francis; she had had such high hopes. Why hadn't she considered what being married meant to a woman? A pregnancy every year or so was what she could look forward to, an uncomfortable, miserable nine months and no time for anything else but her family.

Mary was climbing the steps of the verandah and Eleanor watched as she placed her basket on the low table and walked over to her.

'Would you like a drink, Mrs Tait? By, you do look hot and bothered, I can bring you a cup of tea, or some pineapple juice, what do you fancy?'

'Water, that's what I fancy. A long drink of cold, cold water. I hate pineapple juice, it's so sweet it makes me sick.' Eleanor was irritable.

'I can make a pot of tea, how about that?'

Mary didn't bother to say that the water in the bucket would be warm and stale at this time of the day, something of which Eleanor was well aware.

'Oh, go on then, make some tea. Mr Tait will be here shortly, I'm sure he'd like a cup.'

Mary picked up her basket and went through the open door into the main room of the house and on to the kitchen in the back. She added wood to the stove just outside the back door and filled the kettle with the warm brackish water from the bucket. Where was that lazy black bastard now? This was Matthew's job, seeing to the stove and the tea; hadn't she enough to do just looking after Eleanor?

She took down the tin tray from the shelf and put two cups and saucers on it and the battered tin sugar basin with the wooden lid to keep the ants out. As an afterthought, she lifted the lid and fished out a couple of ants that had got in there anyway. Bloody insects, the place was swarming with them. Great giant things an' all, not civilised little things like at home. For a second or two, Mary allowed herself to mourn for Hetton and the colliery rows and her own folk. Likely she'd never see them again. Had Ben got married, did he have a family? He never bothered to answer her letters.

There was no milk for the tea, they'd just have to do without. Matthew was supposed to be bringing a nanny goat in milk from his uncle who had a rackety shack up on the side of the volcano and a herd of goats he'd brought in from Tonga, but he was a long time about it. It wouldn't be so bad if she had Prue – why didn't the lass write? She could easily find out where they were. But no, her and Ben were two of a kind, ungrateful little beggars.

Mary spooned tea into the pot and poured boiling water over it. The tea was almost gone, she noted, and the store was out of it too. Thank goodness the *John Wesley* was due in today. She poured out a cup for herself and left it in the kitchen before picking up the tray and carrying it through to the verandah. Francis was sitting beside Eleanor, leaning solicitously over her and adjusting a cushion behind her back.

'Thank you, Mary,' he said. 'Just what I need.'

Not what I need, thought Mary as she went back to the kitchen. What I need is for Prue to come back. But what I need most is Morgan West getting off that boat today, marching up here, telling me he can't do without me and I must go with him and live with him and have his bairns. He wouldn't have to marry me, I don't care what anybody thinks.

This flight of fancy was interrupted by the appearance of Matthew at the back gate, a water bag slung over his shoulder and with a nanny goat on a piece of twine, its udders so swollen with milk they almost touched the ground. He tethered the goat by the door and turned unsmiling black eyes on Mary.

'Woman milk goat,' he said loftily.

Mary picked up her cup of tea and took a long swallow of the cooling liquid. She gazed at the Tongan; he was smaller than the native Fijians and his bare upper body less muscular but nevertheless he was a strong man and she found herself comparing him with Morgan. Of course, Morgan was fair and his body quite white under his shirt whereas Matthew was as black as the jet beads Morgan had bought for her in Sydney to console her when Prue went missing. And Matthew's body glistened with the everlasting coconut oil all the natives used on their skins and the edge of his loin cloth was stained with it.

She shook herself mentally and put down her cup. What on earth was she thinking about? It must be the heat in this place, the sticky heat that made her feel so different, so conscious of her body somehow. Of course it had been Morgan who had started it, started it and then gone away. Impatiently, she began to unpack her basket of provisions, putting them away in the press by the wall. It was the only cupboard that was proof against the ants.

'Milk the blooming thing yourself,' she snapped, not even looking round at Matthew. 'I'm not here to do your bidding nor any other black fella's, not likely.' She waited for his hiss of outrage and, when it wasn't forthcoming, glanced at him. He had taken a glass from the shelf and was carefully pouring water into it, clear, sparkling water from the water bag he had brought in with him. Then he carried the glass to the door.

'Water not for you,' he warned, pausing for a moment. 'Water for minister's woman.'

'Is it, now?'

Mary waited until he had gone through the sitting room to the verandah and then she took her cup to the bag on the table and poured herself a drink.

By, it was grand. Matthew must have been to the spring high up the mountain; the water was sweet and clear and tasted of cool rain. Hurriedly she poured herself another drink and drank it down before wiping her mouth and following him through for the tray.

But the tray was forgotten as from out in the bay came the sound of a ship's hooter. All around them people were running to the canoes, men, women and children, all anxious to go out and greet the *John Wesley* as it rounded the headland, sails billowing, and turned in the direction of the jetty. Even Francis had got to his feet and was straightening his jacket and white neck cloth. Matthew had already deserted the verandah and was running for the beach with two of his cronies.

Mary smoothed down her dress and put a hand up to her hair. Morgan might be on the ship, he might, he might, she told herself in what was almost a prayer. The excitement of the natives, always the same when a ship came though nowadays one came every two or three weeks, infected everyone, Europeans too. The only one who hadn't risen from her chair was Eleanor. Francis went to the edge of the verandah and paused, looking back at his wife.

'You'll be all right, won't you, my love?' he asked, almost as an afterthought. Catching his wife's slight frown, he added quickly, 'Mary will stay in case you need her, I won't be long. But I must see if there is any communication from the head of the district, you understand? And there might be letters from home, you'd like me to get them as soon as possible, wouldn't you?'

Eleanor looked at him wearily. 'Oh, go on, Francis, go if you must.'

'Yes ... Yes, I'll be back as soon as I can, Eleanor.'

Mary watched as he strode down to the jetty. Oh yes, Mary will stay, she thought, feeling rebellious. Then she looked at Eleanor, how white her face was, how exhausted she looked. Her black hair was glistening with sweat where it peeped out of her cap as she laid her head back against the wooden edge of the chair and lifted her feet on to a stool. Her ankles were swollen again, Mary saw, swollen worse than she had seen them before. Poor Eleanor, it must be truly hellish to be so heavy with a bairn in this climate.

'Will I get you some more water, Mrs Tait?' she said gently, her own discontents forgotten in her pity for the other woman.

'Please, Mary,' Eleanor said, her voice a mere thread of sound. Mary looked at her sharply. Eleanor's face was chalk white, the brow wrinkled; it wasn't just the heat that was bothering her, Mary decided.

'Is something the matter? It's not the baby, is it?'

'No, no, of course not, it's not time yet, the baby won't come for another two weeks at least. No, it's just my back, it aches so badly and the heat ...' Eleanor's voice trailed away as though she hadn't the energy to carry on with what she was saying.

'Howay then, lass, let's have you to bed, that's the best place for you. It'll be nice and cool with just your nightie and a sheet over you and as soon as you're settled I'll bring you another cool drink and mebbe a few drops of laudanum will make you sleep.'

'I don't know ... what about Francis? I don't want to worry him.' Eleanor was fretful, full of objections to anything that Mary suggested, but Mary wasn't listening.

It's not Mr Tait who's having the bairn,' she said calmly. 'Now come on, I'll help you up and we'll soon have you tucked up in bed. I'll draw the blinds and you can have a nice sleep, it'll do you the world of good and the babby an' all.'

Mary had slipped deeper into the sing-song accent of the Geordies, and somehow Eleanor found her voice incredibly comforting. Oh, thank God for Mary, she had a heart of gold, she had. Why ever had she been so critical of Mary Buckle? And it would be so grand just to lie down in the dark bedroom, so grand ... Trustingly, she allowed Mary to help her to her feet and, leaning heavily on her maid, began to walk across the verandah to the French windows of the bedroom, which were standing open to catch any breath of fresh air.

Suddenly she shrieked in agony and slumped to the ground, taking Mary down with her. Eleanor's weight lay across Mary's middle and it took the girl a few minutes of panting effort to get free and when she did, her face flushed and her pulse racing, she saw Eleanor was in a dead faint and her pallor had taken on an ominous bluish hue.

Mary stared round the compound, rushed to the steps and looked wildly up the street but there was no one there, no one at all. Of course not; everyone was down by the water's edge, or actually on the water, all the boats and canoes in the place were out on the water. All greeting the ship as it sailed into the bay. Anyone would think they'd never seen a bloody ship before, she thought savagely, even Francis Tait was there, leaving his poor wife to God and Providence, what did he care about her when there was the excitement of the missionary ship?

She wasn't being fair, she knew she wasn't, and any road he hadn't left Eleanor with nobody and it was up to herself to see to her. Rushing back to Eleanor, Mary saw she was coming round – at least that she was moaning something incoherent and struggling to lift her head.

Bending to her, Mary slipped her forearms under the other woman's armpits and lifted her into a sitting position. 'Now then, what do you think you're doing, giving me such a fright? Another one like that will be the death of me, I'm telling you. Come on now, help yourself, you're far too heavy for me to lift you up on my own and there's not another soul about can help. Howay now, pull yourself together.'

Mary hardly knew what she was saying but somehow she pulled and lifted until she thought her arms would drop off altogether and at last she managed to drag Eleanor on to the bed. But her heart sank as she glanced back on to the verandah and saw the wet trail where they had come. The waters had broke, there was no doubt about it, hadn't she seen it happen when Mam had Prue? And the last little babby, the thin little blue doll of a babby, had whimpered only once and then given up on life before it had even begun.

Eleanor was moaning, rocking herself from side to side on the bed. 'Mary, Mary,' she cried. 'Help me, Mary!'

'I'm doing my best, lass,' said Mary. 'Try and sit up a bit now, let's get your clothes off and a nice cool nightie on, you'll feel better then.'

It took for ever to get Eleanor changed and then it was practically a waste of time for within minutes the nightie was as drenched with sweat as her dress had been. Eleanor sank back on the pillows, evidently having some respite from the pain.

'Get Francis, he'll have to do something,' she panted.

What could he do? Mary asked herself. There wasn't another white woman on Lakeba, not at the moment. There was a midwife on Bau and she was supposed to be coming over to the island for the birth but not yet, not for another week.

'Plenty of time,' she had said, when she had seen Eleanor only last week. 'Plenty of time, another two weeks at least.'

'So much for midwives,' Mary muttered to herself.

'What? What did you say? Oh Mary, it's coming on again, it is. Oh, dear Lord in heaven, what am I going to do?'

'Now don't fret, pet, you'll be all right, I'm here, aren't I? Women have been having bairns a long time now, we'll manage, you'll see. Any road, Francis will be back any minute, he's bound to be, he knows how you're held.'

Eleanor's answer was a deep moan that came up from the depths of her and turned into a shriek. Mary's shaky self-confidence almost deserted her as Eleanor grabbed hold of her hand and squeezed it so tightly she thought the bones would crack.

'Another pain already?' Mary looked anxiously at Eleanor but Eleanor's eyes were fixed at a point near the open windows of the room and Mary turned to follow her gaze. The oldest woman they had ever seen was standing there, barely four foot tall, with skin black and wrinkled like a prune, wizened breasts bare but for a bone necklace carved with strange symbols and wearing a short kilt-like skirt made out of strips of barkcloth. The creature stood calmly, just inside the room.

Eleanor cried out just once and fell into a faint yet again, which was just as well, for the woman walked to the bed and laid her hand on Eleanor's swollen belly. Cocking her head to one side, she palpated the mass gently, cluck-clucking to herself and completely ignoring Mary.

101

'Hey! What are you doing?' Mary shouted at her, wrenching her hand free from Eleanor's and trying to push the black hand off, but the old woman was surprisingly strong. 'Get out of here, do you understand me? Get out, leave her alone.'

As far as the old woman was concerned, Mary may as well not have been there. She flicked her hand once as though despatching a troublesome fly and then replaced it, continuing to palpate Eleanor's belly.

'I help,' she said at last. 'Minister's woman in trouble.'

'Aye,' shouted Mary. 'But not as much trouble as you'll be in, if you don't get out of here. The minister will be back in a minute and he'll send you fleeing all right, putting your filthy hands on his woman.'

'She sleep now, better soon.'

'You gave her such a fright she's swooned, you mean,' retorted Mary but she paused in her tirade as she looked at the woman on the bed. Eleanor seemed to have come out of her faint and appeared to be sleeping naturally, with even a little colour in her cheeks. Mary put a hand on her forehead; it was cooler, she was sure of it, not clammy at all. And her breathing had slowed to an even rhythm, steady and full.

Astonished, Mary looked at the old woman, who was moving away from the bed to the window with an air of having finished what she came to do.

'How did you do that?' she asked but the woman either didn't understand or chose not to answer. Instead she went out on to the verandah before pausing to speak.

'Baby come one day,' she said and disappeared into the undergrowth.

Mary stared after her; had she been real or just an apparition? But Eleanor was sleeping quietly when only a few minutes ago Mary could have sworn she was rapidly approaching the final stages of labour.

Mary went to the edge of the verandah steps and looked out towards the beach. The *John Wesley* was riding at anchor and a small knot of Europeans were walking up the beach with Francis, surrounded by natives. No Morgan, she thought sadly. All the men were dressed in sober black and there was no sign at all of the American's flamboyant hat, nor of his burly shoulders covered in his pearl-grey cotton jacket. She watched as the group went into the church to give thanks for their safe arrival at Lakeba and shortly she heard the sound of singing, the deep voices of the natives somehow altering the hymn and giving it their own peculiar rhythm.

'Speed thy servants, Saviour speed them,
Thou art Lord of winds and waves.'

Mary sat on Eleanor's chair, listening quietly to the music. The singing seemed to shimmer in the hot air and even the parakeets had stopped their noise and were sitting quietly in the trees, waiting for the heat of the day to pass. A pig grunted softly near the doorway of the chapel and a Fijian appeared briefly in the opening and shooed it away.

Aye well, thought Mary, there's nowt to do but wait for the next time the ship comes, maybe Morgan will be on it that time. Or Prue, by, it would be nice to see Prue.

'Mary? Are you there, Mary?' Eleanor called from the bedroom.

Mary got to her feet with a sigh and went in to see what she wanted. Come on, Mr Francis Tait, she muttered, come out of that chapel and see to your wife, this is where you're needed just at the present.

Chapter Twelve

The baby was born a full twenty-four hours later, just as the old Fijian woman had predicted.

'A boy,' said Mary as she swaddled the tiny red-faced little thing in a square of calico and laid him in the waiting cradle. The midwife, a missionary's wife who had luckily been on the ship with her husband, helped to make the new mother comfortable.

'Thank God,' murmured Eleanor. 'Is he all right?'

'A bit red in the face I suppose, but he's got all the parts he should have,' said the midwife briskly. Her husband was the Reverend Langham and he was in the next room with Francis. 'Now, let's get you comfortable and then Mr Tait can come in to see you both. Poor man, he's been at his wits' end this last day.'

Poor man indeed, Mary said to herself. Why, it had been the middle of the afternoon before Francis had returned to the house. 'On parish business,' he had said, never mind that his wife was in labour. Well, he didn't know his wife was in labour, but still he knew she might have been. Mary helped Mrs Langham change the sheets for cool, clean ones and bundled up the dirty laundry to take out to the kitchen.

'You'll wash them through yourself, Mary,' said Mrs Langham. 'After all, we can't have a man doing such a thing, it's woman's work.'

Oh no, we can't have Matthew doing such a thing, Mary thought, of course not. She went through the verandah doors so as to avoid Francis and Mr Langham. On no account could men be allowed to see anything connected with childbirth, they weren't supposed to know anything about it, not even Matthew, black servant that he was. Oh no, as far as they were concerned the baby might have been found under a bush in the garden.

Mary set a kettle of water on the stove in the yard and while she was waiting for it to heat up she grated yellow soap and mixed it with soda. Normally a woman from the village would take the dirty washing to the stream that ran down the back of the compound and pound it on the rocks until it was clean, but she couldn't do that; a man might see it.

Mary smiled to herself, recognising the absurdity of her thoughts. Men could do nothing right for her at present, she was rapidly turning into a man-hater, it was silly. Ah, but if only Morgan would come for her no doubt her opinions would change. She set to rubbing away at the linen in the tub, working with a steady energy despite the heat, pounding away at the sheets. If she tired herself out she might at least sleep the night through for a change.

Behind her, in the house, Francis entered the bedroom, a little fearful of what state Eleanor was going to be in after her arduous labour. But there she was, sitting up in bed, the baby on her arm, looking pale and tired and triumphant at the same time. He walked over to the bed and kissed her forehead before studying the infant carefully.

'Well done, lass,' he said softly. 'A fine strong lad he looks to be.'

'Oh, he is,' said Mrs Langham, and Francis looked up as though he had just remembered she was there.

'I'm sure. Both Eleanor and I appreciate everything you have done for us.'

'It's our Christian duty to help each other, Mr Tait,' said Mrs Langham. 'It's a good thing I was here – the Lord provides in our hour of need, does He not?' She suddenly realised that they were both looking at her politely but obviously waiting to be on their own together. 'Er ... well, I'll just go out and see what Mr Langham is doing. If you want anything, Eleanor, I'll be there.'

She slipped out on to the verandah and Francis turned to Eleanor. 'I'm sorry I wasn't here when you took badly, dear,' he said. 'You were all right with Mary, though, weren't you?'

Eleanor looked at him, remembering how angry she had been that he wasn't there when she may have needed him, but the pain and the panic were already only vague memories. She looked down at the sleeping baby and fancied she could already detect Francis's high forehead, the shape of his mouth. A surge of happiness ran through her and she smiled at Francis, feeling closer to him than she had ever been before.

'Eleanor?'

'I was fine, Francis,' she said. 'After all, everything turned out all right, didn't it?'

Francis relaxed. 'We have to decide a name for him,' he said, leaning back in his chair.

John George Tait was baptised 20 April, 1862. The ceremony was performed in the chapel by the Reverend Frederick Langham and his wife was godmother. The pair had returned specially to the island for the ceremony and afterwards there was a small tea party to celebrate. The two couples were becoming firm friends and Mrs Langham took an almost proprietary interest in the progress of John George.

Afterwards, the two men went out to visit a tribe of local Fijians who lived only a short distance around the coast from the compound. Most of the converts, those who lived in the compound and some who had spread out into the foothills, were Tongans and Francis was anxious to persuade the Fijians to forsake their old gods altogether and embrace Christianity. He went to it with an evangelistic zeal that he had discovered in himself when he met his first group of unconvinced Fijians. He couldn't rest until he had 'brought them into the fold', as he termed it.

'Take care, Francis, please, for the sake of little John,' Eleanor begged him, for she too had found a new cause: it was protecting her child and making sure Francis did nothing that might put him in jeopardy.

'Don't worry,' said Mr Langham. 'We are perfectly safe on Lakeba, why, this was the first island to be Christianised.'

In which case, why are there still native pagans? thought Eleanor but she held her peace; maybe she was just being overanxious.

So it proved to be, for Francis returned jubilant that he had managed to extract a promise from the headman of the group that he would lead his followers to the compound that Sunday and listen to what the Godman had to say.

True to his word, the headman led a string of warriors up to the chapel on Sunday but he refused to lead them in when he realised his group was outnumbered by Tongans. Eleanor watched with baby John in her arms from the safe distance of her balcony. They stood outside in a semi-circle, each man armed to the teeth and naked but for a loincloth with a *i ula kobo* throwing club tucked into it, a fearsome weapon to see even from the distance away she was.

Each man held at least two short spears, which he grasped as though he intended to use them at the least sign of any discord. But the Tongans remained inside the chapel while Francis stood under the overhanging roof speaking to the warriors, for all the world as though he was delivering a sermon in the chapel at home in Hetton or Houghton le Spring and, after a while, the Fijians' grasp on their spears relaxed. Though when Francis suggested they lay them down, for this was the Lord's Day and fighting was a sin, they muttered angrily among themselves and Eleanor hastily retreated into the mission house.

The day came when Eleanor awoke feeling fit and full of energy and she decided that it was time she put her own plans into action. If Mrs Langham could act as a midwife why couldn't she? This was her chance to tend the sick, put the ideas of Florence Nightingale into practice too. Besides, Francis wasn't in a position to object to anything she did; he was off on his travels round the neighbouring islands preaching to the natives no doubt. The opportunity was heaven-sent for her to begin practising, nursing the sick among the natives and teaching them hygiene.

'But what about John? Will you be back to feed him?' asked Mary. Not that she minded looking after the baby; he reminded her of Prue when she was little and at least it gave her a chance to stay at the front of the house away from the supercilious Matthew, who actually thought he could order her about because she was a woman.

'I have expressed enough for you to feed him if I'm not back,' said Eleanor. She pinned on her bonnet with its swathe of muslin that was supposed to keep off the flies and, blowing a kiss at little John, who was sleeping peacefully in his cradle, she went off towards the huts of the Tongans before she could have second thoughts. It was best to start with the Tongans rather than the Fijians, she told herself, one step at a time, that was best.

She walked along one of the myriad paths that crisscrossed the compound towards the area where the Tongan families lived. The huts were deserted, only a few pigs and dogs lying dozing in the sun. But from the beach beyond she could hear laughing and shouting and children playing so she walked on, determined not to give up now. The corner of the beach seemed to be given up to the women and children and they were splashing about in the shallows, the children quite naked and the women either with only a loincloth round them or occasionally a sarong covering their breasts.

She stood for a minute or two, watching them, envying them being able to splash about with next to nothing on. Then someone noticed her there and the whole lot of them rushed out of the sea and surrounded her, laughing and talk-ing, inviting her in a mixture of mime and broken English to join them. One, a grey-haired, matronly woman who Eleanor recognised as Mia, a relative of Matthew, began to unwind Eleanor's muslin scarf and pull at her dress, wanting her to discard it.

'Baby?' said one, looking round in puzzlement. 'Baby?' Most of the younger women had babies wrapped in their sarongs or straddling their hips and Eleanor realised they couldn't understand why little John was not with her.

'Baby in house,' she tried to explain but only succeeded in making them look even more puzzled. She looked around the bathing place; it was a secluded corner of the bay with not a man to be seen. Surely it wouldn't hurt if she took off her dress and joined them in the sea? It looked so invit-ing and Francis would never know. Within minutes, she was splashing around in the shallows, joining in the games with the younger children and feeling cooler than she had felt since coming to Lakeba.

I'm making friends, she said to herself, if I get to know the women better they will trust me, they will let me help them when they need it. But then she gave herself up to the pure enjoyment of the sea and the feel of the damp sand under her feet and the gentle waves lapping between her toes.

Afterwards, the women walked a little further along the beach to where a small stream came down from the foothills and together they rinsed the salt from each other's long hair in the clear water and exclaimed at the fineness of Eleanor's hair. Eleanor took her own ribbons and hairpins and demon-strated with Mia's hair how to pile it on the top of the head so that it didn't fall down and Mia strutted about before them like a queen, showing her new hairstyle off with elab-orate gestures. And it was then that they heard a male voice. Francis is back, thought Eleanor, her heart sinking.

'Eleanor? Eleanor? I can't believe my eyes! Are you really sitting there laughing so shamelessly and practically *unclothed?'* Francis strode forward and, taking off his coat, flung it round his wife's shoulders and the excited hubbub went deathly quiet as the Tongan women backed away into the undergrowth until there was no one there by the stream but the missionary and his wife

Chapter Thirteen

Mary was still sitting on the verandah swing, idly moving it backwards and forwards, when a strange boat came round the headland, a sailing boat perhaps forty feet long. She watched it curiously; she couldn't remember seeing it before though there were more and more boats about lately, apart from the native canoes.

The boat slowly came in to the jetty and tied up. After a short while the figure of a man jumped out and began walking rapidly along the wooden ramp and up the beach. Mary sat up, her heart beginning to beat uncomfortably fast; there was something so familiar about the man. She walked to the edge of the verandah and put up a hand to shade her eyes, straining to see who it was. And then he lifted an arm and waved and she just knew he was waving at her, not any of the people who had gone down to meet him but her, up on the verandah of the mission house.

'Morgan!' she cried and ran down the steps to meet him, but stopped short as a sound came from the cradle. Little John was stirring and she couldn't leave him alone on the verandah, even in her excitement. Hurrying back, she picked him up, held him to her shoulder and ran on down to meet the man from the boat.

'Good Lord!'

Morgan came to an abrupt halt as he saw the baby in her arms, an expression of shock on his face, but Mary didn't notice it at first; all she could see was that Morgan had come back. He wanted her, he hadn't abandoned her as she had feared, he must want her else why had he come? She flung herself at him, baby and all, and he dropped his bag and put his arms around her to steady her, holding her as she laughed and cried at the same time.

The welcoming crowd of Tongans and Fijians crowded round watching the strange goings-on of the couple. Matthew, who was just emerging from one of the huts, took on a look of scornful disdain that the white woman servant should behave so in the middle of the compound, too. White women had no shame, no decorum, he decided.

'Morgan! Oh, Morgan, you came back, I knew you would, I knew it! By, lad, I'm that glad to see you, I thought you'd gone for ever, I did, I did. I thought I'd never see you again, I thought I'd lost you,' babbled Mary in her excitement.

Morgan had been staring down at her and the top of the baby's head but he was suddenly aware of the interested crowd around them.

'Hold on, now, hold on,' he said. 'Let's go back to the mission house away from this crowd of black folk. I think there's some explanations wanted here, I do indeed.'

He freed one of his hands, picked up his bag and began to propel her towards the mission house with one arm around her, steering her, for she still had her face pressed into his nankeen coat. It took some doing but eventually he cleared a way between the natives and got her up on to the verandah and sitting down on the swing.

Mary sat there with the baby, who was beginning to struggle and whimper against the tightness of her grip, still held against her shoulder. All she could think of for the moment was that here was Morgan back and she loved him and maybe, just maybe, he loved her.

'Now then, ma'am,' Morgan said and she was assailed with a sudden doubt. Ma'am? Why did he call her that, as though she was a stranger? She moved a little away from him and looked into his face, trying to read his expression.

But Morgan was looking at little John as Mary sat the baby on her lap and loosened the cotton shawl so that he got one tiny arm free and waved his fist in the air. His face was red with exertion and temper but he was not a baby who cried a lot and when he realised he was free he settled down and began to suck his thumb

'What?' asked Mary, still watching Morgan.

'Why didn't you let me know about this?' asked Morgan. 'I would have come sooner, I wouldn't have left you on your own.'

Mary gazed at him, mystified.

'Is it a boy?'

Mary nodded.

'What's his name?'

'John.'

'Let me hold him.' Morgan held out his arms for the baby but instead Mary took John over to his cradle and laid him there. She busied herself making him comfortable, fiddling with the sheet and pillow. For it had finally struck her that Morgan thought it was her baby, hers and his. A small giggle escaped her – she couldn't help it – and he strode over to her and swung her roughly round to face him.

'Is he mine?' he demanded and she shook her head, unable to stop herself from laughing.

'He's not mine either, you daft lump,' she said. 'I'm only minding him. This is John George Tait, he's the Taits' baby. An' don't tell me you're not glad of it, you didn't care what happened to me, no, you were off on your own, I could have been having twins for all you cared!'

'Mary, Mary, I've come back for you, haven't I?'

She had been working herself up to a proper head of steam, all the frustrations of the past few months boiling up together, but his quiet remark was enough to shut her up and it was her turn to sit down hurriedly. She stared at him, trying to gauge if he really meant what he said or whether it was a ploy to get her into bed. Did he think that all he had to do was make a vague promise and she would fall into his arms?

Uncomfortably, she remembered the first time he had made love to her. It had been in Sydney; he'd caught her at a bad moment when she had just lost Prue and he had pretended to comfort her. Or rather, he *had* comforted her, she thought grimly, he had comforted her only too well. And she knew how weak she was where he was concerned; it wouldn't take much for her to give in all over again.

'Did you really come back for me?'

Morgan looked at her flushed face, the bright blue eyes and shining curls. Of course he hadn't come back for her, though he had to admit that when he was passing by Lakeba on his way to one of the other islands where he had heard there was still a supply of the prized sandalwood, he had thought of her and how pleasant it might be to spend an hour or two with her.

It would be nice to see the other one too, the prim and haughty missionary's wife – the two women complemented each other perfectly. And that had been all that was in his mind when he dropped anchor at the jetty down below and strolled up into the compound.

But he remembered how he had felt when he thought the child was his and the feeling had been different from anything he had known before. Now he felt a pang of regret that the baby wasn't his after all. Thoughtfully, he looked over at the cradle.

'You didn't come for me, did you, Morgan?'

The woman was persisting. But there was something new on his mind. He had his plantation carved out of the jungle now, and there was every reason to think it would be a success. The Manchester cotton mills were hungry for new cotton supplies now that the Southern states had seceded from the Union and his gamble had paid off. With the cheap labour he had brought in from the Philippines he stood to make a fortune. He needed an heir and this sparky English girl was just the right woman to give him one.

'I knew you didn't,' Mary said bitterly. She walked to the edge of the steps and stared blindly out over the bay.

'Oh, but I did,' said Morgan. He walked up behind her and put his arms around her, holding her curves against him, remembering how good she was in bed. He looked across the compound and saw Francis and Eleanor coming towards the mission house, both of them looking damp and bedraggled but he hardly noticed that.

'Will you marry me, honey?' he asked. 'For here's the very fellow to do the job for us, we could be away on our honeymoon this very night.'

'Certainly not, Mary,' said Francis.

'Excuse me, Parson?' said Morgan West, lifting his dark eyebrows almost to his hairline in offended surprise. 'Are you refusing to marry us?'

Francis glanced across the verandah table at the American, feeling at a decided disadvantage. There he sat, looking the very picture of a Southern gentleman like the ones in the illustrations to Harriet Beecher Stowe's novel, *Uncle Tom's Cabin,* which happened to be a book circulating among the Europeans on the islands just at present. He himself hadn't had a chance to tidy himself up and he knew his coat was stained with seawater from being wrapped round Eleanor's damp shoulders and his boots were stained with mud from where the stream met the sea.

'Mary is our responsibility,' he said, trying to keep the irritation out of his voice. 'We brought her out from England and we cannot let her go off with the first man who takes her fancy.'

He was uncomfortably aware that this was exactly what had happened with Mary's sister Prue; the Lord only knew what sort of abandoned life the young girl was leading among the seamen of Sydney. Where was Eleanor? As soon as she saw they had a visitor she had disappeared into the bedroom, taking baby John with her.

'Mary, will you ask Mrs Tait to come out as soon as she is ready?' he asked and Morgan looked even more affronted.

'I think, sir, Miss Buckle is no longer your responsibility, nor is she your servant to do your bidding.'

Francis was genuinely surprised. What did the man mean? Of course Mary was their servant; that was why they were sitting here discussing her future. And the very fact that Mary was sitting with them showed how liberal, how genuinely caring they were.

The situation was resolved when Eleanor came to the open door of the bedroom. In the ten minutes she had been gone she had managed a remarkable transformation from the bedraggled state she was in when she came home. She had changed into a fresh linen dress, creamy and with a deep coffee-coloured lace collar, and her black hair, newly washed at the stream, was piled sleekly on top of her head and topped by a small lace cap. Her eyes sparkled and a rosy flush coloured her cheeks.

The two men rose to their feet as she swept in and Francis moved to hold a chair for her. Mary smiled. Oh indeed, Eleanor made her smile – this was her best dress, the dress that had only been worn on Christmas Day. For the rest of the year Eleanor stuck to the conventional dress of the missionaries' wives, black or dark grey cotton, unadorned. Mary watched as Eleanor looked out of the corner of her eye to see the effect she was having on Morgan. Oh yes, Eleanor made her smile; why, she almost burst out laughing.

Now, my fine lady, she said silently to Eleanor, you can try to charm as much as you like but Morgan West is going to marry me, no matter what you or Francis Tait say. And her smile was broadly triumphant as she looked across at her lovely man.

As it happened, Morgan was watching Eleanor and with a certain amount of admiration, Mary judged, but it didn't disurb her. No, he was the sort of man who would always look at other women but nevertheless he belonged to her. Morgan caught her glance and looked away, coughing slightly behind his hand to cover the moment.

'I don't care for your attitude, Mr Tait,' he said, taking up the conversation where it had been left. 'Miss Buckle is no longer your servant, I said.'

Eleanor blinked. 'But of course she is,' she interjected.

'No, ma'am. Not since she accepted my hand, she is not. She is now the future Mrs West and we have a position to uphold in the society of the islands.'

Mary sat back, taking no part in the argument; indeed, there was no need. Morgan had such a lovely turn of phrase, she thought dreamily. By, it was going to be grand, married to an American gentleman, mistress of a planta-tion. He was quite right, she had finished taking orders from the Taits.

'Mary is not yet married to you, and indeed, I have great doubts about the suitability of the match.' Even in his own ears Francis sounded pompous but he did have a responsi-bility to Mary.

'Mary, please pack your bags, you are coming with me,' said Morgan, rising to his feet and holding a hand out to assist Mary.

'She can't do that! Mary, stay where you are,' command-ed Francis. Mary moved to do Morgan's bidding, thoroughly enjoying the drama of the confrontation. By, she thought, who would have believed there would be all this fuss over a pitman's daughter from Hetton-le-Hole?

'I am taking her away on the evening tide,' said Morgan, 'whether we are married or not. You may be the parson here, Mr Tait, but we are free, white and American, or at least I am and Mary soon will be. We won our independence from the English, sir, a long time ago.'

'A pity your notions of freedom don't extend to our darker brethren!' snapped Francis but Morgan ignored him. Mary disappeared into the back of the house and Morgan walked to the edge of the steps to wait for her.

'Francis!' whispered Eleanor. 'You can't let them go off unmarried. What will our friends think if you do?'

Francis frowned; the story would be all around the islands in no time if he refused to marry the couple. And in any case, they would surely find someone else to perform the ceremony once they landed on one of the larger islands.

'Very well,' he said heavily. 'I will do it. Though I have to say it is much against my better judgement. What time is high tide?'

'Six thirty,' said Morgan without turning round, but from his voice Francis thought he was grinning in triumph.

'I will perform the ceremony at five o' clock.' Francis looked across at Eleanor, who was tracing a pattern on the top of the bamboo table with one finger, seemingly absorbed in it. 'Come, my dear, we have things to discuss,' he said.

Morgan was left on his own on the balcony. He hadn't intended to get married when he woke up this morning, he thought ruefully. But Mary was a beauty and she was young, he would be able to mould her to what he wanted in a woman. And Minister Tait had properly got his dander up, yes sirree, he wasn't going to let a jumped-up Englishman tell him what to do.

A strange wedding, thought Eleanor. The chapel was almost empty; the only person there apart from the bridal couple and themselves was Mr Radley, the Australian store owner, who had been persuaded to close the shop for half an hour so he could be a witness. But the bride was as radiant as brides were supposed to be. As Eleanor watched her coming down the aisle on Francis's arm, she forgot her own confused feelings about the wedding and genuinely hoped her old Sunday School friend was doing the right thing.

Even Francis seemed to have accepted the marriage and changed roles from giving the bride away to conducting the ceremony smoothly.

The late-afternoon sun shone through the open doorway of the chapel and picked out the highlights of Mary's bright hair. White and gold, thought Eleanor, for they had hastily constructed a garland of white wild flowers for a bridal crown and Mr Radley had unearthed a white muslin dress from the depths of his store. It was simple and too old-fashioned to take a crinoline under it but on Mary it looked lovely. And afterwards, when Francis handed them the marriage certificate that they had to take to Bau to get ratified, she had to admit that they made a very handsome couple indeed.

'I'm sorry there wasn't time to organise a wedding breakfast,' she whispered as she kissed the bride and wished her well.

'It doesn't matter,' Mary answered and they all walked out of the chapel into the sunshine. And there someone had organised a feast. The Tongans had got wind of the wedding and they were there on the beach with a semi-circle of bright cloths laid out and covered with food: roast sucking pig and chickens, fruit in abundance, coconut shredded on pineapple and heaps of glistening rice, all presided over by Matthew and the women of the village. There were bowls of fermented coconut milk to drink and Eleanor looked sideways at Francis as she saw them but he was blandly leading the bride and groom to the middle of the semi-circle where the women were waiting to pile brightly coloured garlands round their necks.

'Did you tell them?' Mary asked Morgan but he shook his head.

'Not I,' he answered and then, prosaically, 'I hope we don't miss the tide.' So she was convinced he was telling the truth.

The islanders knew the sea, however. At the very moment when any further delay would mean the couple would have to stay until morning, there was a general movement towards Mary and Morgan and they were lifted shoulder high and carried along the jetty to board the boat.

119

After that, there was little time for goodbyes, though Eleanor clung to Mary for a moment.

'Keep in touch, please keep in touch,' she said. 'We've known each other a long time, Mary.'

'I will,' Mary answered, suddenly feeling unsure of herself. But the anchor was lifted and the little sailing vessel cast off, still carrying a few islanders. No one was worried about it; as soon as the boat was in clear water the islanders dived into the sea and swam for the shore where they resumed the feasting.

Eleanor picked up a sleeping John from his hollowed-out makeshift cradle in the sand under the shade of a coconut palm, and wrapped his shawl more securely round him. Though the evening was warm, still she was frightened of the mist that sometimes came with the dark and she cuddled the baby to her as she and Francis walked back to the mission house. In fact she lived in dread of fever coming to the island and shivered as she thought of the tiny graves already in the churchyard on the edge of the compound, mute testimony to the dangers that lurked on these paradise islands.

'I pray Mary will be happy,' she said as she climbed the steps on to the verandah and sat down on the swing. It was time for John's feed and he was stirring and whimpering and nuzzling his head into her breast. Modestly she pulled her muslin wrap across herself and the baby before loosening her dress to give him what he sought.

Francis looked away. It always made him feel a little uncomfortable when Eleanor fed the baby on the verandah where Matthew could intrude at any moment. He knew it was the coolest and most comfortable place in the house, especially in the evening, but still ...

'Why don't you take him into the bedroom?' he asked. 'Goodness knows what he might pick up from the night air. Didn't you say that Florence Nightingale said disease is borne on bad air?'

Eleanor blanched; for some reason she had thought that when she was sitting on the balcony it was as good as being inside the house and quite safe. Hurriedly she freed her nipple from the baby's mouth despite his protesting cries and carried him into the bedroom.

As she sat in the rapidly deepening gloom, for she hadn't bothered to light the lamp, Eleanor's thoughts roamed over the eventful day. She grinned as she remembered Francis's shock when he found her bathing with the women. It served him right of course; he should never have come to that corner of the beach when it was understood that it was for the use of the women.

It was funny – he hadn't been a bit bothered about the native women and a lot of them had much less covering them than she had; in fact compared to them she was quite decently clad in her shift and voluminous drawers, which tied below the knee. She sighed as she lifted the baby and changed him to the other breast before settling back in her chair again.

Then there had been the business of Morgan West and Mary. There she had been, walking silently up the beach with Francis, her hair all over the place and her dress damp and clinging to her legs. Neither she nor Francis had noticed the strange sailing boat tied up to the jetty. They were too full of their own affairs and wouldn't have noticed if it had been a tea clipper.

She had been preparing what she was going to say to him, for she knew that when they were in the house and by themselves Francis would demand to know what she thought she was doing. He would say that it was all right for the native women, that was what they were used to and it took time to persuade them to dress modestly and decently as became good Christian folk.

Well, she admitted to herself, she knew he was right, but oh, it had been so good to splash about in the water with the Tongan women, so good. But yes, she was a little bit ashamed of letting herself be caught in her shift and drawers and it might have been one of the good-for-nothing beach-combers who had recently come to the island and roamed about a law unto themselves, all rags and tatters, who had come across her.

But not as ashamed as she had felt of her reaction when she discovered that Morgan West was on the island, sitting on her verandah in fact. How her pulse had leapt! She had forgotten all about the row with Francis and rushed into the bedroom to change into her best dress and do up her hair. And how crushed she had been when she went back out, feeling like a queen in her new dress, and found out the reason he had come to Lakeba was because he wanted to marry Mary. By, she had felt like crawling under a stone.

The baby had finished suckling and smelled to high heaven so he needed his nappy changing. She'd have to do the washing of his cloths herself now, she reminded herself. Mary had gone and the only servant she had now was Matthew, whom she could hardly ask to wash a baby's nappy.

It was going to be very strange without Mary but she would just have to get used to it. And now that she had recovered from the shock, she wished her well, both her and Morgan, of course she did, and so did Francis. Why else would he have gone down to the Tongan huts and told them of the wedding? The Tongans were such a happy lot, they were always ready to make a celebration feast.

Eleanor put John down to sleep in his cot and walked tip-toed to the door. The verandah was deserted but there were lights among the trees on the beach and the sound of laughing and people calling to one another. Oh yes, the Tongans knew how to enjoy themselves, she thought. There was a light from the living-room window – Francis must be in there. She would go in to him and make her peace with him; they had only each other now.

Chapter Fourteen

It was towards the end of the following year that Edward, Francis and Eleanor's second son, was born. Eleanor had felt tired and unwell for the whole of the day and, as usual, Francis was away visiting some new converts on a neighbouring island.

'Mia will stay with you, my dear,' he had said before setting off in one of the native canoes the local chief had put at his disposal. When Mary left, Matthew had suggested that his cousin Mia take her place and Eleanor was well pleased to have her. It was so exhausting looking after little John and still trying to find time to visit the Tongan village to put her ideas into practice, something she was determined to do.

This particular morning, despite the fact that she was so near her term, Eleanor had left John in Mia's care and was walking through the compound to the corner of the beach where she had first made friends with the Tongan women. She carried a basket made from pandanus leaves over her arm with bottles of ipecacuanha cough syrup, laudanum drops and clean bandages to bind up a festering wound one of the women had sustained on her leg when she had cut it on a sharp stick in the undergrowth.

Unusual enough, she thought as she strolled along, keeping as far as she could to the shade by the side of the track. One did not often see festering wounds on the local people. She suspected that the fact that they bathed in the sea every day could have something to do with it. She had to admit that the Tongans' idea of hygiene was often superior to that of the whites, who considered bathing once a week ample.

She sighed heavily. The heat was so oppressive that her clothes were wet through before she'd had them on an hour and then they chafed her skin as she walked, creating sore places.

There was not much laughing going on at the bathing place; a few women and children were splashing about in the shallows and one or two even swimming close to the shore. But there were also some just lying on the beach or sitting with their backs propped against the trunks of the palm trees as though they hadn't the energy to do anything.

Eleanor sighed again, her own discomforts forgotten. Since the *John Wesley* had called last, leaving a group of whites who seemed to spend most of their time lounging about on the beach eating coconuts and chasing the local women to the glowering disapproval of the Fijian men, there had been this sickness among the Tongans.

'Really,' she had said to Francis when they saw the ship had such passengers, nothing at all to do with the church. 'Really you should make a complaint to the district, it isn't right that the *John Wesley* should carry people like that.'

'The ship earns a little money with the fares and it covers her maintenance costs,' Francis had answered, shrugging his shoulders. 'You know our funding is often slow to come through.'

Eleanor remembered the many fund-raising events in aid of overseas missions, the faith suppers, the lectures and talks. There were so many even in their small chapel in Hetton. If all the chapels raised that amount of money, and she was sure they did, then surely there should be enough.

It certainly wasn't worth bringing strangers on the ship even if they did pay their passage. Not when sickness was spread around among the very people the Wesleyans were here to help, Eleanor thought. Look at these poor Tongans now.

A Mother's Courage

She listened to the women on the beach, shaking her head, for they were coughing and spluttering and some of them holding their sides or rocking backwards and forwards holding their chests. They were in pain; even the smallest bout of coughing hurt them. The strangers must have brought the sickness with them. Not that the Tongans usually succumbed as easily as the Fijians, but this particular fever was especially virulent.

Eleanor went round the invalids, dishing out bottles of cough medicine and trying to persuade them they would be better off indoors in spite of the heat. The women took the medicine gratefully but simply smiled vaguely at the advice.

The woman with the injured leg was reluctant to let Eleanor examine it. She shook her head and waved her hands to indicate that she didn't want the poultice of leaves taken off – no doubt it had been applied by the little old woman who had appeared in the mission house on the day before John was born – and in the end, Eleanor had to admit defeat.

She got to her feet and arched her back; this new baby was so active he kept her awake half the night, it was no wonder she felt so tired. Besides, a nagging backache was settling into the small of her back and she ought to get back home and rest. Guiltily she realised that Francis would be very annoyed if he knew what she was doing at this late stage in her pregnancy.

She had barely walked twenty-five yards when the pain suddenly intensified, pulling her almost double and causing her to drop her basket so that the remaining medications and bandages fell out and rolled away in the mud. But there were women there, Fijian women she had not even noticed were anywhere near the compound, surrounding her and holding her up, their bare breasts pressed against her arms and shoulders while their short kilts made of bark cloth from the paper mulberry tree wiggled and showed glimpses of firm brown thighs and knees.

Eleanor noticed these things in a detached kind of way for suddenly everything seemed unreal; there was almost a dreamlike quality to everything. Somehow she found herself carried along to the mission house and up the steps to the balcony. She was laid on a cloth on the floor, a cushion from the swing for a pillow, and she was trying to tell them that she would like to get into her own bed; she even indicated the door to the bedroom. Did she ask them to fetch Mia? She wasn't sure whether she had said it aloud and anyway the women were jabbering among themselves almost as if she had nothing to do with what was happening.

A sharp contraction brought her fully awake. She couldn't believe it was happening so quickly when John's birth had taken so much longer, but an old crone appeared – was it the same one who came before? She laid her brown, wrinkled hand on Eleanor's brow and after that she remembered very little except for the feeling of elated relief when the baby came and was laid on her breast, still attached to the afterbirth by a long and bloody cord. And it was another boy; Eleanor saw it for herself before falling asleep or losing consciousness, she wasn't sure which.

When she awoke she was in her own bed and the toddler, John, his hated skirts twisted up round his chest where he had held them to scramble up on to the bed, was asleep beside her and by the side of the bed was the wooden cradle.

Anxiously she looked at it, trying to edge towards it without waking John. For she had a sudden fear: she hadn't yet heard the baby cry, and surely there was something wrong with a baby that didn't cry?

'Francis!' she called, panic rising in her voice, and at once he was there and Mia too. She was lifting the baby out of the cradle and giving him to Eleanor and he moved his head and whimpered a little as though he resented being disturbed.

'When did you come home, Francis?' she asked.

'Not long since,' he replied. 'Well, Eleanor, I've let you down again, haven't I? I am always so anxious to be about the Lord's business but I should have stayed with you until the baby came. And this time you hadn't even Mrs Langham to help you. I would never have forgiven myself if anything had happened.'

'Oh, hush, Francis,' said Eleanor. 'What does it matter anyway? Here we are, both of us doing fine, do you think white people are the only ones who know how to help at childbirth? I was attended very well, I must thank the women who helped me as soon as I am able.'

And it was all true, she thought, as she lay on the pillow, feeling cool and rested and pleasantly lethargic. This birth had been so very different to the last, so completely different.

There were five new graves in the part of the cemetery where the Tongans were laid to rest. For the others, those who had the infection were slow to recover and were but shadows of their former selves for months afterwards.

None of the whites died of the fever that had been brought to the island by the beachcombers, though Francis and little John were among those who suffered mild versions of the illness.

'Why did it happen like that?' Eleanor asked the question every time she passed the cemetery with the new graves, their recently bare soil already covered by the green creeping weed with the pink flowers that grew all around. Why was it worse for the Tongans than those of European blood? But no one knew the answer, nor why, when the infection had spread to a tribe in the foothills, close to where Matthew's uncle lived, a whole village had been wiped out.

When John had fallen ill Eleanor had blamed herself and confessed to Francis her attempts to doctor the Fijians. He had said little, but in her heart she knew he blamed her too. She spent long hours on her knees beside him in the chapel, praying for the cooler weather to come early, for the rains to come and clear the air of infection, and most especially that her two babies should not die.

In fact they were never in any real danger; John soon recovered and Edward, the new baby, never caught the fever. But Francis suffered from complications, and caught the quinsy. Eleanor poulticed his throat with hot linseed and when there was no linseed left she used bread and water, heated until it was as hot as he could bear, and she clapped the poultice on his throat and bandaged it round. He recovered, but his fine speaking voice was never the same again.

Francis was having some success in his forays out to the neighbouring tribes up in the hills and on the surrounding islands. He had been minister in Lakeba for almost four years now and his time there was coming to an end; soon he would be posted to one of the larger islands.

He'd done reasonably well, he said to himself one evening as he sat in the canoe, idly trailing his hand in the clear water, not blue at this time of the day but reflecting the myriad hues of the sunset, gold and crimson. There were two Fijian warriors paddling the boat and even this he took as a sign of his success.

'Praise the Lord,' he murmured, and was startled at the immediate response of 'amen', in the deep tones of the natives. He smiled at them. He would have been perfectly happy to paddle himself home; the journey wasn't far, just further along the coast to one of the further bays of the island. The chairman of the district and the superintendent of his own circuit frowned on the missionaries using the natives as servants unless they were paid the proper remuneration and the fact was it was all he could do to pay Matthew and Mia to help Eleanor in the house. But the Fijians had insisted it wasn't fitting for him to paddle himself, wasn't he the chief Godman on the island?

They paddled round the headland and the missionary compound was in sight, the chapel in the centre, long and low and larger than the living huts. Yet it was becoming too small for the congregation at the Sunday morning service and even the mid-week service sometimes.

A light appeared in a window of the mission house and shortly after that a brighter one on the balcony. Francis smiled, deeply content. Eleanor always had Matthew put a lamp on the verandah when Francis was expected home, even when they were at loggerheads with one another. Thank the Lord, this was not one of those times, and they seemed to have settled down together so much better these last few months.

It was since Mary had married that scoundrel Morgan West and gone off with him to Viti Levu. They had not heard from her since, though Francis sometimes heard of scandalous doings on the cotton plantation Morgan had established in the interior of that island. It was said that he treated his workers as little more than slaves and if they fled he hunted them down and dragged them back despite the remonstrations of the Methodist ministers on the island.

The canoe beached on the firm sand of the cove and Francis got to his feet and climbed out. He thanked the men and they grinned and pulled the boat above the waterline, their strongly muscled shoulders gleaming in the light of the moon that had risen sharply.

'God bless you both,' said Francis. 'Goodnight now.'

Insects were buzzing round the lamp as he climbed the steps of the verandah, some of them so huge as to be unbelievable to any European who hadn't seen them before. Thank goodness he had devised muslin-covered frames for the doorways of the house; at least they kept the insects out and away from the sleeping children.

Eleanor was sitting by the table, engaged in sewing a suit for John, for he was almost old enough to be breeched. A circle of light from the lamp fell on her, highlighting her dark hair where it had escaped from her cap and making the grey of her dress glow softly. She put down her work and rose to meet him.

'Supper is ready, dear, I'll see to it directly,' she said and kissed him lightly on the cheek.

'Can't you let Mia see to it?' asked Francis. He sat down in the wooden rocking chair, which a previous minister had had brought out from England and left in the mission house when his term of service was ended.

'Mia's gone back to her village,' said Eleanor. She carefully folded her work and put it away in a cupboard. 'She's getting married, Francis, what do you think of that? Without giving any sort of warning too.'

Francis sighed. Eleanor sounded crotchety. Mia's defection had obviously affected her.

'I suppose the woman has the right to get married if she so wishes,' he murmured, leaning his head back on the chair and rubbing the spot between his eyes that always began to ache when he was tired.

'Hmm.'

Eleanor went out into the kitchen and after a few moments came back with a tray and began to set the table. She said little more until they had finished their simple supper of pork and pineapple with sweet potatoes and breadfruit. They had already eaten pork three times that week, Francis reflected, but he was too wise to comment on it. The minister's stipend was very low and pork very cheap on the island, whereas beef had to be imported and when it arrived was either already going off or so salty it was barely edible.

Eleanor cleared the table after the meal and went in to the children to check on them before coming back to sit opposite Francis. He had already picked up his worn Bible to continue the reading from Acts of the Apostles that he had begun the evening before. He always read one or two chapters aloud before calling in Matthew for the household evening prayers and he was confident that Eleanor looked forward to the quiet time as much as he did. Tonight, however, she spoke before he even opened the Testament.

'Francis, I have something to discuss with you.'

Francis looked up in surprise before placing the Bible on the table. 'Discuss?' he said. Eleanor's face was slightly pink, he noticed, why, she actually looked guilty, what on earth had she done?

'Yes. I had a letter last month from Mary.'

'Well, that is a surprise. The girl hasn't been in touch since she left, has she? And very ungrateful I think she's been, too. And why has she suddenly written to you, out of the blue, so to speak? Wait a minute, did you say last month?'

'Yes. Captain West brought it. He was on his way some-where, I suppose.'

At the mention of Morgan West's name, Francis felt un-settled, something that always happened when there was anything to do with the American. 'You didn't say he'd been here,' he said, making it an accusation.

'No. Well, you were away at the time.' Eleanor looked down at her hands, which she was twisting on her lap. 'She asked me to get in touch with Wesley House in Sydney.'

'Wesley House?' Francis was so surprised he got to his feet and strode up and down, his hands clasped behind his back.

'Yes. She wanted them to find Prue.'

Francis stopped his pacing and stood directly in front of Eleanor so that she had to look up to see his face.

'I hope you did nothing of the sort!' he burst out. 'I hope and pray that we never hear from that girl again after the life she has led – why, we can't even guess at its depravity!'

'How do you know what sort of life she has led?' Eleanor was becoming angry in her turn. 'Why should you always think the worst of the Buckles? As a matter of fact, Prue married her sailor and they led a perfectly normal life in Sydney. He couldn't get work on ocean-going ships because he had been ill but he worked on the ferry that goes across the harbour.'

Francis stared at his wife, his expression a study in dis-belief. She had been deceiving him, that was what this all amounted to. She must have been in correspondence with the Buckles to know all this; how else would she have found out?

'You have been writing to Prue as well as Mary?' he said through gritted teeth. 'Come on, you've let the truth out now, you've been lying to me!'

'No I haven't!' she asserted, managing to look quite indignant. 'Well, not really. No, I simply wrote to Wesley House as Mary asked and today I had a reply, it came on the *John Wesley*. And there was a letter from Prue enclosed. Oh, Francis, the poor girl has been widowed, she is at her wits' end how to make a living.'

'You wrote to Wesley House without asking me?' Francis couldn't believe any of this. He and Eleanor had been so happy lately; they had got on better than they had done since they left England. They were so much happier without either of the Buckles, why couldn't she see that? 'You didn't think I might not want my name associated with a ... a ...'

'A poor widow? Oh, Francis, where is your Christian charity? For Heaven's sake, consider what you are saying.'

Francis was speechless for a moment or two. Eleanor always managed to make him feel he was in the wrong, even when he knew he was right. 'A woman of low moral fibre,' he continued doggedly. He felt wretched; he had had such a good day and the natives gave him a feeling of worth, a sense that he was doing what God wanted him to do.

'A poor widow,' repeated Eleanor. 'And the thing is, I sent a letter back on the ship telling Prue she was welcome to come here – she can make herself useful in the house, help with the children. You know Mia is getting married.'

'You did this without asking me?'

'You weren't here to ask, were you? You never are, always going away and leaving the boys and me to God and Providence!' Eleanor was working herself up into a state of righteous indignation. Somehow she had managed to turn everything round so that it was Francis who was being unreasonable.

'My work is the most important thing in my life, Eleanor, you know I am dedicated to God's service,' he said.

'I know it comes before your wife and family,' she retorted, 'and what's more, you don't like the Buckles because you're jealous of them, because Mary was my friend, not just my maid. You didn't like me giving my attention to anyone but you.'

Francis sat down feeling absolutely exhausted, incapable of arguing any more. Was it true? Was that the reason he had always felt so antagonistic towards Mary? Surely not, he thought. But there was enough truth in the allegation to make him feel uncomfortable. He made one last attempt at an objection.

'Why can't Prue go to live with her sister? Surely West can afford to keep his sister-in-law?'

'But you would want Prue to live in a Christian home, surely, Francis? Haven't you told me that Morgan West treats his workers as little more than slaves? What sort of example is that to give a young girl, a girl we wish to reform, to bring back into the fold of Jesus?'

Francis glanced sharply at her – was she mocking him? Eleanor never used phrases like that, she was very down-to-earth and practical in her Christianity. But Eleanor was watching him solemnly, not a trace of a smile on her face.

'And besides, my dear,' Eleanor said, and her tone had altered, become soft and womanly. 'Besides, you know how I need another woman about the place now that Mia has gone.' She sat down beside him and put a hand on his knee. 'Francis, I need someone, especially when you have to be away so much. And most especially now that I am almost sure that we are expecting another happy event.'

Francis was defeated and he knew it. 'I suppose it is a simple matter of Christian charity to rescue the girl,' he said. 'You have a good heart, Eleanor.'

She laid her head on his knee and he patted her dark hair. Closing his eyes, he prayed swiftly and silently that no trouble should come of their taking Prue into the household. Then he reached over and picked up the Bible. 'Come now, Eleanor, Acts of the Apostles, chapter three, beginning at verse one.'

The feel of Eleanor's soft body against his legs had roused him and he was looking forward to their time in bed.

Chapter Fifteen

'My darling Mary,' drawled Morgan, tilting his chair so that it was balanced on the back two legs and stretching his long limbs in front of him, looking in imminent danger of being tipped on to the polished parquet floor. 'You will come with me this morning, I have decided. So go and get your pretty little ass into that green silk riding costume or I will carry you up and put you into it myself. Do I make myself clear, honey?'

Mary, who was sitting at the other end of the imported mahogany dining table, regarded him soberly. 'By, Morgan,' she said, 'you're a proper bastard and no mistake. Why can't you leave me here while you go prancing round the place on your bloody great stallion, lording it over those poor blacks. By, don't you just love it, eh?'

Morgan lifted an eyebrow sardonically. 'Because, my sweet, today I want you with me and that's all the reason I need, do you understand?'

Reluctantly Mary rose from the table and walked to the door before trying one last time to get out of the ride round the plantation. She hated horses, had never got used to riding and when she went out with him she spent her time covering up her terror.

'I am tired, Morgan, I don't feel well.'

'Don't you come the fine lady with me, my girl,' said Morgan. 'Remember, I know where you came from and if you're not a good little girl you might find yourself walking the streets of Sydney along with that sister of yours.'

'What do you mean?' asked Mary. 'Have you heard where she is?' She came back into the room and gazed down at him eagerly.

'Don't get excited; no, I haven't heard from her. But I'd wager a thousand that's where she is. No doubt your friend will let you know if she manages to find her.'

'I don't know,' said Mary, the eagerness dying from her face. 'We haven't been in touch much since I left Lakeba. I didn't like to admit ...'

'Admit what, Mary? That being married to me is not all you thought it was going to be?' He grinned at her and even now the sight of the way his eyes crinkled and sparkled in amusement gave her a melting feeling. To hide it she turned her back and walked briskly to the door.

'I'll go and change,' she said.

They rode out of the stable yard into the full heat of the morning and Mary was glad of the shady hat she was wearing. It had a pale green muslin scarf tied round it and looped round her neck so that she could cover her face if the flies got too bothersome.

She rode side-saddle and the long skirt of her habit was draped elegantly across the hind quarters of her mare so that her highly polished brown boots peeped out from under it. She sat ramrod straight as Morgan had taught her, holding the reins in one hand in just the correct manner. But inwardly she was shaking and her other hand grasped the pommel tightly, she couldn't help it; she stared straight ahead at the shimmering heat haze, her face white and strained. And the old mare she was riding knew it and her ears twitched backwards and forwards nervously.

Morgan led his horse up to her and the mare shied slightly at the closeness of the stallion.

'Careful, man!' Mary cried, and he laughed.

'Mary, Mary, don't be such a ninny, she's not going to run away with you. And I wish you would control that abominable accent, do you want everyone to know where you come from?'

A Mother's Courage

'Why not? I'm not ashamed of it.'

'Yes, well, I think you ought to be,' snapped Morgan.

Mary's pulse was still jumping but she wasn't going to let this pass. 'My accent is no worse than yours,' she declared. 'At least it's—'

Whatever she was going to say was forgotten as they came to the first big cotton field. It was harvest time and there were lines of men and women working amongst the bushes, picking the fluffy white balls and putting them in the enormous bags they had slung round their shoulders, supported by a strap on the forehead.

The heat and humidity was intense yet an overseer was striding up and down the lines, shouting at any worker he considered to be slacking. Mary felt sick as she saw a woman slide to the ground, overcome by the heat. The overseer was quick to spot her and was by her side in an instant, but not to help her. He prodded her, none too gently, with his stick and Mary was furious to see it was a version of the native *i ula kobo* fighting club, albeit a small one.

Forgetting her usual fear of having her foot trodden on when she dismounted from a horse, Mary swung herself to the ground and ran over to the woman, bending over her and raising her head, wiping the sweat away with her own handkerchief. She lifted the heavy bag of cotton from the woman, seeing the red weal on her forehead where the strap had bitten into the flesh.

'My God, Morgan,' she shouted, 'look at this poor woman! By, she'd be better off down a coal mine! Where's your humanity, man?'

Morgan was standing beside her now, his eyes like chips of ice and his mouth a hard straight line.

'Get up out of the dust, Mary,' he commanded. 'Wilson, take this woman away. If you can't keep the blacks in good enough condition to do the work you'll have to do it yourself.'

The woman was pulled to her feet and stood swaying for a moment before casting a frightened glance at Morgan and hurrying to pick up her bag of cotton. As she did so, her dirty sarong pulled against her figure, showing an unmistakable bulge.

'She's having a baby!' cried Mary, her outrage growing.

'Nothing to do with me, my love,' drawled Morgan and the overseer smirked. 'These blacks contract to come here and work in exchange for their passage and bed and board when they get here. They'll do anything to get out of their side of the bargain, dirty shiftless lot that they are. Oh, come on, don't worry about it, a drink of water and she'll be right as rain. They don't feel things the same as we do, Mary, really they don't.'

He took her arm to lead her back to the horses, his fingers like bands of iron so that she had perforce to go, but she was not about to forget the incident.

'Aye, the nobs and the mine owners used to think that about the miners,' she said bitterly. She was remembering her father once telling her how his father was bound to the mine by the yearly bond, virtually at the mercy of the owners. And how, before that, the Scottish miners were bound to the pit for life and their sons after them. She began to tell him but he interrupted her impatiently.

'Now don't get maudlin, Mary, these natives really are different, it's not just a matter of princes and peasants as in the story books.'

'You mean they're not really people, don't you?'

Morgan shook his head in mock despair at her attitude. 'I didn't say that, did I?' He helped her up on to her mare and mounted his own horse. 'I suppose it's womanly for you to have some feeling for the brutes,' he said judiciously. 'Come on now, we must get on.' He set off again on his tour of the estate and after a moment she followed him.

What could she do anyway? she thought. Any influence she might have had on Morgan was rapidly running out as time went on and she had to tell him that, no, there were no signs of a baby, not yet. At first he had shrugged, said there was plenty of time. But Mary dreaded that when she had to tell him tonight that his hopes were frustrated yet again, he would get angry and impatient and look at her coldly as though she were a stranger, just as he had last month.

Eleanor was packing up their home of the last four years in readiness to move to Viwa when Matthew tapped on the bedroom door.

'A visitor, missus,' he said, his haughty face full of disapproval.

'A visitor?' Eleanor was surprised until she glanced out of the window and saw that the supply ship was lying at anchor; she hadn't even noticed it coming in. Her spirits lifted. Perhaps it was Mrs Langham or even Mrs Gibson; they often travelled round the islands with their husbands and when they did they took the opportunity to visit the other missionaries' wives. She didn't even notice Matthew's expression but dropped the pile of sheets she was folding on to the bed and rushed out on to the balcony to greet whoever it was.

'Bring tea and ginger biscuits, please, Matthew,' she said over her shoulder, thankful that she had baked a batch only that morning and they were nice and fresh.

'Hello, Mrs Tait.'

At first, Eleanor didn't recognise the woman standing on the top step, hesitating to come nearer as though unsure of her welcome. She stared at the old-young face and the straggly blonde hair bleached almost white by the sun. It was the blue of the girl's eyes that Eleanor recognised in the end.

'Prue Buckle!' she cried. 'You got here then.' Somehow Eleanor had forgotten all about Mary's little sister these last few days, since Francis had got his new placement on Viwa and there was so much to do to get ready. And then there was baby Edward. He wasn't thriving as he should; he looked so pale and wan and she was terrified he was sickening for a fever. She put the thought out of her mind and smiled at Prue.

'Come in, then, don't stand out there in the heat, sit down, Matthew is bringing tea.'

'Thank you, Mrs Tait. But I'm not Prue Buckle any more. I'm Prudence Allan.' Prue moved forward, and as Eleanor gestured towards the bamboo chair, she sat down, right on its edge.

'Yes, of course, Mrs Allan.' Eleanor couldn't take her eyes off Prue; she was barely nineteen, she knew that, yet she looked like a woman in her thirties and, what's more, one who had a hard life. Her face was drawn and lined around the eyes and the black dress she was wearing looked as though it had been made for a woman twice her size, but then she was as thin as a lathe. Her fingers played continually with a black cotton dolly bag she was carrying and as Eleanor looked down at them, she saw that the nails were bitten to the quick, the skin wrinkled and as red as a washerwoman's. But what shocked Eleanor most was Prue's resemblance to her mother, Mrs Buckle, that very first time she had seen her.

'Are you ill?' she exclaimed and couldn't help thinking of her two children; had Prue brought some terrible disease from the slums of Sydney?

Prue laughed shortly. 'No, Mrs Tait, I'm not badly. I lost my man, mebbe you heard that Jack had died? But don't worry, it wasn't consumption nor nowt like that, no, it was his heart gave up, he wasn't strong, like. But I didn't have a penny to bless myself with after I'd buried him, poor lad. Work was scarce and it's hard to get fat on nowt.'

'Oh.' Eleanor's quick sympathy was roused – whatever the girl had done she was still just a girl and life had been hard to her. When Matthew brought the tea she poured Prue a cup, spooned sugar into it and offered her fresh biscuits.

Prue drank the tea and ate the biscuits carefully, reminding Eleanor of the way Mary had eaten so carefully that morning so long ago when she had come to the viewer's house with Prue for food. Afterwards, the girl sat back and gazed earnestly at Eleanor.

'I want to thank you for sending me the money for my ticket,' she said. 'I won't be much more trouble to you, if you will be good enough to tell Mary I'm here – where is Mary?'

'Mary? Why she's on Viti Levu. Oh, I'm sorry, did you think she was here?'

'Living on Viti Levu?' Prue was surprised.

'Mary married Morgan West,' said Eleanor and as it became obvious that Prue knew nothing about it she told her about the wedding and the cotton plantation.

Prue was cast down. 'She's forgotten all about me, then. Now she has a fine new life, married an' all. An' I bet she's not short of a bob, neither,' she mumbled, looking down at her fingers, twining and intertwining in her lap. She was close to tears, Eleanor realised.

'No, she hasn't forgotten you, of course she hasn't,' she said. 'Why, it was Mary who asked me to try to find you, she was worried about you. She's been worried about you since that day you ran off in Sydney. She spent hours searching for you, she was distraught.'

Prue must have heard a note of censure in this last bit for she sat up straight and lifted her chin.

'Well, I don't know why, I'm sure. I left her a note, didn't I? An' I told her I was going to marry Jack, I told her plain enough, she knew I was all right. Jack was a good man, it was just bad fortune he had to die. I'm sure there wasn't a thing for her to worry about, not then.'

'You were very young, Prue.'

'Aye mebbe so, but I was old enough to marry.'

Her truculent tone suddenly collapsed and she bent her head to her hands again and sniffed audibly. 'Poor Jack, poor lad,' she said.

'It was God's will,' said Eleanor, simply because that was what Francis would have said and she couldn't think of any other comfort to give. Prue sniffed again, then suddenly she sat up straight and became businesslike.

'Well, Mrs Tait, I'm grateful for what you've done, like I said. And if you just give me the money to get to – what's that place where Mary's at?'

'Viti Levu.'

'Aye well, if you would do that for me, I'm sure Mary will pay you back. She must be well able to afford it now, that Morgan West is a proper gent, isn't he?'

'I was hoping you'd stay here and help me out in the house, Prue,' said Eleanor. 'I have a new baby coming and my little Edward isn't very strong and anyway, we are moving to Viwa shortly, it will be easy for you to visit Mary from there.'

'I want to go to Mary.'

Eleanor looked at her. 'Of course you do,' she said. 'But don't you think it would be better to stay here for a short while at least? You can help me so much to get ready to go to Viwa. Even just helping with the children. I would be so grateful, Prue. Look, if you like I can send a message to Mary with the next boat, perhaps she will come over to see you. Morgan often comes this way.'

A fretful wailing started up from inside the house and then John's clear piping tones. 'Mammy, Mammy, Edward's crying again. Mammy, can I come out now? I'm all woke up.'

Prue looked up sharply, colour coming and going in her face, but Eleanor didn't notice at first. She was going into the bedroom where John was already climbing out of his bed.

'Be a good boy, stay on the verandah,' she instructed him as she went past to Edward's cot and lifted the baby out. And her brow knitted in anxiety as she felt how light he was – surely he was not only not gaining weight, but actually losing it? What's more, though his eyes were wide open he lay in her arms listlessly and when she lifted his little hand and kissed it, feeling the heat under the skin, he showed no reaction, no pleasure in seeing her, nothing, only the weariness that had become his habitual expression.

'The bairn's not right.'

Eleanor jumped at the voice at her shoulder. Prue had followed her into the room and was watching the baby critically.

'It's just a fever I think, nothing really serious, I'm sure it isn't,' she said cradling Edward against her breast defensively.

'I'm hungry,' announced John, frowning at all the attention his brother was getting. 'Dinner time,' he went on, when there was no immediate response.

'Yes, pet,' said Eleanor, 'Matthew will bring it now and Edward's milk too.'

John pulled a face at his brother. 'He'll only be sick again,' he said. 'Edward's always sick.' Clearly he thought putting milk into the baby only for him to vomit it back was a waste of time.

Prue held out her arms. 'Give me the babby,' she said. 'I'll see to him for you. Don't worry, I'll look after him real good, I promise you.'

John was tugging at Eleanor's skirts now, insisting on her attention, and after a moment she reluctantly handed Edward over and went into the kitchen in search of food for both the children. When she came back, Prue was sitting on the swing, gently rocking Edward and crooning an old Durham lullaby to him. 'Whisht little babby, whisht my bairn,' she sang while Edward watched her solemnly.

Eleanor gave John his meal and Matthew came through with a mug of goat's milk, fresh drawn from the animal tethered in the yard. There was some for Edward, too, for Eleanor had weaned him when she discovered she was pregnant yet again, something she now bitterly regretted. It couldn't have been that which made him fail to thrive, could it? she asked herself for the umpteenth time. But Edward was old enough to do without breast milk, of course he was, and she had the new baby to consider.

Prue patiently spooned milk into Edward's mouth carefully, not rushing him, waiting until he was ready for the next spoonful. She even had to be persuaded to leave him in his cot while she had her own meal, though once she had joined Eleanor at the table, she tucked into the rice and meat with an intense concentration that convinced Eleanor she must have often gone hungry since her husband died. Afterwards, the two women sat beside the cot, which Matthew had brought out on to the balcony so that Edward could have the benefit of any current of fresh air that might be stirring.

They sat together, John playing with his cup and ball at their feet, and watched over the sick baby. In their anxiety, both women seemed to have forgotten that Prue was intending to go to Viti Levu, as soon as she could.

As it grew dark, Matthew lit the lamp and hung it on the balcony and after a while, Francis came home.

'Prudence Buckle,' he said and looked her up and down.

'Hello, Mr Tait,' she replied. But before he could make further comment he noticed the anxiety that enveloped Eleanor.

'What is it? Is it Edward?' he asked quickly, moving to the cot and gazing at the child. 'If only there was a doctor—'

'Doctors are no good any road,' said Prue. 'I spent all I had on a doctor, they can't help.'

'But Jack Allan was different, this is a baby,' said Eleanor. 'But there isn't a doctor anywhere near so what does it matter?'

'My little Jackie was a baby an' all,' said Prue. 'It's all the same, doctors are useless. Everything's useless.'

'We can pray,' said Francis. After a moment, the three of them got to their knees beside the cot and Francis began to pray. Eleanor wasn't even taking in the words he was saying; her whole being was one big prayer: don't let Edward die, please, God.

After a while, Francis helped her to her feet. 'It's in the hands of the Lord now, my dear,' he said.

Eleanor looked at him; there was no emotion on his face. Did he really believe God would save the baby? His expression was so controlled, his lips together, no crease or furrow on his high forehead and he was like a stranger to her. What was he thinking? Then he caught her gaze with his and she saw the torment deep in his eyes and it matched her own suffering.

In an instinctive gesture she reached out and put her arms around him and in that moment they were closer than they had ever been before.

Edward Tait, aged eighteen months, died the next morning just as the sun rose over the bay. Eleanor and Francis had sat up all night beside his cot yet neither of them saw the moment he died. Eleanor felt his forehead and fancied he was cooler; he seemed to have fallen into a natural sleep.

'I think he's a little better, Francis,' she ventured.

The early morning light stole over the verandah and Francis got up and flung the window wide. 'At least it's morning,' he said. 'It's always better in the daytime, isn't it?'

'Yes,' Eleanor agreed and then she looked again at the baby and in that split second he had slipped away.

Edward was buried in the cemetery on the edge of the compound and the Reverend Langham conducted the service. The Tongans walked at a respectful distance behind the family and the children sang in high, piping voices, 'There's a Friend for little Children'. Afterwards Eleanor packed up Edward's clothes for the new baby and the following week, the family sailed for Viwa.

Chapter Sixteen

Francis William rolled about at his mother's feet, making valiant attempts to crawl after her ball of wool and just not quite succeeding. Eleanor watched indulgently as he managed to raise himself on his arms and even bring a knee up under him but his efforts were frustrated by his long skirts and he fell forward on to his face and began squalling with rage.

Eleanor rolled up her knitting but before she could pick him up Prue came rushing through the house and scooped him into her arms, smothering him with kisses.

'Howay, bonny lad,' she cried. 'Whisht now, don't cry. Prue'll get you a nice biscuit and some milk, you'd like that, wouldn't you, Billy?'

'Don't call him Billy,' said Eleanor crossly. 'His name is Francis William.'

'Why, aye, I know that, Mrs Tait,' said Prue. 'It's a long name for a little lad though, isn't it? There's nowt wrong with Billy.'

Eleanor watched a little sourly as the girl snuggled the baby to her. It was a waste of time talking to her, she thought. Francis William had soon stopped crying; he had a sunny nature and he loved Prue, she had to admit it. In fact, sometimes Eleanor felt quite resentful of just how much he loved Prue; she couldn't help feeling it wasn't a good thing.

Maybe it was time the girl went to live with Mary. Prue never suggested it now and there was no denying she had been very useful in the house what with the children and the housework. And it meant she herself could spend more time in the native villages; she was proud of the way the Fijians were beginning to welcome her and trust her. This was what she had come for, wasn't it?

'Give him to me, I'll see to him,' she said abruptly and Prue looked up startled.

'I can see to him,' she said mildly. She settled the baby on her hip and started to go through to the kitchen for the biscuit jar but stopped at the sharpness in Eleanor's voice as her request became a command.

'Give him to me, I said, Prue. Why don't you do as you're told?'

For a moment Prue stood quite still, not looking at the other woman, then she handed over the baby silently. Francis William immediately set up a loud wailing, and twisted and wriggled to escape his mother's arms and get back to his beloved Prue.

'Hush now, hush,' said Eleanor, sitting down and rocking him back and forth. Prue's bringing a biscuit.' But Francis William was weeping real tears, great drops that rolled down his fat cheeks and dropped on to his pinafore, and he was only quietened when Prue returned with the biscuit jar.

Eleanor relinquished him to the girl, defeated. What a fool I am, she thought, he's only a baby, so he likes Prue, he's not old enough to make a proper choice yet. She watched the girl as she put a biscuit in Francis William's hand and sat gravely by while he smeared it all over his face and pinafore, patiently cleaning his chin. She was absorbed in the task and Eleanor felt an uncomfortable twinge. Poor Prue, her own baby passed on just like little Edward and she hadn't even the consolation of having other children. She had to make do with Eleanor's.

At the thought of Edward, a wave of sadness swept over Eleanor and she blinked; sometimes it still took her unawares. Rising to her feet, she smoothed down her dress and patted her hair into position. She was going to the village, she had promised the women she would, and they depended on her helping them, teaching them simple first aid, advising them.

'I'll be back in an hour, Prue,' she said and Prue nodded without taking her eyes off Francis William. Eleanor bent and kissed the top of the baby's head, a gesture that he ignored completely, so absorbed was he in his biscuit. He's getting fat, she thought as she went down the steps and out into the compound so similar to the one on Lakeba with its chapel and circle of huts thatched with pandanus leaves.

Apart from the compound, though, living here at Viwa was different, Eleanor mused as she walked along the well-trodden path that broadened out until it was almost a road. Not so many Tongans here; the congregation was almost totally Fijian, and there were even a few from the hill tribes. She pondered on them; she never could be sure if they were here because they were genuine converts or outcasts from their tribes.

Eleanor's heart gave a little jump of alarm as she came across two of them sitting by the side of the path. Even sitting down they were magnificent specimens of manhood, their black muscled bodies gleaming with the coconut oil they rubbed into their skins, their long legs tucked easily under them.

'Oh! Good morning,' she said, for all the world as though she was walking down a country lane at home. She felt like an idiot, especially when they glanced up at her blankly and then bent their bushy heads over the fire they were kindling with rubbing sticks and pieces of dry bark. Eleanor hurried on her way, feeling as though they were staring after her when in fact she knew that they had probably dismissed her from their minds as only a woman and a white woman at that.

She had looked at them for barely a second, yet she retained in her mind's eye a picture of the tribesmen, so arrogant and masculine despite their ear plugs and bracelets of some sort of animal's teeth. Most of all she retained a picture of the weapons, the heavy throwing clubs laid on the ground beside them and the wicked-looking spears propped against a nearby tree. Of course it didn't mean anything that they had such weapons with them, Eleanor knew that. Tribesmen carried them everywhere, whether relaxing at home or going to war.

Still, there was some talk among the missionaries of uprisings in the north, tribes from the remote hills fighting between themselves and, worse, attacking white settlers and their servants. There were even rumours of cannibalism.

Eleanor felt a sudden fear for her children – should she go back, stay with them? Francis was, as usual, away from home, 'about his Father's business', as he put it. But what if there was an attack?

She shook herself mentally. She was being absurd, of course there wasn't going to be an attack, what a fool she was indeed. They were miles from any petty war between the hill tribes, the natives here were Christians, of course they were, wasn't the chief converted years ago? And Matthew was in charge of the mission house and he was a fighter if ever there was one. He was a famous warrior. Of course the tribesmen would not attack the house.

Eleanor entered the Fijian village and the children came running up to her, laughing and crying out for the barley sugar she carried in her basket. Soon she was the centre of a group of women, dispensing medicine for the runny noses of the children and ipecacuanha for their coughs, which they had caught once again from a new wave of white settlers.

A little later, when she walked back to the mission house, her basket empty, there was no sign of the two warriors, barely a mark on the ground where their fire had been. She was becoming far too fanciful, she told herself; if they had been there to do any harm to the Christian community they would have been much more stealthy about it.

Francis was home when she arrived there and to her surprise they had visitors. Eleanor thought at first it was Mr and Mrs Langham, or even the Calverts or one of the newer missionaries who often came to consult with Francis on circuit business. But no Englishman spoke in just those drawling tones, that lazy, almost affected way. No, it had to be Morgan.

In spite of herself, Eleanor patted her hair into place and dusted down the front of her gown. Then as she got nearer to the steps of the balcony she forgot all about how she looked, for sitting in the bamboo chair was Mary.

'Mary!' she cried and broke into a run for the last few steps. Oh, it was ages since she had seen Mary, not since that wedding on the beach at Lakeba when Mary had sailed away with Morgan and never once been back to see her, not even when Prue had come back.

'By, it's grand to see you, as good as a tonic it is an' all,' said Mary as the two women embraced, both of them so obviously pleased to see the other.

Morgan smiled a superior smile at Francis. 'Women!' he said. 'They are uncommon glad to see each other, aren't they?'

'They've been friends a long time,' Francis said stiffly. Secretly he was thinking that he rarely got so enthusiastic a welcome when he came home – why, Eleanor hadn't even spoken to him yet.

'Have you seen Prue?' Eleanor was saying. She looked around, surprised Mary's sister wasn't there, when it had been so long since they had met.

'She's seeing to the children,' said Mary. 'They are having a nap.' She looked a little puzzled; she and Prue had once been so close, yet now, when they had been apart for so long, there was a distance between them that Mary couldn't understand. Prue had greeted her pleasantly enough but her attention was all on the baby, Francis William.

After the first excitement of seeing Mary, Eleanor was becoming aware of tensions between the group, not just

Francis and Morgan but between Morgan and Mary. She rather belatedly kissed Francis in greeting and sat down beside him on the swing.

'I'll see to dinner in a minute or two,' she said. 'I'm sorry we just have fish and breadfruit, if I'd known you were coming ...'

'I'll come and help you,' said Mary, rising to her feet. Eleanor looked doubtfully at her gown, slim-waisted and low cut so that her breasts swelled above the blue silk, and the skirt wide and sweeping. Eleanor was suddenly conscious of the contrast between the richness of Mary's dress and the cheap cotton of her own. Well, she thought, Morgan must be doing well while Francis's stipend was only enough for the family to live on.

Mary saw her glance. 'I'll just borrow an apron,' she added.

'Once a servant, always a servant,' said Morgan, his voice so low that Mary didn't hear it. Which was just as well, thought Eleanor, giving him a hard stare.

Prue was in the kitchen, or rather at the back door, broiling fish and rice for the children's meal, with John playing in the dust, absorbed in a private game of his own that involved skipping and jumping over stones. He looked up at Mary curiously for a moment but then returned to his game.

'He's forgotten me,' said Mary.

'It is a long time,' answered Eleanor.

'You haven't been to see me before now,' said Prue, not looking up from her cooking.

'It was ... difficult to get away.' Mary watched her sister for a minute or two, silently. 'We want you to come back with us, Prue, your place is with me.'

Prue looked up in surprise. 'Eeh, I can't do that,' she replied. 'I'm all right here, I'm fine, aren't I, Mrs Tait?'

'Well, if Mary—'

'I have to look after the bairns. My little Billy and little John here, they depend on me.' Prue was quite composed, simply pointing out what she thought were the facts.

Eleanor and Mary exchanged a glance. 'I could manage, you know,' said Eleanor. 'There are plenty of women in the congregation and they would be well able to help out with the children, you know what the Fijians are like, they love children.'

'I think you should come back with me, Prue, you won't have to do anything, you'll like it.'

Prue didn't answer for a while as she was occupied in dishing out the children's meals, setting John's on the kitchen table and bringing him in and washing his hands before placing him before it and giving him his spoon. She sat Francis William on her lap and began feeding him, skilfully evading his attempts to grab the spoon for himself.

'Howay, Billy boy, eat it all up for Prue,' she crooned.

'His name is Francis William, Prue, how many times do I have to tell you?' demanded Eleanor, exasperated. She seized the fish that Matthew had cleaned and laid under a fly mesh earlier. Where was he? she thought irritably, and set to with the griddle and cooking oil. She could make the meal stretch to an extra two if she did extra yam.

'Prue, I really think you should come back with me,' said Mary, frowning as she looked from her sister to Eleanor.

'Well, I'm not,' declared Prue, giving Mary a straight stare. 'You have no babbies, have you? Nor likely to have, I reckon.'

'Prue! Why shouldn't I have a baby?'

'You haven't up to now. Why, I fell wrong right from the beginning when I got wed. And I'd have had another soon enough after little Jackie if it hadn't been that my Jack was poorly. I'm telling you, I might come to see you when the lads grow up a bit, but now I need to be here, can't you see that? Any road, Mrs Tait will soon have another, you wait and see.'

Eleanor started. She was late in her courses and suspected she might be having another but she'd told nobody, not even Francis.

'But Prue—' began Mary, but she was wasting her breath as she soon saw. Prue had finished feeding Francis William and was getting to her feet to take the children into the bedroom for their mid-afternoon naps.

'If they sleep during the heat of the day they can stay up a little while in the cool of the evening. I'll see you before you go, Mary,' she said and Eleanor and Mary were left on their own in the hot kitchen.

'You see how she is,' said Eleanor as she deftly turned fish on the hot griddle and fat spattered and sizzled on the hot iron. 'Sometimes I begin to wonder if there's been a mistake and Prue's their real mother, not me.'

'I'm sorry.' Mary tied an apron over her gown and began to set the trays with plates and cutlery. 'I didn't know she'd lost her own baby as well as her man. Likely she's still mourning, that'll be the trouble, she'll get over it.'

Eleanor brought the platter of fish to the table and began to serve the meal. Then she sighed and paused for a moment.

'Look, Mary,' she said. 'Some of it was my fault, I wanted Prue to stay and help me when she first came and I'm not denying that she is very good with the boys and I'd miss her help if she went with you. But maybe she should go with you, for her own sake.'

They went through to the verandah with the food and the four of them settled down to the meal. Prue did not eat with them even though Eleanor suggested she should; she took her plate and went back to the kitchen.

The sun beat down on the roof and the heat was rising from the dried mud of the compound in shimmering waves, but they were used to it after their years in the tropics and the dinner would have passed off pleasantly enough were it not for the stilted way Francis spoke to Morgan and the cool tones of his answers. Eleanor watched them; they were so different yet both so good-looking, Francis with his clear, guileless brown eyes and strong features, and Morgan, fair-haired and blue-eyed with those striking dark eyebrows.

What was it about him that made every woman's pulse jump in her veins?

'I'll just go and see if I can persuade Prue to come back with us after all,' said Mary when the meal was over and they were sitting over a pot of black Indian tea, sweetened liberally with sugar.

'For Lordie's sake, Mary,' drawled Morgan, 'can't you leave well alone? I don't think it's a good idea at all.'

Mary, who was already on her feet, flushed and bit her lip. 'Morgan, you said she could come and stay with us, you know you did, isn't that why we came?' She looked close to tears. Eleanor stared at her in surprise; what on earth was the matter with her? She had never been a girl to cry easily, she was spirited enough to fight for what she wanted.

'Oh, for God's sake, you're not going to cause a scene, are you?' he exclaimed. 'If you are I think we'd better go back to the boat and wait for the tide to turn, we don't want to embarrass the Reverend and Mrs Tait, do we? Go on then, have a word with the chit, though God knows why you want to after the dance she's led you one time and another.'

Mary ran into the house and Eleanor followed; one look at Francis's face had convinced her he was about to explode.

'Don't worry, Mary, it's all right, really it is, I don't mind having Prue, I trust her with the children—'

Eleanor stopped speaking and held her breath as a great roar came from outside and the women looked at each other, startled.

'You come into my house and dare to take the Lord's name in vain like that?' Francis shouted, his voice trembling with rage. 'You eat my food and accept my hospitality and—'

'Land's sake, Francis,' came Morgan's drawl, his voice hardly raised at all. 'What bloody hypocrites you Methodists are, you do nothing but interfere in a man's business, always meddling. Mealy-mouthed, you all are, the curse of the men here trying to make an honest living. But to get at me over a few words that mean nothing, who the hell do you think you are?'

'An honest, God-fearing man, that's what I am!' Francis snorted. 'Which patently you are not. How did you manage to get rich so quickly? Answer me that.'

'Ah, jealous of me, are you? I thought it was something like that,' sneered Morgan.

'Jealous of you?' Francis was fairly bouncing with rage, he was striding up and down the wooden floor of the balcony. Just inside the bedroom the women could feel the floor vibrating with the force of his footsteps.

'Jealous of you?' he repeated. 'A man who got his land by trading guns to the warring hill tribes, may God forgive you for it!'

Eleanor heard Mary's gasp by her side and glanced at her quickly. The girl's face was chalk white, her eyes closed for a moment.

'Stop him,' she said urgently and briefly Eleanor wasn't sure if she meant Francis or Morgan. 'Stop him, Eleanor, don't let him say anything worse, you don't know what Morgan can do if he gets angry.' From behind them, Francis William was roused by the noise and began to whimper in terror. And suddenly Prue rushed past them out on to the verandah and confronted the men, stamping her feet, her face red and her hair falling down over her face.

'Shut up!' she said in a thunderous whisper. 'Shut up the both of you! Don't you know you're frightening the bairns? By, I bet there'll be nightmares the night for them both, and then none of us'll get any sleep.'

Francis stood looking at her, hardly knowing what she was saying, and in the sudden silence he heard the murmuring of people and saw there was a crowd of natives gathered in front of the mission house, looking at him, their expressions grave. Gradually the rage died from his eyes, the flush from his face.

'I'm sorry, Prue,' he said, his voice tight and controlled. 'I'll be in shortly to see the children. I'm sorry if I frightened them.'

'Hmm!' Morgan grinned. 'Of course, you mustn't frighten the children. Not that you stand any chance of frightening anyone else, certainly not a man.' He stepped closer to Francis and thrust his face forward menacingly. 'But if I hear you repeating lies like that again, by God, I'll teach you to be frightened of me, damn me if I don't.' Contemptuously he pushed past Francis and strode into the bedroom and grabbed Mary by the arm.

'Morgan, don't, you're hurting me,' she said as he pulled her after him, out on to the verandah and down the steps.

'Leave my sister alone!' Prue shouted, running after them.

'I'll do what I like with my own wife,' answered Morgan. 'Now we're going home, the tide's on the turn.' He paused and looked down at Prue, who had caught up with them. 'Don't you ever come near my plantation, do you hear? If you do, I swear I'll have you whipped off the property for the whore you are.'

He turned to continue his path down to the jetty but found his way barred by a group of Fijian warriors, scowling ferociously and fingering the throwing clubs they all carried at their waists.

'Let me through, you black bastards,' he growled, 'or I swear I'll clear a path myself. How do you fancy a little present of lead?' Out of his waistcoat pocket he drew a derringer and by the way he handled it showed he was willing to fire it into the group.

'Let him through, it's all right, come now, we are Christians, men of peace.'

Francis had come up behind Morgan and Mary. The men looked at him, uncertain, but in the end, the tension left them and they stood aside, though their hands did not leave their clubs until Morgan and Mary were on the deck of his boat and casting off. They growled in their own language to each other for a while but then disappeared back into their huts.

Francis took the arm of Prue, who was trembling with reaction, and walked back to the mission house, looking white and strained. 'You see, my dear,' he said to Eleanor, 'how easily they can revert to savagery; there is much to be done in the community yet.'

Eleanor was holding the still-sobbing Francis William, while John was clinging to her skirts. 'Hush now, pets,' she said. 'Hush. The nasty man has gone now, Daddy sent him away. Everything is all right now.'

She surrendered the baby to Prue and caught John up in her arms, holding him tight. The two women sat down on the swing and rocked the children gently while Francis sat beside them, staring out to sea as Morgan's boat got smaller and smaller until it became a speck on the horizon and then was gone altogether. Everything was quiet; the compound had returned to its afternoon's slumbers.

'Well, I think I'll have to alter my sermon for tomorrow in light of what has occurred,' Francis said at last, rising to his feet and going inside.

'Yes,' said Eleanor. She shifted the boy's weight in her arms, easing him to a more comfortable position, and looked down at his face, so like Francis's. The savage is in all of us, not just the natives, she reflected.

Chapter Seventeen

'We are to go to Bau next month, there is a conference,' Francis announced one morning in October. The ship carrying the post had come in on the early morning tide and there was a sheaf of business letters for Francis but none from home and she had thought there might be one from Fanny. Yet England and her family seemed so remote this last year or two, and not just geographically.

At first, Eleanor didn't take in what he had said; she was gazing out to the horizon where the sea shimmered blue and silver and to one side the dark-forested hills rose into the sky. The missionary ship rode at anchor in the bay and bright orange and red parakeets flashed from tree to tree, calling raucously to one another while smaller blue and yellow birds sat close together in the branches.

The nesting season, thought Eleanor dreamily, and put a hand on her own stomach though she wasn't far enough on in her pregnancy to show or even to feel any difference.

'Perhaps this one will be a girl,' she said and Francis looked at her over his letter, a little uncomfortable. He would never get used to the way she talked so openly about expecting a child; it wasn't usual to mention them before they were actually born, not in polite society.

'Did you hear what I said, Eleanor?' he asked. 'I was talking about the meeting next month, well, it is actually only two weeks away, the first week in November.'

'Yes, of course, how long will you be away this time?'

'Us, Eleanor, us. We are both to go, all the ladies are meeting there too, there is to be a discussion on the role of the women in the church, especially the Fijians.'

'Francis, I can't go to Bau, I can't go anywhere, not when the children are so small,' said Eleanor.

'Of course you can, what's to stop you? You have Prue, she looks after them very well, she's devoted to them. I never thought she would turn out so well considering—' He caught Eleanor's expression and pulled himself up. 'Well, she looks after them well, which is to her credit. And Matthew will be here, the house and the chapel will be left in good hands, very capable hands.'

'I don't know …'

'We must go, Eleanor, and unless you intend trailing the children with us, you will have to trust Prue and Matthew to look after them.'

Eleanor regarded him thoughtfully. Francis was evidently determined she should go with him and it might not be a bad idea, now she thought properly about it. After all, she had not been away from Viwa since Francis was transferred there and she had never been to Bau. It was the most important of the islands, she remembered, for King Thakembau lived there, the king of Fiji, even if the title was self-bestowed and in dispute. It would be interesting to see the king at least. He had been a Christian since 1847, they said, though there were rumours that his conversion was the result of convenience rather than conviction.

'Are you sure the boys will be safe, Francis?' she asked, wavering as she got used to the idea of leaving the children with Prue.

'Of course I am, the Lord will protect them,' he replied crisply. 'Besides, our people here would never let anything happen to them.'

Eleanor smiled, remembering how the men of the village had gathered, ready to defend Francis against Morgan West.

It was true, the boys would be safe enough from intruders with such protectors.

'There hasn't been a raiding party anywhere near here in years, anyway,' Francis went on, which was a mistake, for Eleanor felt a twinge of fear – she hadn't thought of a raiding party. The warriors from the hills looked so fierce, she would hate to think she might ever meet a tribe on the warpath. Not, as Francis had just said, that it was very likely, she told herself firmly. That was the sort of thing that had happened when their predecessors had first come to the islands; nowadays the Christian communities were well-established and the people round about more civilised.

'Very well, Francis,' she said, her mind made up.

It was with mixed feelings that Eleanor stood beside Francis on the deck of the *John Wesley* and waved to Prue and the children, and their surrounding crowd of villagers. On the one hand there was the excitement of her first trip away for ages, even if it was just to the neighbouring island of Bau. But John's face began to crumple as he realised they were going without him and Eleanor felt like stopping the boat and insisting they took her back.

'Be a good boy and look after your little brother until we get back!' called Francis and he took hold of her hand and held it tightly against his side, well aware of her feelings. And already the ship was making good progress, the sails filling with the late spring winds and the tide running with them.

'There is a qualified doctor at Bau,' Francis remarked as he combed his beard before the tiny looking glass in the cabin that had been allocated to them. Eleanor was sitting on the bed, rolling on her stockings, but she stopped what she was doing and looked at him in surprise.

'There is? But why haven't I heard of him before? Just think what a doctor could have done for our little Edward.'

Francis turned to her. 'He wasn't here then. There was one before, Dr Williams, but he had to go back to Australia and we have only just got a replacement for him. I would like you to have him look at you while we're here.'

'What on earth for? I'm perfectly healthy, there's no reason at all to bother a doctor.' She pulled on her boots and bent to fasten the laces, something she would find difficult in the months to come, she told herself. 'Isn't that just like life?' she asked Francis crossly. 'When we needed a doctor for Edward there was none, now there is.'

'Eleanor, Edward's death was the will of God,' Francis said. 'In any case, there was no time to bring the doctor from Bau, Edward's death was too quick.'

She didn't answer him, merely smoothed down her dress and waited for him to finish getting ready so they could go up on deck, for the ship was entering the bay at Bau. Will of God, my foot, she thought savagely as he opened the door to the short flight of steps that led to the deck. What sort of a God would make an innocent like Edward suffer? But she pushed the thought to the back of her mind, knowing Francis would never understand how she felt.

The beach at Bau was rather different to the others she knew; for a start there was an imposing structure to one side that Francis said was the king's canoe house and, by the number of canoes in there, he seemed to own quite a fleet. As the passengers disembarked, native warriors carried an imposing stool to the high water mark and the king himself, surrounded by his courtiers, came and sat upon it, sternly regal and wrapped around in a gown of brightly coloured cloth tied elaborately around his portly figure under the armpits.

Eleanor kept in the background or at least a few steps behind Francis as she knew was fitting until the formal welcome was over and then followed the party into the church for prayers of thanksgiving.

The church was also bigger than the one in Viwa, she mused as she looked around surreptitiously during the prayers. And then she fell to wondering how the boys were doing without her; were they missing her? Or were they content to have Prue? She suspected the latter.

Afterwards, in the cool of the evening, there was a feast on the beach with baked fish, pork, an abundance of the small island chickens, and yams and cassava roots, boiled until tender. There was coconut milk to drink though Eleanor preferred the fresh spring water that the young men brought down from the hills.

The Reverend Calvert led them in singing the Grace and somehow the Fijians managed to make the old familiar words and tune sound like a Polynesian chant. The sky darkened and the waves lapped on the shore and the whole had a soporific effect on Eleanor.

Long before the official royal welcome was over, she was having trouble keeping awake. The heat, the long day and the rich food all contributed to her exhaustion and she found herself leaning against Francis as they sat on the sand, uncomfortable and longing for bed.

'It won't be long now,' he whispered in her ear. 'Bear up a few moments longer. Mr Calvert will be giving thanks to the king shortly and then we can go to our hut.'

The long day came to an end at last and as she lay in Francis's arms on the hard bed in their hut she felt his hands on her swollen breasts. In spite of her exhaustion a quickening in her veins answered him. Francis made love carefully, gently, because of her condition and whether it was because they were so relaxed after the meal or the fact that no child was going to cry and interrupt at the most inconvenient point, Eleanor responded with a sensuousness that surprised him.

Next day, after much prompting by Francis, Eleanor had an interview with the doctor. She couldn't help smiling to herself as he felt her abdomen through her clothes, and sounded her chest and peered down her throat. How much easier it must have been for him to examine one of the native women, she mused. Nothing between her body and the stethoscope except perhaps a thin layer of cloth.

'How can you hear anything through my corsets?' she couldn't help asking, a question the doctor chose to ignore.

'Mrs Tait is perfectly healthy as far as I can ascertain,' he reported to Francis.

'I could have told you that myself,' Eleanor said when they were once more on their own.

A few days later, when they were leaving the island to return to Viwa, she thought of what a lovely week they had had, almost a holiday in spite of the meetings both she and Francis had had to attend.

'It was as good as a tonic,' she said to him and he glanced around to make sure they were not overlooked and put his arm around her and kissed her on the mouth.

'The nights were the best,' he whispered and she looked at him in surprise; it was so unlike him. He had certainly never referred in daylight before to what was between them when they were in bed together

'Yes,' she agreed, smiling up at him. It was true, they had been closer somehow during this time without the children and she didn't even feel guilty about thinking it.

'There you are, Francis,' a voice said behind them and he hurriedly dropped his arm as he recognised it as Mr Calvert's. 'I wanted a word with you if your good lady doesn't mind,' the superintendent minister continued.

'Not at all,' murmured Eleanor but she doubted if they heard her; they were already walking away along the deck, their heads close together as they conferred about something or other. She sighed and turned back to her contemplation of the sea. There was always Francis's work to come between them, she thought. Yet she was proud of him there and she had noticed at this conference how his opinion was sought after and listened to, realising that his standing in the community was much improved since last she had been among a gathering of his peers. Oh yes, it was all very satisfying, as was the way the other wives had listened to her opinions too.

She did not feel quite so pleased when Francis came back to her and said he was getting off the ship at one of the off-shore islands, as Mr Calvert had asked him to attend to some business for him.

'You don't mind, do you, Eleanor?'

'It would make no difference if I did, would it?'

Francis looked at her uncertainly. 'I won't be too long,' he added. 'Only a day or so.'

'Oh, go on. No, of course I don't mind,' she replied.

But when she landed at the jetty at Viwa from a ship that was turning straight round to go back out to sea and there was no welcoming crowd standing on the beach, no canoes in the bay, no women bathing at their end of the beach, she had second thoughts.

Disbelieving, she walked to the end of the jetty and stepped down on to the firm sand. It wasn't that there were no signs of life; there were thin columns of smoke rising from the cooking stoves behind the huts. Perhaps the women were preparing a meal and the men all out on the sea. Round the other side of the headland, perhaps, after a run of fish one of them had seen?

'Matthew?' she called. 'Hello, where is everyone?'

She turned back to the jetty hastily, sensing there was something wrong, there had to be, she would stop the ship, but it was already sailing out of the bay, helped by the stiff breeze that filled the sails, and no matter how she waved her hands and called, it did not turn back. Oh yes, someone saw her, one of the missionaries' wives – she could tell by the black-gowned form and the white arm that was lifted to wave back to her. But whoever it was must have thought she was simply waving goodbye.

A wave of relief swept over her the next minute as a large canoe rounded the headland followed by another and then another. She had been right; the men had simply been out fishing, and were bringing in their boats loaded with the catch. No, it had been a turtle hunt, and a successful one she could tell; the men were singing their triumph.

Feeling not quite so alone, Eleanor hurried to the mission house and ran up the steps.

'Prue? Prue, where are you? Matthew?'

The bamboo chair was overturned. John's wooden railway engine, which Francis had carved for him only last Christmas, was lying on its side, the wagon it normally pulled squashed into splinters beside it.

'Matthew? Matthew, where are you?' Eleanor was almost screaming now as she ran through the house to the yard, back into the bedrooms, round and into the living room. 'Francis William!' she cried. Oh God, dear God, don't let anything have happened to the babies! 'Where are they, where are they?' The dread within her was growing and beginning to overwhelm her – she couldn't see properly, that was the trouble, they were there, they must be there, where could they have gone?

Chapter Eighteen

'Mrs? Mrs Tait?'

Eleanor swung round as she heard a woman's voice, hope springing in her, for hadn't the women disappeared along with Prue and Matthew and the children? If the women were back then perhaps they were all on their way, they'd just been out together somewhere, maybe higher up the stream, looking for clearer, cooler water.

Within a split second, Eleanor had almost convinced herself that there was nothing wrong, but as she saw the bedraggled group of women, their legs and short skirts daubed with mud and their bare limbs scratched from running through undergrowth, the hope died.

Beside them the men, returned from the turtle hunt only a few minutes ago laughing and singing their triumph, were grim-faced and angry, muttering to each other in their own language. Even as they gathered in a group before the mission house, another woman ran out of the bushes and flung herself at one of the warriors, gesticulating wildly in her hurry to tell what had happened, her words completely incomprehensible to Eleanor.

'What? What's happened? Where are my children?' Jumping down the steps, almost falling as she missed her footing at the bottom but managing to regain her balance though her ankle had turned and a sharp pain shot up her leg, Eleanor took hold of the shoulder of the woman who had spoken.

'Not my fault, missus, not any of us, we couldn't stop it!' the woman said, her already fearful face showing signs of panic. She tried to back away but Eleanor had tight hold of her.

'What isn't your fault? Tell me, woman, tell me, what are they saying?' She was practically screaming with frustration now and as she shook the shoulder she was holding, another woman stepped forward, a woman with a long scratch across her cheek and a trickle of blood slowly creeping down her neck.

'The men were on a turtle hunt, they think God protect the babies,' she said. 'We ran off with our children when the devils came, don't want to be slaves.'

'What do you mean, the devils came? What are you talking about, you stupid woman, tell me what happened to my children!'

Eleanor stamped her foot and pushed her face forward to within an inch of the other woman's nose. Why didn't she say what had happened, surely it was a simple enough thing to do?

One of the men stepped forward, and she saw it was Mala, the headman among the small community of Christian Fijians who lived in the compound. Firmly he removed her hands from the shoulder she still held and turned her to face him.

'War party came,' he said, 'tribesmen from the hills, devil warriors, no good, take white babies and Tongan man and white woman away. Fijian women escape into the trees.'

Eleanor stared at him; even though she had known in her heart right from the moment she had left the ship that something like this must have happened, she was still disbelieving.

'Missus sit down,' he said and attempted to lead her back on to the balcony but Eleanor shook off his hand.

'We have to go after them, we have to get them back!' she cried.

'We go, you stay,' said Mala decisively. 'Warriors do battle, woman stay at home.'

'I'm going. Oh, Mala, how could you go off on a turtle hunt like that and leave my babies unprotected? What were you thinking of?'

Mala looked hurt. 'Turtles in the bay. They good to eat. Always Fijian men hunt the turtle.' He turned to the other men. 'Now we hunt hill people.'

A roar went up from the assembled warriors; their throwing clubs leapt out of their belts and were flourished menacingly in the air. As Eleanor watched she was struck by how different they looked. Their faces were unrecognisable; they looked as fierce as the tribesmen she had occasionally met in the past. And it was comforting, they would fight for her babies, she knew they would, but would they be in time?

'I'm coming, I'm coming,' she shouted as they streamed towards the canoes pulled up at the water's edge and unceremoniously dumped the turtles out on to the sand. Their throwing clubs were once again tucked in their belts and somehow each one was flourishing a short, lethal-looking spear. But the men didn't even hear her or if they did they dismissed it as a woman's hysteria.

'Come back, missus.' One of the women took hold of her arm and tried to pull her back up the beach towards the compound.

'No, I'm going,' Eleanor insisted, running into the waves after the boats, her long skirts becoming soaked and immediately dragging against her legs. She gathered them up in one hand, not caring that the men were there, and still tried to reach the canoes. But it was no good; they were pulling away, paddling in unison to the deep-voiced war chant they had started up as soon as they were in the canoes.

And Eleanor was left, floundering in waist-high water, until a high wave caught her and lifted her off her feet and flung her back to the beach where she would have fallen heavily were it not for the women who caught her and half-carried her out of the water.

She lay in the sand, the breath taken out of her body, gasping and crying with frustration and gradually, as her breathing eased, she became aware of an ache in her back, coming round to her belly, becoming deeper seated and more insistent. Not this one too, she thought, forcing herself to sit up, holding down the panic until it lessened while she stared out to sea after the canoes, which had already rounded the headland and were gone. It was too late to go with them, she had to think about the baby within her, she had to be calm. Getting to her feet, she turned to walk up the beach to the mission house.

'Ship!'

At the cry from the group of women Eleanor whirled round and sure enough, as though by a miracle, there was a ship coming into the bay, a proper ship, not a canoe.

'Thank God! Thank you, God, thank you, I swear I'll never doubt you again,' she said aloud, starting back to the water. 'Francis!' she called. 'Francis?'

He had come back, of course he had come back, he had heard of the raid and had come back. But even as she ran, she was berating him in her mind; why had he not realised there was something wrong when there was no one on the beach when the *John Wesley* went away? He couldn't even have been watching her disembark, far too full of his work, that was it.

Suddenly she slowed down and stared at the ship coming in to the jetty; it wasn't the *John Wesley,* and where would Francis have got himself a different ship? It wasn't a missionary ship at all, it was a sloop. She had heard that there were boats like this one going round the islands, sailed by opportunists looking to buy land off the natives in just the way Morgan West was rumoured to have done, land to grow cotton.

What did such people want with their settlement? They were Christians here, they would not be tempted by the offer of guns, they were at peace with their neighbours. The panic was beginning to rise in her yet again as the sloop drew slowly alongside the jetty and a figure jumped lightly off the deck and tied the boat up. She glanced around quickly but she was alone on the beach. The native women had had enough for one day; they didn't want to meet another threat and had melted away into the undergrowth once again.

'Eleanor? What on earth are you doing out here on your own? Just look at you, you're soaked through. What is Francis thinking of, doesn't he know there are unfriendly natives in the area?'

As Morgan West strode along the jetty and took hold of her arm, Eleanor let out a great sigh of relief and sagged against him so that he had to catch her in his arms. He stood there for a moment, gazing round the deserted compound, then he picked her up and carried her back up the jetty and on to his boat, depositing her on the deck where she stood leaning against the wheelhouse, swaying ominously. Swiftly he cast off again and took the sloop back out into the bay before turning back to her.

'Now then,' he said, 'tell me what happened. And don't act the weak woman with me either, I want to know it all and as soon as may be.'

Eleanor stared at him; he looked so strong and dependable, so exactly what she needed at that moment, that it was only his brisk tone of voice that stopped her breaking down altogether.

'There's been a raid,' she said, 'they took my babies. Oh, my Lord, Morgan, I wasn't here, neither of us was here, we were returning from Bau. We weren't here when our children needed us, God forgive us, God forgive us.'

'Oh, pull yourself together, woman,' said Morgan. 'We'll go after them; my crew and I are perfectly capable of seeing off a bunch of these black heathens. Where are the men of the settlement anyway? And where the hell is Francis?'

'Francis had to go off with Mr Calvert, well, how was he to know? It's not his fault this has happened, we should have been warned that there were war parties about.' Eleanor was on the defensive about Francis though in truth she felt he was to blame. Why did he go off so quickly, why did he not see there was something wrong? Despair welled up in her; how were they going to find the warriers, how?

'The men – where are the natives?'

'They've gone after them, just now, it's a wonder you didn't see them as you came in, did you not? They seemed to know where to go. Oh, can you find them, Morgan?'

He didn't waste time in answering her; he was shouting orders to the man at the wheel and to another in the rigging. The wind was fresh, fresher out on the open sea, and the sails fairly billowed out as they skimmed across the surface of the water.

'Go below, Eleanor.'

'No, I can help.'

He didn't bother answering her, simply took her arm and pushed her down into the cabin, closing the door after her.

'And if you know what's good for you, you'll stay there,' she heard him say as he went back on deck. Rushing to the tiny porthole she peered out to sea. Dear God, the light was going already, how were they to catch up with the Fijians if they couldn't even see them? And surely the raiding party and her poor babies were already ashore, already hidden away in the hills?

Chapter Nineteen

Prue held John close to her as she sat in the corner of the hill village. Incredibly, Francis William was asleep on her shoulder, completely worn out. John was staring wide-eyed at the group of tribesmen in the centre of the clearing, his little face white and drawn, but he was very quiet, not a whimper, not a movement.

Neither of the children had cried after the first shock of the warriors from the hills swooping down on the village, flourishing their spears and shouting their war cries in deep, guttural voices. The women had picked up their children and run for cover and Prue had done her best to follow them but, before she knew what was happening, the warriors were running for the mission house, ignoring the native women and the rest of the compound.

Matthew rushed through the house, his throwing club already in his hand. 'Back, woman,' he cried. 'Run!' But they were the last words she had heard him say, for a well-aimed club whizzed through the air and knocked him off his feet, sending him to land with a sickening thump on the ground, where he lay still.

Both John and her little Billy stopped in mid-cry and stared, solemn-eyed, at the blood oozing slowly into his thick black hair until Prue pulled their faces round and into her skirts.

And that was it, the rest of the day was surely unreal, it couldn't have happened, the war party rampaging through the mission house, smashing everything, looking for she didn't know what. They were dragged down to canoes lined up on the shore, Matthew's body unceremoniously slung in one and, as Prue gazed out over the ocean desperately looking for the turtle-hunting village men, they began to pull away swiftly into the bay.

The children cuddled in closely to her as Prue sat in the bottom of the canoe. She looked back at the shore. There was not a sign of anyone; the village was deserted and silent, even the parakeets had stopped their eternal racket, even the pigs had fled into the undergrowth.

What was she going to do? Prue stared wildly at the men in the boat, their heads with a thick shock of black hair sticking out so it looked like a wig, necklaces of what looked like sharks' teeth round their necks that gleamed white against the black oiled muscles glistening so powerfully as they pulled the oars against the tide.

The man nearest her saw her watching him and he grinned. Almost without breaking the rhythm of his stroke he touched her blonde hair, even lighter nowadays as it was bleached by the sun, and said something to his neighbour and they laughed.

'Don't touch me!' For a moment Prue forgot her fear as rage rose blindly in her and she spat at him. Casually he lifted a hand and swiped her across the head, rocking it back on her shoulders, making her ears ring. The children burrowed deeper into her lap, bringing her to her senses. She had to look after the children first; no matter what else happened, she couldn't let anything happen to them.

Anything more, that is, she thought, feeling her little Billy's body trembling against her thighs, for all the world like a puppy she had once found in the pit yard at Lyon Pit at Hetton. Oh, God, why in hell had they ever left Hetton?

'Suffer the little children,' Mr Tait had said only last week at Sunday School, and they did sure enough, poor canny bairns. But nothing was going to happen to these two, no it wasn't, the black heathens would have to kill her first.

She looked over at the boat in front, the one that held Matthew's body. What did they want with Matthew's body? Why hadn't they just left it where it fell? But her thoughts came to a sudden stop as the implications of them bringing it with them hit her and a shutter closed off the worst of her imaginings.

Bending to the children, she stroked their heads, lifted up their faces and wiped their noses. 'It'll be all right,' she whispered, 'Daddy will come for you, you'll see, we'll just get to wherever we're going and Daddy will be there in the big ship. You know it can go faster than these canoes, and Mala and all his men will come and, you'll see, they'll punish these naughty men for taking us away.'

The walk, more a climb than walk, up into the hills after they beached the canoes in a hidden cove on the north of the island, was a nightmare she thought she would never recover from, Francis William clinging to her back, supported by her apron tied under him and John clinging to her skirt as he stumbled along beside her and a fierce-looking warrior chivvying her every now and then, pushing her none too gently, threatening her with his spear to hurry her along. She stumbled over her skirts until she caught her foot in the hem and ripped almost half of it off altogether and then at least it was somewhat easier.

Behind her were a couple of men with Matthew's body slung on a pole, pushing her, complaining at her slowness. A stitch started in her ribs and she was catching her breath in long desperate pants. At last they stumbled into the clearing of a native village, a circle of huts not dissimilar to those they had left behind but with a long house to one side that, judging by the activities going on there, seemed to be a communal eating place.

As Prue and the children were pushed to one side and told in pantomime to sit down and sit still, she began to take note of her surroundings. Her heart was filled with despair as she saw the strength of the village; there must have been thirty or so warriors in the raiding party but there were some who had obviously been off somewhere else and any number, to her eyes, of women and old men and children.

The children collapsed beside her, little John, whose short legs had carried him all the way from the hidden bay where the villagers' canoes were stowed, sinking to his knees close by her side and turning to face the party of warriors who were talking and gesticulating in the centre of the clearing. The men were relaxed as they told the story of their raid; they dropped the body of Matthew on the beaten mud in the centre of the clearing and were pointing to it, laughing. Prue distinctly heard the word, 'Tonga' and strained anxiously towards them to see if she could glean what they were going to do with the body. Such stories had been going about the islands, she remembered, tales of the cannibalism that used to be practised. Dear Jesus, she prayed, more fervently than she had ever prayed in her life before, even when her mother was dying in the miner's cottage in Hetton.

'Sweet Jesus!'

At first Prue thought the voice was only in her own imagination, in her prayer, but no, Matthew had moved his head; she distinctly saw the black head move against his mud-and-blood-bespattered shirt. Had she imagined it?

Glancing swiftly down at the figure of her little Billy, still fast asleep, the anxious, fearful look now mercifully smoothed from his brow as he slept, to make sure she did not disturb him, she clasped John to her with one arm and edged a little closer, watchful that none of the warriors saw her.

There it was again, not the words this time, but definitely a moan and Matthew's head certainly moved, he even managed to lift it an inch or so off the ground, his eyes opened and he was staring straight at her, his gaze slowly focusing.

'Matthew!'

It was the first word John had spoken since they left Viwa. Matthew heard it and tried to sit up, hampered by the ropes that still loosely tied him to the pole. He managed to get one arm free and was struggling with the other before a tribesman noticed he was moving and raised his club, jumping forward to deliver a blow.

'No!' Prue screamed and in an instant the rest of the warriors were there, calling harshly at each other, and the one who had been going to use his club on Matthew reluctantly lowered it and stepped back, evidently on orders from one man. He must be the headman, Prue realised, for the others were falling back, forming a ring round him as he stood beside Matthew.

'Whisht, John,' she whispered, drawing back and pulling both children as close to her as she could get them and through it all Francis William slept on serenely.

One of the warriors was hauling Matthew to his feet; he swayed and fell once, but was pulled back and this time he stood on his own, still swaying but upright, his right hand automatically feeling in the cloth about his waist, she surmised for his throwing club, but of course it had been left behind in Viwa.

They are going to kill him now, she thought despairingly and she turned John's face away. Incredibly, Francis William slept on, his little body curled up in ball, one fist tight-clenched against his mouth.

Matthew is a Tongan, Prue remembered, a follower of Ma'afu, the Tongan chief in the Lau part of Fiji, and these hill people hated the Tongans even more than they did Thakembau and the Christian Fijians. Her thoughts ran on chaotically – where had she heard that discussed? Mr Langham, when he was talking to Mr Tait, that was it, dear God, they must have known something like this might happen. God damn all missionaries, the bloody fools that they were, putting their own bairns in danger.

Prue suddenly realised she was swearing; would God help her when she was swearing? I'm sorry, I'm sorry, God, forgive me, she prayed, closing her eyes tightly and lifting her face to the sky. Where was God, any road? Was he there guarding them, his little children, or had he gone off for the night, his shift over?

The headman was strutting before Matthew now, asking incomprehensible questions in a broad, guttural dialect, and Matthew was standing, still swaying slightly, but his head was up and he was looking straight in front of him. Prue felt a twinge of admiration for his courage.

A warrior stepped forward and hit the Tongan across the face and Matthew's head rocked back and forth with the force of the blow but he kept his feet. The headman had changed from his own language to English, a type of English, that is, broken but understandable. Did this mean these natives were not so bad as she had thought they were? If they spoke some English, surely they were civilised to some extent? She strained forward to catch the words and then wished she had not.

'Long pig good to eat,' the headman said and the circle of warriors round him laughed and chortled. One or two even executed a little dance, vastly amused they were, Prue saw with a spark of anger.

'Prue? Are we going to have some pork for supper? I am hungry.'

With a gasp of horror she realised that John had heard the headman too, but thank God he hadn't understood properly.

'No, no supper, not yet, pet,' she answered. 'Whisht now, be a good lad, sit perfectly still and don't talk, please don't talk. Daddy will come soon, you'll see he will.' She took hold of his hand and squeezed it gently. 'Close your eyes, John, there's a good lad, don't watch the nasty men, it's long past your bedtime any road. If you go to sleep now, I bet when you wake up Daddy will be here and he'll take us all home in the big ship.'

'I haven't said my prayers,' John whispered.

'It doesn't matter, not tonight, just go to sleep, John.'

Go to sleep! She felt like screaming at him, she didn't know if she could keep up her serenity another minute. But he lay down obediently and closed his eyes, his anxieties forgotten for now, or perhaps Nature had taken a hand and drawn a shutter down on the day.

Prue turned her attention back to Matthew and the warriors in the centre of the clearing; the exchange with John must have only taken a second or two but in that time the women and children and old men of the tribe had settled themselves in a semi-circle round the edge of the clearing, almost as if they were expecting a show, and Prue's heart began to beat painfully. Something was going to happen and it was going to happen to Matthew, that was why they had carried him all this way, it was for this.

Two warriors, their naked bodies glistening with oil and sweat, were supporting Matthew by the upper arms, holding one hand outstretched, and his swaying stopped. Suddenly he was very still. An excited murmuring was going round the women sitting at the edge of the clearing. Prue glanced at them; they were smiling, one or two held out their own fingers and made comments she couldn't follow for they were in their own dialect.

'Ughh!'

It was the only sound Matthew made as some sort of tool grated on bone, whether a knife or an axe Prue couldn't see, but of one thing she was sure: it was two of Matthew's fingers that the headman was holding aloft, shouting out his triumph in his heathen tongue. Prue shrank back to the edge of the clearing, the children gathered up in her arms, desperate to get away. Oh God, were they going to chop him to little bits while he was still alive?

She closed her eyes, her senses swimming; she was helpless, what was she going to do? Forcing herself to look again, she saw that, in spite of the pain he must be feeling from his severed fingers, Matthew was still standing upright, making no sound at all and a wave of admiration for him swept through her. But no, it looked as though they weren't going to cut him any more, at least not yet; they were building up the fire before the long eating house and they were cooking something.

As the full horror hit her, Prue wriggled back, a child in each arm. No one was looking at her, the women were only interested in what was on the cooking fire, she could get away, she could, anything was better than what was happening in this devil village, anything.

The children were waking up, Francis William was whimpering, but the cries were lost in the general excitement, and if they were to get away now was the time. Back they wriggled until she felt a bush behind her and then, rising to her feet, she put Francis William over her shoulder and grabbed John's arm.

'Run!' she hissed and they fled, round behind a coconut palm, down the path by which they had entered the village. No, no, that was no good, the first thing the devils would do when they found them gone would be to follow that path. Swerving to one side and pulling John almost off his feet after her so that her arm felt as though it was being wrenched from its socket, she left the path and struggled through the thickening undergrowth, into the denser cover of the forest.

She had to pause after a while, for her lungs felt as though they were being torn apart by every breath she took, great riving breaths. She had to sink to the ground, bent double with the agony of it.

'Prue? Prue, are you sure Daddy's coming?'

John's voice was very low, very subdued. Poor bairn, she thought, poor little bairn. No little one should have to see what he had seen that day, no one at all.

She took a look around her though in truth there was nothing to see, only trees and more trees and beyond them, blackness. It would be totally dark soon, she realised. She had to get down to the shore line, it was their only hope. If someone was really coming to rescue them, how would they know whereabouts in the jungle she and the children were? No, they had to get to the shore, any boats would be searching the shore for signs of them.

'Prue?' repeated John and she looked down at him and took hold of his hand.

'Aye, pet, of course he's coming. Look now, we only have to go down the hill, we'll get to the shore and Daddy will be looking for us, come on now, you be a brave lad for me, I tell you, it'll be fine. Isn't this a grand adventure though? Better than a story book, this is.'

John looked doubtful but Prue set off again, thankfully finding a path or an animal track but it led down through the trees and then in the distance there was the shimmer of the moonlight on water. She closed her eyes for a moment; please God, let there be a boat, a canoe, anything in which she could get the children away from this nightmare of a place.

'Somebody is talking, Prue,' said John. 'Listen, I can hear someone talking.'

And it was true; away to the left of them they could hear stealthy rustlings and the subdued murmur of voices.

'Whisht!' she whispered urgently. 'Stand still, listen.'

Even the children seemed to hold their breath for a moment but it was no good; she couldn't make out what sort of voices they were, they were speaking too quietly. For all she knew it could have been the hill tribesmen, searching for them, and the thought made her shake with fear.

'Keep down,' she whispered, falling to her knees on the forest floor, pulling Francis William from her shoulder and holding him down on her lap.

'Daddy! Daddy!'

With mounting panic she felt John pull his arm away from her grip and he was running away, threading his way through the trees, falling down once and bumping his head but getting straight to his feet and running on. Within a second or two he was gone, disappearing into the darkness beyond the trees.

'John! John!' She jumped up, holding Francis William under one arm, and raced to follow John but suddenly someone had hold of her, a man, he was trying to take the baby from her; she kicked him in the shins but he wouldn't let go. His arms went round her, strong muscular arms, all those devils were big powerful men, what was she going to do?

'Prue, Prue, it's all right, it's over now, we've found you, come on now, give the baby to me.'

The words finally penetrated her panic and she looked up into the man's face but could only see the outline of him against a gap in the skyline. And then she realised that the arms holding her were clothed, his head was framed in a hat not a head-dress; it was an Englishman. She sagged against him. Thank God, oh thank you, God, she breathed, thank God, thank God, thank God.

Chapter Twenty

'I can lead you straight there,' said Prue. She gazed up at Morgan anxiously. Why was he delaying, why didn't they go straight up to the hill tribe's village, didn't he realise how desperate Matthew's situation was?

Oh, why had it to be Morgan West who came, why not Francis Tait? Morgan didn't care what happened to Matthew or any other native. He didn't care what happened to her when she thought of it, probably not even her sister though she was his wife.

'Captain West?' she asked again, trying to keep calm, knowing she would only put him off if she gave way to the shouting and screaming she felt rising in her. She looked over at the boys; they were in Mala's arms, their faces gleaming white against his black skin, as white as the animal bones round his upper arm. They looked so strange there, Francis William's foot resting on the bulbous end of Mala's throwing club, which was tucked into his waistband, his arm around the headman's neck.

'If we don't go now they might cut off the rest of Matthew's fingers. Captain West, they might eat him,' she said, desperation rising in her voice in spite of herself. 'There's no time to take us to the shore.'

Morgan considered what she had said, his head bent to one side. 'Yeah, I guess you're right,' he said at last. 'I guess we can't leave the Tongan to the mercy of a bunch of cannibals.' The Fijians muttered restlessly among themselves but did not object.

Prue tore off the remains of her skirt, kilted up her petticoat around her waist and she was ready. There was a short argument about what to do with the children but in the end they were given into the hands of the youngest seaman, the cabin boy from the sloop, with instructions that he was to take them back to the ship.

Eleanor stood on the deck of the sloop, peering at the dark shoreline. She was full of despair. Before her, across the dark expanse of the small bay, all she could see were the trees that came down almost to the water's edge then rose steeply behind, one hill seeming to lead to another. There was nothing else, no sign of life, not a light, not a sound. Morgan and the Fijians from Viwa appeared to have been swallowed up altogether by the forest. Perhaps it was the wrong place? Maybe they were wasting their time here while the children were being tortured or killed in another part of the island. How had the Fijians known where to come? Were they right?

She had to admit that the men from the village had seemed positive of their destination. When Morgan and his men caught up with them, they had beached their canoes and clambered on to the sloop with little or no argument, for they had soon realised it would be quicker on Morgan's fast-sailing vessel. They had pointed the way and when they reached this shore on the north coast they had been jubilant, sure they were right.

'Dear Lord,' she prayed, 'make it true, let it be here.'

'Hey, missus, I've made some tea,' said the helmsman, whose name was Pete, the only man left on the boat with her.

'I'll be all right on my own,' she had protested to Morgan. 'You need all the men.' Morgan hadn't wasted time in answering.

Eleanor took the pot of tea from the seaman. 'Thank you,' she said.

'Don't worry, missus,' he said. 'The boss will soon see those black bastards off.'

She ached to go after them, just to climb into a rowing boat and follow them ashore. But reason told her she would only hold them back, they would do better without a woman and a European woman at that.

Then there was the new baby; she could hardly allow herself to think about it now but there was that ache in the small of her back, nagging, persistent. Well, she couldn't worry about that now, there was too much else.

'There, missus, did you see?'

'What? What?'

Pete was pointing towards the shore, to the black mass of the trees. What was it? She couldn't see a thing.

'There was a light, I'm sure there was a light,' he said. But she couldn't see a thing. She began pacing up and down the deck, compulsively striding out despite the ache in her back. She would go mad if she kept still any longer. And Francis, where was he? If he had been home and discovered what had happened there, surely he would come after them? Her thoughts flitted frantically on, so that she felt she was losing her mind. Turning back to the rail she began staring at the shoreline again. Soon, soon, Morgan or the men from the village would find the abductors, of course they would, and the children would be there and Prue and Matthew and all of them unharmed. God was not so cruel as to let it be otherwise. And, as if in answer, there was the flicker of a lantern from among the dark mass of trees, once, and there it was again, yes, it was definitely a light.

'You see it, missus?' asked Pete and she turned to him, she even smiled at him.

'I see it,' she replied. The light was bobbing down the hillside, becoming brighter all the time, and the brighter it became the more hope rose in her.

'They're coming back,' she said to Pete but he shook his head.

'You don't know, missus, it could be anybody, even those heathen devils. Don't make a noise, they might be coming after the ship.'

The light reached the shore and whoever was holding it began to wave it back and forth, back and forth. And then a small boat pulled out into the bay, closer and closer to the sloop but it was impossible to see who was in it and she held her breath until a voice came softly out of the darkness directly below where she stood.

'Pete? For Gawd's sake, Pete, come down and take these nippers up, will ye? Do ye want me to drop them into the sea?'

And then it was an age before the boys were on the deck and in her arms and the surge of gladness that ran through her was so intense it cut like a knife. It was a minute or so before she could see enough to be able to check their faces, she was so blinded by tears, but when she did she saw they were filthy and tear-stained but otherwise they seemed unharmed.

They stood and let her run her hands over them as she checked for any other injury but when she was satisfied that they were all right their extraordinary stoicism broke down. They were little boys again, crying to their mother, complaining, demanding.

'Mam, Mam, where were you? Why didn't Daddy come? I was frightened, Mam.' And Francis William began to wail, loudly and crossly. One minute he hugged her and kissed her cheek and the next he was hitting her and stamping his foot, full of rage. And why not? she thought as she caught him up again and hugged him, she had let them down and so had Francis.

'Hush, now, be a good boy,' she soothed, 'there's some nice milk down in the cabin, you would like some milk, wouldn't you? It's all over now, pet, all over, the nasty men have gone.'

*

In the clearing, Matthew had sunk to his knees. His face was illuminated by the flames from the cooking fire before the long house, and Prue could see his fine profile etched against the darkness of the trees, gleaming red. Anxiously she watched from her hiding place in the bushes – what were the men waiting for? The warriors of the hill tribe were laughing and joking, even the women were joining in with shrill excited voices.

They hadn't even missed her and the children, she realised, or if they had, they must have thought a woman and two children couldn't get anywhere on their own. They were completely oblivious of the fact that they were encircled; they had been so sure of themselves that they had not posted a single lookout.

Prue looked to her left, where Morgan and his men were hidden, and she could just see the outline of one, kneeling on one leg, his rifle levelled at the warrior chief, but they were holding their fire. To the right, the men from Viwa were holding their spears at the ready, standing immobile, staring fixedly at the group in the clearing.

Her attention went back to the hill-tribe. The chief was lifting something from the pot on the fire and there was a smell like pork hanging over everything. She gagged, holding her hand over her mouth so as not to make a sound, and Morgan dug her in the ribs, casting her a warning glance. But the chief was lifting the small pieces of meat to his mouth, tasting them, smacking his lips, mockingly offering a taste to Matthew.

Oh God, strike him dead, the filthy devil, she prayed. She looked at Matthew and so far as she could tell his expression didn't change, he continued to stare ahead and her heart burned with pity for him. Then two men stepped forward again and there was a great deal of laughing and shoving and the women's voices rose again, cackling over the deeper chuckles of the men as the chief picked up his knife. It gleamed in the firelight as he stepped forward.

He was going to chop more bits from Matthew, she knew that was what he was going to do, oh, why were the men waiting? If she only had a gun she would put a bullet through that devil herself, she would! She glanced frantically at Morgan, so close to her now. Why didn't he give the signal for the men to fire? What was he waiting for? Well, if he wouldn't, she would.

'Now!' she yelled at the the top of her voice, the sound cutting across the clearing. The knife stayed in the chief's hand. She jumped up, still yelling. 'Go on, go on!' she screamed and Morgan shot her a venomous look.

But then the air was filled with the deafening roar of the rifles as the seamen fired and the women of the village screamed and the birds rose from the trees in a squawking cloud. Then the men from Viwa were there, their spears flying through the air and each one finding its mark. The hill people were turning to flee into the trees but the men from Viwa had their throwing clubs out and as many fleeing fugitives were caught by their skulls being crushed with the hard, bulbous ends of these as were caught by the guns of the seamen.

Yet Prue was only marginally aware of the orgy of killing that was taking place; her mind was wholly on Matthew. He was still on his knees with his hands now tied together, right in the middle of it all. She raced to his side, taking hold of his shoulder, trying to pull him to one side before she realised he was unable to rise to his feet for he was hog-tied with the same rope that bound his hands.

The tribal chief lay across Matthew's legs, and as she pushed and shoved at the body to get it off, she saw the knife he dropped as he died. Desperately she hacked at the rope around Matthew's wrists, but it was sticky with blood from the stumps of his severed fingers and her hands slipped once, horrifyingly, so that she only just missed cutting him more. Then he was free and he snatched the knife from her with his good hand, and hacked at the rope binding his ankles. It fell away and he took hold of her, running for the edge of the clearing, stumbling a little but getting there.

'Stay,' he ordered and she nodded, though she felt she could not have moved again of her own volition. She had begun to tremble with shock and the blood was pounding in her veins so that she could barely see.

The clearing was empty of women – whether they had fled or were among those who were cut down, Prue couldn't tell. Some of the men had surrendered; she could see a group of them on their knees before the Fijians who were tying them roughly together with loops of twine around their necks, their hands behind them.

She watched Matthew, a club in his uninjured hand, walking behind them, checking the knots and she could hardly believe his forbearance as he came to the two who had held him as the chief cut off his fingers; he treated them exactly the same as the others. All the excitement seemed to be over, the party from Viwa businesslike in their actions.

Morgan West and his handful of seamen were standing taking a breather, leaning on their guns, when one of them spied a woman hiding in the bush.

'Here's a bit of sport, lads!' he cried and dragged her out by one leg and the others were soon searching for her companions, whooping and shouting.

'Tally ho!' someone shouted and seized a girl with a baby in her arms and the men who a moment before had been kneeling abjectly before their captors were jumping up despite their bonds and trying to get at the Europeans. Morgan West calmly levelled his gun, aimed at one of them and fired, bringing him down in the mud and his nearest companions, still tied to him by the neck, on top of him.

The men from Viwa stood and stared at him as Morgan lifted his rifle to his shoulder once again and calmly took aim for the next prisoner in line while the women shrieked and the seamen whooped their approval. Prue cringed inside herself, oh, dear God, was he going to kill off the whole village? It certainly looked like it. A grinning seaman was dragging off a young girl who could not have been more than twelve right in front of her, the girl's eyes large and staring, limbs frozen in fright.

Galvanised into action, Prue jumped forward and took hold of his arm. 'Leave her alone, you monster!' she cried but the seaman only shook her off, grinning.

'I will, lass, willingly if you'll take her place,' he said and laughed before taking the girl off into the undergrowth.

Chapter Twenty-one

Francis had not long been ashore on the small island that was his destination after he had left Eleanor at Viwa when Matthew's uncle paddled a small canoe on to the beach and, hardly waiting to make the canoe safe, chased after the party of missionaries, arriving breathless and barely able to stand after his exertions.

'Mr Tait, Mr Tait,' he cried. 'A raiding party! I visit my nephew and he gone, and the woman and the babies, all gone!'

Francis stared at him, unable to move at first. No, it wasn't true, there was a mistake, hadn't he left Eleanor at Viwa only an hour or two ago? It was Mr Calvert who stepped forward.

'Calm down, man,' he said. 'Now tell us what you mean, take a deep breath and try to speak plainly.'

The Tongan did as he was told and all the while Francis listened, still disbelieving but knowing at the same time it was true. He thought back to the minutes the ship had been at Viwa, only so long as it was necessary to leave Eleanor and to catch the last of the tide and get out into the bay again. It had been a very quick turn around and even so he had noticed how empty the beach was; why hadn't he thought more about it?

But there had been smoke coming from the native huts and, if he had thought about it at all, he had thought the women must be cooking and the men out on some hunting expedition; he certainly hadn't guessed that there was anything wrong – why should there be? And he had been eager to discuss the building of a new church on this island, newly evangelised and very exciting. Nothing had alerted him to the idea that there had been a raid.

Yet in the back of his mind he knew he had not been sufficiently on his guard and he should have been alerted. He was well aware there was trouble with the hill tribes who were in dispute with the king and his Christian advisers. In fact the hill tribes hated the Methodists, hadn't he heard that only last week when he was at the conference on Bau? Dear God, he prayed, let nothing have happened to my boys, please God, don't punish them because of my negligence.

'We must go after them,' Mr Calvert was saying and Francis looked at him.

'Yes, yes, of course, we must, there's no time to lose,' he answered and turned back to the shore but Mr Calvert stopped him.

'Wait, Francis, wait, consider what we need. The local men, I think, they are our only chance of finding where they are.'

Francis halted. Of course, it was pointless simply dashing off with no idea where they were going. His mind was beginning to clear, his initial despairing panic subsiding and being replaced by a cold determination.

It was not until they were approaching the third small bay, hidden among the rocks of the northern coast, that the native Fijians among them began to show excitement and as they rounded the headland Francis could see why. A sloop was anchored in the bay, a sloop he knew well.

'That is Captain West's ship,' observed Mr Calvert. 'Now what is he doing here?'

Francis didn't answer; he was straining forward against the rail, staring at the figure of a woman only just discernible against the starlit sky. It was Eleanor, he was sure it was Eleanor; she hadn't seen their approach, she was standing with her back to them, gazing at the shore. What was she doing on Morgan West's ship? The question ran through his mind even as he was preparing to lower a boat to go over to her.

'Eleanor!' he called and Mr Calvert joined in.

'Halloo, Mrs Tait!'

Eleanor turned and walked slowly to the opposite side of the deck and stood waiting as the two men climbed aboard. Francis's heart dropped as he saw her face, her eyes still red and her cheeks streaked with tears.

'Eleanor, my dear, we came as soon as we heard, our Fijian friends knew where to look, thanks be to God,' he said, going towards her with his arms outstretched. He put his arms around her but she was unyielding, her face set.

'Mrs Tait, have you heard anything of the children?' asked Mr Calvert, who was hovering beside them.

Eleanor didn't answer; indeed she hardly heard him. When she had first seen Francis coming over the rail a terrible wave of bitterness had washed over her so she couldn't speak for a moment. And Francis saw it in her eyes and he felt he deserved it; he had done the unforgivable by allowing the boys to be put in danger. He did not say how sorry he was; what good were apologies now?

'Mrs Tait?'

This time Eleanor heard the older missionary and pulled herself away from Francis's arms so that they fell to his sides.

'Thank you, Mr Calvert,' she said formally, almost as though she were replying to a polite inquiry at a social meeting, and he blinked and cast a swift glance at Francis. After a slight hesitation she continued and to Francis it was almost as if she didn't want to tell him, as though she wanted him to suffer.

'Mala and his men found the boys, Mr Calvert, they were with Prue, she had managed to escape from the tribesmen.'

Francis broke in. 'Eleanor? Are they harmed? Tell me, Eleanor, for the love of God.'

'Perhaps love of your children would be more appropriate at this time,' she observed and Mr Calvert stepped back, shocked by the venom in her voice. 'They are unharmed in body at least, though no doubt they will suffer nightmares for the rest of their lives.'

'Oh, thank God!' breathed Francis. 'Where are they? I must go to them.' He heard her last remark, of course he did, but almost as an aside, for the important thing was that they had not been injured.

'I think not. They are asleep in Captain West's cabin. I think sleep is a good thing for them, don't you? I don't wish them to be disturbed.'

'Oh yes, indeed,' Mr Calvert interjected, nodding his head as he did his best to lessen the tension between the couple. 'Sleep is the best thing for them.'

'They were calling for their daddy,' Eleanor went on, gazing at Francis stonily. 'Evidently Prue kept their spirits up by saying their daddy would come after them and rescue them.'

Every word a stab at him, thought Francis, and how could he blame her?

'Instead it was Captain West who came. I don't know what I would have done without his help. And Prue too, I know you thought little of her but she saved the boys and now she has led Captain West and his men to the village. The heathens still have Matthew captive.'

'We must go at once, you'll be all right here with a couple of men?'

Eleanor smiled for the first time, cold-eyed. 'I usually am, Francis, I have to be.' She turned abruptly away from him and stared landwards, looking for signs of life among the trees. After a moment she spoke again. 'Of course you must go, though I'm sure Captain West and his men will bring Prue and Matthew back safely; they are well-armed. And there are Mala's men too.'

Francis wasted no more time. Goodness only knew what was happening on shore, he thought. Before long the men were embarked in the canoes for the short row ashore. He glanced back once at the ships anchored in the bay but there was no sign of Eleanor.

'I don't know about West,' said Mr Calvert as he toiled up the hill on the now well-worn track to the village. 'I have my misgivings about him, I don't think he will go out of his way to rescue a native, even a Christian.'

Francis agreed with him. There were disturbing stories of the cotton planters and Morgan West in particular. It was said they had little regard for human life if the human in question was not white.

Their fears appeared to be justified as they approached the site of the native village to be greeted by the screams of the women and the sound of rifle fire.

'In the name of God, what is going on here?' he cried as, almost in mid-stride, he grabbed a man who was molesting a girl.

'Just as I feared,' murmured Mr Calvert. 'Well, Francis, we have to stop it and stop it now.'

Prue couldn't believe her ears; the voice came from behind her, from the path that led into the clearing. And it was Francis Tait who strode forward, his hand round the neck of the seaman who had gone off with the girl, dragging the smaller man after him, stumbling and held up only by the strength of Francis's arm. Behind him came the Reverend Calvert and half a dozen men, Christian men from the south of the island.

Morgan paused; lowering his rifle, he turned to the newcomers.

'Why, Francis, what do you think is going on? We've been saving your family from kidnap and murder and the Lord knows what else, and a good thing too, when you were away leaving them to fend for themselves. Now, come on, Reverend Mr Tait, aren't you going to say thank you?'

'If you or your men kill one more I will personally take you in charge and hand you over to the authorities on Bau,' said Francis. 'Now call your men in, I will have no more innocent girls molested, do you hear me?'

Morgan laughed. 'Oh? And who is going to stop us doing exactly what we damn well like? To the victor the spoils, say I. And if either of you two holy joes think you're going to stop us I'll soon send you lickety-split into the jungle with the aid of my friend here.' He patted his rifle and grinned at Francis, who was still holding the seaman in his grasp almost as though he had forgotten he was there.

Francis stared thoughtfully at him and away at the men from his own compound, who were standing in a group watching him expectantly. Mala, the chief, was listening to the exchange intently and was fingering his club, frowning.

'It's over now, Mala,' Francis said calmly. 'Now we must see to the dead. The prisoners we will take down to be dealt with by the king. You agree, Mr Calvert?'

'Haven't you forgotten something, Francis?'

Francis turned back to Morgan, his eyes hard in an otherwise expressionless face. 'Have I?'

'Thanks, for instance? If it hadn't been for me and my men what do you think would have happened to your children?'

'I don't think they would have actually hurt the children,' Mr Calvert intervened. 'In all the years we, as a Society, have been in Fiji, we have never had a child harmed by the natives. No, I think they may have been held to ransom but not harmed. The tribes' fight is against the king's sovereignty, I believe, and his conversion from the old gods.'

Morgan snorted. 'They are nothing but savages, animals. I don't think them capable of reasoning at all. They simply love fighting and killing and eating their enemies, any excuse will do. Look at what they did to your man. They're all the same underneath, Christian or pagan, I wouldn't trust them an inch. I would be doing you all a favour if I rid the island of this lot!'

'But you will not,' said Francis. 'Now call your men together, we will give thanks to God for the deliverance of our people and then we will bury the dead and go home.'

Morgan looked as though he was about to argue but in the end he did as he was bid and the party eventually made their way back to the shore where there were now two ships in the bay, the missionary ship anchored close to Morgan's sloop. Francis must have found out what had happened and chased after them, Prue surmised. At least little John would know his daddy came, after all.

The prisoners were loaded on to the canoes of the Viwa men, still tied together. The village was left with old men to guard it and women and children lamenting over the graves of their dead. Despite the horrors she had witnessed in the clearing, Prue couldn't help feeling sorry for them and for the few who trailed after them down the forest path, some with babies in their arms, looking for a last glimpse of their men.

Matthew, the Tongan, walked with his head held high, both arms swinging by his sides, and Prue knew what it must have cost him in pain in his injured hand, now covered with a piece of bark cloth but otherwise untreated.

Eleanor will see to it as soon as we get home, thought Prue, Eleanor has healing unguents and ointment that will help it to heal cleanly. She shuddered again as she thought of how he had lost his fingers and smiled into his face as he happened to glance her way. Matthew, of course, as befitted a warrior, ignored her completely.

Chapter Twenty-two

Mary paced up and down the verandah that stretched the whole length of the front of the new house Morgan had built. The day was hot, even hotter than usual, and the serving women had retired to their own quarters now that lunch was over. But Mary ignored the heat. She was working herself up into a fine temper.

Morgan was with another woman, she was sure he was. By, she thought, if she could only find out who it was she would tear her hair out, she would that. She stopped her pacing suddenly and sat down on a white-painted armchair and stared out at the lines of labourers working the cotton fields, hoeing weeds, she supposed, even now when the sun was at its hottest. A wave of sympathy tinged with guilt because she did not do more for them swept over her.

'These blacks are not like us, Mary, how many times do I have to tell you? They don't feel the heat like we do, they're used to it. They get twenty minutes for their dinner and that's enough, now shut up about them.' Morgan had almost lost his temper with her again the last time she had suggested that it might be better to let them rest more when the sun was at its highest.

'They'll work better when it's cooler,' she had said.

Dark anger had clouded his face and she had shrunk back from him but in a moment his expression had cleared and he had smiled at her.

'Leave the workers to me, Mary,' he had said and in spite of his smile his tone was steely and she knew she dared say no more. 'All you have to do is look after yourself and my son in there.' He had patted her stomach, which was just beginning to bulge for she was four months gone by her own reckoning.

Oh yes, she thought now, remembering. He had been so solicitous for a while then but as her pregnancy developed and the baby quickened within her, he had begun to go journeying round the islands more and more and now when he had been away for almost a week, she was sure he had a woman hidden away somewhere.

Not that she cared for herself, she thought savagely, not now. In fact she was beginning to dread the nights when he came to her bed, he was always so insistent and wouldn't brook any refusal for whatever reason.

'It won't hurt the baby, the doctor says so,' he always said. And then he would complain about her 'lying like a log' and fling himself out of the house and she knew he went down to the huts of the indentured women. Oh yes, Mary thought grimly, he might think them sub-human when it came to work or feeling pain and treat them like coolies or slaves but when it came to *that* particular use, they were human enough.

But now it was different, he had a white woman, she was sure he had a white woman, a mistress, a whore from among that crowd of drifters and their followers that camped out on the beach nearby. Or if not that beach, some other. Not that there were a lot of unattached women but any one of them would think Morgan West, the rich cotton planter, a great catch.

They wouldn't stand much chance of a permanent arrangement with him but what if he took up with a woman from a better way of life, someone who expected more and usually got it? Not many could resist his charm, as she well knew. And now she had her son to think about. She wasn't going to have his inheritance taken away for any other woman's brat, that she was not.

Mary laid her hand on her stomach and as she did so the baby moved and kicked and, by, it was strong; her lad would be a proper bruiser and she would defend his rights, oh aye, she would. She grinned to herself; Morgan was so convinced it was a boy that he had her thinking the same.

She paced up and down until she was tired, then sat and dozed in the chair on the balcony until the sun began to drop over the waters of the harbour a mile away and a slight breeze sprang up and cooled her down. And Rosie, her fat, middle-aged maid, came out with the tea tray and clucked about her, arranging cushions to make her comfortable while she drank her tea. Still Morgan did not come home.

'I'll walk down to the harbour, I think, Rosie,' she said to the maid, whose name was not really Rosie but one that Morgan found heathenish and unpronounceable. Rosie looked worried.

'Don't go, missus,' she said. 'Captain West be angry, baby come soon.'

'Why, man,' snapped Mary pettishly, 'the bairn's not due for another four weeks. And any road, some of the women work in the fields right up to the day they have the babby. I'll be all right, walking is good for me.' Mary liked to relapse into the idiom of her own north-east when Morgan wasn't about. It was comforting somehow.

'Wait, I go with you,' said Rosie, admitting defeat.

Mary washed her hands and face, changed into a loose muslin dress and set off through the plantation on the track that led to the harbour. She walked in the middle of the track to avoid the ruts made by the cotton carts. It was dusty today but when the rains came, they became so thick with mud they were almost impassable. Rosie trotted beside her.

As she walked, Mary called out greetings to the labourers she recognised by sight and Rosie cast anxious eyes at her;

master didn't like the missus to be familiar with the hands, as he called them.

Mary found herself enjoying the walk and she slackened her pace and drew in deep breaths of the fresher evening air. As she neared the harbour she could smell the sea so she paused and closed her eyes for a minute, trying to pretend it was the North Sea, tangy and salty and with white-caps breaking and spraying on to the harbour at Seaham as they loaded the coal on to the collier boats from the staithes.

Abruptly, she opened her eyes and walked on. There was no way she could really conjure up home; there were too many other smells, alien smells, and certainly not the smell of new-mined coal. Just brown dust and coconut oil and strange spices and cotton. A wave of homesickness would have overwhelmed her if she had allowed it but she pushed it to the back of her mind with determination. Sometimes it was an indulgence she could wallow in but only when she was alone in her bed, not in the day.

Of course there was no sign of Morgan's sloop in the harbour, nor in the bay beyond; it had been stupid of her to think there might be. There was only a cargo ship, dropping off something or other for the cotton gin that Morgan was building on the estate.

'Good evening, Mrs West,' said a voice so close to her right ear that she jumped and Rosie snorted. It was Wilson of course, Morgan's overseer. No doubt he had been supervising the unloading. He was watching her with a slightly amused expression on his face, one eyebrow lifted in enquiry.

'Oh. Hello, Wilson,' she said, rather ungraciously. He was the only man she consciously tried to treat as an inferior, mainly because he always acted so bloody superior, she thought savagely.

'If you're looking for your husband, I'm afraid you won't find him here.'

He grinned, as one would at a child who does something innocent and so funny to the adult mind. Mary stared at him;

she wasn't going to admit that he had hit on the reason for her walk even if it was highly unlikely that Morgan would be here.

'As a matter of fact, I am simply out for a stroll and walked down here for a change of scenery,' she said coldly. 'Of course I'm not expecting to meet Captain West, I don't expect him back for at least a couple of days.'

Wilson raised his eyebrows further. 'Oh? Funny, I expected him back yesterday, something must have come up to detain him.'

'I must be going, good evening, Wilson,' Mary said abruptly and turned on her heel. 'It will be dark soon.'

'If you wait a moment or two, I will give you a lift. I'm afraid there is only the cart, but perhaps it's better than walking.'

'Thank you, I prefer to walk,' she snapped. 'Come along, Rosie.'

As she set off back up the track she could feel his eyes upon her and imagined what he was thinking. He would be laughing at her, she was sure of it, a silly little miner's daughter with ideas above her station and a husband who went with anybody in skirts. She put her hand on her stomach as the baby shifted his position and kicked at her bottom rib; oh Lord, perhaps she should have ridden back on the cart, she hadn't considered that the walk back to the house was a mile long and all of it uphill.

Halfway back, Mary and Rosie had to stand aside as the cart came up behind them. This time she was glad to accept Wilson's renewed offer of a lift and hadn't even the energy to argue when the offer wasn't extended to Rosie, who plodded on behind them, puffing and panting. When she reached the house, Mary went straight to bed and lay awake, lonely and exhausted. Suddenly she longed for Eleanor. By, she wanted desperately to talk to another woman from home.

It was about two o'clock in the morning when Mary woke up and knew that her labour pains had started. The house was deserted except for Rosie so there was no one to send for the doctor, as Morgan had commanded she should do. She daren't let Rosie go and leave her on her own; the pains were too strong and too frequent for that.

Which was just how she wanted it, she told herself. Rosie knew what to do, she insisted she did, hadn't she had ten children herself? And any road, Morgan wasn't here, it was his fault that she had to get on with it in her own way. She was not worried; none of the miners' wives in Hetton ever had a doctor at their lying-in, what did they want with a man there? It wasn't decent.

At ten past ten in the morning, Mary's daughter was born, a little scrap of a thing, more blue than red like Eleanor's babies had been so that Mary was instantly struck with a terrible fear for the tiny thing. How could such a weak scrap of a baby have kicked so hard at her ribs as to make them sore?

But Rosie took the infant and smiled and said, 'Baby fine,' and wrapped her in one of the delicate embroidered sheets that Morgan had brought home one day for his son. As Rosie brought a basin of water to wash Mary, who was lying in her dishevelled bed, sweat-stained and smelling of blood and childbirth, Morgan walked in.

Rosie paused for a moment and then her movements, which up to then had been deft and sure, became hesitant and she slopped a little of the water on to the sheet.

'Get out of here, woman, I want to see my son,' he snapped at her.

Rosie hesitated and looked at Mary, lying exhausted and uncomfortable in the bed.

'Out, you idiot!' shouted Morgan and she put down the basin and scuttled from the room.

'I told you to get the doctor,' said Morgan without really looking at Mary. 'I told you I didn't want my son delivered by a heathen nigger.' He went over to the cradle and gazed down at the baby. 'He's mighty small,' he observed, sounding disappointed.

'She's a month premature,' said Mary and watched for his reaction closely, half-fearful and half-pleased that he had not got what he wanted. At first she thought he hadn't caught on to what she had said but then he took hold of the sheet in which the mite was swaddled and unwound it, none too gently.

'A damned girl!' he burst out, leaving the child unwrapped and turning on the bed in a fury. 'You had the nerve to give me a damn girl! You never were any blasted good, you barren sow!' He bent his body over her until his face was only an inch away from hers and spat out his insults. Mary quailed – surely he wasn't going to hit her now? But as she stared at his handsome face made ugly with fury and cruelty, something sparked within her and, weak as she was, she sat up in bed and, taking him by surprise, pushed him away. For she had to make a fight, there was the baby to think of now; she couldn't afford to be frightened for herself.

'I'm hardly that, am I?' she shouted at him, her voice weak at first but strengthening. 'What are you, a bloody animal? That is your daughter in the cradle and if I ever catch you being rough with her again I swear I'll swing for you, I swear by all that's holy!'

Morgan had stepped back in surprise and now he opened his mouth to say something but evidently thought better of it and with an oath he flung himself to the door; but when he got there he turned.

'I wouldn't touch the little beggar, she's not like to last more than a few hours at any rate as far as I can see. I'll just let nature take its course. You'd better watch your tongue in future, madam. I'm off now, this room stinks worse than a battlefield and don't expect to see me until you've learned what side your bread's buttered on!'

He could not have said anything better designed to take all the fight out of Mary and she collapsed back on her pillows sobbing her heart out, but not until Morgan had slammed the door and gone out of the house, shouting for his crew as he went.

After a while, Rosie ventured back into the bedroom, washed her, changed the sheets and made her comfortable, and Mary began to recover some of her spirit. The maid washed and dressed the baby in a lawn gown and laid her in Mary's arms and as she gazed down at her daughter she saw that a faint pink was brightening the baby's cheeks, that she turned her head and even waved a fist in the air. She nuzzled at Mary's breast and cried in frustration as she couldn't find the nipple.

'Whisht now, babby,' Mary crooned softly. 'Whisht now, my bonny bairn.' I'll call her Ruth, she decided all of a sudden as the name popped into her mind. And she thought of the story of Ruth, who went into a far country with her mother-in-law.

'Baby strong,' commented Rosie. 'She live.'

'Oh, aye, she will,' said Mary. 'She'll live to go back to Hetton with me.'

Chapter Twenty-three

Despite her worries and the dragging backache that plagued Eleanor during the whole of her pregnancy, her baby was born having gone full-term and was a perfectly healthy boy.

'It would have been nice to have a girl this time,' she said to Francis when he was allowed into the room to see mother and child.

Francis smiled at her as she lay on the pillow with the baby by her side. 'It doesn't matter, my love,' he said in the rather rough voice that he had developed this last year or so. 'The main thing is that he is such a fine baby.'

Eleanor nodded her agreement as she gazed at the new-born's unfocused eyes and plump pink cheeks. He was larger than her other boys had been, she was sure, though she had no scales to weigh him.

'Perhaps we will call him Edward?' suggested Francis rather diffidently, and was instantly sorry he had. He didn't want to upset Eleanor on this day of all days by reminding her of the child they had lost. But Eleanor wasn't upset; she simply looked thoughtful.

'Edward Wales Tait,' she replied, surprising him by the inclusion of her grandmother's name. 'It will remind us of our other dear little Edward.'

'A good idea,' Francis said quickly. 'Now I will go and let you get some rest.'

Eleanor lay with her baby beside her, enjoying the quiet time before Prue came back from the beach with John and Francis William, reflecting on the last few months. They had been angry, bitter months for the most part with the anger mainly on her side and directed against Francis. She knew she was going too far sometimes but he had not retaliated, simply left the room or even the compound until he thought she had quietened down again.

He had insisted that she travel back with him on the missionary ship and Morgan and his men had gone off in another direction.

'We are all right here, Morgan will see us safely home and the boys are asleep down below,' she had protested.

'I wish you to come with me,' Francis had insisted and he carried John while Prue carried Francis William aboard the missionary ship, both boys still asleep. Morgan looked on silently, with a sardonic half-smile.

'I can never thank you enough, Captain West,' Eleanor had said as she left the sloop. 'If it hadn't been for you ...' She didn't finish the sentence, she couldn't. Francis thanked him too, formally, his voice cold and distant. He ignored the mutterings of the seamen, especially the one he had man-handled out of the bush.

Eleanor had held her peace on the journey because of the boys and the presence of Prue and the Fijians but once they were by themselves in their own bedroom, she had let her anger spill over.

'You let us down, Francis,' she said. 'If it hadn't been for Morgan West, my boys might have been dead. I'll never forgive you, Francis.' She hurled insults at him, insults that got wilder and wilder and Francis stood, white-faced, not even trying to defend himself. She stopped at last, exhausted and tearful, and sat down on the bed full of despair.

'Dear God,' she whispered at last. 'How could I marry a man who cares nothing for me or my children?'

Francis's head had jerked up. 'Eleanor! How can you say such a wicked thing?'

It's true,' she insisted. 'All you care about is God and how many natives you can bring to Him. Your family doesn't even count against that.' Even as she said it, she knew she was being vastly unfair but she was driven, she had to hurt him as badly as she had been hurt, she had to. She could not believe that he had been as frantic about the kidnapping of the children as she had been.

What might have been said after that she didn't know, for just then there was a scream from the children's room, a scream so terrible she was convinced that something else was happening to the boys. Jumping to her feet, she fled to the door with Francis close behind her to find John running down the hall to the outside verandah, dragging his little brother after him.

'John, John, what are you doing?' she cried but he couldn't hear her; he was deep in some dream, some nightmare of his own. She snatched up Francis William, who was heavy with sleep and hardly knew what was happening, and hugged him to her while Francis caught hold of John.

'Stop now, stop!' Francis said, holding on to John as he fought and struggled to get away, panic and fright giving him a wild strength.

'Let me go!' screamed the boy, and Eleanor knelt beside him, the younger boy still in her arms. 'They're going to hurt us, we have to get away!'

Francis put his arms around John and held him close. 'No, no, John, no, it's Daddy, we're not going to let anything happen to you, we're not. This is just a bad dream, wake up, John, wake up. You're safe now.'

Gradually the unseeing panic left the boy's eyes, he stopped screaming and began to tremble with reaction and Francis swept him up and carried him to bed.

'Don't go away, Daddy, you won't go away?' John was weeping quietly now and Francis looked at Eleanor, who had followed him into the bedroom with Francis William, who went back to sleep as soon as she laid him down.

'I won't go away, son,' he said. 'I'll stay here until you go to sleep.'

'No, don't go away at all,' insisted the boy.

'I'll just be in the next room,' Francis assured him and after a while the boy's trembling stopped and he slept.

They waited a few minutes to make sure John was all right and then tip-toed from the room.

Outside, Prue was hovering, dressed only in her nightdress, over which she had thrown a shawl. Behind her stood Matthew, his bandaged hand showing white against his dark skin.

'Poor bairn,' whispered Prue. 'It'll be a long day before he forgets. No doubt we'll have our work cut out with him.'

'Go to bed, Prue,' Francis said rather sharply, averting his eyes from her attire. Then, obviously feeling he was being a bit hard, 'You need your sleep too, you have had a bad time as well. But don't think we're not grateful for what you did for the boys, we will never forget it.'

Eleanor was tired to death but she couldn't help a bitter dig at him when they were back behind the closed door of their bedroom.

'No, what would we have done without Prue? Do you find it galling to have to thank her, Francis? After all you have said about her in the past, I mean.'

'Come to bed, Eleanor,' Francis replied wearily. 'It is the shock of what has happened which is making you say such terrible things. You will be sorry for them in the morning.'

'I will not,' said Eleanor as she slipped into her side of the bed and turned her back on him.

John's nightmares had continued for the rest of the summer. They occurred with monotonous regularity two or three times a week and each time they involved Francis William so that in the end Eleanor had moved the younger boy into

208

Prue's room and had Prue sleep in the same room as John. Eleanor's thoughts turned to John as she lay with her new baby in her arms; she thought about his troubles at least once a day, worrying, trying to think what to do. Should she take him to Australia, back to Sydney to see a doctor who knew about these things?

It was Francis's attitude when he was with the children that had gradually calmed her bitter feelings towards him. He so obviously loved them; he had such great patience with them. For their part, the boys loved Francis with an uncritical devotion; their eyes lit up and they would throw themselves on him every time he returned to them from one of his trips round the islands. John had even come to accept the trips, knowing his father had to go away on the Lord's business from time to time.

And besides, Eleanor thought wearily as Prue came in and took the baby from her, she and Francis had to live with each other, hadn't they? Though they did not sleep together, not now – Eleanor was still too bitter for that and Francis did not press her.

'Try to sleep,' Prue advised. 'You need all the rest you can get. I'll take the baby on to the verandah for now.'

'Thank you, Prue,' Eleanor replied and turned on her side, thinking how the experience had changed the girl. She was brighter somehow, more self-assured and not so obsessive about the children. And then, she and Matthew were getting on much better now. Although, she recollected sleepily, it had been Mary who had argued with him more than Prue.

'Ship coming!'

Eleanor looked up and smiled at Francis William as he ran up the verandah steps to her.

'*John Wesley!* Daddy's coming.' He caught hold of her hand and tried to pull her out of her chair.

'All right, I'm coming,' she laughed, knowing better than to ask how he knew it was the missionary ship. 'Where's John?'

'He's gone to meet Daddy,' said Francis William, still pulling at her impatiently.

Eleanor felt a tug of fear and gazed at the ship, which was coming in to the quay. 'He shouldn't go by himself,' she said sharply. 'Haven't I told you both you have to wait for me?' Hurriedly she got to her feet and walked rapidly through the compound to the beach, Francis William trotting by her side.

Despite the fact that the whole of Viwa was buzzing with activity, the men fishing in the bay, the women and children at their own end of the beach splashing about in the shallows, she was anxious until she caught sight of John at the end of the quay. He was waving enthusiastically at Francis's black-clad figure on the deck of the ship.

'What are you doing here?' she said sharply, taking hold of his shoulder and swinging him round to face her. His happy smile disappeared abruptly and he looked ready to cry. 'How many times have I told you not to go off on your own?'

'I was with him, missus,' said a quiet voice beside him and she noticed Matthew for the first time.

'Oh.' Eleanor could think of nothing else to say. She had spoilt the homecoming for the boys, she thought, oh, when was she going to get rid of this fear? The tribes in the north were quiet now; there was nothing to worry about. She had to conquer her fears, she knew.

'Well, you should have told me, John,' she said lamely. 'Now, go on, you can go on the quay to meet Daddy.'

Francis had news. After he had swung John up in the air and lifted Francis William on to his shoulders for the walk back to the mission house, they sat on the balcony drinking tea before it was time to go down to the church for the mid-week service. Already they could hear the notes of the harmonium that they had recently acquired and the voices of the choir as they practised an old Charles Wesley hymn.

> 'Love divine, all loves excelling
> Joy of heaven to earth come down—'

Briefly Eleanor wondered how much of it the singers really understood. She glanced at Francis but he seemed untroubled by such thoughts; he was smiling slightly at the sound of one of his favourite hymns and humming the tune softly in his now husky voice. When it was finished he turned to her.

'We are to be transferred to Bau,' he said. 'In September.'

'Francis, that's good news indeed!' A wave of thankfulness washed over Eleanor. She was sure she would feel safer at Bau, where the king lived, the Christian king, she reminded herself. No rebel tribe would ever dare attack Bau.

Edward, whom Eleanor was convinced would be their last child, was baptised on Bau by the Reverend Langham. The church was full to overflowing; even the king and all his retinue condescended to attend. Mr and Mrs Calvert were there, and Mrs Langham stood as godmother and Eleanor felt surrounded by friends and, above all, safe.

John and Francis William stood beside her looking positively angelic in white cotton and with their hair cut short because of the heat. Eleanor glanced behind her at Prue, who was standing by Matthew looking happier and plumper than she had since she arrived newly widowed from Sydney. As she watched, she saw Matthew and Prue exchange a glance that was startling in its intimacy and then she thought immediately that she must be mistaken; of course there could be nothing between the two, it was simply that they were often together, it was in the nature of their work.

'Who brings this child to be baptised?' asked the Reverend Langham and Eleanor forgot all about Prue and Matthew as the ceremony got under way. The rest of the afternoon and evening was taken up with the baptismal supper, which the king insisted on providing and which went the way of all the native feasts, held on the beach and lasting until the stars came out and the subject of the celebration had been tucked up safely in his bed for hours.

Prue was not at the feast for she was needed to stay in the mission house with the children and Matthew was not in the habit of attending the Fijian celebrations either, being a Tongan. Which was a pity, really, Eleanor reflected as she walked back home with Francis; there were not many Tongans on Bau, it being the home of the Fijian king.

Eleanor picked up a sleepy Edward and brought him into the bedroom that she still shared with Francis; she wanted no gossip about them and it was amazing how such things got about. She sat down on the nursing chair that Francis had recently had brought in from Australia and, turning slightly away from him for modesty's sake, began to breastfeed the baby, drawing a thin scarf over her bared breast to make sure there was no part of it to be seen.

Francis watched her; he couldn't help himself. Did she not realise what she was doing to him? he wondered. She looked up and caught his eye and he hurriedly began to prepare for bed. The same bed as she would lie in, he thought moodily, though she would be at one extreme and he at the other. Just as well it was a wide bed, he thought and smiled mirthlessly.

Eleanor felt the tension in the air and did her best to ease it. 'It went very well on the whole, didn't it, Francis?' she asked him.

'Oh yes, very well. In fact, Mr Calvert was saying how friendly the king is becoming. That bodes very well for the church, you know. It was good of him to provide the feast, was it not?'

Eleanor pulled a face. 'Oh, the church. Yes, of course, you would think of that first.'

Francis sighed; he had said the wrong thing yet again. 'It's important, Eleanor.'

'And so is the baptism of your son. I would have thought this was Edward's day, he should come first.'

'But he did!' Francis was genuinely bewildered but he said no more, just climbed into bed and lay in the shadows watching as she winded the baby and then put him to her other breast.

'The boys were very good,' he ventured after she had taken Edward back to his cot and slipped into bed. He sat up and put out the lamp and then lay stiffly for a few moments. But his feelings were too strong and in the end he reached across the bed to her, his hand coming in contact with her body just under her breast, not totally by chance.

'Don't, Francis.'

He didn't hear, perhaps because he didn't want to. He could feel the beat of her heart as it quickened and thought for a moment it was because she wanted him as much as he wanted her.

Moving closer to her he kissed her lips, groaning slightly in anticipation. It had been so long, so long.

Roughly Eleanor pushed his hand away and jumped out of bed and in his fever he hardly knew what was happening.

'Eleanor? Come back, my love, what is it?'

'You know very well, Francis,' she said harshly. 'I've told you, I don't want you touching me, do you hear? If you can't leave me alone I will have to sleep elsewhere, I don't care what other people may think.'

To Francis her icy tone was like a cold shower. He had told himself all during this time since the boys had been kidnapped that Eleanor was acting as she was because she was in a certain condition, and afterwards that it was too soon after the birth of Edward. But he could no longer deceive himself. The truth was that she didn't want him near her. Rising from the bed, he walked to the door that led on to the verandah.

'Go back to bed, Eleanor,' he said. 'I won't trouble you again.'

He lay down on the cushioned swing, having to curl up his long legs to do so, and lay, sleepless and uncomfortable, until dawn.

'You had better have a cot made up in the bedroom,' he said to Eleanor next day. 'You're right, after all, there is no need to have anyone gossiping about us. You can say— oh, make some excuse, I'm sure you'll think of something.'

Chapter Twenty-four

'There is the most dreadful news,' said Mr Calvert. 'Bad tidings of the worst kind. I was really on my way to Lakeba but in view of what has happened I felt I should come and tell you myself. After your maid servant and two boys were abducted last year, I mean.'

Eleanor's ears pricked up as she heard this mention of the kidnapping of her boys. She was bringing the tray of coffee from the kitchen herself as Prue had taken the children with her to milk the goat tethered on the edge of the garden at the rear of the mission house. Now she paused and rested the tray on the back of the sofa just inside the sitting room and listened unashamedly.

'Bad news?' Francis said.

'Yes, I wanted you to know before everyone else, most especially your lady wife. I know – we all know – how badly affected she was by what happened. I felt you were the best one to break it to her.'

Break what? Eleanor wanted to scream. Why didn't he get on with it?

'Perhaps you are right,' came Francis's patient tones. 'But Eleanor is stronger than you think, you know.'

'Perhaps, perhaps. Oh dear, I hardly know how to tell you.' He glanced at the open door that led to the sitting room and Eleanor stepped back out of sight. 'It is Mr Baker. You know, of course, that he went to Navosa, up in the hill country. Well, he and his seven companions have been slain by the people he wished to serve.'

Eleanor put down the tray on the green chenille cover of the dining table and sat down on the couch. The hill tribes, they were in revolt again then, oh, thank God she and her family were on Bau, where there was a Christian king. She closed her eyes as her head swam and a pulse rose in her throat, threatening to choke her.

She jumped to her feet again in an instant. Where were the boys? She must have them with her, she couldn't let them out of her sight. No, they were with Prue, they were safe, as safe as they would ever be in Fiji, of course they were. Her reason began to take over, telling her it was silly to panic. She strained to hear more of the conversation.

'—worse, I'm afraid. I know what a narrow escape your poor man had. Mr Baker was not so blessed. He and his companions were—'

Here Eleanor had to lean even closer to the door as Mr Calvert lowered his voice.

'—were cooked and eaten. It is said that the chief even sent bits round to the neighbouring tribes, as a rallying call, I suppose. Poor Mr Baker. His poor family, too, I don't yet know how they are taking this tragic news.'

'His companions too? They were Fijian, were they?' That was Francis.

'They were, Christian Fijians, all had given their hearts to the Lord and were willing to risk their lives in His cause.'

And now they'd given their hearts and other parts to cannibals, Eleanor thought, hysteria rising in her.

'Now all have gained the martyr's crown,' said Francis. 'We must see to the families, not let them suffer.'

Eleanor snorted and this time the men heard her.

'Is that you, Eleanor?' Francis got to his feet and walked to the sitting-room door. 'Give me the tray, I will carry it out for you.' As he took it from her, he studied her face and he could see at once that he didn't have to break the news to her;

she had heard. He said nothing however, simply brought out the coffee tray and handed her into a chair.

Eleanor was dumb. She stared out across the bay, over the heads of the people in the clearing that was rapidly becoming a street, with a proper store and even a small hotel. The church was larger than the one at Viwa, more imposing though still thatched in the manner of the islands. The king's house was not in sight, although his boat house was and she saw there was unusual activity going on around it. The king's warriors were forming up already.

Of course, the news would spread like wildfire and King Thakembau would not let this challenge to his authority pass. He was struggling to have his claim to sovereignty over all the islands recognised, especially by Europe. Now that most Fijians realised that Fiji was not the centre of the world, not even very important in relation to other countries, the king needed a European protector, preferably Britain.

'Eleanor?'

She looked away from the bay and realised that Francis was handing her a cup of coffee. She should have been do- ing her duty as a hostess but she was glad to sit back and let Francis hand the plate of Yorkshire parkin cakes to Mr Calvert.

The two men discussed the forthcoming conference when the ministers and lay workers would converge on Bau once again and, after a while, Mr Calvert put down his cup and rose to his feet.

'I must be going,' he said. 'I have a long way to go today.' He looked from Francis to Eleanor, who was stirring her cof- fee absent-mindedly, staring into the liquid thick with goat's milk. 'Aren't you going to drink your coffee before it gets cold?' he asked her gently.

Eleanor put down the cup quickly and stood up. Making a great effort, she smiled at the kindly middle-aged minister. After all, though he was older than Francis and herself by at least fifteen years, he had braved the dangers of the hill tribes to go with Francis in search of the children.

'I don't think I will, Mr Calvert. I'll tell you a secret, shall I? I never have got used to coffee, nasty bitter stuff I think it. Tea's so much more refreshing, don't you agree?'

Mr Calvert was relieved; for a moment or two he had thought she had heard him tell Francis about poor Mr Baker. It was much better that such news should come from her own husband. 'Now, don't come with me, Francis, you stay here and enjoy the— Well, you stay here and have a little chat with your wife. I'm sure you have few enough opportunities for it.' He said his goodbyes and went off down the muddy road to the ship waiting at the quay.

Francis and Eleanor watched in silence until he was out of sight. Then she began gathering up the cups and saucers, putting them on the tray and the Yorkshire parkin in its airtight tin to save it from the ants.

Francis watched for a moment before speaking. 'You heard what Mr Calvert came to say, didn't you, Eleanor?'

Her hands stilled. 'I did,' she said tightly.

Francis continued looking at her; what he wanted to do was put his arms around her and comfort her, hold her to him and promise that nothing was going to happen to her or the children, with God's help he wasn't going to let anything happen.

'It couldn't happen on Bau,' he ventured at last.

Eleanor kept her head bent, refusing to look at him. 'Couldn't it?'

He couldn't bear to look at her any more, she seemed so vulnerable. His Eleanor who was so capable, whose heroine was Florence Nightingale, that redoubtable woman. Eleanor who went among the Fijians doing all she could for them, often acting as doctor and nurse to the sick. He went to her and took her in his arms, holding her unyielding body close against him, one hand holding her head in the crook of his neck.

'Eleanor, it's all right, it is, really,' he said and his already husky voice was almost breaking. 'We can mourn a comrade-in-arms, eight comrades-in-arms, but this is a war, Eleanor, a war against the forces of evil. And you'll see, as we go on the Lord will prevail, we will be triumphant and cannibalism will be banished from these islands. The Lord will protect us, Eleanor.'

Eleanor moved, breaking away from his embrace. 'Will He?' she asked. 'As He did the Reverend Baker and his companions? Now please, Francis, I must get on, I was going down to the village this morning. I promised to look in on a poor girl who scalded herself when she was cooking a meal yesterday. I have to get my basket ready. Now, where did I put the jar of boracic ointment? Oh yes, I know, it is still in the kitchen with the supplies.'

She went into the house and began packing her basket with rolled bandages she had made from old cotton petticoats and pillow slips. She added a bottle of liniment for Lia, the old lady with a painful shoulder joint, and then started for the kitchen to pick up the boracic ointment.

'This ointment has only recently come into use for the treatment of burns,' she said, seeing Francis still standing watching her. 'I read a report of it in one of the medical magazines a month or two ago and sent for a jar. I'm so pleased it has come so quickly.' She walked out on to the balcony with her basket before turning back to him. 'Oh, and Francis, I think it would be better if you didn't put your hands on me in full view of any passersby. I don't think public displays set a good example to the younger Fijians, do you?'

Chapter Twenty-five

There was a letter from home, the first letter Eleanor had received from her family for more than two years. She gazed at the envelope with the address written in the copperplate script of her brother James. Trouble, she thought.

'Best open it, my dear,' said Francis, looking up from the sheaf of correspondence from the Wesleyan Missionary Society that had come on the same ship.

'Yes.'

Eleanor opened the envelope carefully, making sure the stamp with the head of Queen Victoria was not damaged any more than it had been by the franking machine, newly acquired by the infant Fijian Post Office. John was an avid collector of stamps.

'Dear Sister, (she read.)
I hope you and your family are well. Alice and I and the children are all in good health.'

'Bad news, is it, Eleanor?' asked Francis.

Eleanor nodded for, having got over the preliminaries, John came straight to the point.

'I regret to have to tell you that Mother passed away on November 11th. She will be a great loss to us, especially Fanny, but she had a good life despite being widowed so young and has now gone to her Just Reward.'

He had signed it, 'Your loving brother, James.'

James, thought Eleanor. She would hardly know him if she saw him now.

'Mother has died.'

Francis put down his correspondence, went around the table and put his hand on her shoulder. 'I am so sorry, Eleanor,' he said.

'Yes.' Eleanor studied the letter as though searching for more information than it actually carried. But James had never been a great correspondent; in fact this was the first letter she had received from him in all the time she had been in Fiji. There had been greetings at Christmas from his wife but that was all.

'Poor Mother,' she said softly.

'Yes. She was widowed for many years and never complained,' said Francis.

'Oh, she complained right enough,' said Eleanor. 'She complained all the time. In fact, I should say it is probably a happy release for the family.'

'Eleanor! How can you say such things and at a time like this!'

Eleanor looked up at him and sighed. 'It's how I feel. But yes, you're right, I'm sorry, Francis,' she said.

'I'll get Prue to make some more tea, you are upset, of course you are, I shouldn't take any notice of what you say.' Francis went to the door of the kitchen and called for Prue but there was no reply. 'Now where is that girl?' he asked of no one in particular.

'I expect she's gone out with the boys,' said Eleanor. 'Don't worry, I don't want more tea in any case, I'm quite all right. Go on to church, you'll be late for your meeting.'

After he had gone, Eleanor sat on by the uncleared breakfast table, looking out on the street with unseeing eyes. For once she was allowing herself to think of home, of Houghton le Spring and Hetton-le-Hole, the beauty of the hills and dales of Durham and the dirt and smoke of the mining villages. And the viewer's house at Hetton where she had lived with Grandmother Wales and Uncle John. Would she see it all again? Not her mother, not in this life.

Perhaps she had not been very tolerant of her mother when she was younger, too quick to see her faults. It could not have been easy for her, a widow. Now she was a wife and mother herself she could understand more. It was too late now, she realised sadly. There was a hole in her life where her mother had been.

'Till we meet, till we meet at Jesu's feet.'

The line ran through her head and she could almost hear the choir at Hetton singing. Shaking her head, she stood up and began to pile the breakfast dishes on the tray. What was the use of pining for home, Francis would never leave his beloved Fijians, never. And she didn't want to either, she told herself, she was well liked in the village, the women looked forward to seeing her, they trusted her, she didn't treat them with condescension like some Europeans, she was one of them.

Hearing noises in the kitchen, Eleanor picked up the tray and went through. Prue must be back from taking the children to the Sunshine Corner that Francis had recently started for all the children at the church. Matthew and Prue were standing close together, very close together. Eleanor almost dropped the tray as she saw them and realised just how close they were.

'Matthew!' she cried. 'Prue!'

'Yes, missus?' The Tongan did not even move away from the girl; he didn't even look guilty. If anything he looked proud and aloof, almost as if she was an unwanted interloper in her own kitchen. She looked at Prue – the chit was actually smiling!

'Matthew and me, we want to get wed,' Prue said.

'But— But you can't!'

Prue continued to smile, though her eyes grew wary. 'Why?'

'Well, because—' Eleanor stopped. Why couldn't they?

They stood before her, Matthew, with his maimed hand held behind his back, out of sight, was tall, straight and almost aristocratic in his pride. But oh, his skin so dark against the whiteness of his shirt. And Prue, the miner's daughter from the other side of the world, just as proud, her golden hair curling on her forehead, a white cap perched on top and her skin so creamy white where it met the neckline of her dress.

Prue was beautiful, Eleanor thought; she hadn't really noticed how beautiful she had become. Her dimples had come back, she was more rounded than she had been since landing here from Australia and her bright blue eyes shone with health. She even had a saucy gleam in her eyes, as she had had on the ship coming over, the gleam that had captivated the seamen. She was plumper and she had let out the seams of her dress for there was the deeper mark where the sun had not faded the material. An awful suspicion came to Eleanor; oh, surely not, not in the minister's house, no, Prue wouldn't. Eleanor was driven to ask.

'Prue, you're not—'

'We want to get wed right away,' Prue interrupted. She moved away from Matthew and began to empty the breakfast tray, her movements deft and sure but her voice nervous. Or was she just excited? Dear Lord, what was Francis going to say?

'I don't know ... You will have to speak to Mr Tait,' Eleanor said at last. 'Ask him if he will marry you.'

Prue and Matthew looked at each other and smiled and Eleanor saw that they were in love, truly in love. How could she have been so blind as not to notice before now?

'You stay here, Prue, I'll walk down for the children. I'll have a word with Francis for you if you like.'

Matthew stepped forward. 'No, missus. I speak to Mr Tait myself.' He turned to Prue. 'Come, woman,' he said and she bowed her head and followed him out of the door, through the garden and around the house to the street.

Eleanor watched, bemused. She had never seen Prue humble in her life before, not even when she was a child starving at the back door of the viewer's house. Not even when she returned from Sydney after the death of her husband and baby. Now she was not only humble, she was positively submissive, which boded well for her future with Matthew. Polynesian men would brook no insubordination from their wives.

'I am pleased for Prue,' said Francis that night when they were in their bedroom together. He spoke softly, for the children were asleep in the next room. Matthew and Prue had gone off to visit his relatives at Lakeba, evidently something that Matthew considered essential as soon as the marriage was announced.

'Are you? I wasn't sure how you would take the news.'

Eleanor watched him as he carefully folded his clothes and laid them in the clothes cupboard, something he did every night. She herself was already dressed in her voluminous nightgown, her long hair brushed and shining down her back.

Francis put on his nightshirt and picked up his Bible before answering. He had taken to reading a chapter aloud in bed every night lately, after their prayer-time and before retiring to his cot.

She considered whether to tell him of her suspicions concerning Prue or should she wait until after the pair were married? It was so difficult to talk to Francis about such things.

'I think perhaps the marriage ought to be as soon as possible,' Francis observed. He lay on his back in bed, his Bible unopened beside him.

Eleanor turned her head and stared at him. It was the nearest he would get to actually saying he thought Prue was expecting a baby – so he had guessed. Francis had seemed a different man today. He had not once mentioned the cultural differences between Matthew and Prue, something that was often used as a cover for objecting to black marrying white. But not by Francis, she thought suddenly, never by Francis.

'They are in love,' she said, dreamily gazing into the shadows cast by the lamp on Francis's night table. The house was very quiet, no sound from the boys' room. It was a long while since John had had one of his nightmares; she prayed they had seen the end of them. A nightbird called outside the window, low and musical.

'You don't blame them, Francis? You're not judging them?' Francis turned towards her and raised himself on one elbow.

'It is human nature, Francis, we are all weak.'

She saw he was looking at the curve of her neck, just above the high-buttoned frill of her nightgown, and she didn't turn away or huddle under the sheet as she was wont to do.

'Are you not worried about the future of any children they may have, Francis?' she asked. 'They might have a hard time in the world.'

'They will survive.'

It was hard to see Francis's eyes, they were just dark smudges in the lamplight, but she thought he was gazing at her with that intent look she remembered so well. It was a long time since he had approached her, put his hands on her in that way. He had given up, she supposed. And she had been hard on him, she had reneged on her marriage vows. The thought surprised her; she hadn't looked at it like that before.

Somehow tonight she had changed; she smiled gently and put her hand on his arm. It was as much of an overture as she was able to make but it was enough.

'Eleanor.' Francis breathed her name as he took her in his arms and kissed her. He felt her response and began undoing the buttons of her nightdress, at last reaching her breasts, still firm and full in spite of nursing four children. And he was completely lost, his movements getting more urgent as he carried her along with him in his passion.

She had denied her needs for so long, the strength of her feeling took her completely unaware; it was almost as though it was the first time for her. No, not the first time, she thought sleepily as she lay afterwards with Francis still breathing hard and still collapsed half across her, but the first time she had really tasted the glory it could bring.

A lovely drowsiness was creeping over her, forcing her eyes closed. The last thing she heard was a thump as Francis's Bible fell to the floor. Well, the Lord would not be offended, she was sure of it.

Prue and Matthew were married the following week at Lakeba and Francis conducted the ceremony just as he had officiated at her sister Mary's wedding.

'Most of Matthew's family live at Lakeba,' said Prue by way of explanation. She was with Eleanor at the cloth counter of the village store, for Eleanor had offered to buy the material for her wedding dress.

'Well, we have old friends on Lakeba too,' Eleanor answered. 'Now, what do you think of this muslin? Such a lovely cream colour, the colour of old lace. In fact, I have some old lace in a drawer, we could trim it with that, it will make a lovely wedding dress and easy to sew too, we haven't much time to spare if it's to be ready next Saturday.'

Prue looked a little embarrassed. 'I don't think I should have a white dress,' she said.

Eleanor understood; it wasn't the thing when a girl had been married before and especially when she was already— no, best not to think that.

'But it's cream, not white,' she protested. 'I'm sure there can be no objections to it.'

'Oh, no, not that, it's just that I don't want that kind of a wedding dress at all.'

Eleanor looked mystified.

'I'm going to wear what the Tongan women wear. I thought Matthew would like that.'

So there was not much sewing to be done for the wedding dress after all and Prue went down the aisle on the arm of Francis, who had two parts to play that day, and she was dressed in a sarong with flowers in her golden hair and more round her neck rather than in a bouquet in her hands.

Matthew was waiting surrounded by relatives; the only concession he made to European dress was the white shirt that he had tucked into the brightly coloured cloth wound round his waist.

Eleanor stood, her boys by her side, all of them unnaturally clean and solemn in their Sunday best. She watched Francis proudly, thinking how tall and handsome he was. She couldn't understand how she had missed noticing how distinguished he had grown with his dark eyes and full beard.

'—cleaving only unto him,' he was saying to Prue, 'as long as ye both shall live.' And she remembered the night before, how ardent he had been, so different from his cool, dignified self today and she felt warm all over, tingling warm. She picked up the paper fan from the ledge in front of her and fanned herself vigorously. 'God is Love' it read in English and in the local Fijian. Well, she hoped so.

The ceremony was over and the newly married couple were in the tiny room off the church that was used as a vestry, signing the register, when there was a murmur of sound from the door behind her.

The whole congregation was sitting, waiting to spring to their feet as the bridal party made its way out, and some heads turned in curiosity to see what it was. Eleanor was watching the vestry door, which was opening, and she was far more interested in that than any stray dog or pig or whatever coming into the church, but the boys had turned fully round and Francis William even stood on his seat to get a better look.

'It's a lady, Mam,' he announced loudly.

'It's Mary, Mam,' shouted John who was a big boy now and should have known better than to shout in church.

But the congregation was rising to their feet as the harmonium began to sound the wedding march, wheezing and spluttering a bit for the damp atmosphere of Lakeba was already affecting its parts, and Matthew strode down the aisle, though not with Prue on his arm; that would have been making one concession too many to European custom. She was only half a step behind him, however, and smiling with such brilliance that she rivalled the sun.

Chapter Twenty-six

'Come on, Ruth, eat your breakfast and afterwards we can walk down to the harbour,' said Mary. They were sitting on the verandah of the plantation house, the tiny girl drawing rings in her porridge and watching as they filled with milk. She looked up at her mother and attempted to make a bargain.

'Can I play with Juli if I eat it up?'

'You know Daddy doesn't like you to play with the children from the huts, Ruth,' said Mary. She bit her lip as she saw her daughter's disappointment. Ruth was so lonely without other children to play with but the last time she had allowed it Morgan had come home and there had been an almighty row that ended in her getting a black eye; Ruth had screamed and screamed and she had had to pick her up and run to stop him hitting Ruth too.

Ruth put down her spoon and left her seat to climb on Mary's knee where she peered over her shoulder at the track through the cotton fields.

'Daddy's coming,' she said and her hand curled into a tiny fist clutching at her mother's shoulder. A shaft of pain ran through Mary as her stomach knotted. She did not turn to see Morgan dismount from his horse and run up the steps.

'What's the matter with the brat now?' he said, striding over to the chair opposite and flinging himself down. The riding whip he was carrying started to tap rhythmically on the floor and his dark brows met in a scowl. He did not bother with any greeting.

'Nothing. We were just going for a walk, Ruth's looking forward to it.'

Morgan didn't reply; he hadn't even been listening to her answer, she realised. He was staring moodily at the cotton fields.

'There were only three buyers at the auction,' he said. 'And they were from Australia looking for a cheap bargain. Manchester doesn't want our cotton now, not since the South began to pick up.'

Mary felt a surge of joy; oh, how she would have loved to be there at the auction, to see him frustrated and humiliated. And he was all the arrogant businessman only last year. By, it was grand to see him brought down, she'd like to see him bankrupt.

Except it was Ruth's inheritance and she didn't want Ruth to end up penniless. And herself, she deserved to get something out of this marriage after all she had had to put up with over the years. But she had thought Ruth would be a real heiress and that they would go back to England triumphantly in diamonds and tiaras, whatever they were. No, if Ruth was to suffer it spoiled all the pleasure of seeing Morgan's enterprises going down.

'Haven't you got anything to say, you stupid peasant?' said Morgan.

'I'm sorry the business isn't doing well,' said Mary.

'I'll wager you are, if it means there's nothing for that mewling brat,' he snapped, surprising Mary by how close he was to what she had been thinking.

Mary felt Ruth tremble; poor bairn, she knew exactly who Morgan was talking about when he said brat. She probably thought it was her other name. Rising to her feet, she shifted the little girl's weight on to her hip.

'Where the hell are you going now?' Morgan asked.

'I promised Ruth—' she began but he interrupted impatiently.

'Oh yes, the little darling's walk. I don't matter any more, do I? Well, get out of my sight, the pair of you.'

She was going past his chair when he stuck out his leg to bar her progress. Now what? she thought. Was this some cat-and-mouse game he was playing just for his own amusement?

'Let me past, please,' she said, trying to keep her voice pleasant.

'I will, I will.' He thrust out a hand. 'I forgot, this letter came for you yesterday, you might as well have it.'

Yesterday. He had carried it around for a whole day. Mary snatched the letter and hurried off down the track, for if she had stayed she would have said what she thought and there would have been another row and Ruth couldn't stand that.

Once into the fields, she put Ruth down so she could run and skip about, talking to herself as she played another of her solitary games. There was no one in sight as Morgan had not sown so much cotton this year; there was not the work for the labourers and he had turned some off. Even the cotton gin was silent and there was an air of abandonment to the place though the storage sheds were still stuffed with last year's cotton.

Mary watched as Ruth began to pick wild flowers, then she sat down on a rock and opened her letter. It was from Prue, an invitation to her wedding. Wedding? Mary was surprised; she didn't even know Prue was courting.

'I am marrying Matthew. You will remember Matthew, the house man who works for Mr and Mrs Tait. Wish me happy, Mary, and try to come and bring little Ruth.'

Matthew? That arrogant Tongan, the one she herself had quarrelled with so often? How could Prue marry *him?* Mary was thunderstruck.

She glanced up automatically to check on Ruth. 'Don't wander too far, pet,' she called.

'No, Mam.'

Prue hadn't mentioned Morgan, but then she would know that he wouldn't go to her wedding. Mind, he'd be fit to be hog-tied, as he called it, if he thought his sister-in-law was marrying a Tongan. Mary grinned to herself at the thought. Best not tell him then.

The thing was, how to get over to Lakeba herself with Ruth. She wanted to go to her sister's wedding. She would have to find a way to get there without Morgan knowing about it. Rising to her feet, she dusted off her dress and called Ruth to her.

'Come on pet, we'll go to see if there are any ships in the bay, you like ships.'

They walked down to the quay but it was deserted; there was only Morgan's sloop riding at anchor and apparently no one aboard her. If only she could sail a ship, Mary thought dreamily, she would take Ruth and sail away and never come back to this God-forsaken place.

During the next few days Mary's mind worked endlessly on the problem of how she was going to get to Lakeba and time was running short. Morgan, unusually for him, stayed around the place, drinking himself silly then rolling down to the workers' compound, no doubt after women. She didn't inquire; she didn't care about that any more.

No ship entered the bay, though she and Ruth went down every morning to check. Not until Thursday of the following week, when, as they rounded the bend in the track, they saw it, a cargo ship, and the estate workers helping to load it with cotton bales, Wilson on the quay, shouting orders. Morgan must have sold some cotton after all.

The ship was Australian, registered in Sydney; she could see the inscription on a metal plate on the bow, half-obscured by rusty streaks. If she could only get aboard, surely the captain would take her, all the ships trading in these islands took the odd passenger. But there was Wilson to consider and she had no luggage with her though she already had a bag packed and hidden in her cupboard, just in case.

'Come on, Ruth, I'll see if the captain will let us go on board, would you like that?'

'Ooh, yes, Mam.'

The little girl took hold of Mary's hand and trotted by her side to the gangway.

'Where are you going, Mrs West?' demanded Wilson. 'Don't get in the way of the workers, I want the loading finished this morning. Anyway, the child might get knocked.'

Mary picked up Ruth and held her protectively. He was right, she couldn't risk that. 'Ruth wants to go on board, she likes ships,' she said.

'Aye, well, you can come back this afternoon, she's not sailing until high tide and that's not until six. You'll have to ask the captain though. Now, kindly get out of the way.' As usual, Wilson was showing her no respect at all but Mary disregarded it this time; she had more important things to think about.

The captain was at the top of the gangway and he heard some of this exchange.

'Aye, missus, bring the little lass down this afternoon, I'll show her round,' he called out in a strange mixture of Australian twang and Scottish. 'A nice dainty little lass she is.' He frowned his displeasure at Wilson and switched instantly to a friendly smile for Mary and Ruth. 'I'll enjoy having ye both.'

'Thank you, Captain. I'll see you this afternoon then.'

Now she had to find a way to get her bag down here without Morgan noticing, Mary thought, as she went back up the track with Ruth skipping by her side. As they neared the house and the figure of Morgan was apparent, sprawled on a chair, a glass of brandy in his hand, Ruth stopped skipping and moved in closer to her mother.

Mary looked down at her and her heart ached to see the anxious look that had appeared in Ruth's eyes; her lip quivered and she stared at her father compulsively. There was no reason to warn the child not to mention going on the ship, thought Mary. She never said anything to Morgan unless he forced her to.

Morgan grinned and sat up straighter in his chair. 'Come and sit by me, brat,' he said to Ruth. 'Why you always look so blasted scared of me I don't know. Come on now, come and sit by me.'

'Leave her alone, Morgan,' said Mary, putting a hand on Ruth's shoulder and feeling her trembling.

'Come and sit by me!' he roared suddenly and the child jumped with fright and scuttled to do his bidding.

'Morgan, don't—' Mary began. It didn't happen often but occasionally he had taken it into his head to tease the child, his idea of harmless fun, she supposed.

'Don't you tell me what to do, woman,' he growled. He got to his feet and filled his glass from the bottle on a side table. A bottle now almost empty that had been three-quarters full when she went out, Mary noticed. Dear Lord, don't let him hurt Ruth, she prayed. I'll kill him if he does, I will, I'll swing for him.

Morgan tossed the empty bottle into the bushes beneath the verandah and sat down by Ruth. 'Now then, Ruthie, talk to your pa.'

Ruth stared dumbly at him.

'Go on, you can talk, can't you, Ruthie?' He prodded her in the shoulder and her tiny frame fell back against the cushions.

'Don't touch her, Morgan,' Mary warned, starting forward. She stopped when Morgan took hold of the child and lifted her forward, thrusting her down hard on the edge of the chair. The bamboo frame must have hurt her but she didn't cry, simply carried on staring at her father, her blue eyes wide.

'Go to hell,' he snarled at Mary. 'This is my young'un, the only one you've seen fit to give me, poor brat of a female that she is. I'll make something of her yet if I have to kill her in the attempt.'

'And well you might, you're a bloody monster, a flaming cruel sod of an excuse for a man—'

Mary's temper, fuelled by anxiety for Ruth, broke but her tirade was cut short as he lurched to his feet and swiped her across the head with the back of his hand, making her stagger. She kept her feet however though her head was ringing and dark patches clouded her sight. She closed her eyes and when she opened them again she saw he was back in his seat beside Ruth.

'Mam! Mam!' cried the terrified child and he turned back to her but, before he could do anything more, Mary grabbed his gun, which was propped against the wall, and swung the butt at his head. The crack as the rifle met skin and bone was loud but Mary hardly heard it; she had picked up Ruth and carried her down the steps and round the corner into the uncleared brush.

'Stay still, pet, stay still,' she whispered, her breath ragged as she tried to control her panting. If he came anywhere near he would hear it, she was sure he would.

They must have stayed in that small hollow in the brush for hours; the sun was beginning to descend behind the hills when Mary finally moved.

He had not come after them; perhaps she had knocked him out cold. She had to get back into the house to get her bag – there could only be an hour or two before the Australian boat sailed.

'Stay here,' she said to Ruth, 'I won't be long, pet.'

Ruth whimpered softly but she nodded her assent, fear lurking in her eyes. I'll take that look away from her, vowed Mary to herself as she cautiously crept out of the underbrush so that she could see the verandah of the house.

Morgan had not stirred. The whole area was quiet; only Morgan's horse, still saddled and with reins dangling, grazed quietly by the side of the house. Dear God, had she killed Morgan? Mary went to him, kneeling before him to see. His eyes were closed and he was pale under his tan, a vivid bruise on his temple where she had struck him with the rifle, some blood oozing. He didn't appear to be breathing.

Mary sat back on her heels, thinking furiously. She had to get away, and the cargo ship was the perfect opportunity. Wilson would not come up to the house to report to Morgan until after supper, that was his custom. There was the horse though; he would give everything away unless she saw to him.

Fighting her fear of the animal, she managed to catch hold of the reins and tried to pull him away. He lifted his head and regarded her, then calmly went back to his grazing. He had her summed up properly, she thought savagely. Grabbing a hold of the ring close to the bit, she pulled again.

'Come on, you brute!'

Surprised as much by the tone of command as by her show of force, he followed her obediently. She took him round the back of the house to the stable and fastened him in and sped into the house by the kitchen door. The bag was in the cupboard; now all she had to do was pick up Ruth and go. She glanced once at the verandah as she went past, seeing Morgan still lying there, exactly as he was before. Then she turned away resolutely, determined not to look back. Which was a pity, for if she had she would have seen him turn his head, groan and lift his hand to the bruise at his temple.

Ruth was still sitting where she had been left, her thin face looking even more pinched and blue shadows under her eyes.

'Come on, pet,' said Mary and the little girl ran to her. 'We're not just going to see the ship, we're going for a sail on it to see your Aunty Prue.'

*

As she had thought would happen, the captain was pleased to take her and Ruth to Lakeba. 'It's a wedding,' she said to him. 'My sister is getting married.'

'Captain West isn't going with you?' he asked, but it was only with a mild interest; no doubt he thought Morgan had business elsewhere.

'Not this time,' she answered. Not ever again, she thought, feeling a stab of fear that was an actual pain in her stomach. It was not for herself but Ruth; what would happen to the child if her mother was hanged for murder? Her mind shied away from the thought.

Still, she would be with Prue, Prue was family, and she would see Ruth came to no harm. And then there were the Taits. Francis was an upright man, he would make sure the child got what was due to her, she could depend on him and Eleanor. If she asked Eleanor she would send Ruth home to her uncle, of course she would. If the worst happened.

A knock on the door of her cabin broke into her dark thoughts. She had been awake all night going over and over it all, she realised.

'Come in.'

It was a seaman who was acting as steward. 'Captain says to tell you we will be docking in Lakeba in an hour or so,' he said, poking his head round the door.

Mary felt a surge of gladness. Thank God they had made it, now Ruth would be all right no matter what happened to her.

Chapter Twenty-seven

A photographer had set up his studio on the main street in Bau and he had followed the wedding party to Lakeba. So Prue stood proudly in her wedding finery, first with Matthew and then surrounded by his family, uncles and aunts and cousins besides brothers and sisters. Then she stood with her own sister by her side.

'Mary looks terrible,' Eleanor whispered to Francis. In fact, Mary was hard to recognise she was so gaunt, with hollows in her cheeks where before there had been dimples. Fortunately, the bruise on the side of her head was fading; perhaps it wouldn't show up on the photographs. Eleanor shuddered to think how she had got it; only a heavy blow could do that.

Ruth went willingly to Eleanor while her mother posed with Prue, though she shrank away from Francis at first and wouldn't look at the boys.

'She's shy, that's all,' Eleanor said to Francis William, who was fascinated by the tiny girl and wanted her to play a game with him.

'She's like a little doll, Mam,' he said and Eleanor agreed. Ruth was far too small for her age, she looked as though she could do with a few good dinners; why, she was almost as thin as Prue had been at her age. Surely Ruth had been getting enough food? No, it was something else that was holding the child back, putting such shadows in her eyes. It bothered Eleanor, both as a nurse and a mother. Why, the child hardly spoke except to her mother, she was so painfully shy.

She did speak once, however, when the wedding party sat down to the feast, a traditional Tongan feast with sucking pig, succulent island chicken and fish and exotic vegetables.

Ruth was feeling a little emboldened; she saw the other children running around, laughing and shouting at each other and she saw that neither Francis nor any of the other men seemed to be angry about it. Why, Francis even smiled when John bumped into him, making him stagger to keep his balance.

'Are these black bastards eating with us?' she asked her mother. And it would happen there was a lull in the music and chattering noise and her piping voice was heard clearly around the wedding party.

Francis William's mouth dropped open. The doll had spoken, she had not just spoken, she had said a bad word, a very bad word.

'You won't go to heaven,' he declared, shocked to the core.

Ruth felt every eye upon her, blushed a fiery red and hid her face in her mother's skirts.

'I'm sorry,' said Mary, almost as embarrassed as her daughter. 'It's just something she has heard, she doesn't know what it means, really she doesn't.' She was mortified. Morgan had talked like that all the time but she hadn't realised that Ruth had picked it up.

'You mustn't say such things, pet,' she whispered to Ruth.

The child lifted a woebegone face and whispered back, 'Pa does.'

Mary couldn't deny it. 'Yes, but Daddy shouldn't say it either.'

'Children who say nasty things to hurt other people should be whipped,' observed John in exactly his father's tone of voice when he himself was in trouble. He had never been whipped in his life but Ruth had. And she began to weep, great heartrending sobs that shook her small frame convulsively.

'Boys! Come away now,' said Eleanor, rising to her feet and taking charge. 'Now, do you hear? As you can't mind your own business you will have to sit at the other end, away from nice polite people.'

It was Matthew who brought the situation back to normal. Leaving Prue, he went and sat down beside Mary and Ruth. He picked up a snowy ball of sugar flavoured with coconut and held it out to the little girl.

'You like sweets, Ruth?' he asked. She peeped at him from behind a fold in her mother's skirt.

He picked up another, a dark brown one flavoured with chocolate. 'Maybe you like this better?'

Ruth looked up at her mother and saw she was smiling encouragement. She nodded and sniffed and Mary wiped her eyes with her handkerchief.

'You mean you like this one? Or this one?' Matthew held one sweet out and then the other. Ruth pointed at the chocolate one.

'You like the *black* one?' Matthew managed to put just the right degree of incredulity into his voice.

'Yes,' said Ruth. She stared at the sweets and her mouth watered.

'You're sure you don't like the white one?'

'Yes, yes I do, they're both nice,' said Ruth a little louder. 'But I like chocolate the best.'

'Well then, I think you'd better have both,' said Matthew and handed them over before rising to his feet and going back to the seat of honour.

'The colour doesn't matter, does it?' he said over his shoulder. He didn't wait for her reply and in any case, her mouth was stuffed with a gooey mass of chocolate and coconut.

Around her, the noise had started up again, the incident over. The Tongans were far too polite and understanding of children to take offence at what Ruth had said, Mary realised. She watched Matthew as he sat down beside Prue and saw the smiling welcome she gave him. Prue would be all right, she thought. She is in love.

There was little chance for her to speak to Prue privately before the newly-weds embarked in Matthew's canoe for the tiny island where they were to spend their honeymoon. But, as she hugged her sister goodbye, Prue whispered in her ear.

'That bloody Morgan West has done something to you, I can tell. Promise me you won't go back to him, Mary, promise me.'

'Well—' Mary thought briefly that she would be taken back as soon as Morgan's body was discovered. She desperately wanted to tell Prue all about it, she felt she would lose her reason if she didn't but how could she spoil her sister's happy day?

'At least until I get back to Bau?' Prue was insisting and Mary nodded.

'I won't,' she said and stood back as the canoe was launched and the couple set off in a sea of flowers. Eleanor came and stood beside her.

'Come with us to Bau, Mary, you and little Ruth are welcome to stay for as long as you like. It will be lovely to have you,' she said, slipping her arm through Mary's. 'If Morgan is coming for you, he can easily come on to Bau and he can stay too.' Though I hope he doesn't, she thought. Francis and he would argue again, she knew it.

'I don't think Morgan will come,' said Mary. 'But I'll be glad to, Ruth too.'

They sailed back to Bau with the evening tide on a soft and balmy night under a sky sparkling with stars. Francis and Eleanor sat on deck, enjoying the quiet after the noise and clamour of the wedding day, and Mary was down below persuading Ruth to go to sleep without her.

'Promise me you'll stay beside me, Mam,' Ruth said.

'I'll stay until you go to sleep, then I'll just be on deck.'

'The bogey man might get me if I'm on my own and you won't get down in time to save me.'

'I'll look after you, Ruth,' said Francis William. The boys were bedded down in the top bunk.

'But Daddy says that the bogey man will get me if I don't watch out.'

The boys thought about this in silence then John said, 'Well, *our* daddy says there's no such things as bogeymen. He says that Jesus and the angels look after us when we are asleep. He looks after all children.'

Ruth digested this for a moment or two. 'But you will look after me an' all,' she said.

'Me and Francis William, both.'

'You can sit up on deck, Mam,' she decided. 'But you'll be at the top of the stairs, won't you?'

'Of course, pet,' answered her mother and Ruth settled down, comforted.

'There is something very wrong with Mary,' Francis observed to Eleanor. 'I don't just mean her physical condition either, she looks so unhappy.'

'I know. Ruth too, she worries me a lot.'

Just then Mary came on deck and they began to talk of other things. But Eleanor was determined to get Mary to confide in her; she had brought the sisters out to Fiji and somehow she still felt responsible for them, quite apart from the fact that Mary was a friend.

'I hope you can stay a while with us, Mary,' she said. 'We have so much to catch up on and it's nice to talk over old times back in Hetton.'

Mary looked up at the moon, three-quarters full and casting a silver track over the sea. 'I hope so too,' she said. Hetton seemed as far away as the moon, she thought, and just as difficult to reach.

It was three days later on a sunny Tuesday morning, made even more brilliant by the bright red parakeets flying among

242

the trees, that it happened. It was a quiet morning; Francis had been summoned to see the king and Mary and Eleanor were sitting on the verandah of the mission house as they did every morning. Ruth was playing with Edward and Francis William, who was by now her devoted servant. They were in the corner of the verandah playing a complicated game that involved upturned chairs forming a canoe and an old shawl of Eleanor's as a sail.

'Francis is doing so well here,' Eleanor was saying. 'The people like him.'

'He deserves to do well. He works hard, I've seen that since I—' Mary broke off what she was saying and Eleanor glanced up inquiringly as she saw her friend was staring out to sea.

'There's a sail,' she said. 'Oh, I think it's Morgan's ship. What a shame, do you think he wants to take you home today?'

Mary didn't answer; she had one hand to her throat and the colour had left her face. She looked over to Ruth, who had a walking stick and was pretending it was a paddle; she was paddling with all her energy while Francis William fiddled with the sail, which would insist on falling down.

'Mary?'

Eleanor frowned. Mary was terrified but what was so terrifying about Morgan coming today?

'What is it?' she asked. Mary suddenly jumped to her feet.

'Eleanor, take the children somewhere, will you? Out of the way, I mean. Anywhere will do, so long as they don't see.'

'Don't see what? What are you talking about?'

'Please, Eleanor, just do as I ask you. Please! Take Ruth and the boys, just take them away.'

Eleanor bit her lip. 'If something's going to happen, if Morgan's angry with you – did he not know you were coming here? – surely he won't be *so* angry? Don't worry, Mary.'

'Take the children!' Mary was almost shouting now and Ruth stopped her paddling and dropped the stick. She came to her mother's side and took hold of her hand, her tiny face suddenly older with a furrowed brow and anxiety in her eyes.

'Mam?' she said. 'Is Daddy coming?'

'No, pet, he isn't,' said Mary as she put Ruth's hand in Eleanor's. 'Now go with Aunt Eleanor and be a good girl, the boys will go with you.'

'I don't know what it is but I don't want to leave you,' said Eleanor doubtfully, then she saw Mary's expression. 'I'll go, I'll go, come on, boys, we'll go to the king's house to meet your daddy, shall we?'

For a moment Mary thought Ruth would make a fuss and refuse to go but the little girl was used to hurrying out of the way of trouble and in the end she went off, with Eleanor holding one hand and Francis William the other.

After they had gone, Mary sat where she was as the ship docked, feeling strangely calm. I wonder why they are using Morgan's sloop? she asked herself but she didn't really care. They would come up the street for her; perhaps she ought to go inside, she didn't want to be arrested on the balcony of the mission house, in full view of everyone, that wouldn't do Francis's prospects any good.

Francis. She should have told him all about the fight with Morgan but she hadn't even got around to telling Eleanor, somehow the words wouldn't come. Rising to her feet, she went inside and sat down on the sofa with her back to the open door that led on to the verandah.

She sat quietly, straining to hear the first sound of approaching footsteps, but all she could hear was the ticking of the grandmother clock on the wall. Then abruptly the silence shattered and she felt someone standing behind her, blocking out the morning sun.

'Come out of there, you murdering female, or, by God, I'll force you out with this whip!'

Morgan, it was Morgan's voice! Oh, she must be dreaming, Morgan was dead. She was dreaming or it was his ghost come back from the grave to get her. She sat immobile with shock. And he was towering over her, grabbing her upper arms and dragging her to her feet, holding her almost off her feet, only her toes touching the ground.

'Yes, it's me, your loving husband,' he said. His dark brows met over his nose as he glared at her and yet smiled at the same time. 'You useless, barren peasant of an excuse for a woman! You would kill me, would you? You couldn't even manage to finish that job properly.'

Mary stared up into his face; she couldn't say anything. He loosed his grip on one arm and held her in the air with the other as he pulled his riding whip from his belt. Flinging her down on the sofa, he grinned.

'I'm going to give you the hiding of your life, and, boy, am I going to enjoy doing it!'

He lifted the whip and brought it down with all the force of his arm across her breasts and Mary screamed; she couldn't help herself, the pain was agonising. She tried to scramble from the sofa but he caught her with one hand and laughed.

'I told you I would enjoy this,' he said, 'go on, struggle, it makes it all the better.'

'Leave her alone!'

Mary opened her eyes in horror and what she saw almost made her forget the pain. It was John who shouted – he must have been in the house somewhere, she had forgotten about him. And he had launched his slight frame on to Morgan's back and was clinging to him with all the agility of a monkey. He tugged at Morgan's fair hair, pulling his head back, poking him in the eyes, the ears, anything.

Morgan dropped the whip and growled. Putting one hand over his shoulder, he caught hold of John by the scruff of the neck and pulled him off, holding him in the air for a moment before flinging him on to the floor.

The boy lay stunned for a second and Mary found her feet and flew at Morgan, head down, catching him in the stomach. He grunted and went back an involuntary step.

'Run!' she cried. 'Run, John, go!' He was beginning to get up but instead of running, he was turning back to Morgan. Oh dear Lord, he was going to be killed! Morgan would snap him in two, he was in such a drunken rage he would do it. She had to keep his attention on her.

'Yes, I thought you were dead,' she shouted. 'I wanted you dead for what you did to us, me and my bairn, I wanted you in Hell!'

She was backing away from John all the time, trying to draw Morgan after her, through the kitchen, anywhere away from John, but suddenly he had hold of her again, she couldn't move and John was trying to jump on his back again.

She had opened her mouth to scream when suddenly, miraculously, John disappeared and in his place was Francis. He threw his arm around Morgan's neck in a hold that turned his face purple until Morgan loosed his grip on her and she fell to the floor as the whole world went black.

When she came round she was lying on the sofa and John was sitting beside his mother. Eleanor's arms were around him and he was holding on to her hand as though it were a lifebelt.

Cautiously, Mary lifted her head, wincing as she felt the stinging of the weal across her breasts where the whip had struck.

'Francis?' she asked shakily. 'He's not hurt, is he?'

'No,' said Eleanor and Mary could see that she too was trembling with shock. 'He's just making sure Morgan is properly secured until the police come.'

Mary went to the door and gulped in great breaths of fresh air before rushing back in. 'Ruth? Where's Ruth?'

'Don't worry, she's safe. I left her, Francis William and Edward in the village, the women will look after them.'

Mary closed her eyes for a moment. 'John saved my life,' she said.

'He's a brave boy,' agreed his mother. But Mary could see she was haunted by the thought of what could have happened to him. Did Eleanor blame her for not warning them of what might happen? She couldn't blame her if she did.

Chapter Twenty-eight

Francis, despite his respected position in the islands, was not able to have Morgan kept in custody for long.

'She is my wife and I have the right to chastise her if I think she deserves it,' Morgan said to the police chief and Francis had to agree. Civilisation had come to Fiji and with it, western laws.

'You had no right to touch my son,' Francis insisted. At least he could do something about that; hurting John had been an offence, surely?

'He attacked me,' Morgan pointed out.

The policeman smiled at the idea of a seven-year-old boy attacking a mature man. 'A seven-year-old boy is a warrior?' he asked.

Francis went back to the mission house. 'In return for suspending the charge of bodily harm against John, Captain West is to be deported,' he told the two women. 'He will be allowed to return to the plantation only to collect his personal belongings.' He did not say that the deal had included Morgan leaving his wife and child in the care of himself. That part of the bargain was unofficial. Morgan had laughed when Francis proposed it.

'I don't want the pair of them hanging round my neck,' he had said. 'The brat is unlikely to reach womanhood and I want a real heir. I'll find me a southern woman, a lady, not poor white trash.'

Naturally Francis did not report Morgan's comments at home.

'What about the house and plantation?' asked Mary, thinking of her old dream of Ruth's inheritance.

'You can go back for your personal belongings too,' he said. 'But the fact is –' he glanced at Eleanor, feeling embarrassed at being the bearer of even more bad news – 'the fact is, there has been a lot of trouble with foreigners coming in and practically stealing land from the natives. Obtaining it fraudulently at least. And now there is some speculation about the islands being ceded to Britain, the government at home want everything to be strictly above board.'

He paused before adding gently, 'I'm sorry, Mary, you will get very little from the plantation. Morgan had no proper title to it. But you need not worry, you are welcome to make your home with us, both you and little Ruth.'

Mary looked down at the floor for a moment. That was that then, no fortune for Ruth, nothing. Strangely she didn't feel as disappointed as she had thought she would.

'All gone, eh? Like snowflakes on the oven top as my gran would say. Grandda was a great one for pitch and toss on pay night, many's the time he'd come home with all his pay gone. I don't think the Buckles were meant to be rich. Still, at least I'm rid of that b—' She stopped abruptly as Francis lifted his eyebrows in shock.

'Well, I am,' she mumbled. 'I don't think I'll go back to the plantation, there's nothing there I want.'

It has all worked out very well, really, thought Eleanor as she walked down the street to Matthew's house one morning with the usual basket of medical supplies over her arm, for afterwards she was doing her rounds. Mary had slipped easily into her old position in the household though she, Eleanor, was older now and treated Mary more as a friend than a servant.

Prue and Matthew lived out since their marriage and Prue's baby was due any day; in fact Eleanor was going to check her out to see if she could gauge when the birth would happen.

Every time Eleanor saw Prue, she was struck by how happy she was. She was plump, even considering she was heavily pregnant, and she wore her hair long so that her blonde curls hung down her back. With her tanned complexion the effect was striking, Prue was an extremely beautiful woman.

'I'm still waiting, you see.' Prue stepped back from the door so Eleanor could come in. 'Mala's wife says I will have the baby soon, probably today. Though if that's right there are no signs so far.' She laughed and the sound was contented and musical.

Eleanor examined her on the sleeping mat that Prue had woven herself, with some help from Matthew's female relatives. It was covered with intricate patterns in bright colours and, to a western woman like Eleanor, surprisingly comfortable.

As she palpated Prue's abdomen she could feel that the baby's head was indeed well down; it would not be long now.

'Mala's wife is probably right,' she said.

Prue looked embarrassed. 'Er ...' she began and stopped.

'Is there something, Prue?'

'Yes. Matthew, well, Matthew thinks I should have her to help me when the baby comes.'

'Who, Mala's wife? Oh, but ...' Eleanor started to protest, then stopped. She was disappointed; she had thought that naturally she herself would help deliver Prue's baby. But, of course, it was not her right if Matthew did not want her to. And she didn't want Prue to be upset at all, not just now.

'Well, if that's what you want,' she said, turning away and busying herself with her basket to hide her disappointment. 'It is up to you and Matthew, Prue. Did I tell you my John was delivered by the local women? They are very good of course.'

As soon as she could, Eleanor made her excuses and went on her way. Prue was leaving them, she thought sadly, she was leaving them as surely as she had left the time she ran away with that seaman. She hadn't even asked after her sister Mary.

'I have something important to tell you,' said Francis that afternoon. They were sitting at dinner, Eleanor, the three boys with the youngest, Edward, propped up on two cushions, and Ruth. There was a place set for Mary but she was busy serving the meal of chicken and vegetables before she sat down. The days were long gone when Mary or Prue had been expected to eat in the kitchen.

'Leave the tray there, Mary, don't go out, I want you to hear, it too,' said Francis. He waited until she slid into her seat before continuing.

'Now that the hill tribes are more or less quiet –' he gave Eleanor an anxious glance but she seemed not to be disturbed or reminded of the boys' abduction by mention of the tribesmen – 'well, now that things are quiet, the king is to be crowned. There is to be a grand coronation.'

'Will there be a feast, Daddy?' asked Francis William.

'Don't interrupt your father,' Eleanor said automatically.

'There will be a feast. But first of all I have been asked to preach at the service. I am to give the coronation address and also the sermon. The king has asked for me in particular to do it.'

'Oh! Congratulations, Francis, I'm sure it's a great honour,' Eleanor exclaimed, leaving her seat to kiss him on the cheek, whereupon Francis looked embarrassed and glanced at Mary to see if she had noticed. She, however, was thinking of what his news meant to her and was in too much turmoil to notice anything.

'I'm sure I'm very pleased for you,' she murmured and rose to take the tray out to the kitchen.

Francis was doing so well here on Bau, she thought. It didn't look like he would ever want to go back to England.

Oh, they were so good to her, of course they were, and it was ungrateful of her but she so wanted to go back to England that it felt like a disease, a canker, eating away at her.

Back at the table, John was looking puzzled. 'I thought he was king already,' he said.

'Yes, he is,' agreed his father. 'But they will put a crown on his head and I will give a speech and then there will be a service in church. The crown will be something like the queen wears on the stamps that come from England. Now, boys, hurry up, it's time for your lessons.'

Recently Francis William and Ruth had joined John in the mission school that was now run by Miss Tookey, the teacher who had come out from England on the same ship as the Taits. She ran the school with a rod of iron and the children scrambled from the table and rushed to get ready, for any child who was late was liable to get a sore bottom from her cane.

Francis, too, had to hurry off and when she was alone, Eleanor went into the kitchen where Mary was washing up the dishes in a galvanised dish and Eleanor was dismayed to see that she was weeping, the tears falling into the washing-up water unheeded. When she saw Eleanor's face, she dried her eyes on the corner of her apron.

'Don't take any notice of me,' she said. 'I'm just feeling homesick. I'm so heartily fed up of the heat and the damp and the insects and the rats ...'

'Oh, stop,' said Eleanor. 'Or you'll have me joining in. But I didn't know you were so unhappy.' Though why she shouldn't, she didn't know. Mary had plenty to be unhappy about; this land had not treated her very well.

That evening, when she and Francis were alone in their room, she brought up the subject of Mary and her unhappiness.

'I wish we could find enough for her fare home,' she said wistfully. 'I feel responsible for everything that has happened to her.'

'The Lord gave us free will,' commented Francis. 'Mary too.'

'A lot of good free will is if you haven't the wherewithal to do what you want to do,' retorted Eleanor. Francis regarded her solemnly but held his peace until the lamp was out and she was in his arms.

'I will see what is to be done,' he said.

Not much, thought Eleanor. Though his quarterly stipend had arrived, it was much too small to allow for such extras as two tickets back to England. And Mary would need money when she got to England; she and Ruth would have to travel by rail from the south coast to Durham and then she would have to rely on her brother to provide a home for her until she could obtain a position. Something that might not be easy when she had Ruth with her. Oh yes, a lot of money would be needed, she thought sleepily.

Prue had her baby during the night, a healthy boy. The first the women in the mission house heard of it was when Matthew came to work the next morning. Mary and Eleanor walked down to see the mother and child. To their surprise, Prue was already sitting up in a chair, looking as if nothing had happened, except that she was thinner.

The baby was in a sort of crib, suspended from the wooden beams of the roof and swaying gently in the wind.

'Oh, he has blue eyes, just like yours,' exclaimed Eleanor, surprised.

'They will probably darken, don't all babies have blue eyes?' Prue smiled gently. She looked so happy it made tears spring to Eleanor's eyes, for surely happiness such as Prue's couldn't last.

'Oh, he's so beautiful,' sighed Mary. And it was true; his skin was olive, contrasting with the fuzz of fair hair on the top of his head.

'Mind he is, isn't he?' said Prue, jumping up and moving to the crib, gazing down at her son, and he gazed back at her with unfocused eyes.

'Prue! Sit down at least, it's far too early for you to be up.' Eleanor was horrified but Prue simply laughed and picked up the baby and took him back to her seat where she commenced feeding him, quite unabashed.

'I am taking things easy,' she said, 'for today at least.'

'We'll go and let you get some rest,' said Eleanor. 'If you need anything, just ask Matthew to let me know.'

'I don't think she needs anything from us,' Mary remarked as they walked back to the mission house. 'Prue has all she needs.' Eleanor glanced at her; did she sound a little wistful? Prue had been almost a daughter to Mary when they were young.

The coronation of King Thakembau was a great success, especially from the point of view of the children, who had a holiday from school.

Representatives from the king of Tonga came and all the petty chiefs of the islands, as well as most of the missionaries and their families so that Bau was teeming with people. The sombre black garb of the Methodist ministers mingled with the bright colours of the others.

But it was Francis whom Thakembau kept by his side throughout the actual ceremony of the coronation, held, as was the custom, before the long house in the open air. Francis was the king's confidant and it was he who gave the coronation address. Eleanor realised, as she sat with Mary and the children to watch the spectacle and afterwards in the church to hear the blessing, also given by Francis, that her husband was most important to the king.

She felt a touch of anxiety as he started his sermon; he had used his voice quite a lot already that day and he had to clear his throat a few times. But even though he was husky, he was commanding in his address and in any case, the congregation was quiet and attentive. Sometimes she wasn't entirely convinced that all of the Fijians had truly accepted Christianity, though she wasn't sure what made her think so. Perhaps it was simply fear of the king that kept them in order.

'At least the children enjoyed the feast,' remarked Mary afterwards. 'I only hope they aren't sick during the night.'

Next morning Francis, along with his fellow missionaries and the other guests, was off on his travels again.

'I will be away a full week, Eleanor,' he said as she was packing his bag. 'You know there are still some of the mountain people who still believe in the old gods. We must do what we can for them.'

Eleanor walked with him to the ship, her hand on his arm. She waited until they cast off and waved to him as the sails billowed out in the breeze and it began to make speed. At last she was beginning to know him, what he did and why he did it, after all these years. Ten, was it? Yes, almost ten.

It was time to fetch the children from school, almost midday. They always had a rest in the middle of the day, especially in the hottest part of the year.

They were singing a hymn, as they always did at the end of the morning session, their voices shrilling out over the hot air of the dusty street. She waited, content to stand in the shade of the overhanging roof, thinking about Francis. The verse from Acts 14 ran through her head:

> 'I have set thee to be a light of the Gentiles,
> That thou shouldest be for Salvation unto
> the ends of the earth.'

Even the savage hill tribes of Fiji, that meant. But still, the thought that Francis might be going in their direction sent a shiver of apprehension through her.

Chapter Twenty-nine

Eleanor was sweating with terror; she fought to rise from her bed but she was bound hand and foot, there was nothing she could do. The warriors were here, in the house, in the bedroom, they were running through the house, smashing the furniture with their clubs, laughing and yelling at each other. She opened her mouth to scream but no sound came out. Dear God, the children, please don't let them get the children, she thought frantically. Mary, where was Mary?

'I'll save you,' said a voice and she managed to turn her head to see Morgan West, strolling almost casually to the bed, leaning over her. The smell was rank as he grinned and reached out a hand and he was holding a knife with a long, curved blade, it glinted as it came nearer her neck. Suddenly she got her voice back and screamed and the sound reverberated round the house.

She opened her eyes and the room was quiet, the furniture was not smashed to pieces and Mary was standing by the side of her bed, a glass of water in her hand.

'Please, Eleanor,' she said. 'Take a drink, come on, you will feel better for it. You must be thirsty.'

'I am,' said Eleanor but it came out as a croak. She caught hold of Mary's hand, held the glass to her mouth and drank; the water was sweet and cool; Matthew must have brought it from the spring.

She lay back on her pillow, panting slightly, and Mary wiped her mouth with a napkin. The nightmare was still with her, on the edge of her consciousness, and she looked around the room anxiously. The sun was filtering through the muslin curtains, lighting up the corners. There was nothing there, nothing but the familiar things, no tribesmen, no clubs or spears, no Morgan West.

'I was dreaming,' she said shakily and smiled in self-deprecation. 'I didn't alarm the children by screaming?'

'No, you didn't scream, you must have dreamed that an' all,' said Mary. She had a bowl of water and a piece of flannel and she began to wash Eleanor's face and neck; the water was cool on her skin.

I've been ill.'

'Yes. But you're all right now, the fever has broken.'

'Fever?'

Anxiety rushed through Eleanor. What about the children? Dear Lord, she prayed, not the fever, not the cholera? Please God, not the cholera.

'The children are all right, Francis has taken them to Lakeba with him, away from the infection. Dysentry. Whether it came with the crowds that were here for the coronation—'

'Francis has been back?'

'The day before yesterday. You have been ill five days.'

Eleanor was silent, thinking about it. Absently, she let Mary take off her nightdress and sponge her body, lifting her head obediently as clean linen was put on her.

> 'Blow the wind southerly, southerly, southerly,
> Blow the wind south o'er the bonnie blue sea.'

The sound of the old Tyneside song brought Eleanor's rambling thoughts back to the present; Mary was singing softly as she worked, barely breathing the words. Her face had a bloom to it, something that Eleanor had not seen in many a long day; she actually looked happy. It was positively indecent when she herself felt so weak and ill.

'I'm glad you're so happy about me having the fever,' she said peevishly. 'Is there anything else I can do for you?'

'Eeh, I'm sorry, I wasn't even thinking of the fever.' Mary was stricken. 'And there have been some deaths in the village an' all and here am I, singing. I don't know what it's like with the folk that were here, Mr Tait says Mr Calvert was ill but he's recovered. Any road, you're getting better now, aren't you?'

Eleanor sighed. 'I'm sorry, Mary, and after you've cared for me. I just feel so weary and worn, I shouldn't have snapped.'

Mary collected the dish and towels and went to the door. 'Aye, well, you go on to sleep now, I'll do some chicken soup for your dinner and no doubt you'll feel a lot better the morn.' She went out, closing the door quietly behind her, and Eleanor sank down into the bed and closed her eyes. As she teetered on the edge of sleep, she felt comforted somehow by Mary's words, '... you'll feel a lot better the morn.' That was what her mother used to say when she had had some childish ailment back in Durham. Mary still talked like that even after all these years and it sounded so good, the sound of home.

There was something else about Mary though, she had forgotten to ask her, what was it? But the thought was lost. Eleanor fell into a deep, untroubled sleep.

Eleanor was wrapped in shawls in spite of the heat and sitting in the bamboo chair in a corner of the balcony, well out of the reach of draughts, when Francis and the children came home. John saw her there as he walked up the street by his father's side.

'Mother!' he cried and broke into a run. Francis William was hand in hand with Ruth and they followed at Ruth's slower pace while Edward, sitting on his father's shoulders, waved and shouted and struggled to get down.

'You're better then, praise the Lord,' said Francis as he reached the house and climbed the steps to her. The boys were scrambling over her, hugging and kissing her, shouting over each other about where they had been and what they had done.

'Now, John, take your brothers out to the kitchen and tell Mary I want to see her,' he said. Only when they were alone did he kiss her gently and take her hand. 'You do feel better? I had the note from Mary to say you were, but I must say you look very pale and haven't you lost weight?'

His voice was very husky today, Eleanor noticed; sometimes it was getting difficult to hear what he had to say at all. As she reassured him about her own health, she couldn't help a shiver of apprehension; surely he wasn't going to lose his voice altogether? That would be too cruel when his whole life was built around his preaching.

'You wanted to speak to me, Mr Tait?' Mary interrupted her thoughts.

'Yes, come and sit down, Mary, I have good news. It's about the property, the plantation.'

Both women looked at him in surprise. Mary had already told Eleanor that Francis had managed to sell the machinery from the cotton gin to a buyer from the Philippines. That was why Mary had looked so happy that day. The money was sufficient for the tickets back to England and also there would be a small amount left over. Mary had already written to her brother in Hetton, asking him if she could stay with him until she found a position as a housemaid or, perhaps, a children's nurse.

'Of course, I will have to make certain that Morgan cannot claim anything, though I have made inquiries and I am assured that he cannot, not in the circumstances. No, it belongs to Ruth, and you, Mary, as her guardian have control.'

Eleanor was puzzled. 'But surely, Francis, once Mary has bought her tickets, there will not be enough left to make it worth Morgan's while to claim anything, will there?'

Francis smiled and sat back in his chair looking pleased with himself. 'Well, as it happens, there will. At least fifteen hundred pounds over. I have sold the remainder of the cotton that was stored in the warehouses. To the same buyer as I sold the machinery.'

'Fifteen hundred pounds? Francis, you're joking!'

It was Eleanor who spoke; Mary was too stunned.

'I am not joking, Eleanor. I told you I would do my best, didn't I?'

Mary found her voice at last. 'Fifteen hundred pounds? You mean to say I have fifteen hundred pounds? Over and above the price of our tickets home an' all?'

'That's right. Quite enough for you to buy a little house in Hetton or Durham or even by the sea. I'm sure you will be able to buy a nice little house, with a garden if you wish, for three hundred pounds. Why, if you're careful, you should have enough to live on, at least while Ruth is a minor.'

'Eeh, but . . .' Mary paused, the elation that had lit her face for a few moments dying. 'What about Morgan? If he hears, he'll likely come for it, won't he?'

'He won't, take my word for it. In any case I had the bank draft put in your name, as Ruth is a minor.' What Francis didn't say was that there was a rumour that Morgan's sloop had been shipwrecked on its way to Hawaii. He thought about telling her but decided against it; after all, there was no absolute proof. He ran over what he had found out in his mind.

Hawaii was reported to have been Morgan's destination and from there he was supposed to be going to San Francisco. Francis had even written to the church in Hawaii asking for news of Morgan's movements, for he didn't trust him not to sneak back to Fiji if he saw any advantage in doing so.

A report had come from a minister in Hawaii to the effect that the sloop had never arrived and nothing had been heard of Morgan West.

'There is talk of a wreck of an unknown sloop on an island not thirty miles from here,' the minister had written. 'It must have happened during the last typhoon, I believe. I regret to tell you this if the owner was a friend of yours. Please let me know if you need any further information.'

'You really think he will have no legal claim?' Mary was persistent and Francis thought for a moment before answering.

'Well, you would have to ask a lawyer about that to be absolutely sure. But I have consulted with the authorities here and I am convinced that he will not make a claim. After all, he cannot come back to Fiji without laying himself open to the charge of bodily harm to John, and fifteen hundred pounds is not enough for him to chance that.'

'Fifteen hundred! By, it's a fortune to us, though,' said Mary, sinking back into her chair and already beginning to plan how to use the money. She and Ruth might not be going home in diamonds and tiaras, but, by, they would make a splash in Hetton-le-Hole.

'I'll never be able to thank you enough, Mr Tait,' she said formally as she rose to her feet. 'An' little Ruth an' all.'

After she had gone back into the kitchen where she was preparing fish for the afternoon meal, Eleanor kissed Francis on the cheek, automatically glancing down the street first to make sure no one was watching. That was something else she was beginning to respect about Francis; he didn't like public displays of affection from her, so why should she embarrass him?

'You went to a lot of trouble to do that for Mary, didn't you?' she asked.

'Well, if I start something I like to see it through,' he replied, but nevertheless he wore a small, pleased smile.

'I remember how you were so against my bringing the two Buckle girls in the first place.'

Francis pulled his chair close to hers. 'We all can be a little foolish when we are young.'

He began gazing down the street at the people walking about, going into and out of the store or stopping to talk to each other on the shady side. Most of the Fijians were dressed in a mixture of western dress and Fijian, a shirt on top of a wrap-around, bark-cloth skirt in the traditional pattern, though some were in trousers. A few were still practically naked but for a loin cloth and armlet of shark's teeth but the sight of a bare chest no longer bothered him as it had at first.

'There are more people on the street than there have been since the king's coronation,' he said. 'We must give thanks that the epidemic is over, on this island at least.'

'Yes, dear,' said Eleanor.

The community got back to normal eventually, as it did after every visitation of one fever or another, though the particularly virulent type of dysentry had claimed quite a number of victims. The cemetery on the outskirts of the village, which was fast becoming a town, had a row of new graves, both in the Fijian section and the European. It had claimed a number of fatalities among the beachcombers, mostly white, mostly English, though there were Australians and South Africans and some from the Philippines amongst them.

Mary planned to leave as soon as Eleanor got her strength back.

'You can go on the *John Wesley* the next time it is journeying to Sydney,' suggested Francis. 'There are ships leaving for England at least once a week now, you won't have any difficulty in getting a berth.'

There was one difficulty: Ruth was flatly refusing to go.

'I want to stay here with Francis William,' she announced, nodding her head to emphasise what she was saying. Then she walked over to where he was and stood with him, both children gazing stubbornly at the grown-ups.

Wisely, Mary didn't argue, simply went ahead with packing for the sea voyage. She didn't think she would need many of their old clothes when they got back to England as she meant to buy new as soon as they touched land, clothes good enough to dazzle the miners of Hetton.

A Mother's Courage

Eleanor said nothing; she spent most of her time now-adays sitting in the bamboo chair on the verandah, dozing some of the time and the rest just feeling tired to death.

'I'll go for a walk tomorrow,' she said every now and then. 'I've got to pull myself together, this is plain silly.'

'There's plenty of time, you don't have to do anything,' said Francis. But both of them were thinking about Mary's imminent departure. Of course there was Prue, but she was so wrapped up in her own baby and Matthew that she would have little time to spare for helping Eleanor.

The *John Wesley* came and went, and came and went again, and still Mary was not on it. Lines were appearing between Francis's brows and Mary, though she said nothing, was slowly losing her recently acquired sparkle.

'You must go next time the ship puts in,' Eleanor said to Mary. 'It's not fair that you should be tied here, I'll get a girl from the village, or perhaps one of Matthew's relatives.'

Then something occurred that changed everything. Francis came in one day after one of his regular visits to the king.

'Pack your bags, Mary, the ship comes in on Friday and there is now no reason why you shouldn't be on it.'

Mary and Eleanor looked at him in astonishment and he laughed.

'I didn't want to tell you until I was absolutely certain, but the king has appointed me as his European advocate. I am to travel to London to speak for him.'

'London?' For a moment Eleanor couldn't take it in. 'But ... what will we do if you go to London?'

Francis smiled. 'I have expressed myself badly. I must do better when I'm talking to Her Majesty's Government in London, mustn't I? No, my dear, what I meant to say was that we are all going to London.'

'But ... your work here, what about—'

Francis was striding up and down in his exuberance; he couldn't stay still. 'It's all worked out, my love, I have permission from the district, they are putting in a temporary man in my place. I have leave of absence for however long it takes.'

Eleanor stared at him; he hadn't breathed a word about all this, he must have been planning it for weeks. I can't go, she thought, I'm not well enough. How can I get the children ready and everything packed, how can I go?

'You'll have to go without me,' she said, forlorn. 'I'm not well enough.'

'Nonsense, the sea voyage will do you the world of good.' Mary, who had stood in the kitchen doorway with her mouth open all this time, suddenly came to life. 'All you have to do is walk up the gangplank and on to the ship. I will do everything else, packing, seeing to the children. It's not so much after all.' She was now as excited as Francis and desperate to tell someone, Prue in particular.

'First I'll just slip down to Prue's house, I have to tell her. I won't be long, there is so much to do. What a good thing the children are in school, I can get on without them getting in my way.'

She put on a sun bonnet and hurried off down the street to her sister's house.

'You can manage it, Eleanor,' said Francis when they were alone. 'For if you don't go, I won't, and you know how disappointed I will be. It's such an honour for the king to choose me.' He looked sideways at his wife; he knew her too well. She wouldn't be able to hold out against such an argument.

Chapter Thirty

Eleanor walked slowly round the deck of the *Fair Maid of Perth* on Francis's arm. Francis held on to Edward's leading reins as the boy strained to reach the rail and behind them walked Francis William and Ruth. Mary was sitting in a deck chair with a rug over her legs, for she was not travelling steerage this time, oh no. She and Ruth had a first-class cabin next to the Taits.

She smiled as they passed her for the second time, her smile turning to amusement as she saw Francis William with Ruth hanging on to his arm in exactly the same way as his mother hung on to his father's. As they passed the captain's wife, Francis lifted his hat to her and Francis William copied the gesture exactly though his hat was imaginary. This time Mary couldn't help herself; she burst out laughing and Francis turned and caught the children in the act.

'Francis William, you are supposed to be studying,' he said severely though his eyes danced. 'You don't want to be way behind the others when you go to school in England, do you?'

'Yes, and you too, Ruth,' said Mary, hiding her smile. She got out of her chair and took the girl's hand. 'Come on, I'll come down to the cabin with you and hear your reading.' Ruth was not yet five but both she and Francis William could read, so long as the words weren't too lengthy and difficult. Just now, they were reading a heartrending story about a small orphan girl in London and how she came to be saved by a poor but Christian lamplighter.

265

'I'm not going to school in England,' the boy confided to Ruth as they followed Mary below deck. 'I won't be there long enough, I'm going back to Fiji.'

Ruth began to cry. 'I want to, I want to!'

'Not if you don't come,' he said quickly. 'I'll stay if you're staying.' Ruth smiled through her tears. Mary felt a twinge of foreboding – the time was coming when the two had to part; it was inevitable.

'She'll be all right when the time comes,' said Eleanor when Mary confided her fears. 'There'll be so much else for her to think about.' It was the same afternoon and they were sitting on deck. The sun cast a golden path on the water as it slowly descended and a fresh breeze began to quicken from the west, bringing colour to Eleanor's pale cheeks. They were about halfway between Sydney and Capetown and already the voyage was working its magic on Eleanor; she felt better than she had been since before she took the fever.

Mary wasn't so sure that Ruth wouldn't mind parting from Francis William but there was nothing else to say. The ship glided north through the water and she gazed up at the sails, filled with a wind blowing from the south.

'The captain says we are making good time,' she remarked. 'We should be in England in plenty of time to shop for Christmas.'

Eleanor watched her animated face, the hollows filling out after all these weeks away from Morgan West and the plantation.

'You can't wait, can you?' she said and laughed. 'You're dying to get to the shops.'

Francis came up and took a seat beside them. 'London will be the best place, Mary,' he said. 'But I hope you're not going to spend *all* of Ruth's inheritance.'

'It won't cost so much for a few new dresses, I'm not so daft as to pay over the odds.'

Mary gazed out over the water. Oh, she was grateful to Francis for all he had done for her and Ruth, but she sometimes wished he wouldn't take it for granted that she couldn't look after the money. She didn't need him to tell her to be careful. But she'd been without too long not to enjoy spending a small part of the money at least.

The voyage passed uneventfully; they touched on Capetown and waited impatiently for the ship to get under way again. There was a storm that lasted for two days after they set sail again, which meant the children had to be kept amused below decks and Eleanor was so seasick that she felt worse than she had when she was ill with dysentry. But just when they were beginning to think they would never get to England, there it was one morning, a dim grey line in the distance.

They disembarked at Southampton on a day when the sun shone as brightly as it ever did in Fiji.

'I don't need a muffler, Mam,' Ruth had protested as Mary dressed her to go ashore. 'Look, it's a sunny day, it will be warm.' She pointed to the blue sky showing through the tiny porthole. But when she finally did stand on the dockside with the boys, waiting for their parents to sort out the luggage, all three of them began to shiver.

'I don't like it here, it's too cold,' Francis William said. 'Why don't we just go back home?'

'Don't be a baby,' said John. 'You know we can't do that.' But even John hunched his shoulders and thrust his hands deep inside his pockets and his nose gleamed red.

The cold was forgotten when they boarded the train and it steamed and puffed its way out of the station and gathered speed for the journey to London. The children stared wide-eyed at the countryside, the neat fields and hedgerows, the villages with their stone and brick houses.

'The roads look funny,' pronounced Francis William as the railway ran across a bridge over a metalled road.

'It's tarmac so that the road doesn't get ruts from all the carts,' John told him. John had been reading all about England in school. 'The surface is very hard, you see.'

'Not even when the rains come?'

Listening to the conversation, Eleanor was surprised by how little the children knew of England. But, after all, why should they know much, even John with his books. Reading about a place wasn't the same as seeing it.

Alighting at Waterloo Station, even the three adults were completely silenced, it was so long since they had been in such a hubbub. The crowds, the noise from the engines, the train whistles, people shouting at each other above the rest of the racket; to people coming from a place such as Fiji, it was overwhelming, not to say deafening.

Out on the street it was not much better, the horse buses and hansom cabs and water carts competing for space in the smelly, overcrowded street. The children clung to Francis, because he was the largest perhaps, the one most likely to protect them from the dangers they saw all around them. And they were right, of course, thought Mary as he found them a cab large enough to take them all and somehow the driver found his way to the Temperance Hotel in a quiet sidestreet near King's Cross, where Francis had booked rooms through the Wesleyan Methodist Missionary Society.

The children were tired and fretful by the time they got there and for once raised no objection to going to bed so Eleanor and Mary had an early night too.

'I have a meeting at the Missionary Society at eight o'clock,' said Francis. 'You can manage, can't you, dear?'

Eleanor opened her mouth to protest, then closed it again. What difference would it make whether she objected or not? She went to bed and, in spite of the noise, slept through until morning, not even waking when Francis came in.

The next few days went by in a heady whirl, not just for Mary and Ruth, but Eleanor too. One morning at breakfast, Francis announced that he was taking the children out for the day.

'You and Mary have a day to yourselves,' he said. 'I don't have to be anywhere else today, so enjoy yourself, it may be a long time before we are back in London, or even England, again.'

The women explored Oxford Street, exclaiming over the new fashions; dresses were straight at the front and with a bustle at the back, and they discovered that their bonnets were completely out of date and fit only to be consigned to the rubbish.

'The hats, Eleanor, do you see the hats?' asked Mary, turning about to look back at the ladies going by with hats of all shapes and sizes perched on top of their heads. 'Mind, I don't know how they keep them on, no ribbons or strings nor nothing.'

They soon discovered the use of the hatpin, however, and both of them arrived back at the hotel that evening wearing examples of the new fashion. Eleanor felt a few qualms about the cost, but before Francis had left that morning he had handed her ten pounds.

'For you to spend on yourself,' he had said. 'Not the children, mind, this is your day.'

'But Francis, the money—' she had exclaimed. Their stipend had to last until the beginning of the next quarter.

'I had an allowance from the king to cover the expenses of travelling, etcetera,' he explained and she wondered why she hadn't queried how he had paid for everything before now, but she hadn't.

'The stipend is practically untouched,' he added and grinned. 'I don't think we'll starve yet a while, Eleanor.'

Even so, the hat had cost a whole five pounds; it was terribly extravagant of her, she knew. She would have to confess. But somehow, when they got back to the hotel, the opportunity didn't arise. The children were in great spirits and falling over each other to tell of the day they had had in a great house made of glass and afterwards how they had gone to the zoo.

'And, Mam, it was awful,' announced John. 'Not the glass house and not all of the zoo, but do you know, they had some of our parakeets, orange ones and red ones and they were in cages and they could hardly fly anywhere. I wanted to let them out but Daddy said they would die, it's too cold in England.'

'They wouldn't be our parakeets, John,' said Eleanor.

'Yes they were, Mam, it said on the label, parakeets from Fiji, wasn't it awful? You know how they like to fly right to the tops of the trees and round about the bay and in there they couldn't go anywhere.'

'That's enough, John, your mother can't do anything about the birds. Let it be, now, we've heard about nothing else but the parakeets. Didn't you like the rest of the day? The Crystal Palace, for instance?'

'It was all right,' the boy conceded and Eleanor could see that the plight of the caged birds had spoilt the day for him.

'It's no good crying over what we can't help, John,' she said. 'Now take the other two up to wash for dinner, I'm sure you must be hungry. I'll see to Edward.'

On Sunday, they went to John Wesley's chapel in City Road. And John was red with pride when his father was introduced to the congregation as a 'brother returned from labouring for the Lord in foreign fields' and he gazed fixedly at the carving of a descending dove at the top of one of the columns but it reminded him of the parakeets and he felt sad.

'I have done my best to put King Thakembau's case for being recognised as king of all Fiji,' said Francis, the very next morning. 'I intend to go to the station to purchase the tickets for Durham today. We will reserve a carriage, I think.'

'But can we afford it?'

Eleanor was startled; it sounded very grand to reserve a whole carriage. Yet it would be so nice to have plenty of room for the children to wriggle about as much as they liked and still allow the three grown-ups to sit in comfort.

'The advocate of the King of Fiji should travel in style,' said Francis, a trifle pompously she thought, until she glanced at him and saw he was wearing a mocking grin. Well, the King of Fiji did sound so grand; it was only if you knew that being a king on Bau wasn't exactly the same as being a queen in London.

The thought was reinforced when they hired a carriage and rode down the Mall to see Buckingham Palace and saw the Union Jack flying above and the red-coated soldiers on guard. The sight was enough to dazzle all of the children.

'It's good to relax, I feel I am entitled to a real holiday now,' said Francis. 'Now, where else do you want to go?'

'Home,' said Eleanor and Mary together and Francis laughed.

'We'll travel on Wednesday,' he decided.

Chapter Thirty-one

'Durham, this is Durham,' called the porter as he opened the door of the first-class carriage and the children jumped up and down in excitement.

'Settle down, now, settle down,' said Francis. 'Come on now, everyone out, you don't want to get left behind and go to Newcastle, do you?'

There was a scramble for the door; the journey had been far too long for them as it was and they certainly didn't want to go anywhere else, even if it was a castle.

Eleanor's eyes were suddenly damp as she walked along the platform and looked out over the small city with the ancient cathedral towering over the houses. Francis squeezed her hand, knowing exactly what she was feeling. She was not alone, Mary had to take out her handkerchief as the tears rolled down her face.

'I'm sorry, I can't help it,' she said as Francis looked concernedly at her and she blew her nose and sniffed. Little Ruth moved to stand close beside her in sympathy for she didn't know what.

'It has been a long time,' said Eleanor. 'It's funny but in all these years, I've not felt half so homesick as I do now.'

'Hello, Eleanor. Don't you know me?' said a voice and there was her younger brother James. Eleanor had written to him from London to say they were on their way but she had not really expected him to come. After all, they were practically strangers. She hadn't even recognised him when she saw him on the platform and his greeting was formal, as though he hardly knew her either.

Still, they were glad to climb on to the trap he had waiting outside the station rather than stand around while Francis hired a conveyance, and soon they were on their way through the narrow streets of Durham, the children dozy and leaning against their elders and the luggage piled behind them.

'I booked rooms for you at the Colliery Inn, as you asked,' said James. 'I'll drop you there and then I'd better be going back to Moorsley, I'm working tonight.' And Eleanor felt guilty that perhaps she had got him up from his sleep when he was on night shift. How much she had forgotten of the routine of a pit village!

They went down the hill and climbed up Silver Street on the other side, so narrow there was hardly room for two carts to pass. But the road was paved with flagstones and cobbles and the trap made good progress as Silver Street widened out into the market place. They rumbled past Sherburn and out on to the open road.

The light was beginning to fade as they came to the outskirts of Hetton-le-Hole and struggled along the High Street, which was unmade and full of ruts, to the Colliery Inn.

'Ugh!' said Francis William. 'What's that smell?'

'Hush now,' commanded Eleanor. 'It's the coke ovens; when you've been here a while you won't find it so bad. People round here say it's healthy.'

'Healthy as rotten eggs!' murmured Francis.

'Ugh, rotten eggs, rotten eggs,' shouted the sharp-eared Francis William. All the children had woken up properly as the trap bumped along Front Street.

'I'll be along to see you at the weekend,' said James as he helped unload the luggage in front of the Colliery Inn. 'And you'd be very welcome to visit us at Moorsley, any time.'

But Eleanor knew that it could only be Saturday afternoons or Sundays if John was working the night shift and, of course, Francis was very particular about keeping Sunday as a day of rest.

'Thank you, James, you've been so kind,' she said and they all stood and watched as he climbed back on the trap.

'Gee up, Betsy,' he cried to the pony and lumbered away down the street.

There was a smell of beer at the entrance of the Colliery Inn and through the open door that led to the bar they could see the men, some with pint pots in their hands, all staring curiously and unabashed until Francis bade them good evening.

'Evenin', Minister,' they chorused and turned away. Francis and Eleanor exchanged a glance, well aware that the men were probably scandalised that a Wesleyan Methodist minister should be there in a public house. Yet where else could they go in Hetton? There was no other hotel. Eleanor thought sadly of the viewer's house but Uncle John was retired now and gone to live in Marsden.

The smell was sharp and sour, hardly better than the smell of the coke ovens to the teetotal Taits. But the landlady was bustling and welcoming, the rooms clean, the beds comfortable and the whole party was ready to fall into them.

Next morning, Mrs Butts, the landlady, had breakfast ready for them at eight o'clock. Bacon, sausage, eggs and fried bread, and the smell completely smothered any other that might be about. And so nostalgic it was, that Eleanor felt that if she closed her eyes she would be back in the viewer's house of Lyon Pit with Uncle John at the head of the table and Grandmother Wales ringing her bell imperiously for her tray to be taken up.

'Where are we going today?' asked John.

'Not far,' said Eleanor. 'Today is a day for resting, I think. Perhaps a walk round the village.'

Mary had other ideas and she couldn't wait to put her own plans in action. 'If you don't mind, I thought I would go to see my brother, Ben. You know, he's overman at Black

Boy now, over by Bishop Auckland. Then I'll be free to start looking for a house.'

'Black Boy? Isn't that a long way from Hetton? You'll have to go into Durham and take a train to Auckland and then I don't know how you'll get out to Black Boy.' Francis had a map of the county open on the table before him. 'Look, you see what I mean. It will take hours, Mary.'

It was true, she saw, feeling dampened; somehow she had thought it was fairly close. After all, didn't Black Boy have the same owner or general manager or something?

'You're right,' she conceded. 'Well then, today I'll look for a house.'

Eleanor laughed. 'Oh, Mary, you haven't a minute to spare, have you?' Mary hadn't; she felt an overwhelming need to be settled, to buy her house and furnish it before her good fortune was snatched away. Even her shopping spree in London had gone stale on her; she ended up buying only a couple of outfits each for herself and Ruth, wanting to be on her way north.

'Goodness gracious!' exclaimed the old man standing under the newly painted sign that proclaimed 'T.G. Herrington, Chemist.' 'It's Miss Saint, isn't it? All grown up and with a husband and family. I remember now, you married Mr Briggs's grandson, didn't you, and went off to foreign parts?'

'Good morning, Mr Herrington.' Eleanor smiled. 'What a good memory you do have. Yes, I married Mr Tait and we went to Fiji. This is my family, the boys, that is, Ruth is the daughter of Mary Buckle, you remember Mary Buckle?'

Mr Herrington looked vague. 'Er ... well, you'll find nothing much has changed in Hetton. There is a move to have the road made up but it moves slowly, yes indeed.'

Eleanor looked ruefully at her shoes and the hem of her dress, all spattered with mud. As for Francis William's boots and Ruth's too, it was best not to look. 'Yes, well, I'll see you again, Mr Herrington,' she said and shepherded her charges into the general store next door. They all had to have pattens to keep their feet out of the mud.

Mary followed them in, her cheeks red and her eyes sparkling with suppressed excitement. She had her skirt bunched up and held high above the dirt of the street, showing a pair of sensible black boots and white clad ankles. But her skirt was of black bombazine and her bodice slim-fitting and stylish, with sleeves that came down to the wrists and ended in fine lace. Over it all, to protect herself from the cold, she wore a shawl just as all the other women in the shop, but hers was not knitted from undyed grey shoddy but fine, black wool.

'Eleanor?' Her eyes skimmed over the open-mouthed women until she saw Eleanor and the children at the back of the shop, trying on pattens. 'Eeh, I thought I'd missed you for a minute.' She pushed her way through to the back, past the piles of galvanised dishes and pans, past cans of coal oil and scrubbing brushes, hard yellow soap, and brushes and shovels.

'By, Eleanor, you know that cottage down by Easington Lane, the one by itself with a garden round? It's got a "For Sale" notice on it an' I went to see the agent and, Eleanor, it's only a hundred and twenty pounds, even with the paddock at the back. By, I think I'll have it, Eleanor, I do.'

'Don't you think you should look at some more before you make up your mind? You don't have to buy here, do you, what about the coast? I thought you were going to look about there?' Eleanor was taken aback by Mary's hurry; she knew she was enthusiastic but this was really going at things headlong.

'You wanted to see some by the sea—' Eleanor stopped talking abruptly as she noticed, over Mary's shoulder, that practically all the women in the shop and the shopkeeper too had stopped what they were doing and were watching and listening to them.

'We can talk about it later,' she muttered and returned to tying on a patten on Edward's foot.

'Why, man,' said Mary, 'what's wrong with now?'

'Everybody's watching.'

It was John who gave her her answer, his face red with embarrassment to the tips of his ears.

Mary half-turned, 'Mind, you're right an' all, pet,' she said and straightened her skirt ostentatiously and pulled her shawl round her so that the pattern could be seen to the best advantage. She raised her voice and addressed the crowd.

'A very good morning to you all,' she said.

The women looked at each other and mumbled a greeting and then one came forward, middle-aged and shapeless and dressed in a grey skirt, which might have once been black, with a white apron in front. Her boots were black in parts but the toes were scuffed as grey as her dress and the heels practically worn down altogether. In her shawl she had a baby of about five months wrapped up tight and fast asleep against her breast.

'Mary Buckle? You are Mary Buckle, aren't you?'

Mary gazed at her; there was something familiar about her, her eyes maybe, or the shape of her face.

'Why, man, it's Eliza Evans, isn't it?' she cried, suddenly remembering, and the woman nodded. 'Eeh, I would have known you anywhere,' Mary went on, though in reality she was horrified to see a woman who had been in her class at Sunday School looking at least fifteen years older than she actually was. To cover up her feelings, she turned to Eleanor.

'Eleanor, can you remember? It's Eliza Evans from Sunday School!'

'Eliza Hopper now, missus,' said the woman and bobbed an awkward curtsey. 'I'm married with eleven bairns, ten living.'

Ten, thought Eleanor. No wonder she looks so old. 'It's nice to meet old friends, isn't it?' she said, rather for something to say than anything else. 'We just got back last night, Mary too. This is Mary's little girl, Ruth.'

The women stared at Ruth and Eleanor saw the child through their eyes for a minute. She was still small and doll-like for her age but she had filled out recently; her arms and cheeks were plump and a good colour from the sea voyage. She wore a wool dress and cape with a hood, good and warm, and the difference between her and the pale baby wrapped in the old grey shawl was marked.

'By, Mary Buckle,' one of the women said at last. 'You must have done well for yourself, that's all I can say.' She folded her arms and her meaning look at Mary was almost accusing.

'Aye.'

'She has, hasn't she?'

'Right enough.'

The chorus of agreement made Mary flush.

'I mind when she hadn't two farthings to rub together.' One woman nodded her head to emphasise her words.

'Oh, come now,' Eleanor said, stung into springing to Mary's defence. 'It's not a sin to do well, is it?'

The women were turning away, some muttering under their breath, and one whisper was a little too loud and all the shop heard.

'Coming here with a bairn and no man, I can guess where she got her money.'

Mary turned a fiery red and Eleanor seethed with anger. She might have disgraced herself by speaking her mind and so causing a scene were it not for Eliza Hopper, who hoisted her baby up in her arms and came closer.

'Them's only jealous, Mary, take no notice. That lot always were vicious tongues. They were just as bad when your Ben did so well and got his undermanager's tickets. And I mind when I fell wrong with my first and had to wed ... aye, but you don't want to hear that. Any road, most folk aren't like them, they'll be real glad you done well. I'm set up for you, I am.'

Mary managed a small smile and murmured her thanks but she was too full of emotion to say any more and Eliza nodded again and went out.

The morning had lost some of its sparkle after that. Eleanor paid for the pattens and they trooped out of the shop, the children walking awkwardly until they got used to this new kind of footwear. Francis William tripped over his feet and fell flat in the mud and his new suit was covered in the dirty, coaly stuff, so different from the mud by the beaches of Fiji. They had to go back to the Colliery Inn so he could change.

Mary was silent, her enthusiasm dimmed, but she soon recovered after a sustaining cup of tea and slice of buttered teacake.

'You know,' she said to Eleanor, 'I haven't thought of buttered teacake for years, but now I think I must have missed it as much as anything.' She could even laugh at her own contradictory words.

In the afternoon they dressed in more workaday clothes and walked up the street to the corner and round to the row of cottages where Mary had lived with her family.

'Look, there's still the flagstone outside the door,' said Mary. And so it was, but now it had a band of sandstone round it as had the step; someone had been scrubbing and sanding that morning. There was a net curtain at the window too, pale yellow where it had recently been washed with a 'Dolly' dye. The door was open, though there was no one to be seen and, just as she had one morning long ago, Eleanor poked her head round the door and looked at the red brick floor covered with homemade proddy matts, bright and cheerful.

'Now then, were you wanting something?'

Once again Eleanor had been caught prying; a woman had come through from the pantry, carrying a pile of loaf tins. She put them down on the scrubbed table beside an earthenware dish covered by a tea towel, obviously bread dough left to prove. Dusting her hands on her apron, she came to the door.

'I'm sorry,' said Eleanor. 'I—'

Mary came to her rescue. 'We were just looking, I hope you don't mind. But I used to live here when I was a bairn.'

The woman smiled understandingly. She was a thin little woman, not more than five feet tall, and the apron she had on wrapped round her and overlapped so that she had to tie the strings in the front under her practically non-existent bosom. But her smile was big enough and she stepped back and invited them in.

'Eeh, I know what it's like, the men move around from pit to pit, and we have to gan wi' them. Meself, I still have a hankering to go back to Weardale, that's where I was brought up.'

'Well, we have the children with us.' Eleanor hesitated.

'Fetch 'em in, fetch 'em in. I've got some stotty cake in the oven, I'm sure they could eat a morsel, I've got some treacle an' all.'

The smell of baking bread filled the room and the children followed Mary and Eleanor in and sat in a row on the horsehair sofa.

'Good as gold, the canny bairns,' said their hostess, and so they were, their eyes glued to the bread cake as she took it from the oven bottom and tossed it in a cloth before spreading pieces with treacle that melted and ran so that they had to hold the plates under their chins to catch the drops.

'Emily Teesdale, I am,' the woman said after she had seen the children served. 'An' where might you be from?'

'Fiji,' said Eleanor. 'We've just come back from Fiji.'

'Fiji? Is that in Northumberland?' she asked the children solemnly.

Francis William laughed and choked on his stotty cake and spluttered, 'No, it's miles and miles over the sea!'

'Is it now? By, fancy that then, you've come all that way?'

By the time the loosing whistle blew and Mrs Teesdale had got up, lifted the iron pan off the fire and taken out the meat pudding to cool, and the loaves of bread out of the oven, they were all fast friends.

'Mr Teesdale will be in for his tea, he's on back shift,' she explained and the women rose to go. They thanked Mrs Teesdale and the children stood politely and added their thanks and promised to come back another day. They went out into the cold evening.

'We didn't get very far, did we?' said Eleanor as they struggled back to the inn against what felt to them like a howling gale though Mrs Teesdale had termed it 'a bit of a breeze'. But the afternoon had been just what was needed to counteract the depressing effect the women in the store had had on their spirits.

'Did you have a nice day?' asked Francis as they went in. But he didn't need to ask, he could see by their faces they had.

Chapter Thirty-two

'I've bought Wood End Cottage, Ben, you know, the one at Easington Lane.'

Mary sat across the table from her brother in his house on Coundon Road. It was a substantial stone-built house in a row with three others, all occupied by officials at Black Boy Colliery. Ben didn't answer at first; he was filling plates with tinned salmon and fresh salad stuffs from his garden.

Mary looked out of the sitting-room window; the garden stretched away down the bank and beyond she could see the beginning of Coundon Grange, almost at the bottom of the valley, and rising on the other side, the black ribbon through the fields that was where the old Stockton and Darlington Railway line to Shildon had run before they cut the tunnel. A nice view on a sunny day – there were one or two pitheads but even the chimneys and winding wheels looked hazy from here.

She looked again at the sitting room they were seated in; the furniture was solid mahogany, and there was even a carpet on the floor. No eating in the kitchen when Elizabeth had company.

Everything about the room showed that Ben was not short of a bit of cash, she thought; even the fireirons were brass instead of steel and the fender was of wrought iron, twining leaves and roses with a brass rail along the top.

'By, you've done well, Ben, starting as a trapper boy in Lyon Pit and now an overman at Black Boy Pit,' she said and both he and Elizabeth smiled in gratification. And he had his undermanager's tickets an' all, she thought. His wife Elizabeth had pointed that out, her voice full of pride. And he wasn't thirty yet.

Mary accepted the plate passed to her and the one for Ruth, sitting silently by her side.

'Will the bairn have a glass of milk?' asked Elizabeth. She had no children of her own and as she watched Ruth, Mary could see the yearning in her eyes. So she didn't have everything she wanted, thought Mary, poor lass.

Ben finished serving and bent his head to give thanks and then he was ready to respond to Mary's surprise news.

'You mean that old cottage past the old rows?'

'Yes, Wood End,' said Mary.

'Oh, aye.'

Ben took a piece of bread and butter and put it decorously on his side plate. By, thought Mary, they are out to show how they've come up in the world all right.

'Eeh, Ben, remember when Prue broke two plates and we hadn't enough to have our dinner on?' she asked, mischievously. But he wasn't put out.

'Aye, I do. Sometimes it's a good thing to remember.' He held out his cup for Elizabeth to refill. 'I remember going down the pit when I was not much bigger than that bairn there. I won't forget it.' Mary was silent, sorry she had said anything, Ben sounded so bitter.

'Yes. It's a good thing they raised the age to nine for lads to go down,' said Elizabeth. 'I think that's too young an' all.'

'That cottage'll need a deal doing to it,' said Ben.

'Yes. But it belonged to the mine owners and the agent says I can have the use of the pit joiner. Any road, I thought about the coast and I went to have a look but, in the end, I thought Wood End was best. I like Hetton.'

Ben put down his cup and sat back in his chair. He coughed self-consciously.

'Where did the money come from, Mary? I mean, was your husband comfortable?' he asked, and Elizabeth hushed him, murmuring something about it being none of their business.

'No, it's all right, Ben's my brother after all,' said Mary. She hesitated for a minute, deciding what to say. 'Prue's father was an American, he grew cotton and we had a plantation.'

Ruth stopped eating and huddled up against Mary as she had done every other time her father had been mentioned. Ben frowned as he saw it, puzzled.

'The lass misses him, I suppose,' he said, on a rising inflection. 'Would you like your daddy back, pet?'

Ruth shook her head. 'Pa was a bad man,' she declared, her voice barely audible. Shocked, Ben looked to Mary for an explanation.

Mary sighed; she might as well tell her brother everything. But not in front of Ruth. 'When we're by ourselves ...' she said and stopped. Looking down at her daughter's head, she bent and dropped a kiss on it.

Elizabeth was not slow to understand. She rose from the table.

'Come on, Ruth, howay with me. I'm going down the garden to see to the hens. Do you know, we have some ducks an' all, and Uncle Ben has made a pond for them to swim about in. You'd like to see them, wouldn't you?'

'Eeh, yes, I would,' said the girl and scrambled off her seat. She took Elizabeth's hand and went out with hardly a backward glance at her mother.

When they were alone, Mary started on the story of her marriage, right from the beginning, and she held nothing back. When she had finished, Ben went to the fireplace, took a paper spill from the holder on the mantelshelf and lit his pipe, not saying anything until it was going to his satisfaction. Then he walked to the window and looked out to the bottom of the garden where he could see Elizabeth and Ruth standing by the edge of the duck pond, throwing bits of bread for the ducks. The little girl was absorbed in the task, laughing and pointing out a particular duck to her aunt.

'Do you mean to say he hit that little bairn?' he asked, turning back to Mary.

'He did,' said Mary, 'when I didn't manage to shield her.'

'Flaming swine!' said Ben, 'It's enough to make a saint swear.'

He was not a tall man, few pitmen who had been in the pits since they were small were, but he had massive shoulders and arms from the days when he had swung a pick in a three-foot seam as a hewer and his neck bulged. It bulged now with emotion and his face was red with anger.

'Mind, if I could get hold of him, I'd wring his neck,' he said, his fists clenching and unclenching.

'I don't think he'll come here,' said Mary, though to tell the truth she was not completely confident. There was always a little niggle of worry at the back of her mind. 'Mr Tait says my bit of money wouldn't make it worth his while.'

'But Ruth, he wouldn't claim the bairn?' asked Ben. He was thinking that the law didn't favour runaway wives. 'He can say you ran away from him, he's your husband after all.'

'He was, he's not now,' said Mary, and turned away with an air of finality. 'Eeh, Ben, let's forget about it now. I've told you about it. I don't want to talk about it any more.'

'Aye, you don't want to get upset and then upset little Ruth an' all. Howay, we'll walk down the garden, mebbe take her a walk out across the fields.'

'You go, I'll help Elizabeth with the dishes.'

Mary felt all churned up and emotional; she would welcome not having to talk to Ruth, the small girl could be so perceptive sometimes.

There was a brownstone sink set in the scullery cum pantry, and Ben had rigged up one of the new-fangled geysers above it, fuelled with coal gas piped from the pit. Mary exclaimed over it as Elizabeth filled a dish in the sink and began to wash the dishes.

'He's a clever lad, your brother, you know,' Elizabeth said proudly as she handed Mary a tea cloth. 'Mind, it's grand, it's so handy.'

Ben came in with Ruth clutching a twist of paper filled with black bullets and her eyes shining.

'Uncle Ben says I can come next week and bring Francis William and show him the ducks,' she cried. 'I told Uncle Ben I was going to marry Francis William when I grow up so he said mebbe he'd better meet him and make sure he was good enough for me.' She giggled.

'Well, come on now, it's time to go back to Hetton,' said Mary, once again wondering how Ruth was going to take it when the Taits went back to Fiji. Some of it must have showed in her face, for when Ben brought his trap round to the front of the house ready to take them into Bishop Auckland for the train, he took her aside while Elizabeth was saying goodbye to Ruth.

'Don't worry about nowt, Mary, it'll be all right. I remember you used to worry all the time about Prue and me. Ruth will soon forget, she's young enough and she'll have plenty playmates when she goes to school. As for the other, forget about him, I say.'

Mary looked at him with a rush of affection. Ben had been taciturn as a boy and she hadn't often known what he was thinking. But he'd made a fine man, and no mistake about it.

'I'm glad I came, Ben,' she said. 'It's grand to have you to talk to, you're so sensible.'

Ben coughed, flicked the reins and they set off at a trot for the town and the railway station. 'Come back any time you like,' he called as his sister and niece climbed on to the train. 'Elizabeth and me, we like to have you.'

'Uncles are nice,' observed Ruth as the train gathered speed and she leaned against Mary sleepily.

Francis and Eleanor and the boys had been out for the day too. Francis had paid Eleanor's brother James his wages for the week so that he could stay away from work and show them round in his trap. Today they had been to Durham city and the boys were full of it when the party met up for supper in the upstairs dining room at the Colliery Inn.

'We went to the cathedral,' said John.

Francis William spread his arms as wide as they would go. 'It's big, really big, bigger than any place in London,' he told Ruth.

'Now then, don't exaggerate,' Eleanor reproved him. 'It is big though.'

'And we had a picnic by the river and I saw a water vole and there were races on the river, row boats, they were with men from the university, Daddy said. But they couldn't go as fast as Mala and his men,' he added reflectively. 'Their rowboats weren't so good, and the men weren't so strong as the warriors at home.'

This is home, Eleanor wanted to say but didn't. The longer they stayed in England the more Fiji seemed distant; she had said as much to Francis in bed the night before.

'Well, it is distant,' he had answered, smiling.

'No, but – I mean distant, unreal, nothing to do with us,' she had insisted.

'We can't stay here much longer,' he warned her. 'Don't let Fiji get too unreal.'

Eleanor was so much better, though, he thought to himself after she had gone to sleep. He lay and listened to her regular breathing and thought about what to do. Fiji didn't suit Eleanor; ten years there had been enough for her. If she went back, her health could be broken for good. Should he ask for a transfer to Australia? Somewhere in the south, perhaps, somewhere where the climate was more like England's. But he wouldn't say anything to Eleanor until he was sure. He had thought of it at supper that day as the children fell over each other to tell of their activities.

'Eat your suppers, now,' Mary was admonishing them. 'You've plenty of time to talk after.'

If they transferred to Australia, perhaps he could manage another month at home before going, thought Francis. Or even two. There was certainly plenty to keep him busy in the circuit here; all the smaller churches wanted him to give a talk on his work in Fiji and all the women's groups wanted Eleanor to talk to them too.

He glanced across at his wife, who was talking to Mary, her face animated and fresh colour in her cheeks, no doubt from her afternoon by the river at Durham. He couldn't jeopardise her health by taking her back to Fiji, he realised, of course not, the Lord wouldn't want him to. He would write to the Wesleyan Missionary Society in Australia tomorrow.

Eleanor was telling Mary about the day in Durham all right, but she was not discussing the relative merits of the cathedral or the beauty of the river walks or even the excitement of the races between the undergraduates on the Wear. She was telling her of the line of children she had seen being led out of the workhouse on their way to the National School.

'Oh, Mary,' she said. 'I was glad the children were with Francis, he had gone down to Elvet to see the new chapel they have built. It was just James and me, we were buying fruit on the market, for the picnic, you know.' She paused and gazed for a moment at her own children, plump and healthy as they were, thank the Lord.

'They looked like little old men, the boys, in their fustian trousers, mostly too big for them and the girls in shapeless grey frocks and pinafores. They weren't allowed to talk and I didn't see a single smile.'

'Well,' said Mary. 'You knew the workhouses were there, why, man, can you not remember how I fought to keep our Ben and Prue out of it? And Mam, too, when she was so bad after Da was killed in the pit.'

'I can. But do you know, I thought, why, the children on Fiji are better off. At least they're warm and there's plenty to eat.'

'Aye. Well, it's the way of the world.' Mary's face was hard; no doubt she was remembering the bad times herself, Eleanor thought. It was strange, but it was only now, when she was older and a mother herself, that she could really appreciate what Mary had gone through.

Perhaps it was the influence of Grandmother Wales, who firmly believed that if her family could raise itself out of poverty then any family could. But, of course, that wasn't true.

'There's a lot of distress about,' said Mary. 'I dare say the soup kitchens are as busy as ever. Not so much in Hetton now, the pit's doing well, but in some of the villages we came through, I noticed. And mind, the middens! Don't they smell worse than anything in Fiji? I'm sure they can't be healthy. An' do you know, there's cholera in Sunderland? Came in on one of the ships, I should think. Any road, they all have to lime-wash their houses and there's a call for something to be done about the middens. I saw it in the paper.'

Their conversation was cut short as the children claimed their attention but Eleanor had decided she would look closer at what was going on in the pit rows of Hetton. Perhaps she could do something for the people. After all, she had a great deal of experience in nursing now, hadn't she?

'Certainly not,' said Francis, when she broached the subject that night. 'You have just been ill yourself, Eleanor. In any case, we won't be here long enough for you to make much difference.'

'But—'

'But nothing. You heard what I said.'

Eleanor held her peace; she had her own ideas of what she was going to do but there was no sense in upsetting Francis by telling him she was determined.

Chapter Thirty-three

'I'd forgotten about the wind blowing off the North Sea,' said Eleanor, snuggling down behind a sand dune and pulling her wraps close about her.

'Straight from the Arctic, I think,' said Francis.

They were spending the afternoon at Easington, a pretty little seaside village with an unspoilt sandy beach.

'I want to go to the seaside,' John had said that morning and so here they were, only a few miles from Hetton but ten degrees colder.

The boys were down by the water's edge; they had wanted to bathe but Eleanor had taken one look at the whitecap waves on the sea and forbidden it. In the end she had allowed them to take off their boots and stockings and try paddling.

'I'd forgotten all about the sea coal too,' Francis remarked to Eleanor's brother. He gazed out over the beach at the black lines left by the outgoing tide.

It's clean enough, it won't hurt the lads,' said James Saint.

'Why, no, I know that, I was brought up here too, you know. Oh, look here come the sea coalers.'

Carts were coming down the path to the beach, each with a couple of men wielding shovels and carrying sacks. They spread out over the beach and began to collect the sea coal.

'There must be an outcrop offshore,' Eleanor's brother said.

'I think I'll go down and have a word with the men,' Francis decided. 'Coming?'

'No, I'll stay with Eleanor.' James Saint pulled his cap down low over his forehead and thrust his hands deep into the pockets of his jacket. He had taken the week away from the pit so that he could show his sister and Francis round and he was enjoying the holiday himself. But he couldn't see the attraction of standing about on an exposed beach with the wind blowing the water into spray and the sand into his face. It was a sight warmer in the pit, and that was a fact.

Francis walked up to the nearest couple of sea coalers and stood watching them for a minute or two. They worked in silence, picking up the larger pieces of coal, washed smooth as worked jet by the action of the waves, and shovelling up the smaller pieces and putting them in a sack. They worked silently and skilfully, managing to pick up the coal and taking very little sand with it.

The men took no notice of Francis at first, not even pausing in their work. By their side the grey pony — it couldn't have been more than twelve hands, Francis guessed, but broad and sturdy, probably an ex-pit pony — stood quietly, its head down. When an area was cleared, it moved forward itself without any prompting from the men.

'You don't work in the pit, then,' said Francis at last, unnerved by the silence. Both men cast him an expressionless glance. What a fool, he thought, of course they don't. Why would they be gathering sea coal if they did? He tried again.

'Do you live in Easington?'

The older of the two men straightened up, lifted the sack he had been filling and slung it on the cart. Automatically, the pony moved on a few feet.

'Well, Minister,' he said, 'seeing as you're interested, aye, we live in Easington. An' would we be working down the pit when we're fishermen? We gather the sea coal an' all, we've always gathered the sea coal; our family, we have a right. We use it oursel's and sell the rest. There now, is that what you wanted to know?'

Francis was not put off as the men turned back to their work.

'The money must be useful to your families when the weather's too bad to put to sea,' he commented.

'Look, Minister, if you're looking to see us in chapel, you're wasting your time. The only light I'm glad to see is the harbour light when we're coming back in with full nets.'

Eleanor, sitting behind her dune with her brother, heard the last part of the conversation and was full of indignation. Heathens! Why, they were more heathen than the islanders of the South Seas. Well, it was time to bring the boys away from the water line and dry their feet, they must be frozen.

She struggled to her feet, hampered by her skirts, and looked down to the water, but the boys were already coming and even from a distance their feet were red with the cold. Francis was still with the sea coalers, she noticed, going further along the sands. One of them had even loaned him a shovel and he was having a go at separating the coal from the sand, not very successfully as far as she could see.

'Francis has a way with him, all right,' said her brother, shaking his head. 'Those folk have a name for keeping to themselves, they don't mix with the pitfolk at all.'

Then the boys were there, jumping up and down on a rock to get the sand clinging to their feet to dry before putting on their stockings and boots.

'Mind, it's not so cold once you get used to it,' said young John. 'Not warm like the sea at Bau either. Where are we going now, Uncle James?'

'Nay lad, that's up to your father, I go where I'm told,' he answered.

Francis came up looking well pleased with himself.

'I doubt if you made any converts there,' said James Saint, nodding his head at the sea coalers, their cart loaded with dirty-looking sacks, as they trundled off the beach.

'The Lord works in mysterious ways,' Francis replied. 'They are coming to hear all about our experiences in Fiji at any rate. I'm to speak at Easington Chapel tonight. They may yet see the Light. Come on now, do you think the pony won't be too tired to take us to Hartlepool? As I remember, it's not that far, is it?'

'It's late, Francis,' Eleanor said firmly. 'We can go to Hartlepool tomorrow. If you are going to preach here to-night, we'd better be going on home, don't you think? The boys will want their tea. And James has to get back to Moorsley, don't forget.'

'I wasn't thinking of the time,' admitted Francis.

As the trap headed for home, James Saint remarked, 'By, you're a born preacher though, Francis, I'll give you that.'

It was true, thought Eleanor, her husband would not be happy doing anything else. What would happen if his voice gave out altogether, she couldn't bear to think.

Mary was having the time of her life; paintbrush in hand and enveloped in a large brown apron, she was painting the door for the front room of the cottage.

'Blow the wind southerly, southerly, southerly,' she sang as she worked, hardly knowing she was doing so. In the kitchen, the colliery joiner grinned as he measured up the back door for a new frame; the old one was rotted away at the bottom. After that he had the window frames to attend to; the upstairs ones hadn't been opened in years, and the sashes would have to be replaced as well as one broken pane.

Mary stopped singing and looked out of the window into the overgrown garden. Ruth was there, digging away at the weeds in a flowerbed, though sometimes a flower came up rather than a weed. 'An accident, Mam,' Ruth would say, holding the pansy or forget-me-not behind her back.

Going back to her painting, Mary was relieved. Ruth had cried to go with Francis William to Easington, she had even stamped her foot in temper, but her mother had thought it was time to separate them, at least for short intervals. After all, Ruth had enjoyed her trip to Black Boy to see Ben, hadn't she? And Francis William hadn't gone there. And here she was, rooting about in the flowerbed, seemingly quite content, her temper forgotten.

Mary finished painting the door and went out to the pump to fill the kettle for tea. Standing by the pump, she looked about her; the sun was high in the sky, it must be noon, she reckoned. As if in agreement, the noise of wood being sawn at the back of the house stopped and after a moment Henry Hind, the joiner, came round the path that went round the outside of the cottage and stood by the gate watching her.

'Grand day, missus,' he said cheerfully.

Mary picked up the full kettle and walked up to him. He was a nice-looking chap, she thought, tall with gingery hair and bright blue eyes, even though his face was covered in freckles. He spent most of his working days on the surface, keeping the mine property in good repair and sometimes fixing up the miners' cottages, so he wasn't as pale as most of the men of the village but had a healthy tan.

'A grand day,' she echoed as she went past him, feeling his eyes on her back, knowing he was interested in her. She could be interested in him if circumstances were different, she thought. Oh Lord, what was she thinking? She wanted no more complications in her life, no indeed.

She entered the kitchen to put the kettle on the fire and stepped back from the range. It was a bit hot for such a fire today but she had to have it hot enough to boil the kettle. She wondered about the possibility of having gas piped from the pit – she would ask the agent tomorrow.

'You should be able to move in by next week, missus,' said Henry from behind her and she jumped. She hadn't known he had followed her in.

'Yes. I'll be glad to get settled,' she said and began to set the table with mugs from her basket. She had a plate and a packet of roast-beef sandwiches that the landlady at the Colliery Inn had provided, for a price, and she laid these out too.

'Would you like a sandwich?' she asked Henry.

'Thanks, missus, I've brought me own bait,' he replied and took out a miner's bait, or sandwich tin, from the large pocket in his jacket, which was hanging on the handle of a broom just inside the door. He sat down on an upturned box and opened the tin, taking out doorstep cheese sandwiches.

The kettle boiled and Mary made the tea.

'Well, I'll call Ruth,' she said awkwardly and went out into the garden for her daughter. What on earth was the matter with her? she asked herself, irritated. Here she was acting like a young girl instead of a married woman with a daughter. But without a husband, she thought and shocked herself as she found herself thinking what it might be like to be wed to someone like Henry Hind. During the afternoon, she threw herself into her painting and carefully kept away from wherever the joiner was working.

Over the next few days the cottage gradually began to look more cared for, the front gate was re-hung so that it didn't scrape along the ground when opened and all the windows opened easily. The mason came and filled a hole in the wall of the kitchen and put in a new step by the front door. And Mr Hind – she refused to think of him as Henry – offered to paper the walls of the sitting room in his spare time so that by Tuesday evening of the next week they were covered in delicate bunches of pink roses.

'We are moving in on Friday,' Mary told Francis and Eleanor as they sat down to supper in the Colliery Inn. Francis William frowned heavily, put down his knife and fork and crossed his arms before him, something that was strictly forbidden at table. But Eleanor hadn't the heart to say anything to him; she pretended she hadn't noticed.

'I'm pleased for you, Mary,' said Francis. 'It will be so much better for you when you're in your own home.' He sighed. 'I'm sure you have had enough of the stench of beer for a while, as I have.'

Mary, who in truth had given up even noticing the smell of beer or even that of the coke ovens, which hung over the village, looked from him to Eleanor.

'Well, to tell you the truth ... I don't know whether you would want to—'

'Mam wants to know if you would like to live with us!' cried Ruth.

All eyes swivelled to Mary, and even Francis William sat forward.

'Oh, we couldn't impose,' said Francis. 'In any case, there is hardly room enough, is there? And we will be going shortly ...'

'Oh yes, there are three bedrooms and Ruth can share with me,' said Mary. 'You have been so good to me, I would like to pay you back, why not like this?'

'Why not, Francis?' asked Eleanor and it was decided. Francis William picked up his knife and fork and began to eat.

It was certainly an improvement on staying at the inn, thought Eleanor, as she sat on a chair in the rose-decorated sitting room and looked around her. Mary had had the whole houseful of furniture delivered from Durham, solid mahogany pieces that filled the room in the fashion of the day. The chair she was sitting on was covered in a dusty-pink moquette and it was framed in mahogany too.

'Just like Grandmother Wales's chairs,' she murmured, touching the polished sheen of the wood.

Mary laughed. 'Aye, I know. I know this is just a cottage an' all, but it doesn't look too out of place, does it?'

'Not at all,' said Eleanor.

Outside, in the garden, they could hear the voices of the children, laughing and shouting as they played some game. At least they had somewhere to play away from the eternal dust of the street, dust that turned to mud at the first shower of rain.

Eleanor sat back in her chair, crossing her legs comfortably. The only thing that troubled her was that Francis might come in from his visit to the superintendent minister at Houghton le Spring and say they had to pack up and go back to Fiji next week or the week after that. She sighed resignedly. Of course she would go; the mission field was their life, this was only an interlude.

But it would have been nice to find time to visit Eliza Hopper and her children, see what she could do to help them. And there were others in the village she had noticed, two little girls in one family with legs bent grotesquely with rickets, from bad feeding, she supposed. And now Francis seemed to have done all the touring around the county he wished to do, she could have visited Dr Andrews, found out what he thought about the threat of cholera sweeping through the coal field. For she knew it could happen, and if the local Board of Health thought it necessary to put up posters warning the people to take precautions, they must think so too.

Mary's thoughts were completely different. She loved her cottage, she loved buying things to furnish it and she didn't care if anyone did whisper about where she had got the money from. She knew it was honestly come by, she told herself, and she didn't care what anyone else thought. By, she had done what she intended to do and she had enough left to live on an' all. She got to her feet and went into the kitchen for a duster and, coming back, rubbed at a speck of dust on the mahogany table. Satisfied, she took the cloth back and stood at the back door for a while, watching the children playing. They had gone through the gate to the paddock. Well that was all right, the grass had been cut only yesterday evening, Henry Hind had insisted on it.

'Might as well do it, missus,' he had said as he stood sharpening his scythe with a whetstone. And he had grinned down at her.

Mary turned quickly and went back to the sitting room and Eleanor, feeling strangely restless. It was just because all the bustle was over now, she was settled in her little house and now she would find something else to do with her time, something genteel, to suit her position.

Chapter Thirty-four

Ben stood before the sitting-room fireplace, his back to the blaze, his thumbs in the pockets of his waistcoat as he rocked gently backwards and forwards on his heels.

'I will say, our Mary, you've picked yourself a nice canny place. You've made a good job of furnishing it an' all.' He nodded his head to emphasise his words.

'I'm pleased you like it, Ben,' his sister replied. She loved showing off her house.

'It's cold out today,' observed Elizabeth. 'That wind's enough to cut you in two. Do you think it will snow?' It was coming up to Christmas and the north-easter could be heard even inside the house, howling round the chimneys.

Walking to the window, Ben gazed out on the road. The sky was leaden and the last of the brown leaves swirled about in the street while the mud had a coating of ice over it.

'Very likely,' he said. 'We won't be long in setting off back, I reckon. I'm due at the pit the night, any road.'

'I'd have liked to see Ruth first,' Elizabeth said. 'I'm really sorry we missed her.'

'She might not be long back,' Mary put in. 'She's gone to Houghton with the Taits, they don't usually stay out late. I'll put the kettle on and—'

She broke off what she was saying as the pit hooter sounded, loud and long and clear and shocking, blocking out the sound of the wind. The Buckles jumped to their feet, even

299

Mary, who hadn't heard the hooter sound this note since before she went to Fiji.

'It's not loosing time,' she said, rather unnecessarily, for it was only half past two in the afternoon; of couse the shift wasn't ended.

'I'll go,' Ben said and headed for the door, taking his overcoat from the hook as he passed. 'I mebbe can help.'

The women followed him out into the street, the cold all but forgotten, and walked to the end of the road where they could see the pithead. Even as they got there, the winding wheel began to turn.

'The rescue men going down?' murmured Mary.

'Mebbe,' Elizabeth replied, tight-lipped. Both of them thought of the alternative, that they were bringing someone up, injured or dead.

'We'd better get back, no sense in standing here catching our death of cold,' said Elizabeth and they walked back to the cottage.

'We'll soon know, any road,' she was saying as they entered the sitting room. And both women stopped dead as they saw the man, sprawled in one of the pink moquette chairs, toasting his feet before the fire.

'Who the heck—' Elizabeth ejaculated and stopped as she glanced at Mary and saw her face, white as her apron, her eyes wide and staring.

'A very good afternoon to you, my dear,' said Morgan, smiling lazily, not bothering to rise to his feet. 'The door was open so I came on in. Tell me, what is all the excitement about out there? I stopped one of the peasants to ask my way and I couldn't get a word of sense out of her.'

'There's been an accident in the pit,' said Elizabeth, for Mary was still standing in the doorway, staring at Morgan as though he were a ghost. 'Who might you be, any road?'

'Morgan West, at your service, ma'am. I must apologise, dear ... um ... lady,' said Morgan, rising to his feet and bowing elaborately, 'for my wife, I mean, not introducing us. I'm afraid her upbringing was sadly lacking, she knows nothing of the rules of courtesy.'

Elizabeth drew herself up and glared at him. 'An' neither do you, sir, that's plain to see!' She would have gone on at length, for she was remembering what Ben had told her about the American Mary had had the misfortune to marry and she was full of indignation. But Mary stopped her with a gesture.

'What are you doing in my house?' she asked him, her voice low and icy. 'How did you find me? An' any road, why did you bother to look? I thought you were finished with us, me an' Ruth.'

'My! What a lot of questions. But the main thing is, it wasn't hard to find you and I'm here. Wilson kindly gave me the details of how you ran off with my money, you bitch.'

Elizabeth gasped – such language and spoken in such an ordinary tone of voice, even if the accent was outlandish.

'I didn't—'

'Did you not? No, of course, you got that mealy-mouthed preacher to do it for you, didn't you. It was theft, you know that, don't you? I could call the police and have you put in charge. Tait too, I daresay, have him indicted for larceny.' He sat back down in his chair and looked around the room. 'And this is where my money went, is it? Still, I guess I can get most of it back if I sell up. I have other uses for it. I'm certainly not going to live in a filthy mining town, not for longer than it takes to find a buyer, I'm not.'

He reached into the inside pocket of his jacket, pulled out a bottle of Scotch and took a long swallow, draining it. 'Can't even get a decent bottle of bourbon in this Hell-hole,' he muttered.

'You're not going to sell my house,' said Mary. 'You have no right, it's mine, mine and Ruth's.'

Morgan's moods were always volatile when he had been drinking and now he suddenly turned violent. Flinging the empty bottle into the hearth so that the glass shattered and spread all over the hearthrug, he jumped to his feet and grabbed Mary by her hair, pulling it away from the chignon at the nape of her neck.

'You'll mind your manners when you talk to me, bitch,' he said savagely and swung her round so that tears sprang to her eyes with the pain. 'You are my wife, I have every right, I can deal with you exactly as I wish.'

'Leave her alone! By, if my man was here—'

Elizabeth ran forward and beat at him with her fists and he shoved her against the wall so heavily that she was dazed for a moment and slid to the floor. A grazed bruise on her forehead began to bleed and the blood ran down a bunch of pink paper roses, turning them red.

'Get out!' Morgan shouted at her. She got to her feet unsteadily and ran for the door though the room swam about her and a dull pain had started up in her head. All she could think of was finding Ben, Ben would be able to deal with him, he couldn't shove Ben about, no he couldn't.

Elizabeth's head was beginning to clear as she stood by the gate for a few moments, trying to collect herself, for she was so dizzy she couldn't think which way she was going. Ben, she thought numbly. Ben. And then she saw the men from the pit coming off shift, and remembered. No, they weren't coming off shift, they had come to bank because something had happened, that was it, Ben was at the pit trying to find out what.

Some of the men had women walking with them, looking relieved, glad and sad at the same time; she knew the look, she had seen it so often before. My man wasn't taken, it said, praise goodness. Someone was though, poor soul, that was why the men had come out of the pit, they always did that if there was anyone killed.

'Fall of stone,' she heard one miner say. 'Jim didn't move fast enough.'

All this Elizabeth's mind registered as she hurried against the tide of miners and their wives, but for once it was secondary to the terrible need to find Ben, for if she didn't find him soon that fiend from Hell might kill Mary.

A thought struck her as she turned into the pit yard, a panicking thought. Suppose Ruth should walk in, what would he do to little Ruth? Eeh, man, she moaned to herself, she had seen violent men before, men in drink, men who drank their wages and then took it out on their wives and families, but she had never seen anyone quite so cold-blooded about it as Morgan.

There were still some men in the yard. Mr Wood, the viewer, the undermanager and an overman she recognised, the deputy and a couple of hewers, likely the dead man's marras, they would have been working with him at the coal face. There was a cart with a body on it covered with an old blanket. And Ben, talking in hushed tones to the viewer. He saw Elizabeth and took a few steps towards her.

'You shouldn't have come,' he said. 'An' where's your shawl? Do you want pneumonia?'

'Ben, oh Ben, I—'

'Whisht!'

The men stepped back and doffed their caps in deference as the driver – Elizabeth saw it was Henry Hind so it must be the joiner's cart – flicked the reins and the cart began to move out of the yard, the overman at its head. As it turned the corner and rumbled up the street, Ben watched for a few seconds and then looked at his wife and sighed.

'Jim Hopper,' he said. 'Didn't move fast enough, the deputy said.'

Elizabeth nodded; they both had a fair idea why. Since he was sixteen, Jim Hopper had been a wild one, a great one for the beer. And the drink could slow a man up, if he had been drinking the night before ... 'His poor wife and all those bairns,' she said and suddenly remembered why she was here; the tragedy of the Hopper family had, incredibly, pushed it from her mind for a minute. She caught hold of Ben's arm, halting him in mid-stride.

'Ben, oh gracious, I couldn't tell you before, Ben, that man's come, the American, you know, the one that wed your Mary.'

'The American?'

Ben was incredulous; his mouth dropped open and he stared at her.

'Aye, Mary's man! Eeh, you should have been there, he had hold of her by the hair and he pushed me against the wall—'

Ben's bellow was so loud she stopped her explanation. He had looked properly at Elizabeth for the first time and seen the bruise on her forehead, half-hidden by her hair, which had come loose from its pin.

'Mary's man? He did that? I'll have him, by God, I'll have him!'

'Hurry up, Ben, he's knocking her about, he'll kill her if he's not stopped.'

But Ben needed no urging; he was running up the now deserted street and round the corner. Elizabeth hurried after him as fast as she could. When she got to the corner she saw Eleanor Tait and the children, her own three boys and Ruth, standing huddled together, Eleanor with her arms round Francis William and the little girl. Ruth was crying and shaking in an absolute panic of fear.

The shouting from Wood End Cottage told the reason. It was loud enough and profane enough to bring the men off shift out of the nearest colliery houses to see what it was all about.

'What's that? Do they not know a man's just been killed?' one cried in outrage. 'Is that from Mary Buckle's place?' He didn't wait for the answer, which was self-evident anyway; he and his neighbour who happened to be from the end house, Emily Teesdale's husband, strode towards the cottage, still in their pit dirt, one of them with his leather knee protectors still strapped to his legs.

'Francis has gone in to try to reason with him,' said Eleanor. 'We weren't here, poor Mary was on her own, dear knows what he has done to her.'

'Here, let me have Ruth,' said Elizabeth. 'I'll take her into Emily's for now, she wants nothing out here.' She picked the child up and hugged her to her shoulder. 'Whisht now, pet, don't take on, come along o' your Aunty Eliza now.'

'Mam! Mam!' shrieked Ruth but Elizabeth walked on and into Emily's kitchen without so much as knocking, closing the door behind her to keep out the noise. A moment later, Emily opened it and beckoned to Eleanor and the boys and thankfully she took them inside too.

'By, it's a bad business,' Emily said. 'I'll be glad when the day's over, I can tell you. First there's poor Jim Hopper and now— Well, I don't know what's happening over at Wood End but it sounds like there's murder being done. Will I be going for the polis, do you think?'

Elizabeth, who was sitting down by the fire with Ruth cuddled up in her arms, lifted her head. 'Eeh, I don't know ...'

At the same time Eleanor nodded her head. 'I think we'll have to.' She sat the boys down in a row on the sofa where they sat quietly, pale-faced and solemn. 'I'll go now, it's still Constable Blenkin, is it?'

'Sergeant,' said Emily.

Eleanor pulled her wraps around her and went to the door but then had to wait to quieten Edward, who panicked afresh at seeing his mother leaving.

'Sit with John, I won't be a minute,' she said, kissing his cheek, and slipped out into the street.

The shouting from the cottage had died down, she thought, hesitating. Would Mary want the police involved? But then there was some banging and crashing and the tinkle of breaking glass so she lifted her skirts and ran for the police station.

Francis was in there, she thought, fear for him rising in her, making her run harder so that when she got there she was out of breath altogether.

Inside the cottage Francis was kneeling over the figure of Mary, who was lying motionless on the floor. He loosened the wristband of her dress and felt for her pulse – no, he couldn't find it. He tried to find the pulse at her temple and felt a surge of thankfulness as he picked it up, weak and irregular but there and, even as he held his fingers to her head, recovering a little.

'Is she dead?'

Morgan was standing over them, swaying. His words were slurred and he sounded only vaguely interested in the answer.

'No, she's not dead, no thanks to you,' said Francis. Carefully he lifted her and laid her down on the sofa. 'She needs a doctor though, someone will have to go for Dr Andrews.'

Morgan sat down heavily. 'Aw, she won't die, I wish the hell she would. Her and that damned brat—'

'Shut your foul mouth! She needs a doctor, I'm not leaving her here alone with you. Go and get a doctor!' shouted Francis. 'Perhaps you don't care if she dies, but if she does, you'll hang for it, man, it's your own skin we're talking about. Are you too drunk to see that?'

'Aye, and you, you damned hypocrite,' Morgan went on, completely ignoring what Francis was shouting, as though he hadn't heard. 'You stole my cotton, God damn it—'

Francis looked at Mary; was she coming round? Maybe she had concussion, but if she had cracked her head on the solid leg of the mahogany table as she went down, she could have fractured her skull. He couldn't wait any more. He rose from where he had been kneeling by her and flung himself at Morgan, grasping him around his chest, pinning his arms to his sides, and attempted to drag him out of the cottage.

The chair went over with a crash and they lurched towards the fireplace where Morgan managed to get an arm free and swung it wildly at Francis's head, connecting instead with the looking glass hanging on the wall and bringing it to the ground, where it shattered into a hundred silvery shards.

They were both big men, though Morgan was more used to fighting, but he had been drinking and was unsteady, so Francis eventually had the advantage, was actually managing to get his opponent to the front door. On the way Morgan's fist caught him a blow on the head and he staggered into the window and more glass went tinkling out on to a flowerbed. And then there was the problem of getting the door open without leaving hold of Morgan.

Red-faced and grunting, they were struggling when the door burst open and Ben came hurtling into the room. He saw his sister lying motionless on the sofa, the fist that Morgan swung at Francis, this time catching him full in the face as Francis was distracted by the door opening. Both men fell to the floor, Morgan pulled down by the tight grip that Francis still had on him.

Ben's fists were hardened by years of using a pick and shovel in the mine, and if he could have reached Morgan he would probably have killed him. But as he jumped into the fray, he found his shoulder gripped in a hand almost as strong as his. He was swung round and found himself facing Sergeant Blenkin.

'Now then, if you're thinking of joining in, best not,' the sergeant said heavily and Ben stood panting and blinking, his arms swinging. Desperate as he was to give Morgan a hiding, his ingrained respect for the law held him there.

'Right then, what's this all about?' demanded the sergeant. Francis was staggering to his feet, still holding on to Morgan. On the sofa Mary moaned and moved her head, a little colour coming back into her face.

The room was quiet for barely an instant and then Morgan saw the policeman's blue uniform cape and helmet and, making a desperate effort, shook off Francis's hold and ran for the door, knocking into Sergeant Blenkin and bouncing off him, out of the door and into the street. Even as the sergeant turned to follow him there was a wild scream and it was hard to tell whether it was the man or the horse as Morgan ran straight under the animal's feet.

'Whoa, there, whoa!' someone was shouting, the horse was rearing and there was the awful grating of brakes on the iron rims of cart wheels. All three men moved to the doorway and stared at the joiner's cart with Henry Hind standing up as he still hauled on the reins and the horse puffing and blowing white steam from its nostrils, its eyes rolling as it tossed its head.

Chapter Thirty-five

'The thing that I'm most thankful for is that we had the children safely in Mrs Teesdale's kitchen with the door firmly closed when it happened,' said Eleanor. She was with Mary in the sitting room of Wood End Cottage. She and Elizabeth had cleared away the broken mirror and other ornaments that had been knocked over in the fight. They had picked up the overturned chairs, straightened the antimacassars and put the cushions back in their places.

She and Mary had just waved goodbye to Ben and Elizabeth.

'I won't leave you, pet,' Ben had said to Mary. 'The Lord knows you have had some terrible shocks today and then being knocked out like that ...'

One side of Mary's face was swollen, she found it difficult to talk and her head ached abominably where clumps of her hair had been pulled out by the roots. But she hastened to reassure her brother.

'I'll be fine, Ben, really. You go, you have to be down the pit, I know and you're late enough as it is.'

'Well, if you didn't have Mrs Tait, I would stay,' he said, unsure what to do. 'And Mr Tait will be back soon, I'm sure he will.'

Francis was at the police station making a statement. He had been in a brawl, after all, and a man had been killed, albeit accidentally.

In the end, Ben and Elizabeth went back to Black Boy, assuring Mary they would be back at the weekend to see how she and Ruth were faring. Much as she loved her brother, Mary was glad when the room was quiet, her head ached so.

Eleanor made a pot of tea and they sat sipping it in silence, each of them thinking their own thoughts. Emily Teesdale had kept the children with her so at least they didn't have to worry about them for an hour or so.

Francis, oh goodness, what would happen to Francis? Surely the church would understand, they wouldn't penalise him for defending a helpless woman against a violent husband? That's what he had been doing, not really fighting but simply trying to hold Morgan, to keep him away from his wife.

Was Mary mourning for Morgan? After all, she had married him, she must have loved him at the beginning. Eleanor looked across at her as she lay, propped up on the sofa with cushions as she drank her tea. Mary's colour was much better now, she saw. No, surely she couldn't be mourning him, not like a bereaved wife normally would.

Dr Andrews had been and examined her. No serious damage, he had said, slight concussion perhaps, the bruising of course, and shock.

'Keep her warm and quiet,' he had said. 'Plenty of hot sweet tea and a light diet. I'll come back in the morning just to make sure.' Eleanor had walked out to the gate with him.

'A bad business,' he had said. 'A bad day altogether. I dropped in on poor Mrs Hopper earlier. All those wee children, half-starved by the look of them.' He paused and closed the gate behind him before asking abruptly, 'Are you intending to stay much longer, Mrs Tait? I have noticed how much good you have done in the village since you've been here. I remember when you were a girl, how you tried so hard to help them. So eager to learn, you were. You could help the Hoppers a lot, I think, and there are others ...' He stopped speaking and gazed across the street pensively. 'Aye, it's a sad world, is it not, Mrs Tait? There's a deal of missionary work to be done here, I'm thinking. But of course you must go where your husband goes. I'll bid you good day then.'

Lifting his hat, he opened the door at the back of his tub trap and climbed aboard. Eleanor went back inside.

'Perhaps you should go to bed before I bring the children home,' she suggested to Mary. 'If your head aches they won't help it.'

'No, I'll wait, it will only worry Ruth, she'll know I'm in bed because I was hurt.'

'Will you tell her how Morgan was killed?'

'I'll have to, she would find out anyway. Best it comes from me.'

Henry had heard the row at Wood End Cottage as he was returning the horse and cart to the stables after taking the body of Jim Hopper home to his wife. He was in a state of shock after the accident and he couldn't stop talking; he had to explain it all to the sergeant, to anyone there.

Poor Henry, thought Mary, what a day he's had an' all. As she lay on the sofa she had heard his voice in the doorway as he explained to the police sergeant. By, what a good job it was that the sergeant was there! At least he had seen that it was an accident and could tell his superiors so.

'I jumped back on the cart and drove straight here, I thought she needed me,' Henry had said, nodding his head towards Mary.

'Mrs West, do you mean?' asked the policeman.

'Yes, well, her being on her own ... And then he just ran straight out at me, I hadn't a chance, the horse wasn't even going fast, we were slowing to stop—'

'Aye, I know, son,' said Sergeant Blenkin. 'I was there, don't forget. But why would she need you in particular?'

Henry's colour changed from white to red. 'Nothing, only, well, I had been working on her alterations, I knew she was a woman on her own, like.'

311

If it sounded lame, the sergeant didn't comment. Just nodded his head in understanding. On the other hand he had been quite curt with Francis.

'You will have to come down to the police station with me, Minister,' he had said. 'We will need a statement from you.' He had gazed at Francis, his eyes expressionless, and Eleanor didn't know whether that was a good sign or not. It bothered her; it was still bothering her.

'I'll go for the children,' she said now, rising to her feet. 'It's dark already, I'll give them their supper and get them to bed. They've had enough for today – I hope there are no nightmares.' Fleetingly she thought of John and his disturbed nights after he and his brother were kidnapped. No, she thought, please God, no more nightmares.

Mary nodded silently. She didn't seem to have the energy to speak. A great weariness had taken hold of her; she was only keeping herself awake because she felt she had to for Ruth's sake. After she had seen Ruth, talked to her and reassured her, perhaps gone to bed with her so that they could lie in each other's arms, then she would be able to sleep.

The children thanked Emily for having them; Eleanor took Edward in her arms and they walked to Wood End Cottage, the older children quiet by her side. But as they neared the cottage, Ruth hung back, unwilling to go in.

'Come on, Ruth,' said Eleanor. The night was cold, the wind biting and she was exhausted, not just because of the happenings of the day, but with worry for Francis.

'Pa's there,' said Ruth.

'No, he's not,' Eleanor said. 'He's gone, Ruth, he's never coming back.'

'You're not just saying that?'

'No, pet. It's the truth.'

But the child could not be persuaded and Eleanor cast about for a way to get her inside without actually forcing her.

'If the boys go in first and make sure he's gone, will you believe them?' she said at last.

Ruth nodded dumbly.

'I'll go,' said Francis William and darted to the heavy door, lifting the sneck and pushing it open with a grunt. After a moment he came out again, Mary by his side. 'He's gone!' he shouted.

'Howay, lass,' said Mary. 'Come inside. It's nice and warm and there's no one here but me.'

It was near on eleven when Francis returned. The lamp had burned low and eventually gone out and Eleanor was sitting by herself in the flickering light of the coal fire.

'How's Mary?' he asked as he closed the door and turned the key in the lock. His voice was barely audible, it was so husky.

'Sleeping. I think she will be all right now.'

Eleanor took down the candlestick that stood on the corner of the mantelpiece and lit the candle. It had begun to snow around ten o'clock and she waited while he went into the kitchen, shook the snow off his greatcoat in the brownstone sink and came back to the fire, sitting down and stretching his hands out to the blaze.

'What happened?' she asked.

'Just a minute, let me catch my breath.'

'I'll bring your supper then, you must be hungry.'

'Just bread and cheese for me, it's a hot drink I need.'

She put the kettle on and went out for the bread board and the cheese and laid a tray for him so that he could eat by the fire. When the kettle boiled she spooned tea into the pot and poured the boiling water over it. All the time she was in an agony of impatience.

Francis took a sip of the tea and cradled his hands around the cup. He cleared his throat and took another sip and then he was ready to speak.

'Sorry, I know you're anxious. But I've been talking for hours, or so it seems, I had to have a drink.' He sat back in his chair, ignoring the bread and cheese.

'You're not in any trouble with the law, are you, Francis?' she couldn't help asking.

'No, no, don't worry, love. But I had to explain everything that has happened. In the end they attached no blame to me, they accepted that I was merely trying to keep Morgan West from hurting his wife. And of course, the accident was no one's fault but his own. He had been drinking, you see. And evidently, there was some trouble with him in Durham, he got into an argument with the police there, he spent last night in the cells, drunk and disorderly. So you see, there was no need to worry about me, none at all.'

Eleanor breathed a sigh of relief. 'Thank God, Francis,' she said.

'Indeed.'

The next morning the whole village lay under a foot of snow and more was falling, drifting softly down and building up on the window sills so that it was almost impossible to see out. When Francis opened the front door there was a wall of snow drifted up against the wood and the children stared in wonderment, everything forgotten but the magic of the changed world. Snow was something they had seen in pictures, but they had not really believed in it.

'Who is going to help me clear the paths?' he asked and there was an eager chorus from the children. Even Ruth appeared to have put the trauma of the day before behind her and she rushed to get dressed as quickly as the boys and stood impatiently while her mother wrapped a scarf round her head and across her chest and tied it at the back.

There was a tremendous crashing and banging as the pit wagon came down the road, dragging the snow plough and tossing snow high in the air to land on the hedgerows.

'A waste of time,' said Francis as he ducked back into the doorway to avoid being covered. 'It's still coming down.'

But the back shift men had to get to the pit, snow or no snow. 'No work, no pay,' said Mary from her place on the sofa.

It was not until the following day that the snow stopped and the pale watery sun picked out sparkling lights on the icicles hanging from the eaves. The road was a horrible brown mush by then, alternating with sheets of ice. But the boys and Ruth joined the rest of the village children and spent the afternoon sledging down the bank behind the paddock. Some intrepid souls had a go down the side of the slag heap when no one was looking and were chased by a banksman with a broom when they were seen.

'Little beggars!' he shouted at them as they fled into the open fields. 'They'll be tipping there any minute, do you want to be covered in slag?'

Eleanor and Francis went to pay their respects to Eliza Hopper the day before the funeral. She sat in her threadbare front room, the coffin set on trestle tables in the middle and her children by her side, a kind of dignity surrounding them. Afterwards the whole village turned out, but for the men on shift, to see Jim Hopper buried.

The next day it was the turn of Morgan West. He was laid to rest next to Jim.

'Accidental death,' the coroner had said at the inquest. 'I extend my sympathies to his widow and child.'

Mary stood by the graveside with Francis and Eleanor beside her and for the first time, she shed tears. Not for the man who was dead, she could not be sorry about him, but for the man she had thought she was marrying, the dashing American who had been so sympathetic when her sister ran away in Sydney. And the dreams she had had, the marriage they could have had. But when the service was over she turned away from the grave without a backward glance and walked away with Eleanor and Francis on either side of her.

Francis was away a lot during the next few days, though Eleanor hardly had time to notice; she was happy going round with Dr Andrews, taking up her old role as voluntary nurse to the miners and their families. Though, with the bad weather, the threat of cholera had receded, there were plenty of diseases that were impervious to the cold.

John and Francis William were attending the Wesleyan School, as was Ruth, though she was upset that she had to go in a separate entrance to the boys and sit with the other girls.

'I have decided to take a house here,' Francis said, almost casually one evening, in the privacy of their own room. 'We really cannot impose on Mary any longer.'

Eleanor paused in the act of rolling down her black woollen stockings, her eyes wide with surprise. 'Take a house here?' she echoed.

'Yes.' He came and sat down beside her on the bed, putting an arm around her shoulders. 'I think we should not go back to Fiji. Australia maybe, I'm not sure.' He paused and looked at her sideways, gauging her reaction. 'There is work to do here.'

'Really? I mean, you really want to stay?' Eleanor asked. He nodded.

She threw her stocking on to a chair and lay back in the bed, holding back the bedclothes invitingly. 'Come to bed, my love,' she whispered. 'Let me warm you.'